MAST

"Part murd... historical nov... element blends neatly with the other parts. 4****."
SFX Magazine

"From page one I was drawn into Acatl's world… a remarkable historically-based fantasy, using the myths and legends of the Aztec people as a background to a twisting murder mystery."
Speculative Book Review

"A gripping mystery steeped in blood and ancient Aztec magic. I was enthralled."
Sean Williams

"I haven't enjoyed a proper detective story this much in ages, and the rich setting, monsters and magic just added an extra layer of delight."
David Deveraux

"Both involving and well written. Acatl deserves to become as well known as that other priestly investigator, Cadfael."
Strange Horizons

ALIETTE DE BODARD

Master of the House of Darts

OBSIDIAN AND BLOOD
VOL. III

ANGRY
ROBOT

ANGRY ROBOT
A member of the Osprey Group

Midland House, West Way
Botley, Oxford
OX2 0PH
UK

www.angryrobotbooks.com
Not enough sacrifice

An Angry Robot paperback original 2011

ISBN 978-0-85766-160-9
eBook ISBN 978-0-85766-161-6

Printed in the United States of America

9 8 7 6 5 4 3 2 1

MASTER OF THE
HOUSE OF DARTS

A Brief Pronunciation Guide to Nahuatl

The present pronunciation guide comes from a phonetic transcription of the Nahuatl language made in the 16th century by the Spanish friars.

Nahuatl words usually have no accent mark, and bear the stress on the penultimate syllable.

Vowels
The vowels are pronounced as in modern Spanish:

a is pronounced "ah", as in "ash" or "park"
e is pronounced "eh", as in "tennis"
i is pronounced "ee", as in "seek"
o is pronounced "oh", as in "old"
u is pronounced "oo" as in "wood"

Consonants
All consonants save *ll* and *x* are pronounced the same as in Spanish, and therefore the same as in English, except for these notable exceptions:

c is pronounced "s" when it comes before e or i

cu is pronounced "kw" as in "query"

c is pronounced "k" when it comes before any other vowel

h is pronounced "w" as in "wild"

ll is pronounced like a long English "l" as in "fully"

que is pronounced "kay" as in "case"

qui is pronounced "kee" as in "keep"

tl is pronounced as a unit like the "tl" in "battle"

tz is pronounced as in "pretzel"

x is pronounced "sh" as in "shell"

z is pronounced a hissy, soft "c", halfway between "zap" and "cite"

ONE
The Army's Return

The day dawned clear and bright on the city: as the Fifth Sun emerged from His night journey, He was welcomed by the drumrolls and conch-blasts of His priests – a noise that reverberated in my small house until it seemed to fill my lungs. I rolled to my feet from my sleeping mat, and made my daily offerings of blood – both to Tonatiuth the Fifth Sun, and to my patron Lord Death, the Fleshless One, ruler of the underworld.

This done, I put on a simple grey cloak, and headed to my temple – more for the sake of form, for I suspected I wouldn't remain there long, not if the army were indeed coming back today.

As I walked, I felt the slight resistance to the air, the familiar nausea in my gut – a feeling that everything wasn't quite right, that there was a gaping hole beneath the layers of reality that undercut the Fifth World. I'd been living with it for over three months, ever since the previous Revered Speaker had died. His successor, Tizoctzin, had been crowned leader of the Mexica Empire; but a Revered Speaker wasn't confirmed in the sight of the gods until his successful coronation war.

Today, I guessed, was the day I found out if the hole would ever close.

The Sacred Precinct, the religious heart of Tenochtitlan, was already bustling even at this early hour: groups of novice priests were sweeping the courtyards of the temple complexes; pilgrims, from noblemen in magnificent cloaks to peasants in loincloths, brought offerings of incense and blood-stained grass-balls; and the murmur of the crowd, from dozens of low-voiced conversations, enfolded me like a mother's arms. But there was something more in the air – a tautness in the faces of the pilgrims, a palpable atmosphere of expectation shared by the cotton-draped matrons and the priests with blood-matted hair.

The Temple for the Dead was but a short distance from my house, at the northern end of the Sacred Precinct. It was a low, sprawling complex with a pyramid shrine at its centre, from which the smoke of copal incense was already rising like a prayer to the Heavens. I wasn't surprised to find my second-in-command, Ichtaca, in deep conversation with another man in a light-blue cloak embroidered with seashells and frogs, and a headdress of heron feathers: Acamapichtli, High Priest of the Storm Lord. Together with Quenami, High Priest of the Mexica patron god Southern Hummingbird, we formed the religious head of the Empire. I didn't get on with Quenami, who was arrogant and condescending – and as to Acamapichtli... Not that I liked him any more than Quenami, but we'd reached an uneasy understanding the year before.

"Acatl." Acamapichtli looked amused, but then he always did. His gaze went up and down, taking in my simple grey tunic.

He didn't need to say anything, really. I could hardly welcome back the Revered Speaker of the Empire dressed like a low-ranking priest. "I'll change," I said, curtly. "I presume you're not here to enquire after my health."

For a moment, I thought he was going to play one of his little games with me again – but then his lips tightened, and he simply said, "A messenger arrived two days ago at the palace, and was welcomed with all due form by the She-Snake."

"You know this–"

"Through Quenami, of course. How else?" Acamapichtli's voice was sardonic. After the events of the previous year, we were both… in disgrace, I guessed. Not that I'd ever been in much of a state of grace, but I'd spoken out against the election of the current Revered Speaker, and Acamapichtli had plotted against him with foreigners, making us both outcasts at the current court. The She-Snake, who deputised for the Revered Speaker, wouldn't have wanted to countermand his master.

"And?" I asked. I wouldn't have been surprised if Quenami had given us only part of the information, to keep us as much in the dark as the pilgrims milling in the Sacred Precinct.

"Other messengers went out yesterday morning," Acamapichtli said. "With drums and trumpets, and incense-burners."

I let out a breath I hadn't been conscious of holding. "It's a victory, then."

Acamapichtli's face was a careful blank. "Or considered as such."

What did he know that he wasn't telling me? It would be just like him: serving his own interests best, playing a game of handing out and withholding information like the master he was.

"You know it's not a game."

11

Acamapichtli stared at me for a while, as if mulling over some withering response. "And you take everything far too seriously, Acatl. As I said: the Fifth World can survive."

I had my doubts, especially given that the death of the previous Revered Speaker had resulted in city-wide chaos – which we'd survived only by a hair's breadth. "What else did Quenami tell you?"

Acamapichtli grimaced. "Quenami didn't tell me anything. But I have... other sources. They're saying we only won the coronation war because the Revered Speaker called it a victory."

I fought the growing nausea in my gut. A coronation war was proof of the Revered Speaker's valour, proving him worthy of the Southern Hummingbird's favour, and bringing enough sacrifices and treasures for the coronation ceremony itself. The gods wouldn't be pleased by Tizoc-tzin's sleight of hand, and I very much doubted they'd make their displeasure felt merely through angry words. "And prisoners?"

"Forty or so," Acamapichtli said.

It was pitiful. Without enough human sacrifices, how were we going to appease the Fifth Sun, or Grandmother Earth? How were we to have light, and maize in fertile fields? "I hope it suffices," I said.

"I said it before: you worry too much. Come, now. Let's welcome them home."

I pressed my lips together to fight the nausea, and stole a glance at the sky above us: it was the clear, impossible blue of turquoise, with no clouds in sight. Calm Heavens, and no ill-omens. Perhaps Acamapichtli was right.

And perhaps I was going to grow fangs and turn into a coyote, too.

• • • •

Sometime later, the Sacred Precinct was transformed – packed with a throng of people in their best clothes, a riot of colours – of cotton, of cactus fibres and feathers, with circular feather insignias bobbing up and down as if stirred by an unseen breath.

Everyone was there: the officials who kept the city running, accompanied by their wood-collared slaves; the matrons with their hair brought up in two horns, in the fashion of married women, carrying children on their shoulders; the peasants too old to go to war, bare-chested and tanned by the sun, wearing a single ornament of gold on their chests; the noblemen, resplendent in their cotton clothes and standing with the ease and arrogance of those used to ceremony.

I stood with the She-Snake, Quenami and Acamapichtli at the foot of the Great Temple, surrounded by an entourage of noblemen and priests. Everyone's earlobes still dripped with blood, and the combined shimmer of magical protections was making my eyes hurt. I stole another glance at the sky – which remained stubbornly blue.

"There they are," Quenami said.

I could barely see over the heads of the crowd, but Quenami was taller. A cry went up from the assembled throng, a litany repeated over and over until the words merged with each other.

"O Mexica,
O Texcocans
O Tepanecs,
People of the Eagle, People of the Jaguar,
Our sons have come back as men!"

13

And then the crowd parted, and Tizoc-tzin was standing in front of us.

He wasn't a tall man either, though he held himself with the casual arrogance of warriors. His hawkish face could not have been called handsome, even if he'd been in good health. As it was, his usually sallow skin was so taut it was almost transparent, and the shape of a skull glistened beneath his cheeks.

So the war hadn't improved him – I hid a grimace. We'd made the decision to heal him three months ago, as High Priests; but clearly some things couldn't be healed.

Behind him was his war-council: two deputies, his Master of the House of Darkness, and his Master of the House of Darts – Teomitl, imperial prince and my student.

"She-Snake," Tizoc-tzin said. "Priests." He said the last with a growl: he'd never been fond of the clergy, but lately his opposition had become palpable. "Tonatiuh the Fifth Sun has taken us up, shown us the way to glory. Tezcatlipoca the Smoking Mirror has smiled upon us, enfolded us in His hands."

The She-Snake bowed, holding the position slightly longer than necessary – he was a canny man, and knew how susceptible to flattery Tizoc-tzin was. "Be welcome, my Lord. You have graciously approached your water, your high place of Tenochtitlan, you have come to your mat, your throne, which I have briefly kept for you. The roads have been swept clean, the mats have been spread out; come, enter into your palace, rest your weary limbs."

Tizoc-tzin's face darkened, but he stuck to ritual, starting a lengthy hymn to the glory of the Southern Hummingbird.

I'd have been listening, even though I wasn't particularly fond of the Southern Hummingbird – a warrior god who had little time for the non-combatant clergy – but something caught my attention on the edge of the crowd. A movement, in those massed colours? No, that wasn't it. Something else…

The nausea in my gut flared again. Gently, carefully, I reached out to my earlobes, and rubbed the scabs of my blood-offerings until they came loose. Blood spurted on my hands, warm with the promise of magic.

My movements hadn't been lost on everyone: my student Teomitl was staring at me intently under his quetzal-feather headdress. He made a small, stabbing gesture with his hand, as if bringing down a *macuahitl* sword, and mouthed a question.

I shook my head. The spell I had in mind required a quincunx traced on the ground – hardly appropriate, given the circumstances. I rubbed the blood on my hands and said the prayers nevertheless:

> *"We all must die*
> *We all must go down into darkness*
> *Leaving behind the marigolds and the cedar trees*
> *Nothing is hidden from Your gaze."*

The air seemed to grow thinner, and my nausea got worse – but nothing else happened. The spell wasn't working. I should have guessed. I'd made a fool of myself for nothing.

Tizoc-tzin had finished speaking; now he took a step backwards, and said, "Welcome back your children made men, O Mexica."

The war-council stepped aside as well, to reveal three

rows of warriors in quilted cotton armour and colourful cloaks, the feather insignia over their heads bobbing in the wind.

There were so few of them – so few warriors who had taken prisoners. It looked like Acamapichtli's sources were right: there couldn't be more than forty of them before us, and many of them were injured, their cloaks and quilted armour torn and bloody. Many of them were veterans, with the characteristic black cloaks with a border of yellow eyes; many held themselves upright with a visible effort, the knuckles of their hands white, the muscles of their legs quivering. Here and there, a younger face with a childhood-lock broke the monotony of the line.

"Beloved fathers, you have come at last, you have returned
To the place of high waters, the place where the serpent is crushed
Possessors of a heart, possessors of a face,
Sons of jaguars and eagles…"

There was something… My gaze went left and right, and finally settled on a warrior in the front row, near the end of the line – not among the youngest, but not grizzled either. He wore the orange and black cloak of a four-captive warrior and the obsidian shards on his sword were chipped, some of them cleanly broken off at the base. His face was paler than his neighbours, and his hands shook.

But it wasn't that which had caught my attention: rather, it was the faint, pulsing aura around him, the dark shadows gathered over his face.

Magic. A curse – or something else?

The warrior was swaying, his face twisted in pain. It wouldn't be long until–

"My Lord," I said, urgently, my voice cutting through Tizoc-tzin's speech.

Tizoc-tzin threw me a murderous glance. He looked as though he were going to go back to what he was saying before. "My Lord," I said. "We need to–"

The shadows grew deeper, and something seemed to leap from the air into the warrior's face – his skin darkened for a bare moment, and his eyes opened wide, as if he had seen something utterly terrifying. And then they went expressionless and blank – a blankness I knew all too well.

He collapsed like a felled cactus: legs first, and then the torso, and finally the head, coming to rest on the ground with a dull thud.

Teomitl moved fastest, heading towards the line and flipping the body onto its back – but even before I saw the slack muscles and empty eyes, I knew that the man was dead.

I made to move, but a hand on my shoulder restrained me: Quenami, looking grimly serious. "Let go," I whispered, but he shook his head.

Ahead of us, two warriors were pulling the body of their comrade out of the crowd. Teomitl stood, uncertainly, eyeing Tizoc-tzin – who pulled himself up with a quick shake of his head, and went on as if nothing were wrong.

Something crossed Teomitl's face – anger, contempt? – but it was gone too fast – and, in any case, Tizoc-tzin was moving, his elaborate cape and feather headdress hiding my student from sight.

> *"To the place where the eagle slays the serpent*
> *O Mexica, O Texcocans, O Tepanecs…"*

Surely he couldn't mean to…

Behind me, Quenami was taking up the chant again, his lean face suffused with his customary arrogance and a hint of contempt, as if I'd been utterly unable to understand the stakes.

The other officials and the warriors had looked dubious at first, but who could not be swayed by the will of the Revered Speaker, and of the leader of High Priests? They took up the hymn, hesitantly at first, then more fiercely.

> *"To the place of the waters, the island of the seven caves*
> *You come back, o beloved sons, o beloved fathers…"*

"A man is dead," I whispered as the hymn wound to a close, and Tizoc-tzin approached the warriors, bestowing on them, one by one, the ornate mantles appropriate to their new status. "Do you think this is a joke?"

Quenami smiled. "Yes. But the war has been won, Acatl. Shall we not celebrate, and laugh in the face of Lord Death?"

Having met Him numerous times, I very much doubted Lord Death was going to care much either way – He well knew that everyone came to Him in the end, no matter what they did.

"It's a lie," I said, fiercely, but other hymns had started, and Quenami wasn't listening anymore.

The morning dragged on, interminable. There were chants, and intricate dances where sacred courtesans and warriors formally courted each other, reminding us of the eternal cycle of life and the order of the Fifth World. There were drum beats and the distribution of maize flatbreads to the crowd, and songs and dances, and elaborate speeches by officials. And through it all presided Tizoc-tzin, insufferably smug, as puffed up as if he'd been one of the captive-takers.

I stood on the edge, mouthing the hymns with little conviction – my mind on the warrior and on his fall. People did collapse naturally: from weak hearts, or pressure within the brain that couldn't be relieved; reacting to something they'd eaten, or the sting of some insect. But there had been magic around him, strong enough for me to feel it.

I doubted, very much, that it had been a natural death.

After the ceremony, the officials of the city went into the palace, where a formal banquet was served: elaborate maize cakes, roast deer, white fish with red pepper and tomatoes, newts with sweet potatoes... Tizoc-tzin, as usual, ate behind a golden screen; Teomitl was sitting with the other members of the war-council, around the reed mat of the highest-ranked, the closest one to the window and the humid air of the gardens. Beside him was Mihmatini, my younger sister – as his wife, she should have been sitting at a separate mat, but she was also Guardian of the Sacred Precinct, agent of the Duality in the Fifth World and keeper of the invisible boundaries, enough to give a headache to any protocol master. Beneath her elaborate makeup, her eyes were distant: she didn't like banquets anymore than I did, though she could hardly afford to ignore them.

Between them was a thin line I could barely see – a remnant of a spell they'd done together, a magic which kept them tied even though the spell had ended.

Though Teomitl was obviously glad to see Mihmatini, I could see him fidget even from where I sat between Quenami and Acamapichtli, doing my best to avoid speaking to either of them. I could feel his impatience – which mirrored my own.

Further down, several Jaguar Knights were sitting around their own reed mats – among them was my elder brother Neutemoc, smiling gravely at some joke of his neighbour. It looked as though the campaign had enabled him to re-establish ties with his comrades, and other things besides. He looked plumper, and the jaguar body-suit no longer hung loosely on his slender frame: perhaps he was finally getting over his wife's death.

I let my gaze roam through the room, waiting for the banquet to finish. Amidst the colourful costumes, the faces flushed with warmth and the easy laughter there was something else, the same undercurrent of unease tightening in my belly. The atmosphere was tense: the laughing and smiling Jaguar Knights carefully avoided looking at the golden screen, while the warriors clustering around Tizoc-tzin – richly dressed noblemen, with barely a scar on their smooth legs – huddled together, talking as if they were in the midst of enemy territory.

All was not right with the world.

As soon as the last course of the banquet was served, I got up.

"Leaving so soon?" Quenami asked.

"I want to see the body," I said.

Quenami raised a perfectly-plucked eyebrow. "Always the High Priest, I see. Forget it, Acatl. The man had a sunstroke."

I shook my head. "Magical sunstrokes don't exist,

20

Quenami. Someone cast a spell on him."

I expected Acamapichtli to say something, but he had remained worryingly silent – as if lost in thought. Probably thinking of how he could turn the situation to his advantage.

Quenami smiled. "Look at you. Such wonderful dedication." His voice took on a hard edge. "Nevertheless... today we celebrate our victory, Acatl – the return of the army, and the confirmation of our Revered Speaker. Tizoc-tzin needs his High Priests here."

An unmistakable, utterly unsubtle threat. But I'd had enough. "This isn't the confirmation," I said. "As you said – today we celebrate our victory. I don't think the absence of one person is going to make a difference." Especially not one High Priest with dubious loyalties, as far as Tizoc-tzin was concerned. "I don't stop being High Priest for the Dead when we celebrate."

Quenami made a slow, expansive gesture – one I knew all too well, the one which suggested there were going to be unpleasant consequences and that he'd done all he could to warn me.

And, of course, the moment I had my back turned, he was going to go to his master and denounce us.

At least I knew where I stood with him.

The dead warrior had been taken deep within the Imperial palace – on the outskirts of Tizoc-tzin's private apartments. The sky above us had the uncanny blue of noon, with Tonatiuth the Fifth Sun at his highest.

A slave took me to a small, dusty courtyard with a dry well – I'd expected it to be deserted, but to my surprise two people were waiting for me there. The first was Teomitl, still in full finery, looking far older than his

21

eighteen years. Next to him was a middle-aged man, whom I recognised as another member of the war-council. Though he wore rich finery, the lower part of his legs was uncovered, revealing skin pockmarked with whitish scars. He nodded curtly to me – as an equal to an equal.

"I didn't see you leave," I said to Teomitl.

He grinned – fast and careless – before his face arranged itself once more in a sober expression, more appropriate to the Master of the House of Darts. "We were right behind you."

"Tizoc-tzin–" I said, slowly.

"Tizoc-tzin can say what he wants," the other man interrupted. "I have no intention of abandoning one of my own warriors."

"This is Coatl," Teomitl said, shaking his head in a dazzling movement of feathers. "Deputy for the Master of Raining Blood."

And, as such, in command of one quarter of the army. "I see," I said. I pulled open the entrance-curtain in a tinkle of bells, and slipped inside.

It was dark and cold, in spite of the noon hour: the braziers hadn't been lit, and the dead man lay huddled on the packed earth, abandoned like offal – an ironic end for one who had worshipped Huitzilpochtli, our protector god: the eternally youthful and virile Southern Hummingbird.

Automatically, I whispered the words of a prayer, wishing his soul safe passage into the underworld, for his hadn't been the glorious death of a warrior, the ascent into the Heaven of the Fifth Sun, but rather small and ignominious, a sickness that doomed him to the dark, to the dryness of Mictlan.

"You knew him," I said to Coatl.

He made a curious gesture – half-exasperation, half-contempt. "Eptli. Yes. I knew him."

"Did he have any enemies?"

"Eptli was one of the forty honoured warriors, out of an army of eight thousand men. I'd say there would be strong resentment against him."

"Yes," I said. "But why single him out? Why not any of the others?"

Coatl spread his hands. "I knew Eptli because he was under my orders, but no more than that. His clan-leader was responsible for his unit."

There was something – not quite right in the tone of his voice, as if he was going to say more, but had stopped himself just in time. What could it possibly be?

Eptli had been a four-captive warrior: with this, his fifth capture, he could aspire to membership of the Jaguar or Eagle Knights, the prestigious elite of the army.

I was about to press Coatl further, when the entrance-curtain tinkled again. I started – surely Tizoc-tzin wouldn't search for us that soon – but instead a covered cage landed on the floor with a dull thud, startling whatever was inside so it gave a piercing, instantly recognisable cry.

I knelt and lifted the cover – to stare into the bleary, murderous eyes of a huge white owl, who looked as though only the wooden bars prevented it from terminally messing up my face. It screeched once more, disdainfully.

Acamapichtli strode into the room, rubbing his hands together as if to wash away dust. "There you go. Living blood. You can use it." It wasn't a question.

"We're–"

"– certainly not going to wait for Tizoc-tzin to find us,"

Acamapichtli said. "He died of magic, didn't he? That's something serious."

"It might be," I said, carefully. I searched for a diplomatic way to say the words on my mind, and gave up. "What in the Fifth World are you doing here, Acamapichtli?"

"Why," his smile was sarcastic. "The same thing as you. Investigating a suspicious death."

Which, in and of itself was suspicious. Was this another court intrigue? I'd have thought that with the disaster of the previous one, Acamapichtli would have known better than to try causing another. "I don't think curiosity is enough to justify your presence here. Quenami made it quite clear we were angering Tizoc-tzin."

"You forget." He smiled, revealing rows of blackened teeth. "We're in disgrace. It can't really get worse."

I rubbed the mark on the back of my hand: the whitish trace of a fang, a reminder of a prison where it had been a struggle to think, a struggle to even breathe – a cage of beaten earth and adobe where Tizoc-tzin's enemies were reduced to drooling idiots. I'd spent only a few hours within, four months previously, accused of treason by Quenami – a handy excuse to keep me out of the way. I didn't want to go back there. "With all respect... I think it can."

Teomitl snorted. "You sound like an old couple." He didn't sound amused. "You have our permission." His voice made it clear it was the imperial "we", the one that put him on an almost equal footing with his brother Tizoc-tzin. As Master of the House of Darts, he was not only responsible for the armouries and for his quarter of the army, but also heir-designate – the one with the best chance of ascending to the Gold-and-Turquoise Crown, should Tizoc-tzin die.

Which, Smoking Mirror willing, wouldn't be happening

for quite some time yet. There had been enough fire and blood in the streets with the death of the previous Revered Speaker.

Acamapichtli bowed. "As you wish, my Lord." Of course, he knew the lay of the land.

Teomitl was looking at the dead warrior, with an expression I couldn't place. Regret? The dead man hadn't perished in battle or on the sacrifice stone; his fate would be the same as anyone else's, the same as any priest or peasant: the long, winding road into the underworld, until he reached the throne of Lord Death and found oblivion.

Coatl, more pragmatic than any of us, was already kneeling by the dead man's side, examining him with the expertise of a man who had seen the aftermath of too many battles. "No wounds," he muttered, and set to removing the elaborate costume the man had worn.

In the meantime, I took the cage with the owl to a corner of the room, next to one of the huge braziers. Acamapichtli, I couldn't help but notice, hadn't brought back anything of his own – but he was watching the corpse as if considering his next best move.

I took one of my obsidian knives from my belt – even in full regalia, I never neglected to arm myself – and glanced at the owl, which looked even more ill-tempered than before. Why in the Fifth World hadn't Acamapichtli brought back spiders or rabbits?

Bracing myself, I opened the cage, grasped the owl by the head – and, ignoring the flurry of wings and claws, slit its neck just above the line of my hands.

Blood pooled out, red and warm, staining the tip of the knife, spreading to my fingers. I set the knife against the ground, and drew a quincunx: the five-armed cross, symbol of the Fifth World, of its centre and four points leading outwards – of the Fifth Age, and the four ages that had come before it. Then I chanted a hymn to my patron god Mictlantecuhtli, Lord Death:

> *"All paths lead to You*
> *To the land of the Flensed, to the land of the Fleshless*
> *No quetzal feathers, no scattered flowers*
> *Just songs dwindling, just trees withering*
> *Noble or peasant, merchant or goldsmith,*
> *Death takes us all through four hundred paths*
> *To the mystery of Your presence."*

A veil shimmered and danced into existence; a faint green light that seemed to make the room larger. I felt as if I were standing on the verge of a chasm – at the *cenote* north of the city, where glistening waters turned into the river that separated the living from the dead. A wind rose in the room, but the tinkle of the bells on the entrance-curtain seemed muffled and distant. The skin on my neck and wrists felt loose, and my bones ached within the depths of my body as if I were already a doddering old man. Gently, carefully, I turned back towards the room – moving as through layers of cotton.

In the gloom, Teomitl shone with a bright green light the colour of jade – not surprising, as his patron goddess was Chalchiuhtlicue, Jade Skirt, Goddess of Rivers and Streams. Acamapichtli was surrounded by the blue-and-white aura of his own patron god. Around Coatl and the dead warrior though, the room pulsed with the same shadows I'd caught a glimpse of earlier. I saw faces, distorted in pain... and flailing arms and legs, all clinging to each other in an obscene tangle of limbs... and hands, their fingers engorged out of shape, and everything was merging into a final, deep darkness which flowed over the face of the dead warrior and into his body, like blood through veins.

It was like no curse or illness I had ever seen.

I closed my eyes, and broke the quincunx by rubbing a foot against its boundary. "I'd step away from the body, if I were you," I said.

Coatl leapt as if bitten by a snake. "You think it's contagious?"

"It's a possibility," I said, carefully.

Acamapichtli was leaning against the wall, his hand wrapped around something I couldn't see. Another of his little amulets, no doubt: he was in the habit of carving ivory and filling its grooves with the blood of sacrifices to make powerful charms. My hand still bore a whitish mark where one of them had touched me, the year before.

"So?" Teomitl asked.

Coatl shook his head. He'd stepped away from Eptli's body, letting us see quite clearly that although the warrior was covered with scars, there was indeed no wound whatsoever. Eptli had shaved his head, an odd affectation for a warrior, but it did mean we could see there was no wound there either.

Not that it surprised me. "It's some kind of illness," I said. I thought of the shadows again, and shivered. "Brought on by magic."

"Can you recognise the source?" Acamapichtli asked.

I shook my head. Every magical spell was the power of a god, called down into the Fifth World by a devotee, and it should have had a signature as recognisable as the light of Jade Skirt on Teomitl's face. "It's decaying." I would have knelt by the corpse, but what I'd seen of the light made me wary. "Breaking down into pieces, as if the Fifth World itself were anathema to it."

"That's not magic," Acamapichtli said, sharply.

"Star-demons?" Coatl asked. The star-demons were the enemies of the gods, destined to end the Fifth World by consuming us all in a great earthquake.

"I've seen star-demons," I said, slowly – my hands seized up at the thought, even though the event had been more than four months before. "This doesn't look anything like their handiwork."

Acamapichtli's grip on his amulet didn't waver. His eyes were cruel; amused. "I've seen it before."

"And?" Teomitl asked, when it was obvious Acamapichtli wasn't going to add anything further.

Acamapichtli had a gesture halfway between exasperation and pity. "If I remembered, don't you think I'd be telling you?"

"No," I said.

Acamapichtli shook his head, as if to clear out a persistent annoyance. "Let old grudges lie, Acatl. We're allies in this."

By necessity – and I still wasn't sure why. "Why the interest?" I asked.

The ghost of a smile. "Because I don't think you understand Tizoc-tzin. When his banquet is over and he wakes up and realises someone deliberately spoiled his wonderful ceremony, he is going to want explanations. And right now, neither of us can afford to fail at giving them."

Footsteps echoed from the courtyard: the slow, steady march of guards. It looked as though our time alone with the corpse was drawing to a close. I hoped it wasn't Tizoc-tzin, but I didn't think we'd be so lucky.

Before leaving, I took a last glance at the body, lying forlorn and abandoned in the middle of the room, its rich clothes discarded at its side. One moment honoured by the Revered Speaker himself, on the verge of becoming a member of the elite – and the next moment this: cooling flesh in a deserted room, probed openly by strangers. From glory to nothingness in just a few moments... a cause for regret, if there ever was one.

But then again, I was a priest for the Dead and I knew we would all come to this... in the end.

TWO
The Affairs of Warriors

"You mock me," Tizoc-tzin said. His sallow face was puckered in anger, making him seem even gaunter than usual. "Leaving in the middle of the banquet, before the feast was over? One would think" his voice was low, malicious "that you didn't care at all about the fate of the Mexica Empire."

"My Lord," I said, stiffly, "I maintain the balance of the Fifth World. The fate of the Mexica Empire is of paramount importance."

Tizoc-tzin looked dubious. He had come with his sycophant Quenami and, rather to my surprise, with a priest of Patecatl, an elderly man who had slipped into the room unobtrusively to take a look at the body. I had warned him about the possible contagion, but he had only snorted and continued – as if the word of a youngster like me had no value.

"As to you…" He looked at Teomitl, his face caught in an odd expression. They were brothers, yet they couldn't have been more different: there was bad blood between them – had been for four months. "You ought to have known better."

"It's important," Teomitl said. "For Acatl-tzin, and perhaps for me. He was a warrior." Now that Teomitl was Master of the House of Darts, he was most definitely no longer my inferior, and didn't have to add the "tzin" honorific after my name. But he'd kept the habit, all the same.

"And you're Master of the House of Darts," Tizoc-tzin said, curtly. "Head of the army, and heir-presumptive to the Mexica Empire. Do you know what it looks like when you walk out in the midst of the celebrations for our safe return?"

I had to admit he had a point – for all his exalted status, Teomitl had a tendency to behave as though he were still a mere warrior in a regiment – just as I, when I made no effort, had a tendency to behave as a mere priest for the Dead.

Teomitl's face darkened. "The coronation war was a failure."

Quenami winced, and next to me, Coatl looked as though he would rather be anywhere else. It was Acamapichtli who spoke up, his aristocratic face creased in amusement. "You forget. We must appear strong, especially in the present circumstances."

Four months before, in the scrabble for the succession, Tizoc-tzin's court intrigues had led to the death of the entire council, and the intrusion of star-demons into the Sacred Precinct – and the Great Temple's altars had been slick with the blood of our own noblemen. All in front of the foreign dignitaries gathered for the designation of Tizoc-tzin – dozens of neighbouring city-states who had paid exorbitant tribute to Tenochtitlan, and dreamt of a day they could cast us down into the mud.

Whatever angry words Teomitl might have had were cut short by the re-emergence of the priest of Patecatl,

31

who looked preoccupied. "This is no natural death, my Lord."

Tizoc-tzin looked from Acamapichtli to me – but it must have been clear we couldn't have bribed the priest. "What is it, then?"

"I don't know," the priest said, which wasn't surprising. Patecatl was god of herbs and potions: He was powerless against spells. "It looks like a curse."

Tizoc-tzin looked back at me, his lips tightening. "Someone did this, then. Someone cast a spell to kill a man in the midst of the celebration."

"It would seem so," Acamapichtli said, with a meaningful look at me.

Tizoc-tzin threw him a suspicious glance, but more as a matter of principle, it seemed. "There is a sorcerer out there, seeking to destabilise the Mexica Empire."

I winced – and, under Quenami's disapproving gaze, did my very best to turn it into a cough. "My Lord, surely the people love you."

"The Empire goes from coast to mountains, from marshes to valleys. We have our enemies, only waiting for a moment of weakness to pounce."

Tizoc-tzin had always had a slight tendency to paranoia; unfortunately, this had turned out to be justified four months before, when his rashness had got him killed at the same time as the council. I and the other two High Priests had pooled our powers to bring him back from the threshold of the world beyond, but he'd never been the same since. If anything, the paranoia had got worse. He saw assassins in every shadow, every canal bend, every courtyard and in everyone bold enough, or foolhardy enough, to approach him too closely.

The murder looked more like a case of personal

vengeance than political intrigue – not that it was made more legitimate by that, of course. "I don't think–"

"Acatl never thinks." Acamapichtli's voice was dismissive. "That's always been his trouble. We'll of course investigate this as thoroughly as we can, my Lord."

As usual, I wasn't sure whether to thank Acamapichtli or to strangle him. And, by the smug look on his face, he knew my feelings all too well.

Tizoc-tzin frowned. At the point where his eyebrows met, I could see a thin white line: the arch of a broken bone in the skull. His eyes were deeper than they should have been, shadowed like empty sockets.

Southern Hummingbird blind me, we should never have brought him back. No wonder the hole in the Fifth World wouldn't close: the dead weren't meant to rule the living, or to walk in sunlight.

"Very well," Tizoc-tzin said. "I trust this will be solved quickly."

And he swept away, without sparing us a further glance. Quenami lingered behind, looking at us both as if he might add something in his capacity as High Priest of the Southern Hummingbird and our superior, but then shook his head and followed his master. Teomitl, after talking briefly to Coatl, also left – presumably going back to the banquet. From the tense set of his shoulders, he didn't look altogether happy about the situation.

Acamapichtli swore under his breath. "He's not getting better."

"We didn't have any choice," I said, with a conviction I couldn't feel. "We had to keep the Fifth World whole."

"Oh, it will work out, don't worry. Perhaps not for us, though," Acamapichtli added speculatively. I didn't like the tone of his voice – at a guess, he was once more trying to work out the best possibilities for his own advancement.

I decided to take the fight to a terrain I was more familiar with. "Can you look into where you saw that magic last?"

"What magic? Oh, the one on the corpse?" Acamapichtli shrugged. "Why not?"

"You don't sound very enthusiastic," Coatl interjected. He looked paler than he had at the beginning of our interview, and he was shaking. It was all due, however, to barely-contained anger rather than ill-health. "One of my warriors died. I'll have justice for it."

Acamapichtli appeared unfazed. "I usually leave Acatl to deal with matters of justice," he said maliciously. "He's got much more experience than I."

"Do you really think this is a good time for quarrels?" I asked.

"Quarrels? We're not quarrelling," Acamapichtli said. He threw his head back, and abruptly appeared to grow taller and larger, with a shimmering shadow over his face, and his voice echoing like the sound of thunder over a storm-tossed lake. "Trust me – when we quarrel, you'll know."

And he, too, swept away from the courtyard – leaving me alone with a corpse and an angry warrior.

"What helpfulness," I said. I could have done much the same trick, had I wished to, but it would have been disrespectful to Lord Death: a waste of His power for nothing more than the posturing of turkeys. I turned to Coatl. "You have my word," I said. "By my face and by my heart, I'll bring you justice."

Coatl grimaced, but said nothing. He couldn't accuse me of being an oath-breaker, but clearly he didn't trust priests anymore than he had to. A typical warrior. I suppressed a sigh and resumed the interview I'd started during the examination of the body. "You said you didn't know much about Eptli. Are you sure there isn't anything you can tell me?"

Coatl spread his hands again… and then shook his head, as if coming to a decision. "Teomitl-tzin would have told you, in any case. There was – a problem with Eptli."

"A problem?"

"The warriors on that line were those who had captured a prisoner unaided in the course of battle."

"Yes," I said. I couldn't see what he was getting at.

"Eptli – " Coatl shrugged. "Another warrior claimed the same prisoner as Eptli. It happens, in the course of the battle. Things get a little frantic, you can't find any witnesses, and there you are with a prisoner and two men claiming him."

"Doesn't the prisoner know who captured him?"

Coatl's lips tightened. "You've never been on a battlefield, have you? As I said: it's fast and frantic, and all the warriors have painted faces and similar feather-suits. Who's to tell the difference between them, unless they have standards of their own? Which," he added, "neither Eptli nor the other possessed."

"And how do you resolve this, if there are no witnesses?" I asked.

"As you said: you ask the prisoner." Coatl didn't look happy. "Ask other warriors of the unit to see if you can trace the troop movements and see who is more likely to have been there at the crucial point." He didn't sound altogether pleased.

"You don't like doing this?"

He grimaced. "Discipline I can deal with. Warriors should set a higher example than commoners, and if

35

they go so far as to forget themselves, and steal or betray, or retreat in battle, they only deserve what happens to them. This…? The stakes are high, we're not sure, and everything depends on our decision."

"When you say 'we'?"

"The war-council handles all criminal matters connected to warriors while we're out on a campaign." I caught the implication: whoever the guilty party was, they would likely be tried by the tribunal in the palace, thus relieving him of his responsibilities.

I could have asked him if he thought he'd taken the right decision, but there would have been no point. What we needed wasn't the truth of what had happened on this battlefield, but evidence of someone being a strong enough grudge to cast a curse on Eptli. "The other warrior who claimed the prisoner–" I started.

"Chipahua? He wasn't happy. Not at all." Coatl seemed to realise the import of what he'd said. "Not that he'd do anything. I'd be very much surprised. Chipahua has always abided by the rules."

Clearly, he'd defend his warriors to the death, and I wasn't sure I blamed him. Were our situations reversed, I'd have done the same for my priests. "What kind of a warrior was he?"

"What do you want to know?"

"Young or old?" I asked.

"Middle-aged." Chipahua grimaced again.

"But he'd already taken a captive before."

"Four."

"Like Eptli." And, like Eptli, he'd have stood on the verge of admittance into the Jaguar or Eagle Knights. Two warriors, vying for further status and prestige, and only one prisoner. It could definitely get ugly fast.

"Look," Coatl said, "as I said, I don't like doing this. Accusing people without proof."

I drew myself to my full height, letting him see my oak-embroidered cloak, the polished skull-mask on my face: the paraphernalia of a High Priest for the Dead, one who patrolled the invisible boundaries, one who defended against magical incursions. "It's a serious matter. Magical spells are one thing; spells cast under the Revered Speaker's nose, so to speak…" I had no doubt Tizoc-tzin was going to hold Acamapichtli and I accountable for all of it. The Southern Hummingbird knew he needed little excuse, those days.

Still, I stood by what I'd said a year ago. Our Revered Speaker might be a poor warrior with too much ambition, and didn't have the stature to wear the Turquoise and Gold Crown. But when the alternative was star-demons loose in the palace – as we'd had during the drawn-out change of Revered Speaker – I knew where I stood. I would preserve the balance and learn to live with my rancour.

Coatl's face was expressionless. "As I said, you'll want to talk to the commander of his unit."

"I don't think so," I said, slowly. "There is something more you're not telling me, isn't there?" I knew the signs, had seen them too often. Coatl was far from the first uncooperative witness I had questioned. In fact, for a member of the war-council, one of the highest authorities in the army, he was surprisingly amiable. Then again… then again, he wasn't a nobleman by birth – from his build and numerous scars, he had risen through the ranks to attain his current position. His parents, just like mine, would have been peasants.

Coatl's face twisted, becoming distant, expressionless, as if he were being careful not to display a strong emotion – hatred? I very much doubted it was affection. "Eptli could be... difficult to get on with."

"I see. Anyone in particular he didn't get on with? Apart from Chipahua, I presume."

Coatl didn't rise to the bait. "He got into a quarrel with a merchant, three days out from Tenochtitlan."

Merchants and warriors got on about as well as warriors and priests – very seldom. "About the usual things, I presume?" Though not as highly considered as warriors, merchants were often more prosperous, and tended to displays of wealth the warriors found obscene and undeserved. More than one merchant had been beaten to death after returning from a trading expedition with a few too many quetzal feathers, cacao pods or jewels.

"I don't know." Coatl sounded distinctly weary now. "I've seen too many of those cases to tell them apart. The merchant was one of the advance spies, bringing us word of the situation in Metztitlan and of its weak points. He'd barely come into the encampment when Eptli came along and started insulting him."

"Was he hot-tempered?" I asked.

"Eptli?" Coatl hesitated – deciding how much untruth he could get away with. "No," he said, regretfully. "He was a cool-headed man."

Hmm. Either Eptli hated all merchants, or there was something particular about this one, something that had caused him to lose his calm. I added this to the growing list of problems to tackle.

"Where can I find Chipahua?" I asked. The warrior who had vied with Eptli for the prisoner looked like the most likely person to arrange a fatal accident. "At the feast?"

Coatl shook his head. "His rank isn't high enough for him to attend the feast in the palace. You'll find him at his house." He gave me an address in Cuepopan, one of the four districts of Tenochtitlan.

As I left, I could feel his eyes on the back of my neck. He was a singular man – few people had the courage to stand up to an increasingly erratic Tizoc-tzin. I liked him, and I knew I shouldn't have, for in all he had said to me, it had become clear he hadn't cared much for Eptli, and perhaps even resented him for taking away the glory of another, more worthy warrior. He had insisted on obtaining justice – but could he have done otherwise, if he hoped to pretend innocence?

I took a boat from the temple's dock to get to Chipahua's house. Like most of our crafts, it was a small, sleek assemblage of reeds, with a simple frieze of spiders running along the prow. The priest who was polling it through the canals was someone I didn't know: a young man barely into adolescence – probably a novice who had recently entered the clergy. He wielded the pole with the ease of someone born on the lake, effortlessly inserting us into the dense traffic of the crowded canals and navigating between ornate barges three times our size without a second thought.

I sat at the back, wishing I'd thought to change out of my High Priest regalia. It would undoubtedly impress a warrior more than a simple cloak, but the sun was high in the sky and the cloth of the embroidered cape was already uncomfortably hot. Sweat ran down my cheeks in rivulets, and the skull-mask wedged on my face kept being dislodged by the jolts of the boat as it turned into yet another canal.

Most boats were going the opposite way, their oars and poles splashing into the water with the familiar rhythm of rowing. On the land adjoining the canal, a crowd walked in companionable silence: women with baskets of poultry and vegetables, and men bent forward against the band on their forehead which supported the burden on their backs.

Chipahua's house wasn't far from the centre of the city, on the edge of the noblemen's quarter. The buildings here were lower, not having the two storeys that only high-ranking noblemen were allowed, but they were brightly-painted adobe, not wattle and daub, and what they lacked in height, they made up with sheer scale. Every house we passed seemed to sprawl interminably, their gates open to display their outer courtyards, every one more magnificent than the last: a mass of high trees and vibrant frescoes, every building vying with its neighbours with tasteful decoration reminding the viewer of their owner's wealth.

At length, we stopped before a house that seemed almost shabby compared to its neighbours: the outside frieze was a simple portrait of Tezcatlipoca, the Smoking Mirror, god of war and fate, and the single slave at the entrance wore a white loincloth with no insignia or adornment.

He took me to his master without demur, leading me through a courtyard with a well and two pine trees, in which slave women wove cloth, keeping a wary eye on the children, who were playing with dolls and wooden chariots. The rhythmic sound of their looms against the mortars followed us inside – though not the heat, thankfully.

The reception room was supported by columns painted with ochre, and a single quetzal-feather fan seemed to be the only concession to the wealth and status of its owner.

Three warriors and three women were sitting at the far end, gathered around the remains of a meal. When the entrance-curtain tinkled, the warrior in the centre looked up, straight at me, and gestured for the slave to bring me closer.

I'd expected him to remain seated, but to my surprise he rose and bowed to me. "Acatl-tzin. Do join us."

He knew my name, too, which was surprising. Warriors and priests seldom mingled, unless at court, but he wasn't high enough in the hierarchy to be at court on a regular basis. I threw a glance at his companions, who appeared to have swallowed a live ember. Well, at least *their* reception wasn't unexpected. "Chipahua, I presume?"

He smiled. Like Eptli, he wasn't a young man, and battles had left their mark on him, not only in the long scar that slashed his face from right cheek to temple, but also in the wariness with which he held himself. But the smile, spreading to every feature, made him seem almost boyish. "Honoured to meet you, Acatl-tzin." He pointed at the food, spread out on the mat before him. "Do eat with us."

Most of the food was already gone, though the maize cakes and the fish in lime and spiced sauce smelled delicious – not fit for the meal of the Revered Speaker, but simple, robust fare such as I ate every day. "I already ate," I said, regretfully.

"A pity. I'd expected to have more time to idly chat," Chipahua said. "But I very much doubt you came all this way for my sake."

I studied him, but his weathered face gave nothing away. He had to know about Eptli, didn't he?

"You know what happened."

41

Chipahua's gaze didn't waver. "Yes. Someone fainted during the ceremony."

"Not fainted. Died."

"I see." His lips tightened. "And once again we're not informed."

I felt obscurely embarrassed, even though none of it was my fault. Chipahua smiled – but it was a smile tinged with anger. "What did you do with the body?"

"It's still being examined in the palace. Why?"

"Because he was one of us. He should be given a proper funeral."

"He'll have one." A wake, a pyre and a dog's sacrifice, and the hymns for the Dead – no more, no less than what any man was entitled to.

"I don't think you understand," Chipahua said. His gaze was still amused – but it was tinged with the contempt of warriors for priests. "He was one of us. We will be at his funeral, and it will be done properly."

I acquiesced, rather than let myself be drawn into a loaded discussion. "You haven't asked me which warrior it was."

Something passed in his gaze, too fast for me to grasp. "No. It doesn't matter who he was."

A lie. A good one, but still a lie. "The warrior was Eptli of the Atempan clan."

One of the other warriors sniggered. "Got what was coming to him."

"Zacayaman!" Chipahua said, sharply. "Be silent. The dead are owed respect." But he didn't sound as outraged as he ought to have been.

"I've seen sadder reactions," I said.

Chipahua picked up a maize cake, and looked at it as if it were a lump of jade. "If you're here, you know what happened. I can't exactly be sad."

"But you're also the one with the strongest motive."

"Motive?" This time, the surprise sounded genuine, but I'd already seen what a good liar he was. "I don't see... you mean the death wasn't natural? I assumed–"

"You assumed wrong. Someone cursed Eptli, and he died."

Chipahua tore the cake into two neat pieces. "Curses are serious matters," he said.

"So is ascending into the Eagle or Jaguar Knights."

He wasn't looking at me anymore. "It takes more than four prisoners, as you well know."

"I'm not that familiar with army procedures," I said carefully, though in this particular case I did know. My elder brother was a Jaguar Knight.

"The Knights have to accept you as a brother." He shrugged. "I don't think either I or Eptli had much of a chance, to be honest."

"Why?"

"I'm a commoner," Chipahua said, simply.

"And Eptli wasn't?"

"Eptli's father was a commoner before the Revered Speaker elevated him. It gave Eptli a great deal of... arrogance?"

"Which was totally unjustified," the warrior on my left said.

I suspected arrogance was the wrong word. Warriors were arrogant as a way of life. There had to be more to explain why Eptli was so disliked.

"Commoners have ascended into the Jaguar Knights before," I said, thinking of my brother. We were the sons of a peasant family on the outskirts of Tenochtitlan; he'd risen through feats of arms, and I through the clergy.

43

Chipahua grimaced. "The new commander isn't as open as the previous one."

"Southern Hummingbird blind the Jaguar Commander," the right-hand warrior – Zacamayan – said. "We know your worth, as does everyone in the clan-unit." His accent and dress were those of an educated man: he was either a nobleman himself, or the son of an elevated commoner, afforded all the privileges of the nobility.

I ignored the interruption. "You want me to think you had no motive for killing Eptli," I said to Chipahua. "But taking a fourth captive brings other benefits besides entry into the Knighthoods." The haircut that marked them as veterans; distinctive insignia and cloaks; the right to more of the tribute, and the title which would give them the higher status they coveted.

"I won't deny that." Chipahua's face was blank. "If you're going by motive, then yes, I do have one, and a strong one. You'll know I wasn't the only one."

I refrained from glancing at his two supporters. "Giving me names to save yourself?"

Chipahua looked thoughtful for a moment. "You've talked to Coatl," he said finally.

I thought, uneasily, of the tone in Coatl's voice when he'd talked about Eptli. "He didn't approve of Eptli?"

"Eptli mocked the old. He rejected their authority – he said they were spent, and they had nothing more to teach us."

I winced. Given the little I'd seen of Coatl, I very much doubted he'd have liked that. Eptli was sounding more and more like a thoroughly disagreeable person.

Not that I was surprised. It was rarely the likeable men who were murdered. Murder – especially magical murder, with the lengthy preparations, the shedding

44

of living blood and the calling on the power of the gods – required premeditation, and that in turn meant a strong motive. Few innocent men inspired such destructive passion.

"Very well. Do you have anything else to add?" This included the two warriors on either side of me, who watched me with undisguised hostility. Whatever Chipahua thought of priests, they didn't share that opinion.

"No," the left-hand one said.

"No," Zamacayan said. "But you should look elsewhere, Acatl-tzin." He put a slight pause after my name, as if he were adding the honorific only as an afterthought.

"I will give it some thought," I said as I rose. My cloak brushed against him for a bare moment – and I felt a palpable jolt of magic – a strong pulsing power that could only belong to Huitzilpochtli the Southern Hummingbird.

It might have been a ward: many warriors and noblemen had them – including my own student Teomitl. But the throbbing energy climbing up my arm was no standard ward. Zamacayan was either a magic-user, or he had access to one – not the tame priests at court or in the army, but someone prepared to cast a strong, elaborate spell.

I said nothing as the slave took me out of the house, and my priest started rowing us back to the temple. But I was preoccupied. Chipahua himself might have no knowledge of magic, and the two warriors no motive to kill Eptli – but put them together, and bind them with the strong comradeship that kept a unit together in the heat of battle…

"Acatl-tzin!"

I looked up, startled out of my reverie – and almost fell over when I saw Teomitl, leaning on the prow of a narrow-nosed boat. He'd discarded his regalia in favour of a mantle with a red brim, and a dark cape, though his face was still painted black and blue.

"How did you find me?" I started, but then saw the green glow of his patron goddess Jade Skirt etched in every feature of his face. I was on a boat, in the water that was Her province – of course She'd know where I was. I shifted conversation subjects. "What in the Fifth World are you doing here?"

"Telling you that you were right." Teomitl reached out, taking my hand to drag me into his own boat. "Come on, we'll go faster with this one. It's larger, and it's got the imperial insignia."

"Teomitl," I said, struggling not to capsize. "How about explanations?"

"Oh." He looked surprised for a moment. "It's the dead man."

"I shouldn't think he could get any deader," I said darkly, manoeuvring to bridge the gap between the two boats. Behind us, the traffic in the canal had completely jammed – and I guessed it was only the imperial crest that prevented people from screaming at us.

"You don't understand, Acatl-tzin." Teomitl steadied me as I set foot onto the floor of the boat. "Whatever he had, he's been passing it on to other people."

A contagious disease. In the palace. Where the rulers of the Triple Alliance were gathering for Tizoc-tzin's coronation; where the highest-ranking noblemen and priests would be discussing the coronation war and what it meant for the Mexica Empire.

I took a deep breath, but it didn't remove the leaden weight in my stomach. "Lead on," I said.

THREE
Further Victims

Teomitl took me to the same wing where we'd put Eptli's corpse earlier. The atmosphere was curiously subdued, with an over-abundance of black-garbed priests of Pate-catl, and the blue and white cloaks that could only mark priests of Tlaloc the Storm Lord.

I wasn't that surprised: among His many attributes, the Storm Lord was responsible for the spreading of diseases – pouring them down from one of His jars as he poured rain and lightning upon the Fifth World.

Acamapichtli was waiting for us in front of a closed entrance-curtain. On the ground behind him was a half circle, inscribed with blood-glyphs. Even from a dis-tance, I could feel the heat radiating from the tracings. Something large – perhaps even a man – had been sac-rificed here.

"Is it that bad?" I asked. Teomitl's explanations had been confused: I gathered there had been at least one victim, but the sheer number of priests made me suspect it was somewhat worse.

"I don't know," Acampichtli said. "That fool priest of Patecatl should have listened to you in the first place."

"He didn't," I said, though I was as angry with the priest as Acamapichtli himself was. Contagion was a serious matter – and, once started, the illness would be harder to contain. "You can't change that."

Acamapichtli pursed his lips, a familiar gesture halfway between amusement and contempt. "Two victims so far. The priest of Patecatl who examined the body, and Coatl."

They'd both touched it, I recalled. "And the warriors who carried it?"

"We're looking for them." Acamapicthli shook his head. "But they went back to their houses, and no one paid much attention to them after they left."

No, indeed not. But I knew better than to let him cow me through shame. "And the illness?" The warrior hadn't had many symptoms, other than the fluttering shape of shadows over his face, like dappled light coming through trees – no, that wasn't it. I'd seen that somewhere, too – but where?

"Their body temperature is high, and they keep shivering. No other symptoms, but those can take time to appear."

He might have been right – I wouldn't have known. I was called in after there was no hope, after the remedies of ground pearls and white earth had failed, after the patient had taken on the visage of death, after the blood had poured over the heart and spread into all the limbs, quenching life as it did so. And few illnesses came from corpses.

Angry voices brought me back to reality. Teomitl was arguing, loudly and arrogantly, with Acamapichtli. "I don't see why–"

"It's a precaution."

"He didn't touch the corpse."

"What in the Fifth World are you talking about?" I asked, with the feeling I wasn't going to like the answer.

"He wants you to be isolated, with the others!" Teomitl blurted out.

"Only for a few days."

A few days? "We don't have that kind of time," I said. What was he thinking of? "You pick an odd time to be conscientious. What happened to the survival of the Fifth World being assured?" And he seemed to conveniently forget about including himself in his isolation – typical.

He looked at me for a while, and for the first time I heard utter seriousness in his voice. "I am High Priest of Tlaloc the Storm Lord, His voice in the Fifth World. If the god has chosen to break His third jar, and pour the waters of epidemic upon us, then it is my responsibility to beseech Him for mercy – and to isolate those He has touched, to see if They have been chosen to go to Tlalocan, the paradise of the Blessed Drowned, or if they are destined to remain in the Fifth World."

"This is all about appearances, isn't it?" Teomitl asked, angrily. "About looking good in front of the city."

"Teomitl." I raised a hand. I could be mistaken – I could never read the slippery son of a coyote – but there was something genuine in what he was telling us. Acamapichtli believed in his personal gain, but unlike Quenami he wouldn't dismiss the gods out of hand. "Has the god spoken to you?"

"Not yet," Acamapichtli said. And then I did understand: if it was indeed the will of Tlaloc, and he, Tlaloc's priest in the Fifth World, ignored it, then he would have more to contend with than angry mortals.

I suppressed a bitter laugh. We'd weathered the anger

of the Southern Hummingbird the year before – which had resulted in the massacre of the whole imperial council by star-demons; I could understand why Acamapichtli wasn't keen to try Tlaloc's patience.

"I don't think it's Him," I said. "It's magical."

"You presume to know the will of the gods?"

I shrugged. "No. But if it's just the will of a mortal, then I'm oath-bound to go against it. I keep the boundaries of the Fifth World, and the balance that maintains the Fifth Sun in the Sky, and Grandmother Earth fertile. Will you go against that?"

"If I must." Acamapichtli's face was pale. "For a few days, at least."

"We might not have a few days," I said. I hesitated. I didn't know much about illnesses, but still – "Why is it becoming contagious only now? We haven't heard a report about Eptli's comrades falling ill, have we?" And Chipahua and his companions had looked perfectly healthy, with none of the symptoms of the disease.

Acamapichtli looked taken aback. "It may only be contagious after death. I've seen odder things."

"Doesn't matter," Teomitl said impatiently. "Surely you're not suggesting my brother and I should be subject to this, as well?"

Acamapichtli looked as if he might argue for a moment, but he was too canny a politician for that. "I shouldn't think so, my Lord. Your protections – and Tizoc-tzin's – are the strongest in this palace. Nevertheless, I would recommend… caution."

Teomitl grinned, an utterly bleak expression. "One doesn't become Revered Speaker through caution, priest." He looked almost like his brother in those moments, with the same stern mannerisms, and the same

51

way of spitting out words as if they'd offended him. I didn't like that – I'd always known he'd grow away from me, my young and precocious student, but I hadn't thought I would lose him to Tizoc-tzin's shadow. "You overstep your limits."

Acamapichtli's face twisted, as if he'd swallowed something bitter. "My Lord… I differ. As Acatl said, those are the numinous boundaries of the Fifth World. They shouldn't concern you."

Oh, for the gods' sake, the whole business was increasingly ridiculous. "It's too early to start acting so cautiously. Give us some of your amulets, and you can come pick us up if we collapse."

Acamapichtli looked as though he might protest, but in that precise moment he was approached by a young priest of Tlaloc.

"Acamapichtli-tzin," the priest said. He bent his blue-striped face to Acamapichtli's ear, and whispered something. I saw Acamapichtli's face go from mild annoyance to surprise, and then – for a brief moment – to naked fear.

"What is it?" Teomitl asked.

"None of your–" Acamapichtli bit back the sentence with great difficulty. "Since you're both so keen to risk further contamination…"

"Someone else died," I said.

"Not any 'someone else'," Acamapichtli said. "Eptli's prisoner."

The one that had been contested between him and Chipahua.

"Take us there," I said to the priest – who looked back, hesitating, to Acamapichtli for confirmation. Acamapichtli shook his head with sardonic humour. "It's their lives at stake," he said. "We'll discuss the matter of your isolation later on."

The prisoners captured during a war were normally the property of their captors, and as such were lodged by the clan, fed and taken care of until the time came for sacrifice. But on this occasion, either because there hadn't been enough time since the army's return, or because Tizoctzin had wanted to keep a watch on the forty captives for his confirmation ceremony, they had been accommodated in the palace itself, in a secluded section to the west of the building, away from the bustle of life in either the Revered Speaker's or the She-Snake's quarters. The mood, when we entered, was subdued – but I got the feeling it was usual, and not due to their losing a comrade.

It might have been any warrior camp before a battle: the air reeked of the blood of penances, and several of the prisoners I crossed had bloody earlobes and bloody loincloths, their worship-thorns casually thrust through the upper part of their cotton clothes. Somewhere would be an altar to the Southern Hummingbird or the Smoking Mirror – with an accumulation of worship balls, the grass stained red and shimmering with raw power.

We followed the priest to the back of a small courtyard, where another priest was keeping watch on a closed room, with a gloomy countenance. "Here for the body?" he asked.

"To examine it."

"You have the courage of eagles," the priest said. He jerked a finger towards the entrance curtain, gently swaying in the breeze. "It's in there."

I paused before entering, and slashed my earlobes, taking the time to cast a brief spell of protection calling on

Lord Death's power. I waited until the cold of the underworld spread through my veins like melted ice before I passed the threshold.

For all my protection, I felt it when I entered – and by Teomitl's sharp intake of breath, he did, too. The air was tight, somehow more rarefied than it ought to have been: it reminded me of walking atop Mount Popocatepetl, where everything seemed thinner, and yet more sharply defined than at lake level.

I knelt, and rubbed my earlobes until my recently opened wounds bled again. With the blood, I drew a careful quincunx around myself, all the while singing a hymn to Lord Death to grant me true sight:

"We all must die
We all must go down into darkness…"

The air tightened again – like water, drawing back together after a pebble had been thrown into it. It cut my breath for a single, painful moment; and then everything was back to normal.

Or, at least, as much of normal as was possible, given the circumstances.

The room receded in the background, becoming thin and translucent – letting me see the shadows. They played, lazily, between the walls, passing through the black-painted columns and the clay brazier as if they didn't exist. Again, I caught glimpses of flailing arms and legs within – of raised rashes, covering a torso like the scales of a snake, of pus, spurting out from broken skin while the body beneath contorted in a soundless scream.

Nausea welled up in my throat, and I had to steady myself within the circle.

Teomitl was already kneeling by the victim's side. "Don't touch him!" I said. He jerked back as if burnt. The shadows congregated around him – I couldn't help but be reminded of a curious shoal of fish, gathering around a drowned body. Tlaloc's lightning strike me, I didn't need macabre imagery right now. If I couldn't even focus on the task at hand…

Nothing leapt from the body to him, and I might as well have been invisible for all the attention the shadows paid me. Perhaps Teomitl, who was a warrior protected by Huitzilpochtli the Southern Hummingbird – just as Eptli had been – was a better target?

Cautiously, I stepped out of the quincunx, half-waiting for something to happen, but nothing did. I looked at the body: a young, well-muscled warrior, who looked barely old enough to have left the House of Youth. His face was slack and blank, like all corpses, and I could see no obvious wounds. Though…

I knelt, being careful not to touch the body. The smell of wet earth and burning coal wafted up to me – the corpse itself didn't smell yet, it was too early. The limbs were locked in an unnatural position: the man had been dead for some time. I couldn't find any wounds, but there was a slight raised pattern on the skin, like scales on the skin of a lizard – sores which hadn't yet formed.

"Acatl-tzin," Teomitl said, "the death–"

"I know," I said. "It's not that recent. I don't know who was contaminated first, him or Eptli."

"It's the same symptoms. Or lack of," Teomitl said, sombrely.

I shook my head. "Same symptoms. You can't see them, but the same shadows are in the room."

"And?" He looked as if he expected me to have the answer. Of course. I was still his teacher – never mind that I wasn't sure whether he needed me at all. The Master of the House of Darts, the heir apparent, the joint commander of the army: he seemed to be doing well for himself, regardless of my interventions.

"I don't know." I bit my lips. "But I very much doubt it's one of Tlaloc's random interventions." I'd have to ask Acamapichtli for help, but Tlaloc's fancies ran more to dropsy, leprosy or other disease, the kind that turned a man's skin as loose and as flowing as water, or made their breath rattle in their fluid-drowned lungs.

There was a single sleeping mat in the room, on which the dead man lay, and little else in the way of furniture. I rose from my crouch, ducked out of the room for a moment, in order to address the priest on guard at the entrance.

"Do you know if this was his room?" I asked.

"They all share rooms," the priest said in a bored tone. "But this one didn't."

"Oh?" Why the special treatment?

"I guess he was an important man."

"He was sick," a thickly accented voice said.

I hadn't seen the warrior by the priest's side. He looked… alien, in a way that I couldn't quite place. The coat of hardened cotton was the wrong cut; and the single tuft of hair atop his shaved head reminded me of the Otomi elite warriors, but not quite – it was not long enough and not thick enough, and the man had no stripes of paint across his face.

"You're one of the prisoners," I said.

He nodded. He held himself with pride – and why wouldn't he? He'd die for the confirmation, earning his place in the Fifth Sun's Heaven – the dream of all warriors. Surely the minor wound to his pride, that of having been captured by the despised Mexica, was worth all of this.

"I'm Cuixtli, the eldest." He spoke Nahuatl with a thick, barely recognisable accent – but then Metztitlan, his birth country, was far away, a good six days' march to the northeast. "Their leader, you might say."

"I see. I'm Acatl – High Priest for the Dead."

"I know who you are. We worship Lord Death, too, in Metztitlan." Cuixtli nodded again, almost as one equal to another.

"You say he was ill?" I asked. "Before you arrived here?"

Cuixtli spread his hands. "I don't know. When they put us here, Zoquitl was shivering – that's why we gave him his own space, to be sure."

Sacrifices were meant to be unblemished, and in perfect health – no wonder Zoquitl had been handled with such caution, in case his bad luck passed on to his companions.

"And you noticed nothing before?"

"We were on the road," Cuixtli said. "Marching. I didn't see him lag, but I wasn't paying so much attention."

So, if the prisoner – Zoquitl – had indeed been sick, it would have been barely perceptible. But then again, he was a warrior, and would want to avoid a show of shameful weakness.

Who had been ill first? He, or his captor? "Did Eptli visit Zoquitl? While you were on the road."

Cuixtli shrugged. He radiated a serenity that was almost uncanny – something I knew all too well, the growing detachment of those about to lay down their lives for the continuation of the world. One by one, he would be cutting the bonds that tied him to the Fifth World, preparing himself to die in the Southern Hummingbird's name – just as the gods themselves had died in the beginning of the Fifth Age, to bring forth life from the barren earth, and move Tonatiuh the Fifth Sun across the Heavens. "Eptli?" he asked.

"The man who captured him?"

"The one who was awarded Zoquitl." Serene didn't mean unobservant, either. "He came several times."

Beloved father, beloved son, I thought. That was the ritual for capturing another warrior: acknowledging they were as precious as your own blood, as your own flesh – making them into a living offering. "And how did he look?"

"Angry," Cuixtli said. "Elated. He was a man of many moods."

"You're sure?" It wasn't what Coatl had told me about Eptli, and I could see no reason for Coatl to lie. Unless... unless something particularly large were going on in Eptli's life. The trial before the war-council, to get his prisoner awarded to him? Would that be enough to account for the mood-swings? "When was Eptli awarded Zoquitl?"

Cuixtli shrugged. "Early on, before we set out on the march."

So, not that. Unless the argument hadn't been resolved? But could Chipahua and Coatl both be lying? I made a note to ask Teomitl about the case. With any luck, he'd remember it – though I very much doubted that anything outside of the battlefield would have interested my headstrong, glory-obsessed student. "But Eptli didn't look sick either?"

"Not that I could see. I wouldn't know. But illnesses can be a long time brewing."

"I see."

A rattle of bells cut the conversation short, as Teomitl yanked the entrance-curtain open. "Acatl-tzin!"

"What is it?" I asked.

Teomitl threw a wary glance at the priest – who had resumed his expression of studied indifference – and then a more respectful one to the warrior, as one equal to another. He held out his hand to me, unfolding tanned fingers one after the other for maximum effect.

Inside was a single notched bead of clay – which, unfortunately, meant nothing whatsoever to me. "Would you mind explaining?" I said.

"I found it inside," Teomitl said. "It had rolled under the brazier." He raised a hand, to forestall my objection. "I didn't touch the body, Acatl-tzin. I swear."

"I still don't see–"

"This belongs to a woman," Cuixtli said.

"How do you know so much about Mexica women?" I asked.

He snorted. "How can you know so little about them? Any fool knows that. It's too delicate to be a man's ornament."

Teomitl shook his head, impatiently. "It doesn't matter, Acatl-tzin. Don't you see? A woman was here."

I glanced at Cuixtli, who was looking at the bead thoughtfully. "I didn't know sacrifices were granted spouses." In very rare cases, such as the sacrifice of Tezcatlipoca's incarnation, the victim was granted all his earthly desires – and, as he ascended the steps of the Great Temple, everything was stripped away from him: wives and jewellery, and then finally clothes, to leave him as empty-handed as in the hour of his birth.

Cuixtli spread his hands. "Our last hours are spent with the gods, like those of our afterlife. How men make peace with that varies. I don't begrudge them." But his frown suggested he didn't approve.

"So you didn't know about the woman?"

He shook his head. "No. But I can enquire. Do you want me to send word?"

"Send it to me," Teomitl said.

"Indeed." Cuixtli looked at him, waiting for something – an introduction?

"Ask for Ahuizotl, the Master of the House of Darts."

The man's face froze – it was barely perceptible and didn't last long, but I saw it clearly. "I see. And why does the Master of the House of Darts concern himself with such lowly folk?"

"Lowly? You are the bravest in this palace." Teomitl's voice was low and intense. "You give your life; you give your blood on the altar-stone for the continuation of the Fifth Age. You die a warrior's death for all our sakes."

The warrior's face puckered, halfway between puzzlement and pride. "I see," he said again. "Thank you."

Teomitl made a dismissive gesture, and ducked back into the room. I followed him after bowing to the warrior.

"Teomitl?" I asked, once we were inside.

He was looking once more at the dead man, with that peculiar frown on his face – anger? I'd only seen him truly angry once, when Tizoc-tzin had belittled his wife-to-be in front of the court – but that hadn't been the same. His face had gone as flat as obsidian, his eyes dark. Now he just looked thoughtful – but much like a jaguar looked thoughtful before the hunt.

Southern Hummingbird strike me, I needed to stop this. Paranoia was all well and good, but applying it to those few people I trusted was stabbing myself in the throat.

"Yes, Acatl-tzin?"

"Eptli's case," I said. "What happened? Coatl told me the prisoner was contested between him and Chipahua."

"The case?" Teomitl looked surprised. "I don't remember – there was nothing special, Acatl-tzin. Those two
claimed the same prisoner. They wore near-identical bat-
tle-garb, with similar standards."

"Coatl told me it was a difficult decision to make."

Teomitl's eyebrows went up. "Coatl likes simple decisions. He's a warrior, through and through. There is your
side, and the enemy's side, and you shouldn't have to
wonder about more than that."

"And you're not like him?" I asked. Not that I was surprised: politics couldn't be dealt in such a simplistic
fashion. Mind you, I couldn't blame Coatl: I preferred
my divisions clear-cut, but I was aware that the gods seldom gave you what you liked best.

"I can think," Teomitl said, contemptuously. "At any
rate – we questioned the warriors of the clan-unit, and
the prisoner Zoquitl, and we thought it likely Eptli was
in the right."

"Wait," I said. "Zoquitl was willing to testify before a
Mexica tribunal?" I couldn't see for what gain. Either
way, he would die his glorious death on the altar-stone
– and if there was no conclusive evidence, he would be
given to the Revered Speaker, and the end-game would
be the same.

"He's a warrior," Teomitl said, with a quick toss of his
head that set the feathers of his headdress aflutter. "He
wouldn't cheat a fellow warrior."

I had my doubts. After all, as my brother Neutemoc
had proved, warriors – even Jaguar Knights – were like
the best and the worst of us. They walked tall above us,
but sometimes, like any mortal, they stumbled and fell.
"Fine," I said, grudgingly. "You listened to the testimonies
and decided to award the prisoner to Eptli. Why?"

"You want a detailed argumentation? Now?" Teomitl's gaze moved to the dead prisoner.

"The gist of it," I said.

"He was more likely to be in the area, his description fitted Zoquitl's testimony better, and he was more muscular than Chipahua, more likely to be able to capture him with one blow, as Zoquitl testified." Teomitl's voice was monotonous, bored.

"And you never had doubts?" I asked.

"No. Acatl-tzin, why go over this again? We ruled and there is no appeal."

Why? I frowned, not quite sure why myself. "I thought an inconclusive trial conclusion would explain why Chipahua was so angry at Eptli, and vice-versa."

"Well, it's not that." Teomitl hesitated. "There was someone who didn't agree with this, originally."

"On the war-council?" I asked.

"Yes. Itamatl. He's the deputy for the Master of the Bowl of Fatigue. He was sceptical at first, and argued against the evidence. But not for long."

That didn't sound much like a divided war-council, no matter how I turned it.

"We need more evidence," I said.

"I should say we've got more than enough here," Teomitl said, sombrely.

"That's not what I meant."

I needed to see how ordinary warriors had considered Eptli. I needed inside information, but Teomitl would be useless on this one: like Coatl, he moved in spheres that were too exalted to pay attention to the common soldiers. What I needed was someone lower down the hierarchy.

I needed–

Tlaloc's Lightning strike me, I needed my brother.

I had caught a glimpse of Neutemoc at the banquet, so I knew that not only had he come home safe, but also that he had gained from the campaign. But the formalised banquet hadn't left me time to have a quiet chat with him, and I had been looking forward to visiting him.

I just hadn't intended that my visit – the first for months – to come with strings attached: the last thing we needed was for my High Priest business to interfere in our fragile and budding relationship.

FOUR
Brother and Sister

First, we needed to make it out of the palace – preferably without running into Acamapichtli and his absurd notions of quarantine again.

Luckily, the priest who'd brought us into the prisoners' quarters had vanished, and his replacement at Zoquitl's door was more interested in doing his job as a guard than checking on our departure.

"We'll run into priests," I said as we exited the prisoners' quarters. "The palace was overrun by those sons of a dog."

Teomitl shook his head. "Not if we take the least-travelled paths. Come on, Acatl-tzin!"

Of course, he had all but grown up there in the early years of his brother's reign and he knew the place like the back of his hand. He took a turn left, and then a dizzying succession of turns through ornate courtyards where slaves brought chocolate to reclining nobles – until the crowds thinned, the frescoes faded into paleness and the courtyards became dusty, deserted squares, with their vibrant mosaics eaten away by years of winds.

"The quarters of Chilmapopoca," Teomitl said, laconically. "My brother Axayacatl's favourite son. He died of a wasting sickness when he was barely seven years old."

It smelled of death and neglect, and of a sadness deeper than I could express in words. I shivered and walked faster, hoping to leave the place soon.

And then we were walking past the women's quarters: high-pitched voices and the familiar clacking sound of weaving looms echoed past us – the guard in the She-Snake's uniform gave Teomitl a brief nod, and waved us on.

"Are you sure?"

Teomitl's face was lit in a mischievous smile. "Remember three months ago, when that concubine blasted her way out of the palace?"

The scar on the back of my hand ached. The previous year, in the chaos that had followed the previous Revered Speaker's death, we'd uncovered a sorcerer working for foreigners. In his death-throes, he had opened up a passageway, allowing his employer to escape into the city.

"It was supposed to be sealed up."

"It was," Teomitl said. "But I got them to make me a key."

The women looked away as we walked past, though not all of them. Some were smiling at Teomitl – whether because he was an attractive youth or because his uniform marked him as Master of the House of Darts, I didn't know. But Teomitl, lost in his current task, didn't even appear to notice them.

As for me... I'd been sworn to the gods since I was old enough to walk; and the women didn't even raise the ghost of a desire in me. A goddess had once accused me of being less than human, but she'd been wrong. I saw them as people – not for what they could bring me in bed, or the status they symbolised, but merely as the other half of the duality that kept the balance of the world.

At length, we reached another courtyard, which was entirely deserted. Teomitl breathed a sigh. "Good. I hate throwing women out of here. They always make such a fuss."

The building at the back of the courtyard was a low, one-storey structure, an incongruity in a palace that almost always had the coveted two floors. Columns supported its roof, creating a pleasant patio for summertime, though we were barely out of winter and most trees were bare.

In the centre was a patch of clearer adobe, clear of all frescoes: Teomitl reached out for it, and I felt more than saw the discharge of magic leap to his hand, the jade-green glow characteristic of his goddess. The adobe lit up from within, as if exhaling radiance – and then it seemed to sink back onto itself, receding until it revealed a darker entrance. The air smelled of that peculiar sharp smell before the rain.

"It's not the same passageway, is it?" I asked. The one I remembered all too well had torn through the neighbouring quarters: looking through it had merely revealed a succession of courtyards and quarters.

Teomitl grimaced. "I... used an opening in the wards, to keep it simple. Come on, Acatl-tzin."

He laid his hand on my shoulder as I entered, and a tingle went up my arm – like a mild sting by an insect, moments before it started itching.

That feeling, too, I knew – not the exact same one, but close enough. "Your shortcut is through Tlalocan."

Tlalocan, the land of the Blessed Drowned; the territory of Tlaloc and his wife Chalchiuhtlicue, Jade Skirt, Teomitl's patron goddess. A land anathema to me, the power of which ate away at my body and my magical ability.

"Yes." Teomitl said.

"Do you have any idea–"

"–how dangerous it is? Please, Acatl-tzin, I don't need a lecture."

That wasn't what I'd wanted to say. If he'd cast the spell and the Fifth World had still failed to collapse on us, then he'd got the tunnel contained. And he hadn't breached any boundaries – strictly speaking, the breach had been made by the original creator of the passageway. Sophistry, but the gods that guarded the boundaries, such as the Wind of Knives and the Curved Obsidian Blade, thrived on such rules.

"You have a passageway into the palace," I said, following him through the tunnel. It was dark and damp, and reminded me of too many unpleasant things – I knew too well the tightening in my chest, the growing dizziness, the gradually blurring field of vision. "Do you have any idea what Tizoc-tzin would do if he found out?"

I guessed more than saw him grin in the darkness. "Unpleasant things," he said. "My brother's paranoia hasn't improved." He sounded cold. His relations with his brother had always been as complex as mine with my own brother, but they hadn't been good for a while.

The pressure against my chest grew worse as we went deeper – the tunnel was dark and murky, as if we were at the very bottom of Lake Texcoco, and there were things moving in the darkness, shadows that would vanish as soon as I focused on them. The air smelled of mould and mud, and greenish light played on the back of my hands and on Teomitl's clothes, washing everything into monochrome insignificance.

Ahead was a thin beam of light, which didn't seem to grow any closer – and I was finding it hard to breathe, struggling to put one foot after the other; it was as if I were moving through thick sludge, as if I breathed in only mud…

"Acatl-tzin!"

I trudged on. Teomitl's silhouette wavered and danced within my field of vision, and – just when I thought I couldn't take it any longer, that I would have to sit down and recover some of my strength – the light abruptly flared, and grew larger – and I stumbled out, into a world washed orange by the late afternoon sun.

We were in a street I didn't recognise: the back of the palace; not the Sacred Precinct, just an expanse of dirt with a canal running alongside it. It was deserted, both the canal and the streets, with not a boat or a pedestrian to be seen.

"Let's – not – tarry – here," I said. Each word hurt like a burning coal in my throat.

"Get your breath back." Teomitl was scanning the street. "Curses. I was hoping there'd be a boatman."

"So you could commandeer it?" I asked. "That would be hardly discreet."

"If we're going to your brother's, it's quite likely Acamapichtli will figure it out sooner or later."

"I'd rather it were later," I said. "It would give me time to ask questions." I'd forgotten, in the months when the army was gone, Teomitl's tendency to rush in first and ask questions later. It was all well and good for the battlefield, but elsewhere it tended to be a little less efficient, and a little more likely to hinder us, or make us enemies.

Teomitl sighed. "As you wish. We can walk."

Since neither I nor Teomitl had changed out of our regalia, we made an imposing sight on the way: about half the people we crossed stopped, unsure whether to bow. As we went deeper into Moyotlan, one of the four districts of Tenochtitlan, I reflected somewhat sadly that for once he'd been right. Acamapichtli would likely find out where we'd gone in a heartbeat.

However... it was approaching evening, the streets slowly growing darker and the first parties of night-visitors coming out with lit pine-torches, going to a banquet, or a celebration of a birth, of a wedding, or even a party for the return of the warriors. The first snatches of flute music filled our ears, along with voices raised in speeches, and the distant beating of temple gongs in the clan-wards. With the sun gone, the weather was markedly colder and I was glad for the thick cloak of my High Priest's regalia. Teomitl, of course, barely seemed to notice anything so trivial as the change in temperature.

Neutemoc's house was brightly lit, the leaping jaguars on its façade seeming almost alive. But there were no more torches than usual: no visitors, then. I wasn't altogether surprised. Neutemoc's reputation had been badly damaged a year before, when he'd been accused of murder and had lost his wife in a matter of days. Neutemoc himself hadn't been the same – less given to boisterous parties, or even to participating in the clan's daily life. He might have regained some of that on the march, but the damage went too deep to be removed at one stroke.

The burly slave at the entrance knew both Teomitl and I, and gestured for us to go inside.

The reception room was more sober than it had been the year before: gone were the feather fans, and the silver and jade ornaments had been put away, presumably in the wicker chests against the wall. The only things that hadn't changed were the huge frescoes of Huiztilpochtli, the Southern Hummingbird and the Mexica protector god, trampling bound enemies underfoot.

"Teomitl! Acatl!" My sister Mihmatini rose from where she was sitting. She wore the simple garb of a priestess: an embroidered tunic over a skirt, with the fused-lovers symbol of the Duality set over her heart. She positively glowed – not all of it was my imagination, or my pride as her brother. A faint, radiant thread snaked from her feet to Teomitl – who stood, smiling at her.

"You're not at the palace anymore?"

Technically, they were married: Tizoc-tzin himself had set up the betrothal banquet, and had brought the stone axe to the priests – the axe which signified Teomitl's release from the education owed a youth, and his entrance into adult life. The wedding itself had been a grand, lavish ceremony, performed just before the army had left for the coronation war. Mihmatini herself had a room in the women's quarters, but of a common accord, she and Teomitl had moved into the Duality House, where Mihmatini continued her training as Guardian. I wondered how much of this was due to Tizoc-tzin's presence.

Mihmatini grimaced. "I've had enough of the palace. The atmosphere is so tense I'd rather be out, honestly. And banquets are all well and good, but they won't protect the Fifth World."

Teomitl shrugged, though he looked unhappy. "I know it's hard, but things will sort themselves out. Don't let that get to you."

"I know, but..."

"Come here."

I left the two lovers locked in an embrace and turned to face my brother.

Neutemoc looked better than before the army had left: a little less gaunt, a little more smiling, his broad face almost back to its boyish look, though his eyes would always give the lie to that. He'd gone through too much to pretend everything was fine. "Acatl."

The children had risen, and were waiting, warily, for the adults to finish greeting one another: Necalli, the only one of Neutemoc's children to be educated in the House of Youth, was calm and dignified, almost more like a priest-in-training than a boisterous warrior, and he'd obviously taught some of that attitude to his younger sister, Mazatl, who stood quivering with impatience but not moving. I couldn't see Ollin, Neutemoc's youngest son, but I presumed he'd be sleeping with the female slave who nursed him.

"You look better," I said.

"I'd be surprised." Neutemoc gestured towards the mat, on which was spread the evening meal: white fish with red pepper, and sweet potatoes baked in honey. "You, on the other hand, look–"

"–regal. I know." I made a brief, stabbing gesture. "I didn't think up the regalia."

71

Neutemoc's lips twitched into a smile. "You look like a proper High Priest, is what I wanted to say. Come on, sit down."

I hugged the children first. Mazatl was all but leaping up and down. "Uncle Acatl, Uncle Acatl! Can I try on the mask?"

I shook my head. "It's the god's face. I don't think He meant it to be a toy."

Mazatl's face fell. "Can I touch it?" she asked and squealed when her hand met the smooth surface of bone.

"You're such a kid," Necalli said, but Mazatl didn't react to his jibe.

"Children," Neutemoc said, firmly. "Your uncle, your aunt and I have to talk. Be quiet, please."

They fell silent instantly. Neutemoc's authority had always been strong, and with his wife gone, it had grown stronger. Mihmatini and I had both urged him to take another spouse – it wasn't healthy, to have a household run only by a man – but he wouldn't hear of it.

Teomitl, who'd finished embracing Mihmatini, sat down, and removed his feather headdress – casually putting it down on the ground, within reach of the children. He glanced at Mazatl with a smile and a nod – she extended a trembling hand, and touched the feathers as if they might bite. I wasn't altogether sure she needed the encouragement: she was wilder than Mihmatini at her age, and undisciplined girls would have a hard time later on in school.

"I presume this isn't a courtesy visit?" Mihmatini asked.

I grimaced. "Partly. I was intending to visit Neutemoc anyway to have news from the war, but I wasn't intending things to turn out quite the way they have."

Mihmatini nodded. "Teomitl told me earlier."

"Earlier?"

Teomitl looked sheepish – a rare enough occurrence. "I went and apprised her of the situation while you were out in the city."

"You could have told me," I said. I understood: she was his wife, and he hadn't had intimacy with her for months – and, for a bare moment, the endless cycle of rituals and ceremonies that made up his life had been torn apart, leaving him free to move as he wished. But still… she was my sister, too.

Neutemoc picked a frog from the plate in front of him, and ate it in a single gulp, as if not paying attention. "The story is making the rounds of all the regiments by now, in any case. There weren't many warriors singled out for promotions this year, and for one of them to die… You won't keep it a secret."

No, but Tizoc-tzin would try, all the same.

Beside me, Teomitl turned his head to stare at Neutemoc with a particular intensity. "My brother will do as he wishes."

"I have no doubt," Neutemoc said, soberly. He didn't sound pleased, either. Was he among those who had lost trust in Tizoc-tzin? How far did the division in the army go?

"Anyway," Neutemoc said. "If you'll permit me this–" Teomitl nodded, curtly, as one equal to another, "you do know none of this is about you. You're not your brother."

Teomitl looked, for a moment, as if he'd swallowed something sour – but only for a moment, and then the familiar, dazzling smile was back on his face. "Let's focus on the matter at hand," he said. "About Eptli–"

"He was just a warrior," Mihmatini interjected. "Aren't

73

you two supposed to have better things to do with your time than investigate every single thing that goes wrong in the palace?"

"It's not small," I said, slowly. "And it might concern you, as well. Eptli's death has started an epidemic."

"Epidemic." Her face had gone flat. "And exactly when was your little cabal planning to inform me of this insignificant fact?"

She was going too far. She was right in that I should have informed her, but I'd barely found out about the epidemic myself. "Look. I was expecting to spend the entire day dealing with the politics of the confirmation ceremony, which would have been more restful than this mess. I can't be expected to send messengers all over Tenochtitlan to anyone who might happen to have a stake in this. Besides, Acamapichtli is the one handling the situation at the moment," I said, with a touch of malice. Acamapichtli hadn't had to deal with Mihmatini since she'd become Guardian.

"Right." Mihmatini had a dangerous gleam in her eyes, one I recognised from our childhood – when she'd rowed the boat to the Floating Gardens on her own, after Neutemoc and I had both refused to accompany her. "I'll go see Acamapichtli, then. Don't think this absolves you of responsibility."

I forced myself to drag the conversation onto more neutral ground: better have the investigation-related questions solved first, and then we could move on to a more relaxed dinner. "Neutemoc – did you know anything about Eptli?"

Neutemoc shrugged. He sipped at his cup of cactus juice, thoughtfully. "Not our clan. But still, rumours can fly far from the encampment." He wrinkled his eyes, as if considering a particularly knotty problem. "Eptli. Eptli's father was of the Pochtlan *calpulli* clan."

"The Pochtlan clan? But that's…"

"Merchants and messengers. Yes." Neutemoc said. "Hence Eptli's tendency to lord it over merchants."

"That's unusual," I said, finally. "A merchant, becoming a warrior." Merchants, like artisans, were a world apart. Unlike warriors, who could come from any strata of the society, the occupation of merchant was hereditary, a merchant's trade being taken up by his sons or close relatives upon his death. The merchants were tight-knit to the point of obsession, holding their lavish feasts within their blank-faced compounds and seldom mingling with the rest of the populace.

"It happens," Neutemoc said. "But, yes, it's unusual."

"He had a hard time, in his training?"

"I don't know," Neutemoc said. His eyes looked away from me – almost ashamed. "Warriors aren't gentle."

And they would have mocked him, for not following the path of his family; for the blood he couldn't deny or purge from his veins. What a lovely little family the army was.

I knew a little of how things worked – and I could guess how it would have turned out. Eptli would have sought to outdo the warriors in arrogance and fanaticism, and leapt at any chance to mock his shameful heritage. "That's why he got into the shouting match with the Tlatelolco merchant?"

"I wasn't present at the time," Neutemoc said, "so I can't help you there. But I wouldn't be surprised. Eptli was proud to be a warrior and working for the greater good of the army; he couldn't see that it's more than warriors who ensure the success of the Triple Alliance." He said this without irony, although less than a year ago he'd thought warriors were the beginning and the end of the Fifth World.

"He wasn't liked, then," I said.

"No." Teomitl's voice was dry. "Some arrogance is expected, but Eptli took it too far."

"It was justified, to some extent," Neutemoc said. "He captured one prisoner in each campaign he took part in."

I recalled the warrior's face – not that of a youth, barely out of training. "He entered the ranks old, then."

Neutemoc grimaced. "I think there were some – issues with his family. His father wasn't in favour of his becoming a warrior."

"Not surprising. But why did he want to become a warrior?" That was the real question – why turn his back on his father's trade, why run the risk of ridicule? Warriors had status and prestige, but so did merchants, in their fashion.

"I don't know," Neutemoc said. "As I said – Eptli was acidic, and not pleasant to be around. I can find better company."

Could he, I wondered. Could he turn back time and get back to the easy camaraderie he'd shared with his companions before his disgrace? "I see. Anything else?"

"People he had quarrels with?" Teomitl suggested. "Other than Chipahua." He tugged at his feather headdress, absent-mindedly. Mazatl tugged back with an impish grin on her face.

"Hmm. The merchant, but you know that already. And Chipahua – they never liked each other, those two…" Neutemoc pursed his lips, looking uncannily like a younger version of Father. "I can't think of anyone

76

else. You'll find most warriors knew Eptli, and disliked him, but I don't think anyone would be crazy enough to start an epidemic just to kill him."

Mihmatini had been fidgeting for a while. At last she spoke up. "I don't think you have the right set of priorities, Acatl. Finding out who killed him is important, yes, but we need something else first. We need to know when and how he was contaminated, in order to stop the epidemic."

"You think it's deliberate?" I said. I had a hard time believing that.

"No. It looks like an accident. Not everyone is fluent with magic, especially not large spells like those. Anything that touches the integrity of the three souls needs to be powerful, and power can easily overstep the mark."

"It's a costly accident," I said.

"Precisely. That's why we need to find out what spell was used, and how it was cast. You can solve the murder afterwards. We need to prevent deaths."

"I can do both," I said. "If we find who was responsible…"

Mihmatini's gaze could have cut obsidian. "You don't understand. You need to flip your way of thinking. The contagion first, the culprit last. Otherwise…"

"I know." Gods, when had my sister turned into Ceyaxochitl, her predecessor as Guardian? She had the same natural authority, and the tendency to want everyone to fall in line – too much hanging around Ceyaxochitl's former acquaintances, I guessed. "Fine," I said with a sigh. "Go see Ichtaca – he and my clergy will give you help with this."

Mihmatini shook her head a fraction – placated, but

not enough, I guessed. "You look healthy," she said, grudgingly. She closed her eyes, and I felt a spike of power enter the room: the soft, reassuring radiance of the Duality. "I can't see any sickness clinging to you or Teomitl. But all the same – you need to be more careful of what you do."

"We weren't the only ones around the dead warrior," Teomitl said.

"No, but that doesn't mean you can afford to ignore your protections. Epidemics are propagated by people who feel fine – who don't imagine for a minute that they could be carrying the sickness."

"You don't know what the vector is," I said. "It might not even be people."

"No, but I'd rather be careful."

Neutemoc cleared his throat. "If you children are done with preening…"

"You–" Mihmatini said, shaking her head in the pretence of being angry. But we all knew she wasn't – at least, not seriously.

Afterwards, Teomitl and I sat in the courtyard, watching Metzli the moon pass overheard. The night was winding to a close, though the raucous sounds of banquets still made their way to our ears: flutes and drums, and the steady drone of elders' speeches – and the smell of fried maize, of amaranth and chillies, a distant memory of what we'd consumed.

"What now?" Teomitl asked.

"Get some sleep, I guess." Neutemoc had agreed to lend us a room for the night, though he hadn't been happy.

Teomitl leaned further against the lone pine tree, watching the stars glittering overhead. "Acamapichtli–"

"If we get an early start tomorrow, he probably won't have time to catch up." I didn't mention my other fear: that the reason he hadn't caught up with us yet was that he was busy with the epidemic – and that something else might have come up, in the hours we'd been away.

FIVE
Tlatelolco

The night was short – too short, in fact. I woke up in a
room I didn't recognise – and it took me a moment to
remember I was in Neutemoc's house, and not in a room
belonging to some parishioner, or in some quarters of
the palace unknown to me. I made my devotions, drawing my worship-thorns through my ears to greet the
Fifth Sun, and to honour my patron Mictlantecuhtli,
Lord Death.

From outside came the familiar rhythm of pestle striking mortar – and another sound I couldn't quite place, a
dull knock of wood on wood – but no, not quite either.
I got up, and followed it to the courtyard – where I found
Neutemoc and Teomitl sparring together. Their *macuahitl*
swords, lengths of wood with embedded obsidian
shards, were the ones making that odd noise, every time
they crossed.

"Men," Mihmatini said, with a snort. She'd raised her
hair in the fashion of married women, piling it above her
head to form two slight horns; but her dress still marked
her as a Guardian. "They're going to be at it for a while.
Come on, let's get breakfast."

"I don't think–" I started.

"There's always time."

I didn't agree – I kept having this vision of the blue and white cloaks of Tlaloc's priests overrunning the courtyard, demanding to speak to us, to put every single one of us into enforced containment. By now, Acamapichtli was going to be in full flow – and knowing him and his natural antagonism for warriors, he would want to add Neutemoc's household to his list of potential sickness carriers.

But Mihmatini looked in a mood to make water flow uphill, so I merely followed her into the reception room, where I hastily swallowed a bowl of maize porridge, before pronouncing myself ready to leave.

By that time, Teomitl and Neutemoc had come back. Teomitl grabbed a handful of maize flatbreads, folded them deftly into a small package, and nodded. "We need to go," he said to Mihmatini.

"Why?"

Teomitl shook his head. "I'll tell you at the palace."

"You'd better." Mihmatini grumbled, but she made no further objection.

No, that was left to Neutemoc.

As we left the courtyard, neither Teomitl nor I paid attention to him, beyond a simple goodbye gesture – and we all but jumped when he said, "Acatl."

I turned. He wore a simple feather headdress, the plumes falling down on the nape of his neck; and the sunlight emphasized the small wrinkles at the corner of his eyes, making him older than he seemed, like some kind of family patriarch. "You're going to warn us."

Neutemoc didn't have much of a sense of humour, especially for grave matters. "Yes, I am."

"Go ahead. I'm listening."

He looked surprised. Did he expect me to ignore him? I would have, a year before. But things had changed, and he had to know that. "Look, Acatl. You're not in the army, so you don't have much information on how it's going."

"I am, though," Teomitl said.

Neutemoc stubbornly avoided his gaze. "The army is losing faith with Tizoc-tzin. The deaths of the council a few months ago were bad enough, but the campaign was just one series of setbacks after the other. Some of the higher-level warriors are still with him, some others are wavering. And some never had faith at all."

I didn't ask him which of those categories he fitted into; neither, I noticed, did Teomitl. "And now the death of the warrior and a prisoner… it's a lot. You're going to have touchy people, and not only among the warriors."

"The merchants?" I asked. They preceded the armies on campaigns, and followed them, too, gathering goods from newly conquered provinces.

"Yes. Tensions everywhere," Neutemoc said. "It's a bad time for a priest to come barging in with questions." He raised a placatory hand. "I don't see you that way, but I'm your brother."

I thought about it for a while. Being High Priest didn't make me exempt from the contempt of warriors for non-combatants – but then again, what choice did I have? "It's my calling," I said. "Making sure this stops before it becomes a threat to us all. Keeping the Fifth Sun in the sky, Grandmother Earth fertile. I don't have a choice."

"I know." Neutemoc grimaced. "Nevertheless – Chicomecoatl walk ahead of you, brother. You're going to need Her luck."

• • • •

Mihmatini insisted on giving Teomitl and me amulets to protect against magical attacks. I had no idea how effective they were, but she had had a point on the previous night – much as I hated to admit it, she and Acamapichtli might be right. The last thing we needed was Teomitl and I carrying the sickness everywhere over Tenochtitlan.

I left Mihmatini at my temple – the last I saw of her, she was in deep conversation about the epidemic with Ichtaca, my moon-faced second-in-command. He looked a little dazed, as if unsure of what had happened to him – he had expected her to be meek and compliant, like most women; criteria which had never applied to my sister – and even less now that she had become Guardian.

Teomitl went back to the palace, to find the mysterious woman who had been visiting our prisoner, and I set out to see Yayauhqui, the merchant who had had such a blazing argument with Eptli.

I'd thought that Yayauhqui would be from Pochtlan, like Eptli and his father, but he was unknown there. After spending a good hour enquiring from one blank-faced compound to another, I finally gave up. The man had been with the army and his return couldn't have passed unnoticed: therefore, the more probable explanation was that he wasn't from Tenochtitlan at all. That left Tlatelolco, our sister city to the north – where the largest market in the Anahuac valley congregated daily.

I dared not take a boat from the temple docks, and in any case it wasn't far. I walked on foot through the canals, gave the Sacred Precinct a wide berth – and went on north, into the district of Cuopepan. Then north again, crossing the canals on foot – I stopped to buy water from a porter by a bridge, handing him a few cacao beans.

At last, I reached the markers: the huge grey-stone cacti driven into the ground that marked the separation between Tenochtitlan and Tlalelolco. They were, by now, purely symbolic, since Tlalelolco's last Revered Speaker had perished in a short and messy war, eleven years before – putting the Tlatelocan merchants under the direct authority of the Mexica.

I headed straight for the marketplace, reckoning that a merchant such as Yayauhqui wouldn't waste an opportunity for profit, even after having barely returned from the war.

The marketplace of Tlatelolco was a city within the city, its stalls aligned in orderly rows according to the category of goods sold, so that there was one section for live animals and another for jewellery, and yet another for slaves. At this hour of the morning the crowd was out, humming and murmuring: friends greeting each other in the alleys; men out to pay a debt, loaded under the weight of the precious cloth-rolls; women entertaining themselves by watching an Otomi savage, who had descended from the hills to sell a few deer-hides. I wove my way through the crowd, making for the section of the market reserved for luxury goods.

Everything dazzled: the merchandise was spread on coloured cloths, and encompassed everything from the vibrant feathers of the southlands, to gold and silver jewellery, to mounds of precious items such as turquoise and coloured shells.

Behind one such stall, I found Yayauhqui. The merchant certainly believed in sampling his own merchandise: though his cloak was of sober cotton, he compensated by wearing jewels of translucent jade, from his necklace to the rings on his fingers. I'd expected a man running to fat;

but he was still as lean as a well-toned warrior, his face as sharp as hacked obsidian, his eyes deeply sunk into his tanned face.

The stall was full when I arrived – one serious buyer, engaged in negotiations with Yayauhqui, and dozens more who had come to stare at the wealth on display. When Yayauhqui saw me, though, he dismissed his buyer with a wave of his fingers, pointing to one of the two collared slaves who kept an eye on the merchandise. "See to the details with him. I have other business."

If the buyer protested, I didn't hear it. Yayauhqui pulled himself to his feet without apparent effort, and bowed – very low, almost as a peasant would to the Revered Speaker. "The High Priest for the Dead. You honour my modest stall."

I tore my gaze from the crowd gathered around it. "Not so modest."

Yayauhqui laughed – briefly, without joy. "Perhaps not."

"I need to speak to you," I said. "Privately."

He shrugged. He didn't seem surprised. "Let's go somewhere quieter, then."

We strolled out of the merchants' quarters, into the slave section – the slaves stood with their wooden collars, waiting resignedly for their purchasers – and then further on, outside of the market, into a quieter street bordering a small canal. There was only one old woman there, selling tamales. The smell of meat, chillies and beans wafted up, a pleasant reminder of the meal I'd had. I waited while Yayauhqui bargained for her to leave.

He came back with a tamale in his hand – and a disarming shrug. "She didn't mind leaving while we had our conversation, but she insisted I buy some of the food. I don't suppose you're hungry."

"I ate this morning," I said, spreading my hands.

"Pity." Yayauhqui gazed speculatively at the tamale. "I hate to waste food. So, you're here because of Eptli."

Taken aback by the abrupt change of subject, I said only, "News travels fast."

"I'm not without friends in the army," Yayauhqui said. "I can't say I'm surprised to see officials here. I was expecting something a little more – energetic, shall we say?"

His voice was low and cultured – the accents of the calmecac school unmistakable. Like Eptli, he'd have sat with future priests and warriors, learning the songs and the rituals, the dance of the stars in the sky – all things he might well have found useful in his travels to far-away lands.

"It's only me for the moment. Though the others might not be long in catching up," I said.

One corner of Yayauhqui's mouth twitched upwards. "You reassure me."

I decided to take the offensive – or we'd still be standing there when the Fifth World collapsed. "If you were expecting me, then you know what I'm going to ask."

Yayauhqui shook his head. "Please. My quarrel with Eptli was hardly a secret matter."

"No," I said. "I was a little unclear on what it was about, though."

"Eptli–" and, for a moment, his expression shifted, slightly, into something that might have been anger, that might have been disdain – "Eptli was a conceited fool. His father was elevated into the nobility – do you even imagine how rare that is, for merchants to be recognised that way?"

"I can imagine," I said. His sudden intensity frightened me.

"I don't think you can." Yayauhqui's gaze took in my finery – the embroidered cloak, the feather headdress, the fine mask of smoothened bone – and he shook his head, contemptuously. "Anyway, Eptli's father is another matter. He might have moved out of Pochtlan entirely, but he still kept his ties with us. Never forgot to tell us when a child was born in his family, or to invite us to banquets. Never forgot to consult us for important decisions. Why, I attended Eptli's birth myself – of course, I was a youth at the time, barely returned from my first expedition."

He didn't look young, not anymore, but he didn't look old, either: well-preserved, but there was something about him that bothered me, something I couldn't quite grasp even though it was right there in front of me.

"So Eptli and you–"

Yayauhqui spread his hands, in what seemed like a peaceful gesture, but I wasn't fooled. "Eptli was a conceited fool. I despised him, but I wouldn't have killed him."

"Even when he captured his prisoner?" I asked. "That would have elevated him higher than his father – into the Jaguars and Eagle Knights."

Yayauhqui shook his head. "Eptli wasn't smart enough to see that there is more to life than riches and honour, and the consideration of warriors."

He sounded sincere – but then, he was a merchant, and he would have been a skilled liar. Not only for negotiation with customers, but also because if he was indeed with the army, it meant he was no harmless merchant, no trader obsessed with his own profit. It meant that he was a spy, ranging ahead of the army to gather information on the country we were about to fight. "You quarrelled with Eptli on this campaign," I said. "In quite a visible fashion."

Yayauhqui looked mildly irritated. "I let the young fool goad me past endurance. I was coming back from a thirteen-day gruelling mission into Metztitlan, and here he was, laughing with his cohorts on how merchants were all useless bags of flesh."

I bit my lip. I liked what I heard of Eptli less and less – I could understand his behaviour, but that didn't mean I condoned it.

On the other hand, if he had been well-liked, he probably wouldn't have died in such a horrific fashion. "So you shouted at him."

"We both shouted, to some extent." Yayauhqui appeared peeved – more, I suspected, because he'd lost his calm than out of any sympathy for Eptli.

I looked at him again – something was still bothering me. "I was given the impression that it was far more than an ordinary quarrel. That Eptli was a calm man with no reason for provoking people, and that you'd both been noticed by the whole encampment."

"I don't see what you mean."

"I think you do," I said. I had nothing more than that, and he likely knew it; but I could bring more pressure to bear, and he also knew that. "Or shall we take that up with the war council?"

Yayauhqui's lips pinched into an unamused smile. "As you very well know, as a merchant, I am subject only to the elders of my clan." He looked as if he might add something, but didn't.

"But the elders of your clan are subject to the Mexica Emperor," I said.

His features shifted again – he was too canny to show naked hatred, but I could catch some of it, in the folds of his eyes, in the tightening of his lips. "I haven't forgotten that," Yayauhqui said. His voice could have broken obsidian.

He hadn't liked the question. And I, in turn, couldn't quite understand why. "What did Eptli say?"

It was a stab in the dark, but it worked. "He insulted Tlatelolca. Said we were all cowards, and it was no wonder we'd been thrown into the mud."

"Did you fight in the war?" I asked. Seven years wasn't such a long time, and Yayauhqui looked old enough to have been a hot-headed youth at the time – assuming he'd ever been hot-headed, which wasn't that likely. A man raised by merchants, just like one raised by priests, would learn the value of calm and decorum early in life.

Yayauhqui hesitated. Trying to decide whether to lie to me, or to twist the truth? "We were merchants. Not fighters. And the invasion was unjustified."

I had been much younger then, cloistered in my temple in the small city of Coyoacan, and paying little attention to the affairs of the great. But I remembered some things of how the war had started. The Revered Speaker of Tlatelolco, Moquihuix, had been married to a Mexica wife – elder sister to Tizoc-tzin and Teomitl. When she grew old, he mocked her, set her aside and, crucial to the war, denied her the finery and luxurious apartments which had been her right.

Our previous Revered Speaker, who had long itched for an excuse to invade our sister city, had leapt at the chance and called to arms the whole valley of Anahuac to avenge the insult to his family.

And, of course, we both knew how the war had ended. "Wars aren't just," I said, finally. "Just necessary."

Yayauhqui shook his head. "Still the old lies? That our destiny is to triumph for the Fifth Sun's sake."

I looked at him, aghast. "What do you mean, lies?"

Yayauhqui spread his hands. "It seems to me the gods aren't choosy about who spills the blood."

His words terrified me. "You fought in the war, didn't you? What did you see?"

"A god, abandoning us." Yayauhqui's voice was bitter. "He had chosen me, elevated me – promised me a destiny of glory. But, in the end, when your warriors stormed the temples, took His idols, and set fire to the altars, I saw Him. I saw Him laugh, and turn away. They feed on blood and fear and pain, and it doesn't matter whose…"

"You can't say things like that," I said. Of course the gods weren't fair – of course They expected our offerings and our devotion. But it was right; it was the order of the world. Mortals had no right to expect anything from gods. "The gods can't be judged by your standards."

"Why not?" Yayauhqui shrugged. "The warriors of Tenochtitlan then took my wives, priest. Pierced a hole through their nostrils, and threaded rope through to tie them to the other slaves, and they led everyone away into Tenochtitlan, to serve your hearth-fires. And the god didn't lift a finger to help us. So yes, I judge."

Warriors were killed; women taken as slaves. It was the way of the world – and, had Tlatelolco defeated us, we would have suffered the same fate.

He terrified me. It was as if he had weighed everything that held us together, all the rules and the morality that bound the Fifth World and judged them not worthy to be followed – discarded them as easily as a worn-out cloak.

Such a man would have no compunction on summoning an epidemic to deal with an enemy. He might even relish it – especially if the epidemic worked against Tenochtitlan.

"And so you decided to do something about it. You cast a spell on Eptli." My voice was low and calm – every word dragged from a faraway place. I hadn't thought I'd meet someone like this, I hadn't thought the Fifth World could even hold such beliefs...

Yayauhqui snorted, gently amused. "Look at me, priest. Look at me."

I didn't understand. But he was still standing with the tamale in his hands, thin and harsh, moulded by war and by years of travelling into strange lands, serving the men who had led his people into slavery – helping them to conquer more lands.

I took up the obsidian knife at my belt, and slashed my earlobes.

"We all must die
We all must go down into darkness..."

A grey veil crept over everything: the canal water became insignificant, distant glimmers and the blue sky receded, opening up to reveal the darkness of tar. The wind over the city faded into the lament of dead souls, and the cold of the grave rose up, like thousands of corpses' hands stroking the inside of my arms and legs. I shivered.

Through the remnants of the adobe walls, I could feel the bustle of the marketplace: thousands of souls bartering and trading, the animals and the slaves, the magical amulets and charms – everything combining into a rush of life I could feel, even from the remove of Mictlan. It burned like a fire, shimmering and twisting out of shape, endlessly tearing itself apart, endlessly renewed.

It took me some time, therefore, to tear my sight from the large radiance of Tlatelolco, and to look at Yayauhqui.

But when I did, I forgot all about the marketplace.

91

Human beings usually shone in the true sight – the three souls, the *tonalli* in the head, the *teyolia* in the heart and the *ihiyotl* in the liver combining into a swirling mass of radiance. So, to a lesser degree, did the souls of living beings like animals, or summoned creatures.

Yayauhqui, however, was dark – not merely faded and colourless, like the water or the adobe walls, but completely opaque, as if something had reached out and snuffed everything out of him.

Not something, I thought, chilled. Someone.

"The god," I said, slowly.

His voice was mocking. "As I said. They feed on pain."

He had no souls – he might as well have been dead, save that even in death, some semblance of life would remain in the body, some scattered pieces of soul. He was – cut off from everything in the Fifth World. Was he even able to taste the tamale in his hand, could he even feel the wind on his skin? For him, everything had to have been receding into a numinous, uniformly grey background.

"You should have gone to see a priest," I said. Not one of my order – for we parted the souls from the body for the final time, helping them slip into the underworld. But a priest of Patecatl, God of Medicine, or of Quetzalcoatl, the Feathered Serpent of Wisdom – they would have known what to do.

Yayauhqui's smile was bitter. "I have seen one. Several, in fact. They tried to convince me I was an abomination, and should retire from public life. After that – well, I didn't feel so keen to go back to them. Perhaps the Revered Speaker might be able to do something, but…"

And, of course, he wouldn't present himself to the man who had destroyed his city – even if Tizoc-tzin had been willing to help him. "It was Huitzilpochtli, then, who did this to you?"

Yayauhqui shook his head. "Let me keep secrets, priest. They're of no use to anyone save an old man like myself."

He didn't look old – but then again, without souls, how would he age? How would the Fifth World leave any kind of mark?

"So, you see," Yayauhqui said. "I couldn't care less about spells."

He was dead, or worse. The blood in his veins would have no energy; the *teyolia* in his heart wouldn't dissipate into the underworld, or into the Fifth Sun's Heaven. Magic, such as it was, would be anathema to him. "You could have hired someone," I said. Or used someone's blood, though it would have been a dangerous venture.

"Of course. There's always that," Yayauhqui agreed, gravely.

There was something about him I couldn't pin down. "Why serve as a merchant-spy, then?"

His lips stretched. It would have been amusement with anyone else, but with him it was just a shadow of what it could have been. That was what had been bothering me about him: everything was subdued, lacking the inner fire of the living, or even the weaker radiance of the dead. "I fear you still don't understand, Acatl-tzin. Now that we are one city, the glory of Tenochtitlan is also that of Tlalelolco. My relatives prosper on your coats of feathers, your cacao beans, your precious stones and your war-takings. Why should I wish to upset the established order? We'd be left with nothing."

His speech had the intensity of truth – and for a bare moment, he seemed to shine with the souls he had lost, though it was only an illusion. "You could destabilise us, and hope for Tlatelolco to secede."

Yayauhqui snorted. "And I could expect the Fifth Sun to tumble down. I'm no fool. I've seen what happens when you cross the gods, and you have the gods' protection."

And if we didn't have it anymore, he'd be the first to trample us into the ground. But, all the same – lying, especially in such an impassioned speech, would have cost him a great deal of energy, enough for the strain of it to be visible. Perhaps he was telling the truth, as much as I disliked the possibility.

"You'll want to stay in Tlatelolco," I said, finally. "It's not over yet."

Yayauhqui's lips stretched again in that smile that wasn't quite one. "Of course. It's never over."

SIX
Between High Priests

The afternoon was well advanced by the time I walked back into the Sacred Precinct; the incense smoke rising up from the dozens of temples made the orange mass of the sun waver and shimmer, as if through a heat haze.

I thought about Eptli as I walked, chewing on a tamale – I'd yielded to temptation, and purchased one from the old woman seller. The taste of chillies and spiced meat was a welcoming heat in my stomach.

He hadn't been liked. Possibly, he hadn't ever fitted in: to the warriors, he would be the merchant's son, and to the merchants, the man who mocked them relentlessly. In his pursuit for glory, he seemed to have made enemies – many of them, from his rival, Chipahua, to the merchant Yayauhqui.

The merchant worried me, for all his sincerity. His defence – that he wouldn't seek to damage the Triple Alliance, for it would be sealing his own doom – rang true, and yet...

And yet, a man like that would have no scruples. The kind of man who could disguise themselves and pass as a foreigner – gossiping and trading, all the while hiding that they were advance observers for the approaching army – why stop the game, when they got home?

Out of principle… but Yayauhqui hadn't looked as if he had much of that.

Still in a thoughtful mood, I walked through the northern gate into the hubbub of the religious centre, and went straight to my temple, which was but a short distance from the gate.

I'd expected a normal day – a dead body carried through the gates, grieving families talking to priests, examinations in quiet rooms… But instead, it was chaos: the temple's small courtyard was flooded with supplicants – from peasants in loincloths carrying baskets of ripe corn kernels, to officials with jewellery and caged animals. The combined noise was overpowering, and I only caught fragments as I elbowed my way through the crowd – about reassurances, and dreams, and portents which seemed to herald the end of the Mexica Empire.

I remembered, grimly, what Neutemoc had told me – that no matter how well Tizoc-tzin hid the warrior's death, news of it would travel through the city like wildfire. He had no idea it would be that bad.

At the foot of the stairs leading up to Lord Death's shrine, I found Ichtaca waiting for me – while two harried offering priests made efforts to channel the flow of supplicants into separate rooms, where they could deal with them one by one.

Ichtaca wasn't alone, though. Beside him stood two priests in blue and white cloaks, the hems embroidered with a border of frogs and seashells.

Of course. I'd known what I was getting into, walking back to the temple, but then again, I couldn't run forever.

The leftmost priest, a pudgy man with a blue-streaked face, was mildly familiar: his name was Tapalcayotl, and he was Acamapichtli's second-in-command. "Acatl-tzin," he said, bowing to me. "Acamapichtli-tzin has requested your presence at the palace."

It was couched politely, but the meaning was unmistakable. "I see," I said. "I'll consult with my priests first."

Tapalcayotl looked as if he might protest, and then obviously thought better of it. Like his master, he was acutely aware of social divisions.

I drew Ichtaca apart, careful to stand at a distance, since we still didn't know how the illness was passed on. "What is going on?"

"I don't know yet," Ichtaca said. He grimaced. "Your sister took half the priests and went to do a ritual to protect us against sickness. It's a good idea–"

"But it leaves us short," I said.

"It's just a bad time," Ichtaca said. "The disastrous coronation war and the death of a warrior…" He sighed, not looking altogether reassured. "We'll weather it, I'm sure. We have the Southern Hummingbird's favour."

We might have; after all, Huitzilpochtli was the one who had given us the right to bring Tizoc-tzin from the dead. But He was a capricious god, and he only favoured the successful in war. I grimaced. "We'll see how things work out. Can you–"

He made a dismissive gesture. "Don't worry. We've had to deal with worse during the great famine. This is nothing."

I hesitated – but I needed to ask, all the same. I couldn't manage an investigation on my own. "I need you to find out one thing for me."

His face didn't move. "Of course. What is it?"

"There is a merchant named Yayauhqui in Tlatelolco. He used to serve a god in his youth. Can you find out which one?"

"Consider it done, Acatl-tzin," Ichtaca nodded. "And–"

"And you hold up here," I said, bleakly. "Acamapichtli, Mihmatini and I will see what we can do about the epidemic."

Ichtaca looked reassured by the idea of so many high-ranking priests taking care of the problem. I hoped he was right; on my side, I felt as though I was making frustratingly little progress.

We walked back the way I had come, the two priests of Tlaloc on either side of me, looking for all the world like an escort – or an arrest squad, I thought, bleakly. Acamapichtli, among other things, was vindictive, and he wouldn't have appreciated our little escapade.

We climbed the steps into the palace, and headed straight to what I now thought of as Acamapichtli's wing. And he'd certainly made sure we knew it: the priests of Tlaloc the Storm Lord positively swarmed over the various courtyards. The black cloaks of the She-Snake's guards seemed almost invisible compared with the onslaught of blue and white. The air smelled of copal incense, mixed with the acridity of rubber: I wouldn't have been surprised to find out Acamapichtli had replaced all the entrance-curtains with the dark-blue ones of Tlaloc's temple.

In the largest courtyard, a shimmering lattice of magic spread from building to building – there was a slight resistance when we crossed under the influence of the wards, and then this was replaced with a familiar tightness in my chest. The place had been consecrated to the

Storm Lord – it wasn't quite the Land of the Blessed Drowned yet, but it was close to its antechamber.

Acamapichtli was in a large room on the second floor, reclining on a mat as if he were the Revered Speaker himself. He wore his customary heron-plumes, and his face was painted with the dark-blue streaks of his god – impassive under the makeup. As we came nearer, though, I saw the thin lines of fear at the corners of his eyes; and the slight quivering in his hands – and felt the stronger circle drawn around him.

"Ah, Acatl," he said when I arrived. "Do be seated."

"I'd rather remain standing," I said, curtly. "Do you have a better idea of what's going on?"

"Not much better than you." Acamapichtli smiled, a thoroughly unpleasant expression. "Thanks to you and your protégé, this thing might already be loose in the populace."

I disliked "populace", which he made sound like an insult. "The two warriors who carried the corpse would have passed it on anyway."

"Not if we found them fast enough – we did catch up with one, if nothing else. He's sick, Acatl, perhaps worse than Coatl or the priest of Patecatl. But I fear that's not the point. The point is that when I give orders, you follow them."

"Since when are you my master?"

"Since the epidemic started." It would have been better if he'd looked insufferably smug, the way he usually did, but he didn't. He merely stated a fact.

"And what about Quenami?"

"Quenami is a fool. Nothing new under the Fifth Sun. I expected better of you." Of course, he hadn't.

"May I remind you I have an investigation to run?" I

asked. "Someone cursed Eptli. And, furthermore, containing the sickness is all well and good, but we need to find a cure for it."

"And for all we know, this is the will of the gods."

This time, he'd goaded me too far. "Fine," I said. "You know one way of solving this?"

Acamapichtli's eyebrows went up.

"Summon the dead man," I said.

It was a crazy undertaking – chancy at best, even for Acamapichtli. I could never have attempted it: Eptli had died of a contagious disease, which made him the property of Tlaloc, and I didn't worship the Storm Lord. I could go into Tlalocan, the land of the Blessed Drowned, to see if his soul would respond to my call, but it was a risk. I would be at Tlaloc's mercy, and I had a suspicion the god was as vindictive as Acamapichtli. He wouldn't have forgotten that I'd thwarted His attempt to take over the Fifth World, a year or so before.

Acamapichtli looked at me – I could see his face twisting, his lips preparing words of contempt, deriding my knowledge as a priest.

"You know it's the only way," I said.

"You're a fool," Acamapichtli said. "Most dead men don't know who killed them. Summoning him will be useless."

"He might remember what contaminated him in the first place," I said. "Which is more information than you have."

Acamapichtli shrugged. "I don't need to know what contaminated him. Containing this is good enough for me."

"Not for me," I said. "And if you're so certain it's Tlaloc's will, you can ask Him what He wants." More likely, if it was Him – and I didn't believe that, not with such an odd magical signature to the disease – He didn't want anything. Tlaloc sent epidemics as He sent rain; He sometimes rewarded prayers, sometimes punished, and most of the time did so for reasons we weren't entitled to know.

Acamapichtli grimaced. He didn't like giving in.

"You'll have me under your eye," I pointed out.

"I'm not sure whether to be pleased, or to wonder what you're up to."

"I'm not up to anything. You're much better at plotting and conspiring."

He smiled. You'd have thought I'd just complimented him. "Yes, you're still as hopeless at diplomacy as you ever were. Do you seriously expect me to agree?"

"It's not about diplomacy," I said. Time to be blunt, anyway. "We have a hundred thousand people in Tenochtitlan, tightly packed. If the epidemic gets out, it'll be worse than the Great Famine. We'll lose thousands of people. And while you might think those are acceptable losses for the Fifth World, I for one don't intend giving in to the machinations of a mortal."

"You forget. It might be the machinations of a god." Acamapichtli's voice was malicious.

"Then I'll bow down my head to the inevitable. It wouldn't be the first time." I'd been there, during the whole ceremony that consecrated Tizoc-tzin as our Revered Speaker – wearing my High Priest regalia, watching as Tizoc-tzin ascended the steps of the Great Temple, feigning weakness, as our ally, the ruler of Texcoco, dressed him according to his new station, inserting an emerald into his nose, putting dangling gold bells on his ankles. I'd watched as he made his offerings, as the gathered nations of the Anahuac Valley cheered him on. And not once had I let on what I truly thought – that the man was unfit to wear the Turquoise and Gold Crown, that he would only lead us to further disasters.

But, on the other hand, I had seen the cost of people fighting over the Turquoise and Gold Crown – the star-demons, the chaos, the fear within the palace – and even a flawed Revered Speaker was better than none. For the sake of the Fifth World, I could hold my tongue, and give no voice to my dislike.

I didn't know what Acamapichtli thought, but I guessed he didn't much care for Tizoc-tzin, either.

Acamapichtli said nothing for a while.

"You make your own decisions," I said. "But you'll be the one accountable for them."

He made a brief, stabbing gesture with his hand. "And you'll support me, of course." It wasn't a question, and I didn't answer. "Fine. I can waste some time to satisfy your morbid curiosity. But you'll learn nothing from it, Acatl."

I'd expected Acamapichtli would want to prepare the spell in his quarters, to make good use of the strong foundations of magic he'd laid. But instead, he chose the courtyard to prepare his spell. He had his priests drag five braziers – one at each corner, and one at the centre. They drew lines around them to materialise the sacred quincunx, the fivefold cross that symbolised the order of the world.

Acamapichtli himself remained at the centre, muttering prayers I couldn't make out from where I was standing. He drew out his worship thorns, and stared at them, thoughtfully – but didn't make any gesture to drag them through his earlobes.

He seemed to be waiting for something, but I wasn't sure what.

A growl drew my attention away from Acamapichtli: four slaves were carrying a wooden cage, in which was the largest jaguar I'd ever seen – a mass of muscles and fangs, with a burning gaze that suggested captivity ill-suited it.

Of course, the jaguar was one of the animals sacred to Tlaloc – the god Himself had jaguar fangs, and the sound of His thunder was like the roars of the jungle felines. But still…

The slaves put the cage in the centre, a few hand-spans away from Acamapichtli – who still didn't move. They withdrew, leaving no one but him and the beast in the circle. The jaguar paced within the cage, raising its head from time to time – opening its mouth to reveal glinting fangs. Acamapichtli, seemingly oblivious to its presence, picked up his worship thorns, and drew them through his earlobes. He didn't flinch as they went in: like any priest, he'd been doing this for far too long to pay attention to the pain.

He whispered more words, with greater urgency than before. Then he planted the worship thorns, one by one – driving them into the earth halfway through.

A faint tremor shook the courtyard – as if something were rising up to meet the fresh blood.

At length Acamapichtli raised his head, and saw me, standing outside the quincunx. "Acatl! Come inside."

I eyed the jaguar, doubtfully. I had my obsidian knives, but even I wasn't mad enough to take on a beast like that without preparations.

Or – as the uncomfortable thought occurred to me – without live bait to distract it.

Acamapichtli snorted. "Don't be a yellow-livered fool, Acatl. The spirit will only be visible inside the quincunx. Or do you want me to ask the questions for you?"

And feed me the information he deemed fit for my consumption? Not a chance. I drew my obsidian knife, feeling its reassuring heft and coldness against the palm of my hand – and stepped over the circle.

The earth shivered as I walked, as if it were permanently shifting – as if it didn't know whether to be mud, water or packed dust. My feet squelched every other step, but when I lifted them, nothing clung to my sandals.

I reached the centre, where Acamapichtli stood waiting. Was it just me, or had the sky overhead darkened – far faster than it should have for a late afternoon? I could have sworn...

The jaguar yawned. Its pelt had grown almost featureless in the dim light; its eyes shone yellow, and its teeth glittered like opalescent pearls. I could almost see the saliva beading on the canines. It pressed itself against the door of the cage – and it was bending, the wood splitting up with a sound that resonated within my chest. The jaguar roared, a sound like thunder in the sky.

Acamapichtli hadn't moved. He stood with both hands empty – they were long and supple, and in contrast to the rest of his regalia, quite bare, with no rings that could have caught on anything.

"What are you afraid of?" he asked.

At this stage, I wasn't sure if it was him or the jaguar, or both. He shifted – and all of a sudden his skin shone a dark orange, and his eyes were two black pits ringed with yellow, the same as the animal within its cage. Even the fluid, confident way he moved seemed to echo the beast's.

"Acamapichtli–" I started.

The jaguar threw itself against the door of the cage, and the wood, with a final sputtering sound, gave way. The entire latticework of wood exploded, but I had no time to focus on this, because the jaguar leapt out and ran straight towards me – muscles bunching up for a leap, and all I could see was its open mouth with the fangs glinting – my hand went towards the knife, a fraction of a moment too late – the beast was almost upon me, its jaw extending to clamp around my skull...

And then, abruptly, it was on the ground in front of me, its legs scrambling for purchase, desperate to get up – and Acamapichtli stood over it, holding it down with both hands. He didn't even look to be in a sweat. The beast kicked and yowled, and made a racket strong enough to wake up the dead, and its claws raked the ground, sinking into the earth – but it made no difference. Acamapichtli still held on. He might as well have been a rock.

My heart was threatening to burst out of my chest, but I didn't move, either – just stood there, watching.

At length, the jaguar's struggles grew weaker; its legs quieted, its whole body heaving with huge breaths that didn't seem to sustain it. Then it grew quieter still – the face, flopping back towards me, bore the unmoving glaze of the dead.

Acamapichtli stood away from the beast, withdrawing the noose he'd coiled around its neck. He didn't even spare me a glance. In the darkness, his eyes still shone yellow, and his face had lengthened, with a suggestion of a muzzle. The fingers of his hands, too, seemed to be longer and sharper.

"*O Lord, Our Lord*
O Provider, O Lord of Verdure
Lord of Tlalocan, Lord of the Sweet-Scented Marigold,
Lord of the Smoky Copal..."

Acamapichtli withdrew the worship thorns from the earth in a single flourish, and walked back to the jaguar. He drove them into the pelt, at the height of the spine.

"In the Blessed Land of the Drowned
The dead men play at balls, they cast the reeds,
They sip the nectar of numerous sweet and fragrant flowers,
Grant us leave, O Lord, Beloved Lord,
Grant us leave to call them back."

Mist poured from the jaguar's spine, as if the thorns had opened up some vast reservoir. It pooled around the corpse, a swirling mass of white – and then it stretched, still remaining as thick, until I could barely make out the contours of the buildings around us, and it went upwards, driving even the darkness from the sky. Everything seemed to turn white and clammy, with the particular, watery smell of marshes.

And then, gradually – as a shiver started low in my back and climbed upwards – I became aware we weren't alone anymore.

SEVEN
The Summoning of Spirits

I'd summoned ghosts from Mictlan many times and they always appeared the same: faint silhouettes, with shadows playing over their features until they hardly seemed human anymore. But the ghost that Acamapichtli had called up wasn't like that: I could see the light of its *teyolia* soul, a scorching radiance in his chest that I could almost feel. Like Acamapichtli himself, his skin was mottled, halfway between a jaguar's pelt and human skin.

Other than that, he looked much as he had alive. He no longer wore any finery, but the face bore familiar features – save that his lips were congealed purple, and deep pouches lay under his eyes. When he raised a hand to touch his chin, I saw that the base of his nails too were purple, and the tips of his fingers wrinkled, as if he had remained too long in warm water.

"I–" he whispered. "Where–"

Acamapichtli's smile was the jaguar's, before it found its prey. "I summoned you, Eptli of the Pochtlan clan, warrior of the Mexica."

Eptli's gaze swung between Acamapichtli and I. I had no idea what he saw; I very much doubted that I still looked the same. "I don't understand." He hugged himself, as if he were cold. His eyes were two pits of darkness. "I was–"

"Dead," Acamapichtli said, curtly. "My… colleague here is convinced you know something about that."

"I remember–" Eptli shivered. "So cold. I was so cold when we entered the Anahuac valley. I barely even saw Tlacopan. But I was strong. I hid it, and no one guessed. No one guessed." He laughed – it started low, and climbed to a high-pitched, insane trill.

"For how long were you cold?" Acamapichtli asked.

Eptli shuddered, and the mist seemed to quiver in turn. "I don't know. Three, four days perhaps. I don't remember…"

Great. Much as it pained me to admit it, Eptli was going to be useless. Some people kept their coherence after death, but he clearly wasn't one of them.

"Three, four days." Acamapichtli nodded. "Then we have a little more time. What happened before? How did you catch this?"

"I don't know."

"The disease would take time to become visible," I said.

Acamapichtli made a stabbing gesture with his hands. "No. Remember, Coatl and the physician took barely a few hours to show symptoms. Did anyone die at the camp, Eptli?"

"Die?" He shivered again. The purple was spreading from his lips to his cheeks, marbling them like the skin of a corpse. "So many people died – the wounded and the weak, they all died for the glory of the Empire. It is right, it is proper." He turned the emptiness of his eyes towards me, almost pleading. "It is right…"

Acamapichtli snorted. "See, Acatl? Useless."

I wasn't prepared to admit defeat so soon. "Let's see." I came closer to the man – his face was turning darker and darker, and his eyes were drawing inwards, sinking towards the back of his skull. I focused on what mattered – there was nothing I could do for him. "What do you remember about your prisoner?"

Something lit up in his eyes. "Prisoner? My fourth. I earned him, earned him…"

I resisted the urge to strike him; he was a ghost, and it wouldn't help. "Eptli," I said, gently but firmly. "Your prisoner, Zoquitl. He was ill, too, wasn't he?"

"I don't remember." He shook his head. "I–" His face twisted, and he fell to the ground, with a cry of pain. The warmth in his chest blazed.

This wasn't normal. "Acamapichtli," I said. I could have cast a spell of true sight, but I had no idea what would happen if I did so inside another's ritual.

Acamapichtli was watching Eptli, his fangs closed over his lower lips, his eyes dilated in the mist. "A spell of forgetfulness," he said.

"Something strong enough to endure after death?"

A drop of blood rolled off one of Acamapichtli's canines. "Evidently." He knelt, and took Eptli's face between his hands. "Very strong," he said, with a hint of admiration. "I'm not sure it can be removed, not without dispelling him."

"Then you're useless," I said, not without malice.

"Tsk tsk," Acamapichtli said. "So little faith. I notice you're not leaping to my rescue either."

"You seem to be doing just fine."

He made a sucking noise between his fangs – and, lightning fast, brought his hands together, as if to crush Eptli's head. The radiance at Eptli's heart wavered, and then began to dim; the warrior began writhing as if in the throes of some great pain. Acamapichtli took a step backward, his face dispassionate. I realised with a shock that I'd taken a step forward – as if anything could help the man, when he was dead and gone already.

"Hurts," Eptli hissed. "How dare you–" His voice was low; I could barely make out the words. When he raised his head, I saw that his skin had gone completely purple, and that his hair had taken on greenish reflections, like algae.

"What do you remember?" Acamapichtli asked. "Quick, there isn't much time."

It was, to an extent, his ritual, and I was just a spectator – however, Acamapichtli had a number of disadvantages, not least of which was that he had no context about Eptli. "Was Zoquitl sick, Eptli?"

"No," Eptli whispered. "Strong and young, he was – a strong offering, a man fit enough to hold the glory of the god. But I was – cold. I'd put on all the amulets, all the magical protections I could, but it wasn't enough…"

So Eptli had been the first one. "When was this?"

"I don't know." Eptli shivered. He was growing – darker, more distant. The smell of algae was stronger, and the mist was eating away at the radiance. "I don't know. I shouldn't have–" He shivered again. "I shouldn't have–"

"Shouldn't have what?"

But he was going away from us – subsumed into the mist. "Shouldn't have insulted Yayauhqui?" I asked. "Shouldn't have quarrelled with your comrades? Shouldn't have won against Chipahua?" It wasn't as if the questions lacked, after all. "Eptli!"

His voice came back, floating through the mist. "I shouldn't have taken it – I should have known… said it was for safekeeping, but I should have known… It was so cold when I touched it…" And then another word, which could have been "Father", which could have been something else entirely.

And then nothing.

Acamapichtli reached out, and plucked the worship thorns out of the jaguar's body; and the mist receded and died away, leaving us standing in a darkened courtyard, with the familiar surroundings of the palace. A host of priests in blue and white stood on the edge of the circle, all watching us intently.

"Let's go inside," he said, brusquely. "This isn't fit for all ears."

Inside, he didn't seem much changed, but something in the way he paced by the carved columns suggested otherwise. "He suspected something."

"Yes," I said. "You heard it. Someone gave him something – for safekeeping, he said."

"So not something usual." Acamapichtli bit his lips. "Or else whoever did this wouldn't have needed the excuse. A piece of jewellery?"

"You're the expert on amulets," I said, more sharply than I'd intended.

He nodded, as arrogantly as ever. "I am, but you can put so many things into an amulet…"

"Can't you summon him again?"

Acamapichtli grimaced. "Not until the protective deities change – which doesn't happen for another thirteen days."

By which time it would be too late.

"Do you still think it was Tlaloc?" I asked.

"Possible," Acamapichtli admitted, grudgingly, "but unlikely, given the circumstances. Someone – a human being – gave Eptli something that made him feel cold. It's beginning to sound more and more like a spell directed at him." His eyes were hard.

Eptli had taken the proffered object, and fallen sick. And Zoquitl, who was in regular contact with Eptli, had caught the sickness as well. But why Zoquitl, and none of the other warriors? Did Zoquitl have some weakness we were unaware of – some lack of protection because he was Mextitlan, and not Mexica?

And why Eptli?

Acamapichtli's eyes were hard. "Now I know where I've seen that magic before – but it doesn't look quite the same. Once, I had to arrest a man who'd hired a sorcerer to cast a spell of leprosy onto a rival. A marvel of ingeniousness – it called up the sickness from Tlalocan itself."

Tlalocan, the land of the Blessed Drowned – where the sacrifices to Tlaloc lived in eternal bliss, reaping maize from ever-fertile fields, and listening to the whistle of the wind through the floating gardens. "That's why it kept disintegrating?" I asked. Magic from Tlalocan – raw magic from a god's territory – couldn't be called forth into the Fifth World: it would endure for a short while before the mundane began to assert itself once more. "Because it didn't come from the Fifth World."

Acamapichtli nodded. He sounded distracted. "Yes. Someone called up Tlaloc's raw magic into the world – a spell bound up in death and drownings, if you will. You ought to know that." It was a jibe at me as High Priest for the Dead – but weak and deprived of bite.

"And how powerful do you have to be to cast that kind of spell?"

"Not powerful. Ingenious, as I said. Whoever is behind this has great knowledge of Tlalocan, and of Tlaloc's magic."

"Your clergy?" The words were out of my mouth before I could take them back.

His eyes narrowed. "Of course not. Don't be a fool. My clergy is all above suspicion – and in any case, what motive would they have for killing a warrior they've never seen?" Priests of Tlaloc – the Storm Lord, the god of peasants and fishermen – seldom if ever went to war, for their blessings were reserved for the fields and the harvest.

"I don't know," I said, darkly. "I've seen many things. What about the spell on Eptli's soul?"

"Part of the same curse, I'd say. And tied to the *teyolia* soul, so that it persisted even in death. Again – we're dealing with a smart, resourceful sorcerer."

"But do you know who?" I insisted. "We need facts, not speculation."

Acamapichtli brushed his hands, carefully. Blood still clung to the lines of his palm, but he appeared oblivious. I had no idea how much of it was an act. "I can enquire," he said. "About that, and the sickness. We have priests specialised in diseases at the temple."

"Then why haven't you done so before?"

His gaze, when he raised it, could have bored through stone. "I've dealt with my own affairs. Deal with yours, Acatl."

He was the fool if he thought he could convince me to back down. "As you said earlier – we're in this together. All of the Fifth World."

Acamapichtli snorted. "Fine. Do it your way, if that's what you want."

As if he always did things for the sake of necessity – rather than for his own sake and on his own terms. "I'll keep you apprised," I said, walking towards the entrance-curtain.

"Likewise," Acamapichtli said, but we both knew he was lying.

I was about to take my leave, when the entrance-curtain tinkled and a flustered-looking Tapalcayotl came in. "My Lord, I'm sorry, but–"

He was followed by Mihmatini and her personal slave, Yaotl – and by a delegation of grey-cloaked priests from my order. "Out of my way," she said. Her voice was grim.

Acamapichtli looked from Mihmatini to me – a suspicious expression spreading on his narrow face. "What jest is this?"

Mihmatini shook her head. "You're the one in charge of the confinement?"

Acamapichtli nodded. "I can assure you that no one with the sickness has come out of this palace." He threw a murderous glance at me – he still hadn't forgiven what he saw as imprudence on my part. "But none of that need concern you. I'm sure you have more pressing concerns." His tone was condescending: he was going by appearances only, not even bothering to check. I didn't have the true sight on me, which prevented me from seeing the magical trails in the room, but I was sure that the strong magic which had just entered the room – a strong reassuring rhythm like a heartbeat – could only be Mihmatini's wards.

Mihmatini smiled. "You forget. I am Guardian for the Sacred Precinct, keeper of the invisible boundaries, and agent of the Duality in this world."

Acamapichtli raised an eyebrow. "You have the courage of eagles, girl, but it's useless if you can't follow through with actions."

"Acamapichtli!" I snapped. "Show some respect."

Mihmatini shook her head. "It doesn't matter, Acatl."

She smiled, and it was slow and terrifying and desperate. "I'll tell him what he needs to know. What he does with it," she spread her hands, as if scattering seeds into the bosom of Grandmother Earth, "is his own business."

"Fine," Acamapichtli said. "Have your say, and leave. We're busy enough as it is."

"You won't laugh," Mihmatini warned him. "With the help of the clergy of Mictlantecuhtli, I have beseeched the Duality to smile down upon us, and keep us standing tall, warded against the shackles of disease."

"And you've failed." Acamapichtli's voice was mocking.

From the grim expression on Mihmatini's face, I'd already suspected it hadn't worked, but unlike Acamapichtli, I had more faith in her abilities.

"Why did it fail?" I asked.

"It hasn't worked. But not because of anything in the ritual."

"You're young and unblooded–" Acamapichtli started, but my sister cut him, as savagely as a warrior in a fight to the death.

"I'm old enough to do what I'm doing. The reason it hasn't worked is because someone has sent up their own entreaties into the Heavens."

Surely she didn't mean… "Mihmatini–"

"I told you that you wouldn't like it." Her voice was flat, emotionless. "Someone is deliberately blocking any attempts at containing this. Someone wants this to become a full-blown epidemic."

There was silence, in the wake of her words. "You can't mean…" I started, and then stopped. My sister might be young, might be slightly untrained, and not as well-versed in the subtleties of the Duality's magic as her predecessor had been. But her own magic was strong,

115

and she wouldn't advance such a monstrous hypothesis unless she was sure of it.

"Mistress Mihmatini isn't mistaken," Yaotl said in the silence.

"Then…" I spoke the words as they came to me, desperately trying to piece them into some kind of coherence. "Then this isn't about Eptli as a man. This isn't about personal revenge." Gods, I had been wrong; I had expected this to be small and personal. But it wasn't. It had never been.

One of my priests, Ezamahual, a tall, dour son of peasants, spoke up. "This is about the warrior," he said. For once, he wasn't stammering, or ill at ease, but, like my sister, utterly certain of the truth of his words. "This is about the man who was distinguished in the coronation war, and the sacrifice that should have been made to Huitzilpochtli. This is about making us weak."

I left Mihmatini deep in conversation with Acamapichtli and my clergy – they were discussing the technicalities of the ritual, unpacking everything they had done in order to convince Acamapichtli. I went out into the courtyard, breathing in the cold air of the night, hoping it might steady me.

It didn't.

A deliberate epidemic. This was bad. It had been bad enough when it had just been a side-effect of a spell gone wrong, but if someone was actively opposing us…

No, not us.

As Ezamahaul had said, this was all about Tizoc-tzin – his coronation war, his confirmation as Revered Speaker. Someone, somewhere, didn't want this to happen. It could have been a foreigner – and the gods knew there would be enough of those in the city, because of the upcoming confirmation. It could be Yayauhqui – his protestations had rung true, but perhaps he was a better liar than I'd thought.

Or it could be someone in the palace. Tizoc-tzin was hardly popular, and he had ascended to the Revered Speaker's mat over many rivals. Some of those were now dead, but some were still here: the She-Snake, who professed to believe in order; the noblemen and officials who had supported another candidate...

Gods, more politics. I really didn't want to have to deal with this.

But, in the end, it didn't change much. It was my duty – the one the previous Guardian had given me in spite of my protestations – what I had always done, what I always do. Keep the boundaries, protect the Fifth World and the Mexica Empire – what kind of a man would I be, if I let the epidemic rage within the city?

We had to find out how it had started – what the spell was – in order to counter it.

I stared at the stars – the distant, reassuring patterns fixed in their courses, the demons that couldn't fall into the Fifth World anymore – until they seemed to become the only thing in the world.

A tinkle of bells, and my sister came to stand by my side. "Obstinate man," she said.

"Did he believe you?"

"For now, I guess." She looked tired. "We'll go back and cast one of the lesser spells of protection. It won't work as well–"

"–but it will buy us a little more time?"

She nodded. "Acamapichtli said he'd look into the precise nature of the sickness, which should help us guard against it. But you–"

I spread my hands. "I know, I know. I need to find out who is behind this, and how they're doing it."

Mihmatini grimaced. "It might still be someone with a grudge against Eptli – they might be plucking two limes in one swoop: causing the disease, and getting back at him."

I bit my lip. "It might. But Ezamahual was right: it might simply be that he was a successful warrior, part of Tizoc-tzin's successes."

"All I'm saying is that you shouldn't discount the possibility out of hand." I must have looked dubious, for she laughed, and made as if to punch me. "Don't be so serious, Acatl!"

"This is serious."

"Oh, Acatl, for the gods' sake. We've already had this talk. Better laugh, and smile at the flowers and jade. Life is too short to be spent grieving. You, of all people, should know this."

I shook my head. It wasn't about enjoying life, but rather about my responsibilities, and what I needed to do.

And needed to do fast. For, if the primary motive wasn't Eptli's death, but the epidemic – if someone wanted deaths, many deaths, then what prevented them from directly contaminating someone else? It could all go fast – very fast – with us defenceless against the sickness.

Though the evening was well-advanced, I headed straight to Teomitl's quarters hoping to catch my wayward student before he went to bed, and apprise him of events. If there was something going on against his brother and the empire he was heir to, I felt he ought to know sooner rather than later.

And I wanted to see him, too: with the campaign, he'd been absent for four months, and I couldn't help but feel he was drawing away from me – a thought that pinched my heart. He'd grown up immeasurably since becoming my student, but he wasn't an adult yet – too impulsive, too careless to take his place as Revered Speaker.

His quarters were on the ground floor near Tizoc-tzin's own private quarters: his elevation to Master of the House of Darts had, it seemed, changed little. The entrance-curtain fluttering in the evening's balmy breeze had gone from orange to red and white with a huge butterfly – the colour and pattern reserved for warriors who had captured three or more enemies.

"Teomitl?" I pushed open the entrance-curtain – the bells sewn into it tinkled, a familiar, high-pitched sound – and stepped inside.

The room was as bare as it had always been, the only concession to wealth being the frescoes representing our ancestors in Aztlan, the mythical heartland of Huitzilpochtli the Southern Hummingbird.

I'd expected to catch Teomitl; what I hadn't expected was to find him with someone else.

"Acatl," the visitor said, rising. "What a pleasant surprise."

I found myself wishing I'd removed my sandals, after all. "My Lord," I said, bowing as low as I could.

Nezahual-tzin, Revered Speaker of our ally Texcoco, was a youth of barely sixteen years of age, with a smooth face that could have belonged to a child. The easy, graceful way he wore his feather regalia and turquoise cape, however, served as a useful reminder: Nezahual-tzin was a canny player of politics, who had grown up fighting for his Turquoise and Gold Crown, and he was blessed with the wisdom of Quetzalcoatl the Feathered Serpent. A dangerous opponent, should he ever set himself against us...

A horrible thought crossed my mind. What if he was the one behind it all? The gods knew he didn't like Tizoc-tzin; the man had all but accused Nezahual-tzin of wanting to break the Triple Alliance, four months past. And Nezahual-tzin certainly had the knowledge and the craft to make any spell he wished to – even one calling on the power of Tlalocan, though Tlaloc wasn't his preferred god to call upon.

But no; he was a smart and canny man, and, like me, he had seen the heavy cost we had paid during the change of Revered Speaker. He might have disliked Tizoc-tzin, but he had helped us crown him all the same. No, it couldn't possibly be him.

Teomitl wouldn't meet my gaze. "Nezahual-tzin came to inquire about the dead warrior. We were planning to look for you."

Eventually, I guessed. No – I looked at Teomitl again, seeing the impatience ill-hidden on his features. Those two still had no love for each other, and I guessed Teomitl had been trying to get rid of the unwanted guest for a while.

"I didn't know you had the best interests of warriors at heart," I said to Nezahual-tzin.

He smiled, uncovering teeth of a dazzling white. "Warriors, no. Magical epidemics, most probably."

"I see," I said. "You weren't with the army."

"No." Nezahual shook his head, briefly. "The coronation war is Tizoc-tzin's only. The Triple Alliance won't interfere when he proves his valour." He sounded vaguely amused: he had no illusions about Tizoc-tzin's valour.

"Don't mock my brother," Teomitl said. "I haven't seen you much on the battlefield, either."

Nezahual-tzin rolled his eyes upwards. "To each their own." I'd expected him to elaborate, but he didn't.

I looked at Teomitl, who was fidgeting. "I need to talk with Teomitl. Alone."

Teomitl nodded. Yes. There is plenty to do."

I could see that he wanted to remove Nezahual-tzin from his presence – and Nezahual-tzin saw it as well, because a slightly mocking smile was playing on his broad features.

I didn't know how much I could trust him with any of the details on the epidemic, and in any case, it was better to be prudent. I took the first excuse that came to mind. "If you'll excuse us," I said to Nezahual-tzin. "We have to look for a woman."

"Women tend to be elusive," Nezahual-tzin said, gravely. I remembered, too late, that he might be sixteen years old, and have the wisdom and grace of someone far older, but he didn't disdain the pleasures of the flesh, and his women's quarters already held dozens of concubines.

Teomitl glared at Nezahual-tzin. "You don't know what you're talking about."

His desire to oust Nezahual-tzin from his quarters was palpable, and at length Nezahual-tzin nodded. "I see," he said in a swish of feathers. "I will leave you to your affairs while I attend to mine."

I waited until he had left to look at Teomitl. "We have a problem," I said.

"A problem?"

Quickly, I outlined what Mihmatini had told me. Teomitl's face did not change during the recitation, save that it went paler and paler – and that a green light, like jade, like underwater algae, started playing on his features. "Deliberate?"

"Insofar as I know, yes."

121

"Then who?" The room was bathed in green shadows now; if the culprit had been there, he would have been blasted straight into Mictlan.

"I don't know."

Teomitl grimaced. He looked disappointed – an expression which sent an odd pang through my chest, making me wish I'd been capable of removing it – but he soon rallied. "So we're looking for enemies of the Mexica?"

I shook my head. "Not only that. Enemies of your brother, quite possibly. Remember last year. Someone could well be a Mexica and love the Empire, and yet still want to depose Tizoc-tzin for personal gain."

Teomitl snorted. "You don't remove a Revered Speaker. You kill him." I'd expected him to be outraged, or angry; but he was merely stating a fact all too well-known to him, as if he'd already brooded over this many times.

"Teomitl–" I said, suddenly frightened.

He grinned – careless, boyish again. "Don't worry about me, Acatl-tzin. I'm not a fool. But the fact remains: what does our sorcerer hope to gain with this?"

"Weaken us," I said, darkly. "Perhaps even encourage a civil war." We'd always stood united, but then again, all our Revered Speakers had had the favour of the Southern Hummingbird – their coronation wars a success, bodies piling at the foot of the Great Temple until the steps ran slick with blood.

Teomitl's face darkened – and, for a moment, he looked far too much like his brother. "You go too far."

I shook my head, ignoring the faint stirrings of unease. "You've seen the banquet. We are divided. With enough panic, and enough fear... the gods only know what a sorcerer can achieve."

And there was Tizoc-tzin – who had been dead, and who we had brought back to life. What kind of magical protection could a dead man afford us?

Teomitl said nothing.

"You must know the court. You must see the atmosphere."

His hands were steady – almost too much – his face carefully guileless. "I can look," he said, finally. "Does that mean we stop enquiring about Eptli's enemies?"

I thought of what Mihmatini had told me. "Not necessarily. Whoever the culprit is, they must have hated Eptli – or what he represented."

Teomitl grimaced. "I did have some information, but…"

"What information?"

"The head of prisoners sent word," Teomitl said. "He said that a woman dressed like a sacred courtesan walked into their quarters, not long before the uproar of Eptli's death. She all but barged her way into Zoquitl's quarters, and they had a lengthy conversation."

A courtesan? "You don't know which kind?"

"Fairly high-up in their hierarchy, I should imagine, from what Cuixtli said. Why?"

"Xochiquetzal," I said, curtly.

"Oh."

Xochiquetzal, Goddess of Lust and Childbirth, had until recently been a resident of Tenochtitlan, granted asylum by the grace of the Duality – and of the previous Guardian, Ceyaxochitl. However, in the wake of Tizoc-tzin's ascent to power, She had been exiled from the city, partly in retaliation for her plot against the Southern Hummingbird a year before, and partly because Tizoc-tzin's paranoia wouldn't allow a scheming goddess to be within a stone's throw of him.

I hadn't approved. Like all gods – except Lord Death and the Feathered Serpent, who took no part in the intrigues of the Fifth World – Xochiquetzal was ruthless, and always plotting something. But risking Her anger and resentment wasn't wise.

"Does he know who she was?"

"He didn't remember her name. He thought it was something to do with flowers…" which didn't help, since half the women's names included precious stones or flowers, "and something else. Some kind of food – amaranth, maize?"

"I don't see–" I started, but the tinkle of the bells on the entrance-curtain cut me short.

"Xiloxoch," Nezahual-tzin said, not even bothering with an apology or an introduction. "xoch" was for flower; and "xiloch" was tender maize.

"You were spying on us?" Teomitl asked, indignantly. "You–" He stopped himself with an effort, remembering that he spoke to a superior and an ally. "That's not honourable."

"Honour will see us all dead," Nezahual-tzin said, with that particular, distant serenity that was his hallmark. "Let's be practical."

"How much did you hear?" I asked.

He didn't answer, but by his mocking glance, I could guess he had been outside all the while, listening.

"Don't you dare make this public," I said. I could have asked him not to act on it, but it would have been in vain.

Nezahual-tzin snorted. "Secrets are of value. Why would I reveal something like that?"

"For your own gain," Teomitl snapped.

"Of course I wouldn't." He smiled, with practised innocence – not that we were fooled.

"You'd better not."

I decided to interpose myself, before the conversation degenerated: those two would come to blows easily enough, and it wouldn't help the stability of the Triple Alliance if the heir-apparent to the Mexica Empire and the Revered Speaker of Texcoco fought among themselves. "You said the courtesan's name was Xiloxoch. How do you know, Nezahual-tzin?" And realised, too late, that there was only one possible answer to the question.

A faint, sarcastic smile appeared on Nezahual-tzin's lips for a bare moment, before his face was once more smooth and expressionless. "You know how I know," he said, curtly. "She's a delightful woman, Xiloxoch. Not as young as she used to be, but a treasure-trove of inventions. A pleasure to be with. Almost makes staying in Tenochtitlan worthwhile."

Teomitl's face went crimson. I was less fazed than him – both because I'd expected something like that, and because what women did in the privacy of their chambers had long since ceased to matter for me. "I don't think your prowess as a man is the question here."

Nezahual-tzin's eyes rolled up, revealing corneas of opalescent white. "Of course. You don't feel concerned."

Less than Teomitl, obviously. Ah – might as well question him, and find out what he knew. "As I said earlier, let's focus. What do you know about Xiloxoch that would be relevant?" I stressed the word "relevant."

For a moment, I thought Nezahual-tzin was going to launch into a recitation of Xiloxoch's virtues on the reedmat – but he must have perceived the shadows of jade playing on Teomitl's face, a sure sign that my student was losing hold of his divine powers. "You forget. I have no idea what you want with her."

125

"You know. You were listening."

"I see," Nezahual-tzin said. "Well, I don't know much more than what's already known at the House of Joy." He smiled disarmingly, but neither of us were fooled. "She chooses her mat-partners carefully, and she'll not bend for anyone."

"And would she say she was a devoted follower of Xochiquetzal?"

Nezahual-tzin's eyes rolled upwards again, revealing corneas as opalescent as mother-of-pearl. He was silent, for a while. He was – had always been – a good judge of character. "Her? She has her pick of Jaguar Knights and Eagle Knights, and even of Otomi shock troops. She should lack for nothing – but her chambers are simply decorated, and I've never seen anyone so bored with precious stones. So yes, I would think so. She's a priest-ess, not a greedy woman. She sees herself infused with the essence of the Quetzal Flower – invested with the mission to inflame lust in others."

I had feared so. "Do you know–" I started, but didn't get any further.

The entrance-curtain was slammed against the wall with such force that one of its bells flew off – and landed at Teomitl's feet with a discordant sound.

The She-Snake, the keeper of the palace order, stood framed in the entrance, his black-streaked face almost flush against the darkness. By his side was a group of guards dressed in black – even in the dark, I could see their shaking hands, their pale faces. Something was wrong, and every single one of them reeked of magic, an odour that slipped within my lungs like smoke, thick and acrid.

"Acatl," the She-Snake said. "Teomitl." He bowed a fraction, from equal to equal. "You have to come now."

"There's been another death?" I asked, my heart sinking. But why would everyone look in such disarray, if it was just one of the sick people who had died. "Tizoc-tzin?" I asked.

The She-Snake shook his head. "No. The war-council, Acatl. Someone has just made an attempt on the life of the Master of the House of Darkness."

EIGHT
Master of the House of Darkness

We followed the She-Snake to another part of the palace – less grand than the quarters of the imperial family, though still ostentatious enough, with rich frescoes of gods and warriors, and the smell of pine needles, a pleasant overlay over the harsher odour of copal incense wafting from the huge burners.

To Teomitl's dismay, Nezahual-tzin had fallen in with us, as if nothing were more natural. "Well, that's interesting," he said in a conversational tone.

Teomitl's eyes tightened. "This is a Mexica affair."

"You forget." Nezahual-tzin's broad face still bore that expression of distant amusement. "What strikes Tenochtitlan will strike its neighbours, too – and Texcoco is not just any neighbour, but part of the heart and soul of the Triple Alliance."

The courtyard we entered resembled Tizoc-tzin's private quarters in miniature: at the centre was a pyramid of limestone. Atop the stairway was a squat building, and on the platform that led up to it floated a round feather standard depicting a cactus with red fruit. The insignia was unfamiliar.

"Teomitl?" I asked, my face turned upwards.

My student shed Nezahual-tzin with the quickness and eagerness of a striking snake. "It's his insignia," he said. "Pochtic, Master of the House of Darkness, Lord of the Eagle Prickly Pear."

The entrance-curtain was held open by a slave, who bowed to Teomitl and Nezahual-tzin as they passed. In the antechamber a pile of sandals attested to the presence of several dignitaries: Teomitl and I removed ours, while Nezahual-tzin stood waiting patiently. Of course, he was a Revered Speaker and had no need to appear barefoot before Tizoc-tzin.

Inside the room the atmosphere was hot and oppressive, like the air of the dry season. The smoke of copal incense lay over everything, and everyone present blurred into hazy, indistinct silhouettes. Nevertheless, I counted at least ten people gathered at the furthest end against the featureless wall.

As we approached, I made out the familiar hue of Tizoc-tzin's turquoise cloak. His sycophant Quenami was here, and a host of feather-clad warriors I didn't recognise, probably the higher echelons of the army. In the centre...

I had caught a brief glimpse of Pochtic when the army returned: he'd been standing with the other three members of the war-council, though all I remembered were the crimson feathers of his headdress, and the black-trimmed mantle, held together with a folded rosette. The man lying on the reed-mat, though, had nothing to do with that image.

His face was cut – not lacerated by a knife, but abraded everywhere, deep enough to draw blood. The wounds did not look deep, but they were horrific; circular patches covering his entire skin from cheek to forehead.

His earlobes were torn – not by sacrifice or by penance, but as if a wild animal had bitten them off – and his eyelids were a bloody mass. His chest still rose and fell, though he was unconscious.

"It looks like he's been mauled," the She-Snake said, behind me.

Teomitl frowned and shook his head. "No. That's no wild animal. He'd have wounds with torn edges."

"Then what is it?" Tizoc-tzin's livid face turned towards us. Under the Turquoise and Gold Crown his eyes seemed to have sunk deeper, his cheeks gaunter and paler, giving him the air of a corpse just risen from its funeral vigil. "What is it? No one attacks my war-council in my palace. Do you hear, brother, no one!"

It was getting worse, then – the lack of grace, the paranoia. I sought Acamapichtli with my eyes, but couldn't find him. It seemed he'd stayed with his patients – for once doing the right thing.

"I don't know." Teomitl knelt, throwing his red-and-white cloak behind him – he extended a hand towards the bloody face, and seemed to remember something. In a fluid, violent motion, he tore the jade rings from his fingers, and dumped them on the ground. Then, gently, as if caring for a sick child, he raised Pochtic's head towards him. Blood ran down in lazy streams, staining Pochtic's chin and neck.

I picked one of my obsidian knives, and quickly slashed my earlobes, whispering a prayer to Lord Death – waiting for the familiar cold sensation in my belly, and for the world to recede.

"We all must die,
We all must go down into darkness…"

There was a welter of magics in the room, all the protective spells the warriors and Tizoc-tzin had surrounded themselves with. Teomitl himself radiated the strong, undiluted power of his patron goddess. And from the unconscious Pochtic...

It was faint, like an echo at the bottom of a cenote; like a minute trace of water on the skin, barely shining in the light of the Fifth Sun. A trace of magic clinging to the face: a thread spun in the darkness that went towards...

I moved, slowly, cocking my head left and right. It was coming through the knot of warriors – I pushed my way through, ignoring the glares they shot me.

Behind them was nothing but a wicker chest – but now that I was clear of the knot of entangled magic the feeling was stronger, achingly familiar. I threw open the chest. Behind me, people were whispering, but no one, it seemed, dared to interrupt me.

Inside were codices, papers, folded cloth – there didn't seem to be anything in there that would have that particular aura. Had I been mistaken?

Unless...

I started emptying the chest, dumping on the floor everything from golden ornaments to maps of the city. There was nothing at the bottom of the chest, either – just the knots of wicker that made up the structure. But the feeling of magic remained.

Underneath, then. I shifted the empty wicker chest out of the way – and there was indeed something under it.

I knelt to examine it. It was the oval shape of a mask, with the vague, grotesque suggestion of eyes and mouth – but without any holes. Some image of a god.

My hands were slick and warm – the other side was sticky with some substance that...

Gently, carefully – afraid of what I'd see – I flipped the mask. The reverse was covered with blood. I lifted it to the light: it was semi-transparent rubber, letting me catch glimpses of the room through it. In its grooves and protuberances I saw a human face in reverse – the skin clinging to the mask, the nose and mouth completely plugged, the eyes themselves sealed, until the world reduced itself to the impossible struggle for breath, to a scream that couldn't be uttered through glued lips.

And now I knew how he'd got the wounds.

"The blocked breath," someone said by my side – Nezahual-tzin, looking at the mask as if it were nothing more than a curiosity. "Sacrifices for the harvest and the rain."

But this wasn't a sacrifice. This was – someone had tried to murder Pochtic in his own rooms. "How would they get it on him?"

Nezahual-tzin shrugged. "I can think of several ways, but we'll know more when he wakes up. By the way, your student says that the body is saturated with Tlaloc's magic."

Why did this fail to surprise me? The blocked breath – a mask that mimicked a drowning – not dying of the water, but close enough. Strangled and suffocated men belonged to Tlaloc the Storm Lord, after all.

And Acamapichtli had said the epidemic had been called up from Tlalocan. It fitted – all too well.

I was still looking at the specks of blood against the mask. "He tore it off his own face…"

"He's a strong man." Nezahual-tzin made an expansive gesture with his arms. "He'll survive."

At this stage, Pochtic's survival wasn't what I cared for most. "Coatl," I said, carefully. "And now Pochtic. Someone is targeting the war-council." No, that wasn't possible. The attack on Pochtic had been deliberate, but how could the sorcerer foresee that Coatl would be in the room with Eptli's body and catch the sickness?

Nezahual-tzin said nothing – but somebody else was speaking, in a familiar high-pitched voice. Tizoc-tzin was working himself into a frenzy again. For a brief moment, I considered ignoring him – but I couldn't do this. Whether I liked it or not, he was Revered Speaker, and I had to stand by him.

"I want every sorcerer who uses Tlaloc's magic rounded up," Tizoc-tzin was saying as I walked back to the dignitaries. "Arrest them all."

"Many of them will be innocent," the She-Snake said, coldly. His gaze was turned downwards, to where Teomitl still knelt by the unconscious body. "You can't just accuse whoever you want."

"You dare question me?" Tizoc-tzin's voice rose to a shriek.

The She-Snake – who'd swum in the waters of politics from a young age – wasn't about to be defeated so easily. "My Lord, I am your viceroy, keeping the order of the city just as you keep the order of the world outside. I would never countermand any of your orders, but the people might not understand what you're doing."

"I fail to see where the problem is. They are plotting against the Empire."

Did he even have any idea of how many practitioners of Tlaloc's magic there were in the city – not merely the powerful ones like Acamapichtli, but the hundreds of commoners, casting spells for small favours from the gods – curing minor ailments, improving the harvest, granting children to barren couples? "My Lord," I said.

Tizoc-tzin's head swung towards me – transfixing me with anger and contempt. "Yes, priest?"

Southern Hummingbird blind me, why couldn't Acamapichtli be here? He'd have found smooth, convincing words that, if they hadn't calmed Tizoc-tzin, would at least have not angered him. But all that occurred to me in that frozen moment was the truth. "Tlaloc is but a tool. It's highly likely the sorcerer has access to the magic of other gods. Tlaloc might not even be his favoured god." Only the humble and weak spell-casters were restricted to the magic of a single deity: everyone else tended to cultivate the favours of one or two gods, and to call on the others as needed.

Tizoc-tzin's face contorted, and I realised I'd just given him more targets for his rage. "I see. Good remark, priest. Round up all the sorcerers, then."

"This is impossible," the She-Snake said.

"Impossible." Tizoc-tzin's voice was flat, as cutting as an obsidian blade. "Impossible. I ought to have known I couldn't trust you."

"We do seem to have trust issues," the She-Snake said, gravely. He had guts, that much was certain – I just wasn't sure it would avail him of anything. Theoretically, the She-Snake couldn't be demoted, but it was merely a matter of it never happening before. The Revered Speaker, after all, named the She-Snake – why couldn't he cast him down?

"Don't play games with me." Tizoc-tzin stared at the She-Snake; neither of them said anything for a while. The whole room held its trembling breath.

At length, the She-Snake nodded. "My Lord," he said, slowly. "I will give orders to my men." His face revealed nothing of what he felt, but his whole pose was tense.

"Good," Tizoc-tzin said. He turned, taking us all in. "Dismissed. We'll reconvene after the sorcerers have been questioned."

As he swept out of the room with his escort, I chanced to catch a glimpse of a dignitary – a short man, almost dwarfed by the weight of his quail-feather headdress. His face was set in a scowl and he was staring at Tizoc-tzin's retreating back with withering anger – as if expressing all the contempt the She-Snake had felt, but not dared to make public.

"Who is that man?" I asked Nezahual-tzin, who was closest to me.

He frowned. "The one with the greenstone and snail shell necklace, who looks as though he's swallowed something bad?"

"That one, yes."

"I'm not that familiar with Mexica politics…" Nezahual-tzin's voice trailed off. "Itamatl, if I'm not mistaken. Deputy for the Master of the Bowl of Fatigue."

The fourth member of the war council, then: one of the cornerstones of the army, the one who guided the men through the fire and blood of battle. And he hated Tizoc-tzin that much? I wondered who he had supported in last year's power struggle. For all I knew, he had never expected Tizoc-tzin to become Revered Speaker. And yet… that he should show it openly, at a time like this? This was bad, very bad.

The room was empty of dignitaries now: the slaves were creeping back, and a few women – Pochtic's wives? – looking away from us. Nezahual-tzin threw them his most charming smile, but it seemed to make them even more frightened.

"Teomitl–" I started, but Nezahual-tzin was standing as still as a jaguar on the prowl, looking down at Teomitl.

My student hadn't said anything during the whole confrontation – which was uncharacteristic. Slowly, carefully, he gathered his rings from Pochtic's side – and slid them, one by one, back onto his fingers. His face was the exact double of the She-Snake's – that smooth lack of expression which hid inner turmoil.

His hands, as they manipulated the rings, were steady, but I knew him well enough to see the slight tremor, the almost imperceptible curving of the fingers – the trembling aura of magic around him, hinting at tossing waves, at stormy seas.

I'd seen him angry, in spurts of scalding wrath that never lasted – but this was something else. This was cold, deliberate rage, and I wasn't sure it would ever be extinguished.

It was dark when we came out, with a scattering of stars overhead – the eyes of demons over the Fifth World, contained only by the power of the Southern Hummingbird.

Tlaloc's magic. And the sacred courtesan served Xochiquetzal, who was as close to Tlaloc as goddesses went.

I didn't like this, not at all. I turned to Nezahual-tzin, and asked, "The sacred courtesan. Xiloxoch."

"Yes?" His eyes were on the stars. Could he discern his protector god among them – Quetzalcoatl the Feathered Serpent, Lord of the Morning Star?

"Can you find her?"

"Now?"

There was an itch in my shoulder blades, the hint of a lament in my ears. And, in spite of the precautions we'd taken, I wasn't altogether sure we'd done the right thing – were Teomitl and I immune to the sickness, or merely spreading it throughout the city? "As soon as you can."

"I'll talk to the leader of the prisoners again," Teomitl said, brusquely. "And send word if Pochtic wakes up."

"And Tizoc-tzin?" I asked, carefully.

"Tizoc does what he wants." Teomitl wouldn't look at me. What was going on? It wasn't shame; that was an emotion he barely knew the meaning of.

"Teomitl–"

He made a quick, stabbing gesture with his hands. "I'm Master of the House of Darts. Member of his war-council. His heir. If I don't make sure he follows the right path, who will?"

"Leave that to the She-Snake," Nezahual-tzin said, distractedly. "You can't afford to be among those he distrusts."

Teomitl snorted, but said nothing. He worried me. "Don't do anything rash, please."

"I won't." And, under his breath, "not unless he gives me a reason to."

"Teomitl!" I said.

He pressed his lips together. "You're not my master, Acatl-tzin." And he was gone, wrapping his cloak around him, before I could react.

It wasn't the first time he'd done that, but before, he had been bewildered, or lost – or unsure of Tizoc-tzin. I knew him enough to tell by the set of his jaw and of his eyes that he'd come to some great decision, one that he didn't want me to be privy to.

And, given his anger at Tizoc-tzin's acts, I could guess at the decision. After all, his brother was unpopular with the army, whereas Teomitl's smoke and mist was spreading, his mark on the Fifth World becoming larger and larger. He was Master of the House of Darts, controlling the great arsenals of Tenochtitlan and therefore access to all the causeways that linked us to the mainland – and why shouldn't he see to it that the Turquoise and Gold Crown was held by someone who deserved it, and never mind what the disasters this would cause for the balance of power?

No. He wouldn't. He was more intelligent than that. He had to have absorbed some of what I'd taught him about magic – about the Fifth World being held by a thread until Tizoc-tzin was confirmed.

Surely he wouldn't...

"He's a clever man," Nezahual-tzin said, thoughtfully – as if he had read the tenor of my thoughts. When he saw my face, he smiled. "I didn't use magic, Acatl. You're an easy man to read."

"I don't dissemble," I said, curtly. My relationship with Teomitl might not be wholly private – because of our respective positions – but the Revered Speaker of Texcoco certainly had no business prying into it to satisfy his thrice-accursed curiosity.

Nezahual-tzin ventured nothing. At length, when I didn't speak, he shrugged – a falsely careless gesture, and went downstairs. "I'll see you around, Acatl."

I remained for a while – not because I found the view beautiful, but because I wanted to be sure that he was gone. We'd only had two deaths – a tragedy by some standards, insignificant in the larger frame – and already the fabric of the imperial palace was unravelling.

As if I'd needed further proof that we remained fragile, as the Empire slowly rebuilt itself from the mess of the year before… This wasn't the most auspicious of times for a sorcerer to move against us. I would have prayed for this to bring us together against a common enemy, but deep down I already knew it wouldn't.

• • • •

I walked to my house alone, amidst the looming shapes of the temples. Even at this late hour, the Sacred Precinct was busy: priests sang hymns and made penances, and circled the Serpent Wall, offering their blood at regular intervals. From within the temples came a grinding sound, as novice priests ground the pigments which would be used on the following day to paint faces and arms for religious ceremonies.

My temple was still lit; I entered briefly, to reassure myself that all was well, and to check a few examinations. Ichtaca had made no progress on tracking down information about the merchant Yayauhqui; hardly surprising, since I'd only asked him a handful of hours ago.

I went to bed praying to Chicomecoatl to look favourably upon us – and to bless us with Her luck, to better unravel this skein of magic.

I woke up sore, as if I'd spent the entire day and night walking. My head throbbed, and for a brief moment, as I pulled myself to my knees, the world seemed to spin.

I closed my eyes for a brief moment. The spinning went away and the soreness seemed to recede, but the feeling remained. The onset of the sickness? We should–

Stay inside like old men? No, I couldn't. I had work to do.

Nevertheless… it would have been highly irresponsible to go further without some kind of precaution. Mihmatini's spell had its uses, but, as much as the Duality was arbiter and source of the gods, They were not the ones to whom I owed my allegiance, and Their protection would not be the most effective I could call on.

I made my offerings of blood to the Fifth Sun and to Lord Death, singing the hymns for the continuation of the Fifth World, and pulling my worship-thorns through my earlobes.

On my wicker chest were two sets of clothes: one was a simple grey cloak, appropriate for a priest for the Dead; the other was the ornate, owl-embroidered monstrosity of my regalia complete with skull-mask and feather head-dress. The grey cloak was far more comfortable, likely to be far less noticed, but the days when I could have worn it had all but passed. Ichtaca was right: I needed to show myself, and this included wearing the regalia. With a sigh, I folded the simple cloak back into the chest, putting it under the folded codices I was working on. It was, after all, unlikely I would need it in the days to come.

I walked into the Sacred Precinct in full regalia.

The dizziness did not return, though I watched for it. The world remained crisp and clear, the sky above the Sacred Precinct a brilliant blue, with the familiar smells of copal incense smoke, underlain by the rank one of blood. Ahead, atop the Great Temple, the sacrifices went on un-abated: a body tumbled down the steps, coming to a rest in the grooves that surrounded the pyramid's base – the painted white skin spattered with blood.

Everything seemed well: the Empire strong, the gods watching over us, a Revered Speaker about to be con-firmed in a burst of glory, and his coronation war a resounding success.

How I wished I could be fooled by such appearances.

Ichtaca met me at the temple entrance. I could tell that he was either preoccupied or in a hurry, for the black streaks on his cheeks were slightly curved instead of straight, as if he'd applied them with shaking hands. "Acatl-tzin."

"I presume something has happened."

Ichtaca grimaced. "Teomitl-tzin sent word. Pochtic – the Master of the House of Darkness – has regained consciousness, but there are two further warriors affected. One of them is dead."

Dead already? The sickness was spreading – I rubbed the tips of my fingers together, as if I could wash it away from my skin. How was it contracted? "And the others? The ones Acamapichtli had in confinement?"

"I've heard no news."

Well, there was nothing for it. "Send priests for the funeral rites, and remove the bodies. We need to examine them in an isolated spot. Did they die in the palace?"

Ichtaca shook his head. "I think at the House of Youth, but I'll check."

A group of grey-clad novices passed by us. By the reed-brooms in their hands, it looked they were going to sweep the courtyard, cleansing it in honour of Lord Death. "Do check," I said. "Nothing else?"

Ichtaca spread his hands. His nervousness was palpable. "The merchant: I did find which god he worshipped, but–"

I sighed. Ichtaca had always been a staunch believer in Mexica superiority, and the past few months had hit him badly. "Tell me," I said, gently.

"Tezcatlipoca, the Smoking Mirror."

Lord of the Near, Lord of the Nigh; god of war and youth, protector of sorcerers. Nothing too surprising there, sadly – even the viciousness of Yayauhqui's punishment was characteristic.

"Does it help?"

I couldn't lie to him. "I'm not sure. It certainly doesn't put him at the forefront of suspects: the epidemic seems to be coming from Tlaloc."

"Again?" Ichtaca asked.

Two years earlier, the Storm Lord and a splinter group of His priests had attempted an elaborate plot to unseat Huitzilpochtli's dominance – using the Revered Speaker's weakness to raise up an agent in the Fifth World. They would have succeeded, too, but for our order.

"He's a god," I said, slowly. "The Duality only knows what He's plotting." I paused, then.

"What is it, Acatl-tzin?"

"The Flower Quetzal," I said slowly. Xochiquetzal had been the Storm Lord's ally – as interested as He had been in the end of the Fifth World.

"You think She's involved in this again?"

I thought of Xiloxoch. "I don't know. But it's a possibility."

One I didn't care much for. A scheming deity was bad enough, but an alliance of gods…

I nodded. "Before I go, I need a ritual performed."

"Which one?"

I'd had time to mull it over on my way to the temple. Mictlantecuhtli, Lord Death, was seldom invoked for defensive magic – unless one counted summoning creatures such as the Wind of Knives or the Owl Archer from the underworld. But this particular sickness, it seemed, was under the auspices of Tlaloc the Storm Lord. And the magics of the underworld and of Tlalocan cancelled each other out.

"It's not a ritual," I said at last. "At least, not per se. I just need you to provide a little… help."

We repaired to one of the examination rooms, under the hollow gaze of Mictlantecuhtli. As I'd asked, Ichtaca had gathered only offering priests for this – the novices would have been all too glad to take part in something like this, but they hadn't yet learned the fundamental lesson of the priesthood: that magic might be awe-inspiring, but that the heart of our devotions lay elsewhere. That Lord Death did not give us more than was needed, or grant us our prayers, but that we could rely on Him to stand by His rules, that he was not cruel or capricious, but merely there, awaiting us all.

And it was my role – and Ichtaca's – to teach them the importance of the small things, of the devotions at night, of the examinations of corpses with knives and small spells, of the offerings that came day and night to give their lives the rhythm of faith.

At the feet of each priest lay a pile of quetzal feathers, and a single lip-plug made of jade. On Ichtaca's signal, they cut a thin line across the back of their hands, and let the blood drip onto the feathers and jade.

Ichtaca – who was part of the circle, started chanting a hymn to Lord Death:

"Only here on earth, in the Fifth World,
Shall the flowers last, shall the songs be bliss,
Though it be feathers, though it be jade,
It too must go to the region of the fleshless."

Where the blood touched the feathers, they gleamed – a dark hue of green, the miasma of the underworld. A cold wind was blowing across the room, making the priests' grey cloaks billow like the wings of some gaunt and skeletal bird.

"It too must go to the region of mystery,
Only once do we live on this earth,
We came only to sleep, only to dream,
Only once do we live on this earth."

I took a deep breath, and tightened my grip on my obsidian knife. I had offered no blood, but that did not matter. To call on what I intended, I needed no offerings, merely my presence, there in the very centre of Lord Death's largest temple – I, who had been consecrated High Priest, invested with the breath of the underworld.

I felt it rise within me: the lament of the dead, the grave voice of the Wind of Knives, the careless smile and wide eyes of the Owl Archer, the hulking shapes of beasts of shadows – and everything that presaged Mictlan in the Fifth World: the old folk laid out on their reed-mats, struggling to breathe for yet another day; the peasants feeling the first aches in their backs, the first creaks of their joints; the women in the marketplace with their wrinkled faces and streaks of white in their hair; the children, learning that no year resembled the one past, and that time had caught them all, more surely than a fisherman's net; all those on the road to the throne of Lord Death – and to oblivion.

"In the house of the fleshless,
In the house with no windows,
We go, we disappear,
Only once do we live on this earth."

The world contracted. A cold feeling ran over my entire body, as if I'd just put on chilled clothes after some time standing before a brazier. And the feel of the underworld, instead of abating, continued unchanged. I saw the skulls under the faces of the priests – smelled the coming rot, and the blotches that would spread over their skins as the blood stopped flowing within their bodies.

I wouldn't be able to maintain it for long, for it took its toll on my own energy. I'd expected to be frightened, or disgusted, but I wasn't. Cocooned in a power as familiar to me as the taste of maize, I felt... at ease, relaxed even for the first time in days. I had lived with the awareness of death for years – not as a distant event in the future, but as real as the blank eyes of corpses, as the blotches on pallid hands.

It would have to do.

I crossed the Sacred Precinct as if in a dream. A cold wind blew around me, reducing the bustle of the crowd to the silence of the grave and the crackle of flames on a funeral pyre. Indistinct faces brushed past me, and the only things that seemed real were the shadows of the temples, from the round tower of Quetzalcaoatl the Feathered Serpent to the familiar pyramid shape of the Great Temple dwarfing the Sacred Precinct.

I didn't feel quite ready to face Teomitl yet – what would I have flung at him, save worries I couldn't quite substantiate?

Instead, I made my own way to the quarters of the Master of the House of Darkness and found him awake, tended to by his personal slave. One of the She-Snake's guards was at the entrance; he let me pass, though I knew he would soon be reporting my coming to his master.

The Master of the House of Darkness looked, if anything, worse than on the previous day – his raw skin shining in the morning sun, glistening with the particular glint of pus and scabs. His torn eyelids had puffed up, all but hiding his eyes. With my new, sensitive eyesight, I could trace the incipient rot in every streak on

145

his forehead and cheeks and smell the swelling pus, a rancid odour that threatened to overwhelm the smoke of copal incense.

"My Lord," I said. "I am Acatl, High Priest for the Dead."

"I know who you are." The voice sounded slightly peeved. "I might be on my mat, but I'm no invalid, and certainly not at Mictlan's gates yet."

I wasn't entirely sure I agreed, but I didn't say anything. I sat cross-legged in front of him – an honoured visitor – and spoke as if nothing were wrong. I prayed his diminished eyesight wouldn't let him see the way my gaze wandered downwards – of that, if he did see, he would misinterpret it as a sign of respect.

"So," Pochtic said after a while. "Here to investigate the attack on me, then?"

"Among other things," I said, carefully. He was obviously used to be being in charge – which wasn't surprising, given his high position in the army. "Can you tell me more about what happened? I found the mask on the ground."

Pochtic's ruined face did not move. "He was waiting for me in my chambers. I never did get to see his face – before I knew it, he had me pinned, an arm locked around my neck. And then he slid the mask on." He gave a shudder – the act of memory itself was too painful. "I don't remember anything except waking here, afterwards."

He spoke like a warrior: frank, honest, not mincing words and making no efforts to hide anything.

Or did he? His account was not only fragmentary, but singularly unhelpful – as if he'd worked on it to give as little information as possible.

"Hmm," I said. "He grasped you by the neck. That would indicate a man taller than you."

His mouth set in a grimace – his hands clenched as the split lips contracted, opening up the hundred tiny wounds he'd sustained. "I suppose so."

With him lying down, it was hard to tell – but I remembered the ceremony of welcoming for the army, and the four members of the war-council following one another. Pochtic, in his crimson feathers and black-trimmed mantle, had towered over Teomitl – who wasn't very small himself, either. So either our assailant was uncannily tall, whether he was human or not – I could think of several creatures that would fit that description. Or...

I needed a way to look at his neck – one that would be discreet enough to draw no suspicion. If he was lying, and in some ways involved with the epidemic, the last thing I needed was to be spooking him.

If I rose now – with the words he'd spoken fresh in his mind – he would suspect something. I had to gain time, instead. "Asphyxiation," I said. "It's a common ritual used by the priests of Tlaloc."

"I have little to do with the Storm Lord," Pochtic said, not without disdain. "My service is dedicated to Tezcatlipoca the Smoking Mirror, Lord of the Near, Lord of the Nigh – and to the other gods of war."

"You don't think someone could have attacked you for precisely this reason?" I asked.

Pochtic snorted. "I maintain good relations with the gods and their priests. Nothing particular happened in the last few days that would justify this."

His eyes flicked, just a fraction, as he said that – and for a moment I saw raw fear in the pupils. He knew, or suspected what he'd been attacked for.

What was going on?

"So you didn't know your assailant? You're sure that

you wouldn't have caught a glimpse of him – have any inkling or any suspicion why you were picked for that kind of death?" I rose as I said that, and walked nearer to him – and, as I expected, Pochtic followed the direction of my voice, tilting his head upwards. His cloak slipped, a fraction, uncovering his neck and the top of his shoulders – a fraction, but it was enough for me to see that there was no mark whatsoever there.

No, wait.

There were faint bruises on both shoulders, not far from the neck area. I'd only had a short look at them before Pochtic settled down again, but they were familiar, from a thousand examinations. Palm marks, facing upwards. In other words, someone had forced Pochtic down on his back, and put the mask on – and left him here, flopping like a fish on dry land until the air in his lungs gave out.

Then he had seen his assailant – or a shadow, at least. Why lie about it?

"I've told you," Pochtic said. "I don't have any idea what's going on."

"You're a strong man," I said, slowly. "I'm surprised you were overwhelmed that easily."

Pochtic's eyes glittered with something I couldn't place – shame, fear? "He held me like a rag doll," he whispered. "And then I couldn't breathe. Do you have any idea how horrible it is – your lungs starting to burn, your mouth struggling to draw air through jade? I– all your life, you breathe. Day after day, moment after moment – and suddenly you can't see anything, can't focus on anything but how powerless you are?"

He was Master of the House of Darkness: a rich, powerful man, who had everything he could ever want –

physicians waiting on him, servants to satisfy the least of his desires. Like Eptli, he believed himself designed for greatness – and then, in a moment, everything had been snatched from him. He had been reminded that – like precious stones which cracked and broke – he was destined for Mictlan, the underworld, the place of the fleshless.

I knew the fear in his eyes – I had felt it myself. But in him it seemed to be compounded with something I couldn't place. Did he lie about his assailant because the latter had been small, and he was ashamed? Or was it something else?

Either way, this wouldn't be solved here. To accuse him of lying would bring me nowhere and would only anger Tizoc-tzin further – not the most intelligent of ideas, given his current mood.

NINE
Enemies of the Empire

I was walking out of Pochtic's quarters, when, through a courtyard, I caught a glimpse of Teomitl, walking by a woman in a simple red skirt. She did not wear the two horns of married women, but there was an ivory comb in her hair. Her face was lathered with makeup, giving her skin the yellow sheen of corn, and she walked with the familiar, swaying allure of a woman used to seducing men.

A sacred courtesan. Xiloxoch? I couldn't see any other reason for him to talk to someone of her status – not now that he was married, in the process of founding a household of his own.

Though Teomitl didn't look seduced – if anything, he looked angry, the facets of his cheeks taking on the colour of jade, and his eyes hardening into small, glinting stones. The aura of his patron goddess Chalchiuhtlicue, Jade Skirt, was strong enough to hurt my eyes.

"Teomitl!" I called.

He slowed down a fraction, but barely acknowledged me. He was in regalia – not the peacetime one, but rather the frightful spectre, the war costume of the Master of the

House of Darts. It made him look wild, untamed – from the dishevelled plume of quetzal feathers fanning out from the back of his hair, to his head, emerging from between the jaws of a sculpted skeletal beast. "This is Xiloxoch." He smiled, but the expression never reached his eyes. "Nezahual-tzin brought her to my quarters."

And what pleasure Nezahual-tzin would have derived from it, no doubt. "So you're accompanying her back to the House of Joy?"

Teomitl made a small, stabbing gesture with the back of one hand. "No. I'm taking her to the military courts."

"For visiting a prisoner?" Surely there was no law against this?

The light around Teomitl flared up, became blinding. "You don't understand, Acatl-tzin. Xiloxoch has serious accusations to make."

Against the prisoner? "I–"

The courtesan, Xiloxoch, spoke up. Her voice was that of an educated woman – most of the courtesans who attended the warriors in the House of Youth tended to be commoners, but she had obviously been taught by priestesses in the calmecac school. "Bribery and fraud," she said. Her teeth were black, the colour of unending night; her eyes, outlined with makeup, shone with determination. A driven woman, Nezahual-tzin had said. "Eptli has scratched the jade, has torn apart the quetzal feathers – dishonouring father and mother, and the gods that watched over him."

The sinking feeling was back in my stomach. "What did he do?"

"He corrupted the judges." Teomitl's voice was curt. "The two-faced son of a dog corrupted the war-council, under my own eyes."

But the war-council included him, surely? "The whole council?"

"The Master of the House of Darkness, and the deputy for the Master of Raining Blood." Xiloxoch's face twisted; it might have been a smile, but there was no joy in it. "The other deputy refused."

Pochtic. Coatl. And the other man, the one I hadn't seen more than for a few moments. "And Teomitl?" I asked.

Teomitl's face was a mask, his skin carved jade, his cheeks hollowed, and his eyes dark holes. "I was too much of a fool to catch what they were saying."

"That's a serious accusation," I said, very slowly. "Do you have any evidence?"

"We don't need evidence for the moment," Teomitl said, impatiently. "We need to warn the magistrates, so that they can arrest the culprits."

I raised a hand. Had he learned nothing? "Do you have evidence?" I asked Xiloxoch, again.

Her eyes were dark, and deep; her black-stained teeth shining in the oval of her face. "The behaviour of a dead man. The word of another. It's not easy, as you can see." She didn't smile. Her whole being seemed – taut, with something very like the will to seduce – somehow transfigured, shaped into an instrument of the law. Driven, Nezahual-tzin had called her.

But driven by what? The desire for justice, or one of Xochiquetzal's plots?

"It's a serious accusation," I said, finally. And, if it was true...

No. I couldn't be like Teomitl, and take risks as easily as I breathed.

"It's a serious crime," Xiloxoch said. Her voice took on the singsong accents of an admonition. "'The city has given you a plume of heron feathers, the city has given you paper clothes. You are the slave of the city, the servant of the people. Do not let your words ripen and rot.'"

She did smile, then; and it was terrible to behold, a thing without joy.

I didn't like that. Whatever her motivations – and they had to be more complicated than a simple will for justice – it was still… troubling. "Coatl," I said, slowly. "Pochtic."

"Acatl-tzin–" Teomitl said, "You don't think–"

I wasn't in a state to think, that was the problem. "Eptli is dead. Coatl is in isolation. Pochtic has been savaged."

Xiloxoch hadn't moved – she stood as straight as a thrown spear, waiting with undisguised impatience. Still, she'd moved a fraction at the last – something about Pochtic was either news, or unexpected.

"Whatever testimony you have," I said to Xiloxoch, "it won't last long." And, to Teomitl: "You're wrong."

For a moment – a bare, fleeting moment – I saw the harshness of jade in his features, and the shadow that spread to his eyes – and I thought he was going to reprimand me, to deny my right as his teacher. But then he shook his head, and some of the tension in the air vanished. "Wrong? Prove it."

Think, think, Southern Hummingbird curse me. "I want to know what you have," I said to Xiloxoch. "Once again, it is a serious accusation that you bear. We can't act prematurely on that."

"I slept with Eptli, once or twice. He made – careless confessions, after he was spent." Her lips twisted. "He was so sure of himself, that one. Didn't think for a moment that the captive would fail to be awarded to him." She spat on the ground; her saliva glistened on the dry earth.

"And you still slept with him." I understood her less and less – was her patron goddess Xochiquetzal behind that? The Quetzal Flower's intrigues tended to be far more vicious and far less complicated than that.

"He was handsome," Xiloxoch said, dismissively. "One might as well pick the prettiest ones."

"That's not a very strong reason," I said. "Why did you pick him, Xiloxoch?"

She shook her head, but did not answer.

"Xiloxoch." Teomitl said – his voice was soft, but it was no longer that of the young, unproven warrior. "Someone has been spreading diseases in the heart of the Mexica Empire. This is also a serious crime."

"I wouldn't know anything about that." Her eyes had flared; her hands clenched. She looked more angry than fearful.

"Why pick Eptli, Xiloxoch?"

"I told you. For justice."

"No," I said, slowly. "That's not what you told us. You said you'd learned of Eptli's transgression only after you slept with him."

There was a soft, green light spreading – Teomitl's aura, giving everything the air of underwater caves. The air smelled of churned mud, with the salty aftertaste of blood – and it was thicker too, clogging in our lungs. I could hear Xiloxoch's rising breath – coming in shorter and more laboured gasps. "Why?" he asked.

Last time I'd seen him try this, he'd almost killed a guard – but things had changed now, and he seemed more in control. Though one could never be sure, with the capricious Jade Skirt.

Xiloxoch's face was pale, her teeth drinking in the light and giving nothing back. "He was such an arrogant, obnoxious man. Thinking all the quetzal feathers, all the jade of the Fifth World were his due. So used to riches he thought they could buy anything."

The quintessential warrior – contemptuous of anything so feminine as sacred courtesans. "In other words, the perfect worshipper of the Southern Hummingbird."

Xiloxoch smiled, but said nothing.

"It's a serious accusation," I said, again. "But, if it's true, then they'll uphold the law, and Eptli will be stripped of rank, posthumously. Warriors were held to higher standards than commoners, by virtue of their higher knowledge and education. The war-council – the heads of the warriors, their role-models in the Fifth World – would be held to even more exacting rules.

"Come on," Teomitl said. "Let's see the magistrate, and we'll sort this out."

I shook my head. The pattern was disturbing: if Xiloxoch's accusations were true, we had three people involved. Eptli had offered the bribe, Pochtic and Coatl had accepted it. Eptli was dead, someone had attacked Pochtic, and Coatl had fallen prey to the same sickness as Eptli. As to the prisoner Zoquitl – the prize in all of this – he had also died.

Whether Xiloxoch's accusations were true or not, someone seemed to be killing off everyone alleged to have taken part in the affair.

Was it someone else associated with Xiloxoch? "Who else knows about this?" I asked her.

She started. "I don't understand."

"Don't take us for fools," I said. "As you said – everyone mentioned has died, or been attacked in some way. I find it hard to believe there is no connection."

Xiloxoch's eyes flicked towards the ground. "I didn't mention it to anyone. Why would I?"

Teomitl watched her intently – I wondered if he saw anything else, with the light of Jade Skirt so strong in his eyes – but at length he nodded. "Let's go, Acatl-tzin. We've wasted enough time already."

I thought, quickly. The coincidence was troubling, but then all the men she had accused were members of the war-council and what better way to sow chaos amongst us than target them – the supreme four, commanders of the army?

"No," I said. "We have more important things to do than this." And, to Xiloxoch: "I'm pretty sure you can find your own way to the military courts."

Her smile was wide and dazzling. "Of course. Don't worry about me, Acatl-tzin."

After she'd left, Teomitl turned to me, his face creased in puzzlement. "We could have–"

"No," I said. "She brought nothing but groundless accusations. I'm not about to give her the pleasure of our approval. Let her face the magistrates on her own terms."

"It's a serious matter."

"You've said it yourself: you noticed nothing."

"Yes, but I'm a fool when it comes to matters like this."

I shook my head. "It's not good enough, don't you see? We serve justice; not whims based on scant evidence." Otherwise we would not be much better than Tizoc-tzin.

Teomitl's face took on some of the harshness of jade again, but it was soon gone. "Fine. I suppose you're right. But if it's not true, then what was she was doing in Zoquitl's room?"

I had a fair idea of what she could have been doing in Zoquitl's rooms – what sacred courtesans did best. She was a servant of the Flower Quetzal, goddess of Lust and

156

Childbirth, and sleeping with a promised sacrifice would not only enable her to honour her goddess, but might also leech potency from the Southern Hummingbird. It was small – one sacrifice out of forty – but the Flower Quetzal would have gladly counted it a victory.

Unless She had more extreme plans? Unless She was once more Tlaloc's ally, seeking retribution on the Fifth World?

"What now?" Teomitl asked, impatiently.

There was something going on – someone undermining the Mexica Empire or Tizoc-tzin's leadership. It could have been Tlatelolco; it could have been Xochiquetzal's followers, but it could also come from inside.

Pochtic had seen his assailant and recognised him, which in turn meant that he had known him. And I didn't think that could apply to either the Tlatelolca merchant or the sacred courtesan. But Itamatl – the fourth member of the war-council, who had displayed such hatred for Tizoc-tzin... that was a strong possibility.

"There's a man we have to see."

We stopped by the kitchens first, to get some flatbreads and fried newts. As we ate, I asked Teomitl about Itamatl.

"Honest man," he said with a shrug.

"He doesn't seem to like Tizoc-tzin all that much."

Teomitl grimaced. He looked distinctly uncomfortable, which was unusual for him. "Itamatl had an elder brother who was on the council."

I winced. "So he's dead?"

"And bound to the Southern Hummingbird, like the rest of the council."

And, of course, it had been because of Tizoc-tzin, and because of his fanatic drive to become Revered Speaker, that the council had died – or, more accurately, had been sacrificed to buy the Southern Hummingbird's favour. "And Itamatl?"

Teomitl wouldn't look at me. "Itamatl was very fond of his brother. But Acatl-tzin, you can't possibly think–"

"I don't think. I just follow what I see." Open hostility to Tizoc-ztin, and a motive for wanting the Revered Speaker cast down, denied the Gold and Turquoise Crown Itamatl's brother had died for… "And I can't exempt anyone from suspicion."

Teomitl snorted. "You might as well suspect me."

"Of dubious loyalties to Tizoc-tzin?" The words were out of my mouth before I could think, but Teomitl said nothing. He merely watched his fried frog, as if he could order it out of his sight.

"You have to wait," I said, slowly. "Otherwise…"

"I know." He bit his lips. "I've seen the star-demons, remember. I know you made the right decision, Acatl-tzin. But, still…"

I said nothing. He needed time for things to sink in. He would see the truth of it soon enough.

Itamatl's quarters were not far from Pochtic's – in the same grand and ostentatious part of the palace. They looked much the same: a squat pyramid of limestone with more unfamiliar insignia – that of the Master of the Bowl of Fatigue, I presumed, and the lesser ones, the one with the coyote underneath the red sun, had to be for Itamatl's war prowess.

There were no slaves, no servants to block our way; and the antechamber was similarly devoid of people. From inside, beyond the simple black and red entrance curtain, came rustling noises, like someone turning the pages of a codex with great speed.

Teomitl pulled the curtain open with his customary energy, sending all the bells into a frenzy of ringing – but it was not enough advance warning for the man inside – who rose from his crouch near the brazier with wads of paper still in his hands, and an expression of anger slowly stealing across his face. "What is the meaning of this – oh, I might have known. Good afternoon, Teomitl." He still appeared angry.

"Burning papers?" Teomitl asked.

Itamatl shook his head. He wore nothing but a simple cotton loincloth – no warrior finery here, as if he were uncomfortable with it. But he addressed Teomitl as an equal. "Time to get rid of the old, I should think."

"The old order?" I asked.

Itamatl put the papers down. I caught a glimpse of elaborate drawings – warriors striking at each other, elaborate representations of army units, with their feather insignia and shields. "The remnants of our old wars. Might as well not keep them." He appeared utterly unashamed; at ease. "Especially given how they turned out."

"Be careful what you say," Teomitl said.

"You know what I'm going to say."

"Yes. And I'll listen as a friend, but I am also Master of the House of Darts."

Itamatl shrugged. "Fine." He turned to me, and bowed, brusquely, as if forced to acknowledge someone he didn't much care for. "And you'll listen as High Priest for the Dead."

"It's my role," I said, slowly. "You don't seem to care much for our wars."

Itamatl looked at Teomitl – who said nothing. At length, he said, "There will always be wars, and the Southern Hummingbird will always grant His favours as he sees fit."

"But, here and now, we are the ones holding His favours."

Itamatl's gaze was sardonic. "And this grants us the right to lie and dissemble?"

"If you approve so much of the truth," I said, "then be frank with us. Do you wish for this coronation war to be a success?"

That, if nothing else, caught him aback. He threw his head back, and laughed.

"Just like a priest, to wound with words." He was silent, for a while. "No. Just once, I would like Tizoc-tzin to be thwarted in his desires. To know what it is to lose." He smiled, bitterly, at Teomitl. "I might have tried to make him lose you, but I don't think he would care, either way."

Teomitl's face was a mask; for once, I couldn't read him, no matter how dearly I might have wished to. Did he still love his brother, in spite of the grievances between them – or was there nothing left between them, save duty?

"Be careful what you say."

"Words aren't a crime," Itamatl said. "Not yet."

"But acts are," I interjected. "Eptli's death. The sickness. The attack on Pochtic."

There was a moment of silence, which seemed to stretch into an eternity. Then, a snort and a shake of his head. "I'd have been tempted, perhaps. But I assure you, I have nothing to do with this. If anyone has to pay, it's Tizoc-tzin. I won't drag down other warriors."

And, but for the silence, it might have sounded sincere.

"I see," I said, though all I could see was that we couldn't discount him as a suspect.

Teomitl said, in a brusque fashion. "There have been rumours, Itamatl. People saying we were approached with bribes by some of Eptli's allies."

"Bribes?" The puzzlement on his face looked genuine, but then again, he had had ample time to prepare himself for the question. "I don't see–"

"I didn't either." Teomitl's voice was low and savage. "But that doesn't mean there was nothing."

As we walked towards the entrance-curtain, his voice brought us short. "Teomitl!"

"Yes?" Teomitl didn't turn around.

"He'll drag us down, you know. Bit by bit and lie by lie. You know this."

"I know." Teomitl shook his head. "Come on, Acatl-tzin. Let's go."

Outside, it was early evening and the stars were shining in the sky. Teomitl paused on the platform, staring at them – I thought he might be looking for the Evening Star, the incarnation of Nezahual-tzin's protector god, but when he did speak, it had nothing to do with the Feathered Serpent. "Acatl-tzin... it was worth it, was it not?"

Trust him to get to the heart of the matter. Itamatl had accused priests of wounding with words, but Teomitl could be equally devastating in his naiveté. I stared at the stars – fixed, distant, but it only took a slight effort of memory to remember the rattle of skulls, and the lights plunging down towards us, becoming the eyes of the monsters, becoming large shapes looming over us, bringing the shattering cold, and the sense that nothing would be right again...

"We need a Revered Speaker," I said. "Otherwise the star-demons will come back." I wished I could believe it that easily. Perhaps it was better to weather a period of chaos, if that was the price to pay for a better man? But I couldn't say that. I couldn't agree to pay in blood and deaths, and casually sacrifice so many, as Tizoc-tzin had sacrificed the whole council. I'd had no choice, back four months before: we'd had to bring Tizoc-tzin back into the Fifth World, so that he would ward us against chaos and fire. That he was a man I despised changed nothing.

"He's a bad Revered Speaker. Itamatl is right." Teomitl's voice was low and fierce. "I can't admit it to him because of who I am, but he is right."

"He's not eternal," I said, finally. I started down the stairs, slowly, towards the inner courtyard, which lay in darkness beneath the merciless light of the stars.

"But he's still young." Teomitl scowled. "He could live forever."

He was a shambling corpse – because that was what we'd brought him back as, because I'd held back during the ritual, and left us with only a shadow of who Tizoc-tzin had been. "He won't last long," I said, finally. "Trust me."

"Days, months? A year?" When I didn't answer, he said, "It'll be long enough, then. Look at us. We're already torn apart."

"It's nothing new," I said, but I didn't know what I could tell him. He had seen the star-demons, as I had. He knew the price of being without protection – the price of opening up the boundaries and letting everything that prowled in the space outside the Fifth World walk our streets and swim in our canals. "I hate to say it, because it makes me sound like Acamapichtli, but we'll endure. We always have."

Teomitl laughed, without joy. "Because we're worth it." He shook his head. "Because we trample others into the dust."

"Why the moodiness?" I asked.

"I thought…" He shook his head. "I thought of who might want to harm the Mexica Empire. There are so many people we have defeated and made slaves…"

I thought, uneasily, of Tlatelolco – of the bustling marketplace, which hid the scars of war, and the enslaved people; the bitterness of men like Yayauhqui. I thought of Yaotl, who was a foreigner and a slave, and who wouldn't ever be free. "It's the way of the world. War isn't kind, or fair. You should know this, too."

"I do know!" He made a short, stabbing gesture with his hand – and stopped halfway, as if bewildered by the lack of an enemy. "It's just that…"

I waited for something else, but it didn't come. Instead, his head came up – like an *ahuizotl* water-beast sniffing the wind. "Something is wrong."

"Something?"

There was a faint, growing light at his feet – wisps of yellow radiance which slowly gathered themselves, until a thread of light shone on the floor, snaking through the courtyard, under the pillars of the buildings – losing itself in the darkness.

The thread which tied him to Mihmatini; except that I had never seen it so bright. "Mihmatini?" I asked.

"She's in trouble," Teomitl said. He was out, and running before I could even so much as finish my sentence, and, since he was the one with the link to her, I had to run after him.

I'd thought we would be going to the Duality House, but to my surprise Teomitl headed straight for the low building which hosted the courts of justice.

At this late hour, it was almost deserted – the wide airy room filled only with a few stragglers, trials that had dragged on too long, with clerks furiously drawing glyphs on papers, as if their speed could somehow expedite the magistrates' work.

Teomitl rushed through the room as if it were completely empty – passing dangerously close to a couple of artisans with wooden cangues around their necks. I followed at a more sedate pace – mostly because I was out of breath, not being as young as him.

I couldn't see Mihmatini anywhere – or the courtesan Xiloxoch, for that matter. What kind of trouble would my sister get into–?

Oh.

Teomitl was headed towards the back of the room, where an entrance-curtain of turquoise cotton marked the entrance of the noblemen's sections – which hosted both the Court of Appeals, and the Imperial Audience, that only met every thirteen days.

My work those days seldom took me into the courts, but I still had eyes, and could make out the pile of sandals near the entrance-curtain. It was an Imperial Audience today – reserved for grave crimes which touched on the security of the Empire.

And my sister was inside, and in danger.

A cold hand seemed to have closed around my heart. Surely it couldn't be…? Surely she was safe from Tizoctzin, if anyone was safe…?

Teomitl had stopped at the door, and all but tore off his sandals. I did likewise, my hands shaking on the cotton straps – trying to make out where the luminous thread was going.

The room beyond the curtain was much like the previous one: wide and airy, supported by painted pillars – and with a hint of the gardens through the back, a scent of muddy earth, a faint, raucous cry of quetzal birds seeking each other through the wooden bars of their cages.

It was packed full, as usual: almost every official in the palace seemed to have decided to attend, creating a riot of coloured cotton suits, of feather headdresses and jaguar pelts – of protective magical lattices, which hissed and faded when they met another incompatible magic.

Through the crowd, I could barely see the centre, but it seemed like some kind of hearing was going on – I caught Tizoc-tzin's voice, raised in anger, and another voice – a familiar one…

It wasn't Mihmatini's, but it was familiar all the same. Surely it couldn't be…?

Teomitl pushed his way through the crowd with the same determination he'd have used to ram a spear into a chest. I pushed ahead, oblivious of who I cast aside, of the angry voices that followed our passage, the buzzing of flies in my ears – that voice, it had to be…

"I've said it before: there is no plot against you, my Lord."

And, finally, the crowd parted, and I saw…

Tizoc-tzin, sitting on the high-backed seat of the Revered Speaker – his sallow face distorted in the familiar expressions of fear and anger.

I caught a bare glimpse of the judges to his side: two noblemen I vaguely recognised, and the familiar black-clad countenance of the She-Snake.

But, in the centre – in the centre was Acamapichtli, High Priest of Tlaloc, his clothes torn and bedraggled, looking almost vulnerable – save for his face. He'd raised it towards the judges' dais, looking the Revered Speaker and the other dignitaries in the eye – a forbidden act, sheer defiance that was going to cost him dearly once his hearing was over.

Teomitl had stopped, his gaze going from Tizoc-tzin to Acamapichtli – the greenish cast of his skin receding to show normal colours once more, his eyes the bewildered ones of a boy. He looked right and left, and finally caught sight of Mihmatini, who was standing a few paces away with the slave Yaotl by her side, her face clenched in anger. But she didn't seem to be in any kind of danger.

"What is the meaning of this?" he asked to Tizoc-tzin.

"This isn't your province," Tizoc-tzin said. His gaze moved from Teomitl to me – and in the depths of his eyes I saw only the magic of the underworld, calling out to me with the soothing song of the Dead.

Shuddering, I tore my gaze away from Tizoc-tzin. "My Lord," I said. "Grave accusations have been made–"

"I know." Tizoc-tzin waved a dismissive hand. "Don't worry, priest. They are being taken care of."

"I don't understand," I said. I swept an eye around the room, which was utterly silent. No one moved – save for the She-Snake, and in his smooth, round face I saw the first stirrings of anger. "Why–?"

"Isn't it obvious?" Tizoc-tzin asked. He laughed, and I heard the breath rattling in his lungs – such a beautiful sound, like the wheeze of funeral rattles. "Tlaloc's magic has been spilling out into the Fifth World – into the heart and entrails of my palace, priest!"

"I still don't see–" I said, though in reality it was all too clear. But I wanted him to say it, nevertheless.

Tizoc-tzin waved a hand towards Acamapichtli. "Isn't it obvious? The Storm Lord's emissary is here. It's him we should beware of, him we should cut open, him we should…" His voice dipped, and I couldn't hear the rest.

Acamapichtli hadn't moved. At length, he straight-ened up – slowly, stately, with that infuriating, effortless arrogance. "Will that be all, my Lord? I have the feeling we have explored the question quite thoroughly." I could have cheered.

"You–" Tizoc-tzin started, but the She-Snake interrupted.

"My Lord, I think it would be prudent to adjourn. You grow tired."

While Tizoc-tzin protested, Acamapichtli turned, slightly – until he could see me. "Acatl," he whispered, low and urgent. "They've dismantled everything."

"Everything?" I asked, with a sinking feeling in my belly. "Your sick patients…"

The look on his face was clear enough. The containment, however efficient it might have been, had been breached, and, worse than that, we had a man under accusation of grave treason loose in the palace, if not in Tenochtitlan.

We had to wait until the end of the audience to leave, which was, sadly, all too predictable. Acamapichtli and his priests were to remain in confinement until Tizoc-tzin could figure out further charges to bring against them. He wouldn't even listen to any other accusations – I caught a glimpse of the courtesan Xiloxoch arguing with a magistrate, but it was likely it would all come to nothing.

If it was even true. I had my doubts.

Afterwards, Mihmatini caught up with us.

"I didn't expect to see you here."

"Same goes for you," Teomitl said. He shook his head. "I thought you were in danger."

"In danger?"

Teomitl pointed to the thread coiled on the ground between them, which was now a faint light once more, barely visible unless one knew where to look. "It flared up."

167

"And of course you rushed to my rescue."

"Was I supposed to leave you–" He stopped. "What kind of danger were you in?"

Her face was set. "I lodged a formal complaint with Tizoc-tzin over the arrest of a High Priest. The second arrest in four months," she said, throwing a glance towards me.

"You did what? Are you mad?" I asked. When I had failed to enthusiastically support Tizoc-tzin four months ago, he had arrested me and threatened to execute me. And now she – Teomitl's wife in a marriage Tizoc-tzin hadn't approved of – told him to his face that he was wrong? "Do you want to be killed?"

"I'm old enough to take care of myself."

"Not in that kind of circumstance," Teomitl said.

"You think so?"

She'd always had a tendency to charge into trouble – climbing cacti to get maguey sap, with the firm belief flimsy cotton bandages would protect her against thorns; rowing to the Floating Gardens on her own and wedging her boat so deeply into the mud that she couldn't lift it out; sneaking into the calmecac school to see Neutemoc, never thinking the priests would keep a watch…

"Tizoc-tzin isn't quite a fool," Yaotl said. His face was grave. "Arresting a young woman because she spoke up against him in an open trial would make him look bad."

"She's the Guardian of the Sacred Precinct. Hardly harmless," I said, dryly.

"But she's eighteen, and a housewife." Yaotl smiled. "That's what people will see first, and Tizoc-tzin knows it. And if he doesn't, I'm sure his sycophant Quenami will remind him. He can't afford to do that, not in front of his noblemen."

But, presumably, he could afford to arrest the entire clergy of Tlaloc.

"I'm still free," Mihmatini pointed out. "If he were to do anything, he'd have done it by now."

And that was supposed to make me feel better? "Look–" I started – and gave up. She looked so much like a younger version of her predecessor Ceyaxochitl, and the gods knew nothing had ever stopped Ceyaxochitl once she'd made up her mind – only death, snatching her from us unexpectedly and pointlessly. "Just be careful, will you? You can't go on doing this, and I don't want you to get hurt."

"I appreciate the thought, but really, I'm old enough to take care of myself."

"I'm just worried about you," I said.

Teomitl moved to stand by my side. "The court is no fit place for anyone currently."

Mihmatini's eyes rolled upwards. "Honestly. If I didn't know better, I'd have thought you had prepared before-hand." Someone sniggered: Yaotl, who never wasted an opportunity to mock Mexica. "Now, if you'll excuse me, I have to be elsewhere. I'm lodging a formal complaint with the She-Snake as well."

"I wish you wouldn't do that," I said. Ceyaxochitl had once told me that everyone had to grow up, but why did it have to happen so fast to those around me?

"Thank you for the honesty." Mihmatini grimaced. "Now, you're not going to make me change my mind, and you two look as though you'd better be elsewhere. I'd suggest we both get on with what we were doing."

And, before either of us could answer that, she was gone. Yaotl threw us an amused glance, and turned to follow his mistress out of the courts.

"Acatl-tzin...." I'd never seen Teomitl look so forlorn.

"She'll survive," I said, slowly. She had Yaotl to watch out for her, and probably the She-Snake. And surely she was right – surely, if Tizoc-tzin had wanted to act against her, he would have done it by now? "We'll deal with this later. We have to find the sick men first."

TEN
Contagion

The wing of the palace Acamapichtli had occupied had, indeed, been quite thoroughly dismantled – the white and blue cloaks of Tlaloc's clergy replaced by the familiar black garb of palace guards, and the courtyards filled with feather-clad noblemen instead of dark-faced priests. As I crossed into the courtyard that had been the centrepiece of Acamapichtli's power – albeit temporarily – I couldn't help but brace myself against protection spells, as if some kind of veil would still remain across the threshold.

But nothing happened; I crossed easily, as if nothing were there. We found the room where Acamapichtli had confined his sick men without much trouble: it was wide, swept clean of any furniture save three sleeping mats – and two of those mats were still occupied by groaning bodies. A slave was crouching by the second one – wiping the forehead with a wet cloth; he looked up as we entered, and then bent back to his task.

"They're still here," Teomitl said.

Both Coatl and the priest of Patecatl lay on the ground – their skins as pale as muddy water, their eyes sunken deep into the oval of their faces – and a familiar blue

171

tinge around the lips, like the touch of a drowned man.

I knelt by Coatl, careful not to touch the body. My protection tingled and tightened – how effective was it, really? If this thing was passed on through contact…

Coatl was shivering, beads of sweat pearling at his temples; his gaze swung wildly from left to right, quite obviously not focusing on anything in the Fifth World. He lay curled on the sleeping mat, like a warrior around a mortal stomach wound, and his skin was black as if he'd been charred in a fire – except that it looked smooth, without any of the blisters I'd have expected. The eyes… the eye-whites were a deep red, against which the cornea obscenely stood out.

"Coatl?" I asked, though it was quite obvious he could no longer hear me – lying in the clutches of sickness, his mouth in the earth, his face in the mud, oblivious to anything save the voices of the gods. "Coatl."

A light played on my hands, turning them paler – a radiance as green as quetzal feathers seen through water, first quivering on the edge of being, and then growing stronger and stronger, until it had washed out every colour in the room, making even the painted frescoes on the wall seem of carved jade, gilding the faces of gods and warriors on the adobe until they, too, seemed alien and faraway. Teomitl knelt by my side, his hands outstretched over the body of the priest.

"Coatl," he called, and his voice was the thunder of storm-tossed waves, the slithering sounds of *ahuizotl* water-beasts moments before they fed on a corpse. "Honoured one, keeper of the red and black codices, holder of the wisdom – of the words as precious as wealth. Honoured one, travelling far in the wilderness, in the jungles – the time has come to wake up."

172

Coatl went rigid. "My Lord," he whispered, without opening his eyes.

"Wake up, honoured one." Teomitl's voice had the cadences of ritual – and its pitch was getting higher and higher – deeper, too, no longer the voice of anything human.

Coatl shuddered again. "I can't, my Lord!" Foam pearled up on his lips – his body arched, as if in the grip of a seizure, and then he fell back down again, hitting the mat with a thud.

Teomitl looked as though he was going to reach out and seize the body. "No," I said, laying a hand on his arm – a mistake, for the power within him struck as quickly as a coiled snake – pain travelled up my arm, and for a bare moment I had the feeling my skin was being flayed away, exposing muscles and bones that bent and snapped, sending my arm into spasms...

I jerked back, biting my lips not to scream. "Don't – touch – him," I managed through dry lips. "You–"

Teomitl's gaze moved towards me – held me, and for a moment I saw not him, but Jade Skirt – waiting for me with arms outstretched, to drag me down into the waters that had cleansed me at my birth... "Teomitl!"

"I'm the one you shouldn't touch, priest." His lips quirked into a smile – lazy and cruel, nothing human anymore – and then, as abruptly as She had appeared, the goddess was gone, and we were left in an empty room with an unconscious priest – unconscious, not dead, thank the Duality, for while I could see the shadow of Lord Death hovering over him, his spirit had not yet departed his body.

Teomitl looked at me questioningly.

"I did something foolish," I said, a little more abruptly than I'd intended to. Chalchuihtlicue, Jade Skirt, like most gods, always made me uneasy: pretty much the only god I could claim a modicum of common understanding with was my own god, Mictlantecuhtli – ruler of a place that welcomed everyone, patiently waiting for the corn to ripen and wither, the fruit to fall and rot.

"So did I." Teomit's face was harsh again. He looked down at Coatl. "I don't think he'll be awake for a while."

I didn't think he'd ever been in a state to hear us. On the positive side, though, he wasn't going to walk away and spread the sickness yet further.

My eyes caught on the third sleeping mat, and I froze, remembering what Acamapichtli had said. "There was a third man in confinement, wasn't there?"

"That's the first I hear of it," Teomitl said.

I shook my head. "A warrior, one of those who carried the body. Acamapichtli told me they'd found him, and that he was sick."

I didn't like that empty mat: it made me feel uncomfortable. It was one thing to have healthy warriors possibly passing on the sickness unawares, quite another to have a sick man get up and leave.

"But we don't know where he is," Teomitl said.

"No," I said. And we were obviously not going to find out from either Coatl or the priest of Patecatl. I decided on a more constructive approach: I walked out, yanking the entrance-curtain out of my way in a tinkle of bells, and asked the first guard of the She-Snake I met where the priests of Tlaloc had gone.

He looked at me, hard. "You're not one of them." It sounded halfway between an accusation and a question: he didn't quite know what to make of me.

"No," I said, bowing my head – letting him take in the regalia. "I'm High Priest for the Dead in Tenochtitlan."

"Tizoc-tzin said they were traitors," the guard said.

He– he had arrested the whole clergy of Tlaloc – as thoughtlessly as that? He– What could he be thinking of, cutting away everyone that sustained him?

He–

Focus, I needed to focus. Little good I would do, if I managed to get myself arrested yet another time. "They... might have information we need," I said, gaining in assurance as I spoke. "For the good of the city." I felt soiled, even though it wasn't quite a lie.

The guard looked at me, dubiously. Fortunately, Teomitl chose this moment to join me, and the sight of the Master of the House of Darts – Tizoc-tzin's brother – standing by my side helped the guard decide. "Fine." He gave me a location, which was a set of courtyards reserved for the private usage of officials.

When we arrived there, we found the courtyard had been turned into a jail: wooden cages filled it from end to end. Through the bars, I caught glimpses of the men crouched within – whispering hymns in a low voice, beseeching their god to help them. The hubbub of their voices was almost deafening – there had to be more than a hundred priests in that courtyard. Magic flowed over us: the harsh, pitiless feel of Huitzilpochtli's magic, laid over the cages and the courtyard to prevent the priests from casting any spells.

At the other end, under the pillars, a couple of wooden cages had been set aside for the higher ranks: Tapalcayotl and two other priests sat – it wasn't easy to look dignified and haughty while sitting hunched under a low canopy, but Tapalcayotl managed it. I guessed Acamapichtli had been giving his second-in-command lessons in arrogance.

"Well?" he asked when I came closer. "I assume you're not here to tell me we're to be freed."

"Not exactly," I said.

Dealing with Acamapichtli was bad enough; I didn't have to bear with that kind of attitude from Tapalcayotl, as well. "You're not in much of a position to argue or make demands."

Tapalcayotl grimaced. "Fair enough," he said at last. "What do you want?"

"The third sick man – the warrior. Where did he go?"

"He went away?" one of the priests asked.

"Why? He wasn't fit to walk either?"

The priest shook his head. "He died."

A dead man?

"There was no corpse. Someone took it away." Not good; not good at all. Eptli's corpse had still been able to propagate the sickness; I didn't want to see another instance like that.

Tapalcayotl hadn't said anything for a while. He was staring at the rings on his hands as if they held some great truth, his face pinched and twisted. At length, not looking up, he said, "I think the other warrior took it."

"Which warrior?"

"He came several times to enquire about the health of Coatl and his companion," Tapalcayotl said. "We told him he couldn't have the corpse for funeral ceremonies, and he was angry. He said warriors took care of their own."

Where had I heard that? "Did you know him?"

"No. He wasn't a young man, more like the kind you'd expect to have married already – his thighs were covered in battle scars."

Which about described every warrior who had survived a few battles: their quilted cotton armour didn't protect their legs, and the obsidian edges of the *macuahitl* swords inflicted horrific wounds in the melee. "Anything else?" I asked, struggling to contain my impatience.

"He had another scar. Across his face. A sword must have sliced his right cheek open, and gone upwards to the temple." Tapalcayotl grimaced again. "My guess is that he was happy to be alive after that."

"Acatl-tzin," Teomitl said behind me.

I nodded; got up, as leisurely as I could. The scar was indeed distinctive, and I knew where I had seen it last.

The warrior Chipahua – Eptli's comrade, who had been so frustrated at being deprived of the captive.

We came out of the palace all but running. Teomitl had picked up two Jaguar warriors on the way – we'd run into them outside the aviary, and he'd used his authority as Master of the House of Darts to sweep them up. They didn't look aggrieved; rather, they held themselves with a particular sense of pride – an almost religious devotion, as if they were favoured of some god.

Teomitl's face had taken on the aspect of carved jade again; perhaps it was that, or perhaps his regalia, which was distinctive enough, but the crowd of the Sacred Precinct seemed to part from us, the priests and worshippers shrinking away as if burned by the light.

At the edge of the Sacred Precinct, Teomitl called over two boats with a mere wave of his fingers – two small craft, poled by women taking their wares back from the marketplace.

"We could have taken a boat from my temple," I said as I climbed into one of the swaying craft. The woman's gaze was stubbornly cast down – one did not look the Master of the House of Darkness in the eye.

Teomitl waved a dismissive hand. "Your temple is too far, Acatl-tzin. We would waste time."

The boat slipped into the crowded canals like a knife through the lungs, weaving its way between the coloured craft carrying baskets of vegetables and cages filled with animals. The woman poled in silence, not looking at either of us – it occurred to me that I was just as impressive as Teomitl in my position of High Priest, holder of wisdom and knowledge; so far high above her I might as well have been sitting on the canopy of a ceiba tree.

"What are you going to do?"

"Warn them." Teomitl's voice was curt, deadly.

"It might already be too late." The sickness came fast – faster than it should have, but if it was supernatural, it was only to be expected.

Teomitl's lips tightened. "You're in a contrary mood."

I guessed I was; someone needed to temper Teomitl's blind enthusiasm. My place as a teacher demanded no less.

The boat passed under a wooden bridge, a hand's breath from a porter drawing water for a peasant. The houses thinned, growing larger and larger like trees unfolding from the ground – the adobe walls brightly painted, and the gardens on the rooftops spreading a smell of pine cones and dry wood, a sweetness that reminded me of home.

It docked in front of Chipahua's house: we crossed the small stretch of beaten earth of the street, determined to finish this sordid business.

Teomitl stopped short when he reached the courtyard. "Acatl-tzin."

"I know." There had been a slave, last time, and the sound of pestle against mortar as the women pounded maize into flour. Now there was no one.

No, not quite. There was something… trembling on the edge of existence – a smell, a tightness in the air – something all too familiar that sent a thrill to my bones, and set my heart hammering against the cage of its ribs.

"Death," I said, aloud.

One of the warriors drew his *macuahitl* sword – a thing of glittering edges, of cutting shards, reflecting the sunlight into a thousand fractured pieces. Magic quivered along its body: the warm, unwavering glow of the Southern Hummingbird's power in the Fifth World. "Stay back, Teomitl-tzin."

But Teomitl was already moving – faster than a snake uncoiling, rushing forward. I followed him at a more leisurely pace – taking in everything as if in a daze.

The courtyard, bathed in golden sunlight; three still bodies under the pine tree – no, not quite still, for even as I watched one of them gave a last, heaving gasp, and I saw the *ihiyotl* soul gather itself from its seat in the liver, and unfold wings of blinding radiance, taking flight in an instant like a held breath, vanishing into the world of the gods.

The second courtyard, and the woman I'd seen earlier – Chipahua's wife – lying on her back, looking at me with unseeing eyes.

There was no blood. I might have understood it, if there had been blood – might have thought of sacrifices, of gods gathering back the power that belonged to Them. But everything smelled dry, as stretched as Mictlan the underworld.

The reception room: Teomitl was standing in front of the dais, looking down at a mat filled with food – the smell of cooked amaranth wafted up, terrifyingly incongruous – and the frescoes themselves seemed to have dimmed, their bright colours passing away.

Too late, I saw that it wasn't the colours that had vanished, but the shadows that had appeared, so many of them they covered the whole room, clinging to the pillars and the walls, packed tight against the faces of the gods. I caught a glimpse of screaming faces; of tangled limbs; of flaky skin, distorted by sores, and then they were unfolding like the wrath of a storm, and upon us before we could move.

For a moment – a bare, agonising moment – it seemed my protection would hold; bathed in the familiar stretched emptiness of Mictlan, I saw this as no more than part of the rhythm of the Fifth World – all sicknesses leading, ultimately, to the throne of Lord Death, the place that belonged to us all: stretched and dry and dark, sending us back into the embrace of Grandmother Earth.

And then, with a sound like bones caving in, the protection yielded. It left a faint, cold tingle on my skin – soon replaced by a blazing heat, and a sensation like a thousand bats beating wings around me; darkness rose and enfolded me in a crushing embrace, and I saw nothing but one screaming face after another; glistening limbs, wet with blood and with the white of bones poking out from wrinkled skins; over me, the bodies were all over me, feebly twitching; fingers scrabbling over my eyelids; limbs strewn across my chest, crushing the breath out of me; clammy lips pressed against my thighs and arms and hands, every touch seeming to rob me of more strength.

Everywhere – they were everywhere, in the Fifth World, in the world above, in the world below – there was no escape…

I was on my back, staring into the slack face of a woman, who pressed against me like a lover – her mouth open in a soundless scream, revealing teeth the colour of decayed corn. Her hands – or another's hands, I couldn't be sure – were clawing at my belly; there was a brief, fiery flesh of pain, and the slimy sensation of something wet against my skin, before the pain flared up again, destroying everything else. Distantly, I noted what it had to be, and what its loss meant, but the thought itself vanished in the welter of other ones – in the rancid smell of so many bodies pressed against mine.

Pain. Pain – was–

Pain was an offering. Pain was–

I could hardly focus anymore through the growing haze; didn't know where Teomitl was anymore…

The gods took pain, which was the only sincere sacrifice. Prayers were nothing more than children's wishes, but pain and blood made them real – because it cost to give them, and because they were freely offered.

The gods–

There was a familiar litany in my mind: repeated so many times in the calmecac school, in calmer times, on a hill away from the city, where I'd stood with my bloodied worship-thorns, offering up the truest sacrifice for the sake of the Fifth World and of Mictlan.

I had no worship-thorns, and the stars were all gone – my sight blocked by mottled, bluish skin, by distorted limbs and glazed faces. But the hymn – the hymn always remained.

"We leave this earth,
This world of jade and flowers,
The quetzal feathers, the silver and the jade…"

My voice quavered and broke at the beginning, but soon the familiar words came back and with them some of my assurance. As I spoke, the pain seemed to recede, pushed back into a remote corner of my mind, to be dealt with later.

> "Down, down into darkness we must go,
> Past the rushing waters, past the mountain of knives,
> We leave this earth…"

I was High Priest for the Dead; I had endured worse than this. I would… I would stand.

The bodies were still pressing against me, but now I saw that they flopped weakly, like fish on dry land, the motions of their limbs and fingers nothing more than re-flexes, like the gestures of a man drunk on jimsonweed. I could feel their frantic heartbeat, echoing the mad beat within my own chest.

> "The precious necklaces, the precious feathers,
> The songs and the flowers,
> The marigold and the cedar trees,
> We leave this earth…"

There was… light, after a fashion – a weak, pallid radi-ance that threw everything into stark contrast. The bodies and faces paled, and seemed to recede too, their features growing dimmer and dimmer until they became part of the quivering shadows on the walls.

The weight on my chest was gone; the whole episode feeling like the stuff of nightmares. I pulled myself up-wards, slowly, limb by limb, wincing at the pain. My stomach wasn't bleeding, but I still felt as though I'd been mauled, and the fever wasn't gone – it had merely abated for a small moment, enough for me to regain a small part of my senses. But it would come back when the hymn stopped running in my mind, when I grew too weak to hold the sickness at bay.

I needed help.

In the darkened room, I caught sight of more bodies, spread around the remnants of a meal – none of them appeared to be moving.

"Teomitl?"

My student was lying a few paces away from the body of Chipahua, twitching and shivering and moaning.

"Teomitl!" I reached out and shook him – he had Jade Skirt's protection, he couldn't fall like this, not to something as foolish and as inconsequential… "Teomitl!"

But there was no answer, and his eyes, when they finally opened, were the filmy white of rotting corpses. He hung limp in my grip and didn't answer. I could – with some effort – have stretched out my priest senses, but I could guess that the magic of Jade Skirt had gone from him.

He couldn't die – he was Master of the House of Darts, heir-apparent to the Mexica Empire, agent of Chalchiuhtlicue in the Fifth World, commander of the army… He was…

At the back of my mind ran the litany – the same words, over and over: *Lord Death's lands are vast and deep, and Grandmother Earth awaits; as She does for us all.*

He couldn't die… but Tizoc-tzin had died, too, and come back only through a god-blessed miracle, a spell that couldn't be cast again in the Fifth World.

Somehow – somehow I hoisted Teomitl on my shoulders, and staggered out of the house, calling out for the Jaguar Knights, but whether fallen or fled, they wouldn't answer. I couldn't find the boats we'd arrived in, either. So instead, I turned my face away from the blinding light of the sun, and started to walk back to the Sacred Precinct.

Teomitl grew heavier as I walked, and the world shrank into a whirl of colours and sounds: vague faces, fading in and out of focus; a morass of feather headdresses, black-dyed cheeks, and the glint of gold caught in hair as black as night. My feet dragged in the dust and the sounds of the city seemed far away; the clacking noise of the women's loom no more than a distant irritation. The shadows came back, too, swooping over the canals like *ahuizotl* water-beasts – quivering, always on the edge of leaping.

> *"We leave this earth,*
> *This world of jade and flowers,*
> *The quetzal feathers, the silver and the jade…"*

They were slowly rising – casting the adobe house into darkness, making the coloured clothes dull and insignificant. My world shrank to this: the burning light of the sun – echoed in the itching that seemed to have overwhelmed my skin – and the shadows, the same that had killed Eptli, which would engulf us all…

My hands shook; I held Teomitl tighter against my chest, afraid I'd let him fall into the dirt. I couldn't let go: I had to get him back to safety – he was my student… My whole body was afire, my stomach a mass of pain. If only I could pause, rest for a while, doubled up in a foetal position, until the pain went away…

The shadows shifted lazily over the canals and the bridges, the assembled throng of peasants in loincloths, the matrons holding baskets of tomatoes and squashes close to their chests. Like the wind, they ruffled the cloaks of war veterans, exposing old, whitish scars that took on the appearance of suppurating sores once more. I trudged on, dragging my feet in the earth. The sun beat on my back – and it seemed that the beat was echoed within me, at the junction of skin and muscle, an endless rhythm like thousands of hands hammering from inside, demanding to be let out.

Ahead, I caught glimpses of the Serpent Wall – the shadows congregated around the snakes atop the wall, in the quetzal-red jaws and green bodies, darkening the scales and the crown of feathers around their heads. Almost there...

Abruptly, Teomitl weighed nothing – no, it wasn't that, it wasn't that. Someone had taken him from me. I had to... had... to...

"Teomitl! Acatl!" My sister's face swam out of the morass of shadows – a scant few moments before the fever rose again, and I knew nothing more but the nightmares.

ELEVEN
Bitter Medicines

My dreams were dark and numerous; in all of them I lay on my back, while something crushed my chest, and in every shadow I saw the faces of the sick, opening their mouths to scream. Sometimes I heard them, sometimes I did not – but they were always by my side, blindly scrabbling for the raging warmth of my body.

At some point, sleep claimed me, dark and exhausting, and the bodies faded, to be replaced by the sound of distant chanting, while I lay panting and burning, every breath searing the inside of my throat.

I woke up, and there was still chanting – as my mind cleared, I recognised the words of a hymn to Patecatl, god of medicine.

> *"Come, you the five souls,*
> *I expel from this place the green pain, the tawny pain,*
> *Come, you the nine winds,*
> *I expel from this place the green pain, the tawny pain…"*

They were spoken by a reedy, frightened man who stood some distance away from me, clearly afraid to touch me. He smelled of copal incense and a mixture of herbs I couldn't place, sharp and bitter. The fever had receded, leaving my mind as clear and as brittle as polished obsidian. I noted the pattern of snakes on the ceiling arcing above me, and the frescoes on the wall were of a huge tree to which clung babies, drinking the sap like mother's milk; the hymn washed over me, again and again like waves on the shore, like the embrace of Chalchiuhtlicue Jade Skirt at birth, washing away all the filth and the sins of the ancestors.

I lay quiet, unable to move.

Some time later, an entrance-curtain tinkled; the priest started. "He's awake, my Lady."

"I can see that," Mihmatini's voice said.

There was a silence; the priest's face stubbornly turned towards her, his gaze downcast. "My Lady?" he asked, finally. "You promised I could leave…"

Mihmatini snorted. "I did, didn't I? Very well, you may go."

He was scurrying out toward the exit before she'd even finished her sentence.

"Acatl?" Mihmatini asked. "How are you feeling?" She knelt by the side of the bed – I'd expected sarcasm, or some biting remark about my tendency to get into scrapes, but there was none of that; merely thin lines at the corners of her red-rimmed eyes.

Then I remembered. "Teomitl. Where–?"

"Ssh." Mihmatini laid a hand on my forehead. She grimaced. "What I need to know now is how you are."

"I've felt better," I said, carefully. My tongue scraped against my palate, as abrading as coarse sand, and there was a distant ache in my stomach, like a beast laying low, waiting for the best moment to pounce again. "You haven't told me about Teomitl."

"I need you to rest," Mihmatini said. "Whatever protection you had blocked part of the sickness, but you're not invulnerable, Acatl."

Neither was Teomitl. I watched her – clad in the blue cloak of a Guardian, with feathers hanging down the nape of her neck and black paint, applied to her cheeks and forehead with a trembling hand, leaving large swathes of skin uncovered. And, on the ground beneath her feet, was a thread of yellow light – going straight through the wall, its radiance contracting and expanding with every one of her breaths, like a heartbeat. "It's bad, isn't it?"

She wouldn't look at me, as if I'd somehow turned into her superior. "Whatever it is, it's affected him worse than you. It's as if he had a special affinity with the sickness."

Then why hadn't it struck before? But, of course, he had always been quite far away from the corpses; he had given the first one only a cursory examination, and while he'd stayed in the room of the second one he hadn't cast spells or even strayed close to the body. Then again… for all I knew, he could have been affected already, and not said a word to me about whatever trivial symptoms he might have felt.

Southern Hummingbird blind the man and his pride.

"I need to see him," I said, pulling myself upright. Or rather, trying to. None of my limbs seemed to work properly; it was all I could do to fall back in a vaguely graceful manner.

"You're staying on the sleeping mat," Mihmatini said, in a voice I recognised all too well – reserved for disobedient children, or recalcitrant priests. "You're quite obviously in no state to walk, Acatl, and I will not have you push yourself past your endurance."

"It wouldn't be the first time," I said, knowing what her answer would be.

"You know, that doesn't strike me as something to be particularly proud of," Mihmatini said. "Stay here."

"And what? Wait? He's my student as much as he's your husband. If anything happens…" I wouldn't forgive myself.

"Then what?" Mihmatini's voice was low and terrible, that of a judge about to pass sentence. "You're a priest of Mictlantecuhtli, Acatl. You don't do healing spells."

"No," I said. I pulled myself upwards again, more carefully this time, letting the full weight of my body rest on the wall. "But I know about illnesses."

Mostly as causes of death, granted. But still… still, the priests of Patecatl were quite obviously useless. For something like this – a deliberately cast disease – we needed to fight the sorcerer who had cast it: a man or a woman we still knew nothing about.

Either that, or…

"He's Chalchiuhtlicue's agent," I said.

Mihmatini rolled her eyes upwards. "I've already thought of it. We tried healing or cleansing spells that called on Her power."

"And?" I said.

"They're not working. But then nothing else has."

I shook my head. "It's not spells you'd need, but Her personal attention."

Mihmatini grimaced. "Going into Her own land? We tried that, as well."

"You have?" It was bad, then; for going into Tlalocan, the land of the Blessed Drowned, was far from simple or safe. By going into a god's world, one agreed to be bound by its rules and caprices – to face monsters and magic, and desires that predated the Fifth Age.

Mihmatini's face was pale. "The way was closed. Perhaps She thought us beneath Her notice."

"You'd be beneath Her notice, but Teomitl wouldn't." She had schemes for him – whatever they were. She'd picked him up, chosen to wield Her powers in the Fifth World. She wouldn't have done that without a reason... and I had a feeling the days were fast approaching when we would come to know it. "Unless something has gone wrong." Acamapichtli – abruptly, I remembered the trial. "Acamapichtli's arrest. That's what's gone wrong." And Tapalcayotl in his cage; and probably the whole clergy, all over the city – the Consort, High Priestess of Chalchiuhtlicue, and her own clergy... "The arrest of her husband's clergy must give Her enough to be busy."

Mimahtini shook her head. "I know it's serious, Acatl, but that's not what we're focusing on right now."

No. She was right. One couldn't grasp four hundred stalks of corn at the same time. We needed to shape our minds to a single purpose, or Teomitl would be gone just the same way as Eptli.

I thought again of the corpse – small and forlorn and abandoned, and my stomach lurched within me at the thought of Teomitl's being there, in Eptli's place.

"You don't know healing spells either?" I asked Mihmatini.

"I've thought of something, but it cannot possibly work as it is. Come and see."

She found a cane for me, which looked suspiciously like her predecessor Ceyaxochitl's cane. I used it to prop myself upwards – and half-carried by Mihmatini, half-pushing myself on the cane – I made my way out of the room. Ironic, really – Ceyaxochitl herself had been the fittest old woman I'd known, using the cane mostly for show in order to enjoy the respect and pity accorded to the frail elderly. She'd never been one much for frailty, and she would probably have scolded me for being such a weakling.

Gods, what I wouldn't have given to have her back – overbearing and patronising as she'd always been. The cane was warm under my fingers, but she was gone, down into Mictlan, never to return, her wisdom and knowledge going the way of dust blown by the wind.

The entrance-curtain opened into the main courtyard of the Duality House: like most temples, it had a rectangular layout, with a pyramid shrine in the centre, and various rooms and compounds opening into the main courtyard, their entrance-curtains shaded by a pillared portico.

Yaotl was waiting for us at the entrance, sitting on his haunches in a position of attention. He unfolded himself when Mihmatini came out; she acknowledged him with a curt nod. For me, he had nothing but his usual, mildly sardonic glance – not that I had expected more than that.

"Anything?" Mihmatini asked.

Yaotl shook his head. "No change." He handed his mistress a folded piece of paper. Mihmatini took it, but didn't open it.

"Come," she said, and all but dragged me to another room, the entrance-curtain of which was marked only by a few glyphs.

Inside, an antechamber led into a deeper, more shadowed room – Mihmatini's quarters, in as much disorder as usual. The wicker chests bulged with clothes: colourful headdresses and skirts spilled out from under their lids, and a feather-fan I'd last seen in Neutemoc's house rested on top of one of them. The two sleeping-mats had been unrolled: one was empty; the second one held Teomitl.

He was so pale – his skin so leeched of colours it seemed like pallid gold. His eyes were sunk deep into his face; his hair, curled and plastered with sweat, clung to his scalp in clumps, and he tossed and moaned. I dragged myself closer, and painstakingly crouched down – not so much a deliberate gesture as a gradual sagging of my body, stopped at regular intervals by my grip on the cane – slow and messy.

Teomitl did not move, or give any sign that he had registered my presence; after a while, I realised that he wasn't moaning, but talking under his breath, so fast I could barely follow – delirious snatches of sentences mentioning anything from Jade Skirt's touch to beasts of shadows. I touched the mat; it was already soaked. "You said you had something."

A flutter of clothes, and then Mihmatini was crouching by my side – the thread between her and Teomitl reduced to an arm's length, bright and vivid, like blood in an open wound. Her face was calm, expressionless – like obsidian in the instant before it shattered. "I haven't been idle. We've cast spells of protection in the Duality's name, and we have also been looking into possible causes for the sickness. It's one – or more – of four things. He's carrying something within him, which was put there by a sorcerer. I don't think it's the case: insofar as I can tell, none of the dead men touched anything?"

I thought, uneasily, of Eptli. "It might have started that way, but I don't think it's using a physical vector anymore."

"Hmm." Mihmatini unfolded the piece of maguey paper Yaotl had given her: it was a transcription from a divinatory priest's calendar, listing horoscopes and fates for a particular birth – a beautiful piece, with coloured glyphs swirling around the images of the protector gods.

"His?" I guessed. A man's birth influenced many things, not least of which the healing rituals which would be effective.

"It was hard to find," Mihmatini said. "Fortunately, Yaotl is frighteningly efficient at what he does."

I wasn't surprised. It wasn't only healing rituals that depended on the birth-signs, but also vulnerabilities – naturally, someone as paranoid as Tizoc-tzin would not want his war-council to be on display for any sorcerer to tackle.

"Ten Rabbit. He could have a nahual totem; but he's never been strong enough to materialise one. And none of the other affected men had nahuals – Eptli was born on a Five Knife, his prisoner was a Two House insofar as we could check, and Coatl is quite definitely a Ten Rain. So it can't be that, either."

The words came fast, one atop the other – almost without pause. "Mihmatini. Slow down. It's not going to change anything."

"You don't know that," she said, angrily, but she didn't protest further.

"What about the *tonalli*?" I asked. The spirit in the head, the vital force that sustained us – many spells cast by sorcerers were "frights", which caused the *tonalli* to vanish like a burst bubble, and the victim to enter a slow decline towards death.

"It's weak," Mihmatini said. "But that could just be because the body is weak. Which leaves the last explanation." Her finger rested on the paper, near the head of Tlaloc the Storm Lord. "It's some kind of influence."

I thought of the shadows – this far into the Duality House, under the influence of so many protection spells, they had all but gone – but they had been real enough.

"Given what I've seen of the sickness, I think it's some kind of influence. But I don't think the influence would hold here."

"If he has it within his body, he's sheltering it from our wards," Mihmatini said. "That was my idea: to make him expel it." She stopped; looking at me – for guidance, I saw with a start.

"You're old enough not to need me anymore," I said, though I was secretly pleased to see she still looked up to me.

She rolled her eyes upwards. "Of course I do need you. I can dispel the influence once it's out of his body, but I can't draw it out."

"You need a physician."

"No, I don't. I can't say I've been impressed by the performance of the priests of Patecatl so far," Mihmatini said. "I need someone more competent than that."

You, her gaze seemed to say. "I can't," I said, the words burning in my throat. "I'm no healer. I serve Lord Death – I can sever the soul from the body or call it back, but nothing finer than that. If I cast a spell, it will expel his own life-force from his chest."

She fell silent – Southern Hummingbird blind me, I should have been able to give her another answer. I took the folded paper from her, and stared at it. Teomitl had been born on the day Ten Rabbit in the week One Rain. This put him under the tutelage of Tlaloc the Storm Lord – and given what was happening all over Tenochtitlan, we couldn't possibly hope to call on Him.

Unless…

"Quetzalcoatl," I said aloud, my hand trailing on His image – the Feathered Serpent, Lord of Wisdom and Knowledge.

"I don't see…"

"It was His blood that brought humanity back to life, in the beginning of the Fifth Age. His breath that runs through us." Quetzalcoatl-Ehecatl, the breath of all creation, the wind that no walls, no mountains would ever stop for long.

"It might work," Mihmatini said. "But I'm not sure the priests of Quetzalcoatl have escaped the widespread arrests."

I folded the paper, carefully – back into the shape Yaotl had given it at the start. The arrests – yes, we would need to talk about those, to see if anything could be done…

Focus. One thing at a time. Save Teomitl first – if we could. Tlaloc's Lightning strike me, we had to succeed – I wouldn't lose him as I'd lost Ceyaxochitl. I couldn't.

"It needn't be a priest of Quetzalcoatl," I said, slowly. "I've got just the right person in mind."

I wrote a message with shaking hands – the glyphs drawn askew, the red and black ink running, staining my fingers. A disgrace, my teachers would have said; but we were long past that. Yaotl carried it to the palace, while Mihmatini dispatched other messengers – slaves and priests both – to Chipahua's house, in order to collect the bodies.

The Duality House, as usual, seemed to have become our bulwark against the storm, and my sister was at the heart of it, managing everything with the proficiency of someone born to it.

Ceyaxochitl had once told me she was gifted; and I could still remember my answer. *Gifted, yes – more than you or I – but not, I think, destined for Guardianhood or for the priesthood.*

I'd forgotten how often Tezcatlipoca the Smoking Mirror delighted in twisting fate – sending us down unswept paths, into unexplored wildernesses.

Mihmatini remained in the room, but at length a priest came to her with an urgent question, and with a last, agonised glance at Teomitl, she had to step out.

While I waited for her to come back, I held Teomitl's hand; it was the least I could do. The priest of Patecatl would have frowned, and raised up the spectre of contagion, but what did it matter?

From where I crouched, the sounds of the House – the conch-shells, the hymns and the chants, the wet sound of bloodied grass balls slapped onto altar-stones – all receded away, and I was left alone with Teomitl. He had been moaning and muttering beforehand; I'd assumed it was nonsense, but as time went by, I caught words, a few at first, and then, as moments trickled by like drops of water, I picked up more – bright beads amongst threads – and the pattern itself, coalescing out of darkness, an endless litany of delirious failures.

"Fool, fool, fool, what did you think? Going in as if you were invulnerable – of course you never were, of course you never will be. She'll watch you from the World Below, she always does, what do you think you can prove?"

He could only be referring to his mother, who had died after a long struggle to bear him into the world – leaving him forever unable to prove himself as brave as she had been. "Teomitl," I said. "She'd be proud of you."

But he couldn't hear me – he just went on repeating the same things over and over, the same delirium.

A tinkle of bells announced the entrance of Mihmatini, accompanied by Nezahual-tzin – in regalia at least as fine as the one Teomitl had worn, from the red feather-suit to the finely wrought helmet in the shape of a coyote's head.

"I received your message," Nezahual-tzin said. "Most interesting. It was, ah, lacking a certain amount of flourish, shall we say?"

Mihmatini, I couldn't help but notice, was already glowering at him. What had he said to her, in the few moments in which they had walked through the House?

"You'll have to excuse me. My health isn't what it was at the moment."

Nezahual-tzin nodded, gravely. "Nevertheless... there was a most interesting pattern in your glyphs."

"We're not talking about interesting," she snapped. "We want your help. Are you going to give it, or stand here making cryptic pronouncements?"

Nezahual-tzin removed his feather headdress with slow, deliberate gestures before laying it to the ground. Then he unclasped his blue-green cloak and let it fall onto the floor. He had us all staring at him – and he no doubt knew it.

"Your brother will no doubt tell you that making cryptic pronouncements is a pastime of mine." Nezahual-tzin's voice was slow and stately, as if making a formal speech – every word delivered with the proper stresses, in the accent of Texcoco, the purest dialect of Nahuatl in the whole Anahuac Valley. He moved in a fluid, easy gesture, and before I knew it he was crouching by my side, watching Teomitl.

He smelled of herbs, the same bitter smell as the physician – had he just come from the sweatbaths? He liked going there to restore his strength and increase his power tenfold.

"The *tonalli* life-force is weak, but the *teyolia* soul is still in the body."

"We already knew that," Mihmatini pointed out.

I intervened before the conversation degenerated further. "He has something within his body, and we need you to draw it out."

"And then?" Nezahual-tzin raised an eyebrow.

Mihmatini crouched on the other side of Teomitl's body – straight ahead of Nezahual-tzin. She brought her hands together and twisted them together, as if wringing a rabbit's neck. "Then I'll destroy it. But I can't do anything so long as he protects it with his flesh and with his blood."

Nezahual-tzin nodded. He was still watching Teomitl – listening to the delirium as if he could find some sense within. I wondered how he felt – those two had never liked each other, Nezahual-tzin's detached, almost sarcastic attitude and focus on philosophy and knowledge at utter odds with Teomitl's desire to live in the present and prove his valour on the battlefield.

"So?" I asked. "Can you do something?"

"I can always do something," Nezahual-tzin said. "What's the thing inside him?"

"We're not sure," Mihmatini said – her voice making it all too clear she was losing patience.

Nezahual flashed her his most dazzling smile – a pity it would never work on her. "We'll have to improvise, then. Can you bring me butterflies?"

Mihmatini sent to the Wind Tower, the temple of Quetzalcoatl, for what Nezahual-tzin needed. While the priests of the Duality were gathering cages and drawing blood-patterns on the floor, I retreated towards the entrance-curtain. My presence here, as representative of Mictlantecuhtli Lord Death, was likely to do more harm than good.

Outside, the Fifth Sun beat down on the cracked earth – as if nothing were wrong, as if Teomitl's life didn't hang in the balance by a thread. I struggled to find peace or acceptance; it had been easier the year before, when my own life had been in danger, but this… this was different. He was my student, my brother by alliance, and my responsibility through and through – and yet I had failed him on every level.

Whoever was propagating this illness, they would pay – they would face the curved obsidian blade of justice, and be pierced by darts, and choked by mud until they had paid full price for their offence.

From within came chanting – Nezahual's grave voice, measured and pure, intoning a hymn, as if each word were a flower slowly blooming.

"Down into the darkness You go,
In the place where the bones are broken,
When the flutes and the drums are silent…"

There was a sound like a flag unfurling: thousands of beating wings, sending the entrance-curtain billowing in the damp breeze – and the butterflies flew out of the room, a widening stream of iridescent colours missing me by a hair's breadth, like a continuation of the cotton cloth, their touch on my skin soft and delicate, a reminder of the god who was always there, watching over us, as He had ever done since the moment He'd brought humanity's bones back from the underworld.

"I pierce myself, I make myself bleed, aya!
Burn down the paper stained with my blood,
Return the gift that was given,

I pierce him, I make him bleed, aya!
Burn down the paper stained with his blood,
Wash away the touch of the evil one,
The breath of the sorcerer…"

I heard another sound – a moan that started low, and grew – only to break into a dry, shuddering cough. Mihmatini cried out; I clenched my fingers, my nails digging into the palms of my hands. If I went inside, I would be of no use. I had to remember that – had to–

A duller sound – something large and wet hitting the ground, and Mihmatini's voice, raised in anger.

Then silence. The last of the butterflies lingered in the courtyard, its wings catching the light of the Fifth Sun and breaking it down into four hundred breathtaking colours. I did not move – not even when the entrance-curtain was lifted, and Mihmatini walked into the courtyard, carrying a crushed black thing which looked for all the world like the remnants of a caterpillar.

"This is it? Should you be touching it?" I asked.

"It's nothing," Mihmatini said. Her face was glowing – her cheekbones lit from within with a light like that of the moon, save stronger. Instead of washing away her features, it seemed to make everything sharper, better defined, underlying her gesture with a solemnity that made her seem far, far older than her twenty years. "It's the sorcerer's influence, given body and pulled out of him. By itself, it has no power."

Nezahual-tzin's face was pale. "But it's not the whole of the influence. There is something else inside him, but I can't get it out. You should have asked someone else."

"We asked you." Mihmatini's voice was low and intense. "Acatl trusted you."

"I haven't said I was giving up." Nezahual-tzin's face was set in a determined, most uncharacteristic grimace. "In the meantime... this is for you, Acatl. No doubt you'll find it entertaining." His voice was mocking again.

"Come," he said to Mihmatini – for a moment, he looked as though he was going to offer her his arm, like a man to his wife, but in the face of Mihmatini's glower, he opted instead for a simple, nonchalant wave of his hand.

I knelt, and peered at the black thing. It stank – not the rank, deep smell of the altar of sacrifices, but something closer to a bloated corpse left in the sun for too long. It looked like a lizard – save that it seemed to have little to no tail.

I'd expected magic, but when I extended my priest-senses towards it, I felt – almost nothing. A faint, residual beat perhaps, but one that would take true sight to be prised apart. It looked like–

Southern Hummingbird strike me, I'd seen this before – not the blackness or the stench, but this vague curled-up shape, almost small and pathetic.

A symbol, that was what it was. It wouldn't give sickness: it was just the shadows which had been given a physical body, a physical reality Mihmatini and Nezahual could expel from Teomitl's body.

Carefully, using the tip of one of my obsidian blades, I prised the thing apart – it had vestigial limbs, which I carefully disengaged from the body, and what I'd taken to be a tail were in fact two legs, all but fused together by the violence of Mihmatini's spell. I had seen this before – where had I–?

A human child.

True, the head was wrong – flat rather than round, and slightly too small – but the rest – the rest was unmistakable:

the small limbs just starting to branch into fingers and toes, the sharp edge of the spine with its vertebra. I hadn't attended many vigils for premature children, but several times, I had had cause to examine a woman who had died in childbirth with the child still in her womb – praying all the while that her spirit was at rest, that she wouldn't see the indignity of knives tearing her open from the Heavens where she now dwelled.

That made no sense – carefully, I lifted the thing again, but saw only the same resemblance.

And then I remembered, with a chill – that Xochiquetzal, the goddess who watched over the courtesan Xiloxoch, was not only Goddess of Lust and Desire, but also watched over childbirth.

TWELVE
Recovery

I must have remained there for an eternity, staring at the thing – and not knowing what to do.

Xochiquetzal's magic. And Tlaloc's influence. I had been right: it looked like the plague came from those two – seeking to damage the Fifth World once again. And Xiloxoch had been the self-confessed worshipper of the goddess – doing Her will in Tenochtitlan in Her absence. But still...

Still, all this for revenge?

Xochiquetzal would not remember the Mexica, or Tizoc-tzin, kindly. Neither would She blink at slaughtering dozens to make Her point.

Before rushing out to the temple of Xochiquetzal, I needed – confirmation. Some evidence that the thing had indeed been the result of a spell which called on Xochiquetzal. I needed to cast a spell of true sight, and look for magical traces.

A shadow fell over me – the priests of the Duality? Perhaps even the people we'd sent to Chipahua's house, with more information on what had happened?

The shadow did belong to one of the priests; what I had not expected was that they wouldn't be alone: leaning on their shoulders were two Jaguar warriors – the same ones that Teomitl had so peremptorily recruited on the way out of the palace.

"What happened?" I asked the priests.

They had little to report. The bodies of Chipahua and his household had been taken to a remote spot on the edge of Tenochtitlan, past the Floating Gardens, where Ichtaca and the other priests of my order could conduct more thorough examinations – hopefully with a reduced risk of contagion.

The Jaguar warriors looked pale, and probably felt as bad I did; but appeared unharmed otherwise. I wondered about the sickness – it didn't seem to take time to show symptoms, but its progress seemed... erratic, to say the least? It didn't look natural at all.

"I need you to do one thing," I said.

They looked at each other – with an eagerness I found troubling. "When you go back to the palace, can you arrange for the other bodies – Eptli and his prisoner – to be taken with the others? My order will need to examine this."

"Of course, my Lord."

The entrance-curtain tinkled again: Nezahual-tzin, his face set in a careful mask. He looked angry, or contemptuous, I wasn't sure. "Acatl," he said. "You have to see this."

The first thing I saw when I entered was Teomitl. He was awake, sitting propped against the wall, pale and wan, his eyes dark wells in the beige oval of his face, his hands clenched within his lap in a way that was anything but natural – it was obvious that if he released them, they would start shaking. Mihmatini was by his side, crushing his hand in hers – her face a mixture of elation and relief. The luminous thread between them was all but gone now, faded enough to become part of the beaten earth.

"You're awake," I said.

Teomitl's face twisted; it would have been a carefree smile, if it hadn't suddenly seemed so old. A white light played on his cheeks and forehead – the same one that had been on Mihmatini's face, save that on him, it made his skin recede, until I could see the arch of his cheek-bones, the empty holes of his eye-sockets.

Like Tizoc-tzin – but I caught and crushed the thought before it could wound. "As you can see." His voice was toneless.

"So it worked, then," I said.

"It didn't." Nezahual-tzin was standing away from all of us – leaning against the wall near the entrance, his head level with a fresco of a snake emerging from a man's open mouth. His arms were crossed, in that familiar nonchalant attitude which belied the seriousness of his words.

"You're obviously better at healing than you think," Teomitl said. His voice shook, but the sarcasm was unmistakable.

"I know my weaknesses. There was something left within you, something the spell couldn't catch."

"And yet here I am."

"Teomitl," Mihmatini said. "You're not in any state to make coherent contributions to the conversation."

"I almost died," Teomitl said. He'd obviously meant it as a joke, but his voice caught on the words. "I won't put off things any more. Time is playing against us, isn't it, Acatl-tzin?" His shadowed eyes, roaming, caught Nezahual-tzin – and then moved on to the two Jaguar

Knights, who had followed us inside but said nothing so far.

There was a moment of silence. One of the warriors started to bow, but Teomitl shook his head imperiously. "This isn't the time or the place. I apologise for dragging you into this."

"It is we who should apologise, my Lord," the eldest warrior said. "We ran away when we saw the shadows over the house. You could have died."

Teomitl's face had hardened, in a curious mixture of anger and vulnerability. "Yes, I could have died. Ran out of time, like anyone else in the Fifth World." He shook his head. "I have greater things to do, before I die. Your apology is accepted – as long as you don't run away again."

"You know we won't, my Lord," the eldest warrior said.

Teomitl nodded; I hadn't expected him to be embarrassed, as I would have been had any of my priests said this to me, but I couldn't read his expression – was it anger, contempt? Perhaps merely anger at himself, for catching the sickness in the first place – it wouldn't have surprised me from a man who always strove to reach the Fifth Sun.

"What next?" Unsurprisingly, they all looked at me. But there were so many things, so much that wasn't right. With an effort, I quelled the panic, and forced my thoughts into some kind of order. "Chipahua is dead," I said. "I don't know why, but I intend to find out." That could be taken care of by my clergy. I spread out my hands, counting out matters one after the other. "Acamapichtli is under arrest." And we needed him – we needed my clergy for death, the Duality for protection, and the clergy of Tlaloc, for the epidemic itself.

I lifted the black thing Mihmatini had carried. Teomitl looked at it with curiosity. "What is it?"

"The spell that almost killed you." Mihmatini's voice was low, almost spent.

Teomitl shook his head. "I've never seen it before."

A frown had started spreading on Mihmatini's face; she looked from the thing in my hand to Teomitl – and then back to me. "Acatl–"

"Yes," I said. "It looks like a human child, except smaller."

"I don't see–"

Nezahual-tzin detached himself from the wall, the muscles in his chest rippling as he moved. I could see why he'd have no trouble finding women to marry or bed – he'd have found them even without being Revered Speaker of Texcoco. "Xochiquetzal," he said. "Goddess of childbirth."

"You said Xiloxoch worshipped her."

Teomitl's face hardened. "Let's arrest her."

"It's scant proof," I said.

"Don't be foolish." His voice was harsher than anything I'd ever heard. "We have someone killing off the warriors and the priests of the Mexica Empire. If Xiloxoch isn't involved, I'm ready to apologise to her, and pay her whatever she might want as compensation. But in the meantime, I'm not taking any risks." He made an imperious gesture with his fingers, motioning the Jaguar Knights closer.

While Teomitl was giving instructions to the two warriors, I sidled closer to Nezahual-tzin. "You said you weren't responsible for his recovery."

"I am not."

"Then–"

Nezahual-tzin nodded. His eyes were still on Teomitl. "I don't believe in miracles. If he's cured, someone must have helped."

"Chalchuihtlicue?" I asked.

"Your sister said that she'd tried summoning Her earlier, and that it had been in vain."

"But who–?"

"I don't know," Nezahual-tzin said, grudgingly. He had never liked admitting ignorance. "But I will find out." He looked at Teomitl – who seemed in the middle of an animated conversation with the warriors, with the occasional interjection from Mihmatini. "Can I speak to you outside?"

I felt, suddenly, like a conspirator. "Surely anything you have to say to me–"

"I'm afraid not. It's outside, or not at all."

I sighed, casting another glance at Teomitl. I guessed it had to do with my student – whom Nezahual-tzin had little liking for.

We walked out of the room, and back into the courtyard. The air was thick with the smell and smoke of copal incense; the altar atop the pyramid shrine covered in a mound of maize cakes. Priests with black-streaked faces were sweeping the courtyard with rush brooms, keeping it clean so the Duality would always been welcome.

"What do you want?" I asked.

Nezahual-tzin smiled. "Don't be so hostile. You know I'm working in your best interest."

"Until you decide you no longer need us." He had done it often enough, after all – last year, when I'd had a death sentence hanging over my head, he'd all but sold me back to Tizoc-tzin.

He shrugged. His eyes rolled up in their sockets, revealing the milky white of faraway stars. "You heard Teomitl. Someone is acting against the Empire."

"And?"

"You think a mere courtesan would want this?"

"Why not?" I asked. "You forget. Her goddess has enough of a grudge against the Mexica Empire."

Nezahual-tzin shook his head. "There's something wrong with this."

There was, perhaps – I still needed to examine the black creature, and see if I could identify the traces of magic left on it. And I hated to have to arrest an innocent woman. But Teomitl had a point: the risk was great, and the time for hesitation had passed. "We're the ones investigating this, and as of this moment we don't have any other leads. If you want to investigate, please do."

I'd intended to make clear to him that barging in with his criticism wasn't appreciated, but he took me seriously. Or, knowing him, perhaps he understood and didn't care. "There was a merchant involved, I understood."

I didn't bother to ask how he knew. It was either the blessing of Quetzalcoatl the Feathered Serpent, or his preternaturally excellent network of spies. "Yayauhqui."

"Yes, Yayauhqui. You didn't ask the right questions."

"What right questions?"

"I'm told your Fire Priest was wondering what deity Yayauhqui worshipped as a youth."

"I thought there might be something there." Even if there hadn't been.

"Perhaps," Nezahual-tzin said. "But that's not what matters. What matters is Yayauhqui himself."

"I don't see–"

"He was a member of the Imperial Family. A small and insignificant one: I doubt Moquihuix-tzin ever paid much attention to him. He was never a man to pay much attention to the small fish anyway."

"A member of–"

"You see why it's important," Nezahual-tzin said soberly.

"It could still be something else."

He shook his head. "You don't understand, Acatl-tzin. Tlatelolco will not forget. They'll never forget."

I looked at him curiously. Why such animosity? He had been barely a child at the time of the war that had cost our sister city their independence. "What makes you say that?"

"You have been to Tlatelolco."

"Only the marketplace," I said.

"You'll have missed the most important thing," Nezahual-tzin said. "Their Great Temple."

"What of it?"

"It's a ruin," Nezahual-tzin said. He sounded sad, or angry – I couldn't tell. "The limestone has cracked and dimmed; the frescoes have all but vanished. Not a human hand has touched it for eight years; not a single sacrifice has been offered there. To the gods, it might as well be dead."

"Why?" I asked, and thought of the answer before Nezahual-tzin could speak. "Tlatelolco worships within Tenochtitlan's Sacred Precinct. Tlatelolca shouldn't be allowed to repair something that has no use." The Great Temple: the focal point of worship, the pride of one's city – the beating heart, the entrails.

"And they pay tribute every eighty days; send men to keep the temple of Huitznahuac in good repair, and feathered costumes every year. That, on top of the exactions the Tenochca warriors committed within the city on the day of the battle."

"You weren't there," I said.

"My father was," Nezahual-tzin said. His eyes were brown again, but with a particular, distant glaze, as if he could actually see into the past. Knowing him, it might well be the case. "But for him, Moquihuix-tzin might well have succeeded in his bid to overthrow the Tenochca domination."

"I still don't see–"

"You don't know how the war started."

"Over his wife," I said, slowly. Teomitl's sister, the one Revered Speaker Moquihuix-tzin had neglected.

"No," Nezahual-tzin said. "It started because, when Moquihuix-tzin's wife found refuge in Tenochtitlan after one too many nights of neglect, she brought word of a plot – an alliance between Tlatelolco and Culhuacan – both cities would regroup their armies, storm Tenochtitlan and send every man and woman of Tenochca blood soaring into the Heavens."

"That's–"

"Not something the Triple Alliance boasts of." Nezahual-tzin shrugged. "You can see how ill-informed it makes us seem. That it should take a woman to bring us word of what was right under our eyes."

I couldn't help it. "You don't like women, do you?"

"On the contrary," Nezahual-tzin said. "I think most people underestimate them, often unfortunately. Your sister, for instance, is worth perhaps more than all three High Priests combined, but there'll be few members of the clergy crowding to offer her any kind of official position. But never mind, that's not the point."

"I wish you would get to it," I said between clenched teeth.

Again, that graceful shrug, that mocking smile, and – hovering behind him in the afternoon light – the shadowy form of an emerald-green serpent, with a mane of black and red feathers, and eyes that glowed like pale stars. "Merely that Tlatelolca plot. They've always been good at it, and they can hide their resentment for years if need be – waiting for the best moment to strike."

"You're generalising from one example," I said.

"Perhaps," Nezahual-tzin said. "But the evidence against your merchant Yayauhqui is exactly as slender as that against Xiloxoch."

"Then what do you want? That we should arrest him as well?" And spark off another war between Tlatelolco and Tenochtitlan?

"I want you to consider this, and to remember my warning. There are men you shouldn't cross, Acatl. Beware of Tlatelolca, especially if they seem helpful."

He'd unnerved me more than he knew; or perhaps exactly as much as he'd intended to. "I'll keep it in mind."

"Good. Oh, and another thing," Nezahual-tzin said. "You'll want to keep an eye on your student – for his sake and yours."

"Why?" I said, feeling lectured enough for a lifetime. "You've interfered quite enough in my affairs."

"Ah, but you didn't see."

"See what?"

"The warriors." Nezahual-tzin's voice was slow and gentle, like a mother pointing out a child's failures.

"What about them?"

He shook his head, almost sadly. "One of them started to remove his sandals. He only stopped because his companion gave him a warning glance."

"He started to remove–" I took in a deep, shaking breath. Only in the presence of the Revered Speaker, or of his representative, did one put aside one's sandals. "The army isn't satisfied with Tizoc-tzin. It's only normal they'd want to find someone else to worship – that's hardly his fault." Even to me, the words rang as hollow as rotten wood.

"Ah, but he didn't try very hard to stop them, either."

I remembered what Teomitl had said, when they'd both tried to bow down to him. *Now is neither the time nor the place.*

Now, no. But later, perhaps – once Tizoc-tzin was overthrown, and Teomitl himself crowned Revered Speaker?

When I came back, I found Teomitl still sitting on his reed-matand Mihmatini gathering up Nezahual-tzin's feather headdress and cloak. "Feeling better?" I asked.

Teomitl grimaced. "Not really. And you, Acatl-tzin?"

Every muscle in my body felt stretched and pounded, like maize in the mortar, and without the cane, I wouldn't have been able to stand up. "I've been better." I didn't say anything about Nezahual-tzin's warning; I wasn't sure why. A desire not to worry him – or perhaps a sign that I believed Nezahual-tzin far more than I should have?

I would watch, and wait, and the accusation would prove itself groundless, another of Nezahual-tzin's little games. Yes. It had to be. Teomitl wasn't a fool. He had to know open rebellion would throw the Mexica Empire into more disarray than it could bear.

He had to. "Mihmatini?" I asked.

She paused on her way to the entrance. "Yes?"

"You haven't told me how it went, with the She-Snake. After the trial."

"Oh." She paused. "Nothing much. I complained and the She-Snake notified me I was acting irresponsibly. We both know who put him up to this." She snorted. "If you ask me, Tizoc-tzin still sees me as a young, in-experienced girl."

Did he? It was his loss, then. Both Teomitl and I had got over that stage long ago.

I was watching Teomitl's face as she spoke, and saw the hands clench and the shadow of jade imprint itself over the features. "My brother is a fool." There was something in his voice: a harshness that hadn't been there before, as if being so close to death had stripped away the last of the pretence.

"Teomitl," I started, but at this moment the entrance-curtain was wrenched open – by one of Mihmatini's priests. "My Lady Guardian…"

"What is it?"

"There is a delegation in the courtyard, asking to see you and the High Priest for the Dead."

The delegation was, as I had suspected, mostly priests from my order, Ichtaca at their head. "Acatl-tzin." He looked relieved to see me. "When we didn't see you come back…"

I shook my head, obscurely ashamed. "I haven't aban-doned you. It's just been – a busy day."

"He almost died," Mihmatini said, fiercely. "What is it?"

Ichtaca took a deep breath. "You have to come to the palace, now."

My heart sank. What had happened now? "Why?"

It was Palli, the round-faced offering priest, who spoke

up. "The sickness is no longer contained, Acatl-tzin. It's—" he took a deep breath, "it's got into one of the palace wings. There are dozens of dead people."

THIRTEEN
Sickness in Our Midst

The atmosphere in the palace was tense and fearful – even worse than four months before, when a star-demon had wreaked havoc in the courtyards, killing one councillor and carrying off the soul of a second. The first few courtyards we crossed seemed to be devoid of the She-Snake's black-clad guards, but as we went deeper – towards the affected wing – we saw more and more of them, and heard the growing clamour of the crowd.

"How bad is it?" I asked Ichtaca.

"Thirteen sick, two dead. And it's spreading." For once, he'd agreed to walk ahead of me, casting aside the etiquette which would have seen him defer to me as his superior. And a good thing: I was still weary and slow, limping through the courtyards with the help of Ceyax-ochitl's cane, and of course I only had a vague idea of where we were going.

"And they don't know where it started?"

If Ichtaca had had less of a sense of decorum, he'd have thrown his hands up. "The priests of Huitzilpochtli are quite... competent."

"But not enough?" I guessed, shrewdly. They were

Quenami's order, and Quenami had never had to handle a massive panic.

"You're assuming Quenami will be capable of something beyond court intrigue," Mihmatini said, curtly – she'd insisted on accompanying us, when it had become clear that the emergency concerned her as well.

"To be fair," Ichtaca said with a grimace, "I'm not sure we'd have handled it better. It's work for the clergy of Tlaloc."

Who inconveniently happened to be locked in cages, awaiting Tizoc-tzin's pleasure.

The courtyards we passed were all but deserted, the entrance-curtains closed with the finality of barricades. From time to time, a pale face would peek between the curtains – and withdraw just as fast, as if unable to meet our gaze.

Gradually, the noise grew: it was the priests of Huitzlipochtli arguing with burly warriors, trying to convince them they should stay inside, wait for the contagion to be ended.

"And when in the Fifth World do you think this is going to happen?" One of the warriors waved his *macuahitl* sword, threateningly; his companion laid a hand on his arm. "Let it go, Atl. You know priests are useless."

"I assure you–" the priest said in a quavering voice.

"Great work," Mihmatini muttered under her breath. I winced, but said nothing. Ichtaca likewise made no comment, but quickened his pace – forcing me to stay the same if I wanted to remain ahead of him.

There were more priests in the following courtyards, and the same total lack of mastery: they stood in doorways, arguing with irate warriors and noblemen – with mothers holding out wailing children, and old women who looked totally unfazed by any of their finery. As we neared the centre, it got worse and worse; the quarrels louder, the priests more numerous but equally ineffective, and the people milling outside, hoping to break the containment, becoming more and more dispersed.

And, in the last courtyard, there was a crowd – not densely packed, but at least a hundred people, mostly artisans, judging by their garb, and by the handful of feathers and precious stones scattered on the ground. From somewhere within the hubbub, I caught Quenami's raised voice: "You see, we have to–"

He didn't see. Like most artisans, they worked within the palace, but didn't sleep there. Their workshops were there – and, granted, their whole families had come with them, helping them glue feathers or mosaic beads, or sort out precious stones, but they certainly hadn't expected to be all but imprisoned in the palace.

Mihmatini was already pushing her way towards the centre, and Ichtaca and my priests followed in her wake, but the noise of the crowd was growing – a rolling wave of discontent that wouldn't be quelled by Quenami's words. It was going to burst.

Mihmatini had reached the centre. I caught angry words, presumably coming from one of the priests, and her own voice, raised to carry. "There is no cause for alarm…"

I was still lagging behind when it all broke down: one moment I was slowly making my way through a crowd of angry artisans, the next moment people were pressed against me, trying to hit me, to hit each other, anger palpable in the air. I couldn't see my priests, or Mihmatini, and the noise around me was only the wordless murmur of the crowd.

I tried to reach up with my one free hand, to slash my earlobes and whisper a prayer to Lord Death – which would have endowed me with the cold of the underworld, keeping the mob at bay, but they were too numerous, I couldn't...

Instead, I was all but carried by the crowd to the edge of the courtyard: it wasn't anger at the priests that drove them, but desire to leave the palace. I understood, but I couldn't not condone. For all we knew, several among them were already contaminated, carrying the sickness everywhere within the palace. They had to be stopped – and, indeed, the She-Snake's guards were already pulling up at the entrance to the courtyard, their uniforms a stark black against the adobe, their faces pale in the afternoon light – leeched of all colours, save the glint of their spears, the colours of their feather-shields.

The crowd in which I was caught wavered and came to a stop – and, for a bare moment, I dared to hope I might somehow slip away, turn back, and make my tottering way to Mihmatini and my priests – but then one artisan, more adventurous than one of his fellows, threw an adze at the leftmost guard.

The guard ducked, but the crowd was inflamed: the first ranks flung themselves at the guard, heedless of their spears. They fell back, cut, but there were always more artisans to take their place...

Buffeted here and there, I nevertheless managed to reach up with my free hand and, without a knife, rub at my earlobes, ignoring the growing pain until a sharper stab of pain told me I'd succeeded in removing the scabs from my previous offerings. The blood that stained my hands was only a few drops, but it would suffice.

"In the land of the fleshless,
In the region of mystery,
Where jade crumbles, where feathers become dust..."

Cold rose up, caught me in its embrace – gradually extinguishing every other feeling until it was all I could feel. The people on either side of me – two burly artisans weighing precious stones as if they were weapons – shrank back, and I used the opportunity to make my way out of the crowd, pointing the cane ahead of me like a weapon. I came to rest under the row of pillars surrounding the courtyard. A few hostile gazes followed me: if I didn't move away, I'd be the next person they threw adzes at.

Where was Mihmatini?

A soft, dappled radiance came from the centre of the courtyard: the press of artisans had shrunk there, become almost a huddle. I caught a glimpse of Quenami's haughty face, and Mihmatini in hurried conversation with Ichtaca and two artisans. It didn't look as though they were fighting.

At the courtyard's entrance, the guards were putting up a valiant fight, but they would not last long and I couldn't see how we would prevent them from leaving at all: more carriers of the plague in the heart of the city, further deaths…

Southern Hummingbird strike me, I couldn't see a way out of this. If only I could make my way over to Mihmatini…

I was about to move towards her when something brushed against me: the touch of some magic, like cold fingers lingering on my skin, sending chills into my heart. It might have been one of the artisans, but the spell was unerring, casting aside my protections as if they were nothing. Unless we had a sorcerer hidden among the artisans, it couldn't be any of them. I raised my gaze and, through the corner of one eye, I caught a glimpse of a man at the other courtyard entrance – the one that led deeper into the palace, where only a few frightened servants had lingered. He wore rags, but leant against one of the pillars with the casual, relaxed attitude of noblemen – and the profile. The lean, aristocratic face was achingly familiar.

It couldn't be…

Acamapichtli?

Calling through the din of the crowd would have been futile. Instead, I made my way further in – away from the pack tearing at the guards, the crowd becoming thinner and thinner as I retreated. I'd have broken into a run, if only I didn't feel so weak. Instead, I all but limped to the other end and by the time I reached the entrance, there was no one there.

I looked left and right, but even the servants had left. Had I imagined the whole thing? Acamapichtli was under arrest, like the rest of his clergy – kept in a cell where his powers would be weakened; kept under guard, so he couldn't plot against Tizoc-tzin (futile… Acamapichtli plotted as he breathed).

Just as I was about to head back into the courtyard, the magic came again: a weaker touch, skilfully drawing aside my protections – an invitation to step forward. I followed it into the next courtyard, and then into another, which was bare and deserted, the flowers in the earth wilted. The cane scraped against the ground, the echo of this the only sound within the courtyard.

Footsteps came from one of the buildings around the courtyard. I hobbled painstakingly towards it, but Acamapichtli was pulling the entrance-curtain open long before I finished crossing the courtyard.

"Well, fancy meeting you here." His face was creased in a sarcastic smile.

He looked much as he always had: his face lean and haughty, his eyes deep-set, his lips curved in sardonic joy. Save, of course, that he no longer wore the head-dress of heron feathers that had marked him as the slave of his god, the loyal servant of the city – and that his cloak was of maguey fibres, more suitable for a commoner than for a High Priest. His hair, unbound, fell down to his feet, black and lanky, stiff with the blood of his offerings. Deprived of the black paint on his face, he looked curiously effeminate, the aggression all but smoothed out of his features.

"So it *was* you. How in the Fifth World–?"

He raised a hand. "Later. There isn't much time. Come in, will you?"

"You mean they'll be looking for you?"

Acamapichtli grimaced. "Of course. I used the chaos, but it won't last forever. Don't make me waste my time, Acatl."

"Are you telling me the truth?"

Acamapichtli frowned. "I'll swear it on Tlaloc, if that's what it takes. On the Provider, the Ruler of the Blessed Drowned, the Lord of the Sweet-Scented Marigold, He who holds the jars of rain."

My doubt must have shown on my face, for he added, with the same old impatience, "Don't be a fool. I have mocked you and schemed against you, but have you ever known me to lie to you?"

The worst thing was, I couldn't remember if he had. Unlike Tizoc-tzin, I didn't keep a tally of who had offended me, and when. "Not under oath," I admitted, grudgingly.

I stepped into the room, and Acamapichtli let the entrance-curtain fall. It appeared to be an artisan's workshop:

fragments of feathers and precious stones were still spread out on reed mats, and a half-completed shield, showing the outline of a coyote in red feathers, lay in a corner, against the brazier.

I laid the cane down, and leant against the wall, trying to appear casual – in spite of the rapid beat of my heart. Acamapichtli watched me, smiling sardonically; I doubted he was much taken in by my pretence of calm.

"Fine," I said. "If you're here, you might as well tell me about this." I reached into the small bag I carried with me, and fished out the distorted black thing I'd taken out of Teomitl's body.

"Is that–?"

"Taken from the body of a sick man," I said, unwilling to admit Teomitl had been sick. "You said you only had a few hours–"

"Yes, yes." Acamapichtli waved a dismissive hand. "But this is more important. Give me one of your blades, will you?" He gestured at his clothing with a sharp, joyless laugh. "I'm not quite as well-equipped as I should be."

"It's been dedicated to Mictlantecuhtli," I said, slowly. And the magic of Mictlantecuhtli Lord Death would be anathema to that of Tlaloc – but Acamapichtli shook his head. "It should do. I just need it to draw blood."

If, a year ago, someone had told me I would be standing in a deserted room helping the High Priest of Tlaloc safeguard us against an epidemic… I might have laughed, or railed, or done four hundred other things, but I wouldn't have believed it.

Acamapichtli laid the creature on the floor, with an almost reverent care. Muttering under his breath, he slashed his earlobes and the back of his left hand, and let the blood drip down onto the ground.

223

"By Your will, O, Our Lord,
May bounty and good fortune be unleashed,
May the sweet-scented marigold shake,
May the rattleboards of the mist clatter..."

Mist pooled out from the place the blood had struck the ground, spreading fast, as if someone had pierced a hole in the wall of a steam house. It climbed up, clinging to the back of Acamapichtli's hand where he had cut himself, and the air itself became tight, hard to breathe, tinged with the characteristic, marshy smell of Tlaloc's magic.

"With a sprinkle, with a few drops of dew,
Let us be blessed with fullness and abundance,
May it be in Your heart to grant, to give, to bring comfort..."

At length, Acamapichtli looked up. "It's what I thought," he said. He made a single, dismissive gesture with his hands – as if sending away an underling who had displeased – and the mist fell away, sinking back into the ground as if it had never been. It became easier to breathe once again.

"What you thought?" I asked.

He smiled – a thoroughly unpleasant expression. "The magic does look similar to that of Tlaloc, but it doesn't belong to Him. It's Chalchiuhtlicue's."

"That's not possible," I said, sharply. Chalchiuhtlicue, Jade Skirt; Tlaloc's wife, Teomitl's protector. Goddess of Lakes and Streams – patron of women in labour, She who washed away the sins of newborn children.

"Because you're the expert on the water gods?"

"No," I said. "But I'd thought..." My voice trailed off. "You said it was Tlaloc's magic earlier."

"I was wrong." Acamapichtli didn't look ashamed at all. "A mistake easily made. The spell was an unusual mess, and already decaying."

I couldn't resist. "You're the expert on the water gods."

"Don't push me."

Much as I would have liked to, this served no purpose. "I won't. But I still don't understand why She would…"

"I don't know," Acamapichtli said. His voice was grim. "That was the other thing I wanted to ask you."

"About Jade Skirt? Why do you need to ask?"

"She's your student's protector," Acamapichtli said.

"I don't have any loyalty to Her."

"Teomitl-tzin might, though."

"I–" I started, and then found myself, to my surprise, telling the bare truth. "I don't want to think about this, not now."

I'd expected him to mock me straight away, but instead he cocked his head, and watched me for a while, not saying anything. "Fine. It doesn't have much bearing on this anyway – not yet. Keep your unpleasant revelations cooped up, until they rise up to gobble you up like coyotes."

Still as pleasant a man as ever. "What did you want?"

"It's time we got a better grip on where this is coming from, and why."

"And your idea–"

"You had me summon a dead man, and it didn't work. There is someone much better informed, though."

"Someone?" I asked, already suspecting the answer.

"Tlaloc," Acamapichtli said.

"You – you can't mean to do this." One did not, could not summon gods into the Fifth World. For one thing, They would not be inclined to answer the call of a single mortal; for another, the Fifth World, which was not Their essence, made them weak and helpless, and gods seldom enjoyed being either. Instead, in the (unlikely) event one wanted to speak to gods directly, one went into their country. In my entire life, I had talked to Mictlantecuhtli perhaps a handful of times, and my last journey into another god's land had left me wounded and sick.

That was, of course, discounting the fact that when Tlaloc had tried to seize power in the Fifth World, Teomitl and I had been the ones to stop Him. I would hardly be welcomed into Tlalocan, the Land of the Blessed Drowned. "You can't mean–?" I said, again.

"You want to know what's going on."

"Yes, but calling on the gods–"

"At least we'd be certain."

And I'd certainly be dead. I wasn't keen for that kind of assurance. "It's a great risk."

"Not so great." His voice was sarcastic. "Haven't you noticed rituals have become easier?"

"I don't understand–"

"When I summoned the dead warrior, Eptli, the sacrifice of a single jaguar shouldn't have brought him back for so long."

"Then you knew." He'd intended to cheat me all along; to pretend nothing had worked, that he'd done his best. How typical.

"That's not the point," Acamapichtli said, sharply. "The point is that something is interfering with the boundaries."

"The plague?" I asked.

"I don't know. But it makes going into Tlalocan easier."

I grimaced. "Less dangerous doesn't mean it will be a walk in the Sacred Precinct. You haven't convinced me it's absolutely necessary for the good of the Empire."

"And if it were?" His voice was sharp, probing in all the fragile, vulnerable places of my being as if by instinct, but this time I didn't need to hesitate.

"If you proved to me it were necessary, I would go." To say I wouldn't like it would be an understatement, but I knew where my duty lay.

Acamapichtli watched me for a while. At length he shook his head. "I can't see any other solution. And before you ask – no, I can't go alone. You're the one who has the most information about who died and when. I'm going to need you." He didn't look as if he liked the idea much – more as if he'd swallowed something unpleasantly bitter, like unsweetened cacao.

"And that's meant to be enough? Am I just meant to trust your word?"

His eyes narrowed. "Again? I thought we'd moved past that. I'm no fool, and neither should you be. I know the cost of strolling around a god's country as much as you do – and I don't suggest this lightly. But we're desperate."

"You are desperate. I'm not." And then realised what I'd said. "Sorry. I know the cost of angering Tizoc-tzin."

That stopped him; he looked at me through darkened eyes. "Yes. You do. As I pointed out earlier – I don't have much time."

"You haven't told me–"

"How I got out of the cell? Let's just say I have – unexpected resources." He grimaced; something about his escape had obviously been a source of unpleasantness. Had he ended up pledging a favour to someone? "But that's still dancing around the point."

"Like a warrior at the gladiator-stone," I said, wearily.

"Well?" Acamapichtli took a step away from me, and stood, wreathed in the dimming light of the sun. "If you're not coming with me, I'll be going alone. Just decide, Acatl."

I – I leant on the cane, feeling the ache in every one of my muscles. Going into the country of another god was dangerous enough; it would be worse in my weakened state – the epitome of foolishness.

But still…

Still, what if he was right and this was our only chance? "Fine," I said. The wood of the cane was warm under my fingers. "Let's go see Tlaloc."

FOURTEEN
Lord Death's Gift

The back of the room held a couple of rush brooms: Acamapichtli picked up one, and handed the other back to me.

Under other circumstances I would have protested, but we had already made clear the necessity of the journey.

"You want to dedicate this place to Tlaloc?"

"As small a space as I can." He grimaced. His eyes kept slipping to the entrance-curtain, as if he expected someone to interrupt us at any time. "Because of the plague, it's been touched by Chalchiuhtlicue, which should help. But still, if I can avoid Her..."

"She's your god's wife," I said, though I wasn't entirely surprised. Tlaloc and Chalchiuhtlicue formed a... tense couple, always ready to oppose one another. He had ended the Third Age, the one ruled by Chalchiuhtlicue; She had opposed Him when He'd attempted to rule the Fifth World.

I swept the room in silence – I hadn't swept anything since the days of my novitiate, and the dust, pushed back to each corner of the room, brought back memories of the month of Drought, Toxcatl, with everything cleansed for the arrival of the gods, and the palpable tension in the air, like moments before the storm…

> *"Aya! Paper flags stand in the four directions,*
> *In the place of weeping, the place of mists,*
> *I bring water to the temple courtyard…"*

Acamapichtli knelt, and started tracing two glyphs in the beaten earth – Four Rain, the Second Age, the one ruled by Tlaloc. Then, with a swift, decisive movement, he raised the knife, and slit his wrist – not a superficial cut that would have nicked both veins, but deep enough to hit the artery. It happened so suddenly the blood was already spilling on the ground before I could even so much as move.

"You're mad," I said.

"Desperate," he grated, keeping a wary eye on the entrance-curtain. "Get inside that glyph, Acatl."

"But–" The blood pooled, lazily, at his feet, spreading into the furrows of the glyphs – shimmering with layer after layer of raw magic. Bright red blood, coming from the heart instead of going to it – pressing against the edge of the wound with every passing moment, pumping itself out of the body in great spurts. Acamapichtli was already pale, and swaying.

He was chanting as the blood pooled – not slowly and stately, but a staccato of words, the beat of frenzied drums before the battle was joined – a series of knife stabs into a corpse's chest.

> *"You destroyed the Third World,*
> *The Age of Rain, the Age of Mist and Weeping,*
> *The Age of your unending bounty,*
> *Drought swept across the earth,*
> *The fruit of the earth lay panting, covered with dust."*

And, as the blood hit the floor in great spurts, it turned to mist and smoke – with a faint hint of the stale odour of marshes – sweeping across the room, subsuming everything, until it seemed that nothing of the Fifth World was left. The glyphs shone blue and white for a bare moment, painful across my field of vision, and then faded, and when I looked up again, we were standing in churned mud, at the foot of a verdant hill.

Acamapichtli, however, had lost consciousness – his blood still spurting out from the open wound. Suppressing a curse against ill-prepared fools, I retrieved my obsidian knife from his limp hand, and slashed the bottom of his cloak into shreds – it was either that or my cloak, and I had no wish to argue with Ichtaca about damaging the High Priest's regalia. I worked quickly – there was no time – pressing my fingers against the nearby muscles to stem the flow of blood. He'd lose the hand – there was no way this would heal gracefully, not after he'd spent so much time bleeding.

At last, I was done, and looked critically at my handiwork – I was no priest of Patecatl, and the gods knew it showed. At least he was no longer bleeding, though it felt I'd spent an eternity with my fingers pressed against his cold skin. Now to make a rudimentary bandage…

I–

Was it just me, or was his wound no longer bleeding – the edges far closer together than they should have been?

The air was crisp and clear; I breathed it in, feeling it burning in my lungs, tingling against the mark in my hand. I'd expected to be down on my knees, struggling to remain conscious – as I had the last time I had visited a god's country.

But nothing happened: the land around me was verdant, endless marshes cut through with canals and streams. In the distance, I could barely make out ghostly silhouettes engaged in a ball-game: the dead who had drowned or died of suffocation, or of water-linked diseases, and who had found their final destination in Tlalocan.

Among the myriad destinations for the Dead, the land of the Blessed Drowned was a pleasant paradise – never lacking food or rain, the maize always blossoming on time, the reeds abundant. A warrior would have chafed, but for me, the son of peasants, the wet air reminded me of my faraway childhood spent on the edge of the lake, and even the ghostly boats passing each other in the canals brought familiar memories of rowing at night – when the sky darkened to two red lips above and below the horizon, and everything seemed to hang suspended on the edge of the Fifth World.

A hand shot out, and grabbed my ankle – I all but jumped up, before realising it was merely Acamapichtli, using me as a leverage to stand up. His face was still pale, but the wound I'd tied off was closed, sinking to nothing against his skin.

"You're lucky," I said. "Opening up an artery tends to be more fraught with consequences."

He shrugged – characteristically careless and arrogant. "Different rules."

I shifted my cane in a squelch of mud. "If you say so." He had still spent the blood, regardless, and I very much doubted he would get *that* back. "And those different rules also explain why I can breathe here? Last time, in the Southern Hummingbird's heartland–"

Acamapichtli grinned, unveiling teeth that seemed much sharper and yellower than before. "We're not interlopers here, Acatl. I asked the god for His permission, and He has granted it to us."

"Great," I said. Even with the god's permission, I still felt drained. I leant on the cane, watching the hill. It rippled under the wind, and...

Wait a moment. "That's not grass," I said. It rippled and flexed in the breeze, as green as the tail feathers of quetzal birds – pockmarked with thousands of raised dots, swept through with yellow and brown marbling.

Lizard skin.

Acamapichtli grinned again, an expression I was starting to thoroughly dislike. "Of course not. Come on. The god is up there."

Of course. Gingerly, I set out; when the cane touched the skin, I felt a resistance – not at all what I'd expected from grass or earth. It smelled... musty, like dried skins, and it bounced under our steps with alarming regularity. As we climbed higher past the darker streaks, I caught sight of folds and sharper patches – places where one set of skin overrode another – darker patches with the splayed shapes of claws, and larger pockmarks, and almond-shaped holes where the eyes should have been, opening only on blind earth. I didn't even want to know how many lizards had died to make up the hill.

It would have been an arduous climb, even had we both been fit – which neither of us was. I leant on my cane, and though Acamapichtli arrogantly strode ahead, he was pale-faced, controlling the trembling of his hands only through an effort of will: I could see the quiver in his fingers, quickly masked.

We didn't speak and the only sounds were flocks of herons, wheeling around us with harsh cries, and the distant sound of thunder, like the roaring of jaguars. As we crested a ridge about halfway up, we saw Tlalocan spread out under us, a mass of green and yellow shimmering in the sunlight, the distant rectangles of Floating Gardens interspersed with canals, with the shades of drowned peasants harvesting maize from the eternally ripe sheaves of corn, forever happy in Tlaloc's paradise.

The thunder peals got louder and, as we ascended on the path, storm-clouds moved to cover the sky, darkening the air all around us. I glanced at Acamapichtli, but he was still looking stubbornly ahead.

Tlaloc had given His permission, which meant we walked here without gagging or shedding flesh, but that didn't mean He wasn't saving things for later. I remembered the last time I'd seen the god in the Fifth World: the shadowy figure perched on the shoulder of his child agent; His fanged mouth level with the child's ears; the voice that had shaken like thunder; the words that dripped poison after poison – and I, sinking down with my brother's body in my arms, desperately struggling to come up, to breathe air again...

Ahead, the path flared; the texture of the ground under our feet had subtly changed. I paused to catch my breath and saw the curling pattern beneath us: a single skin going all the way to the top, and...

Outlined against the darkened sky were the head and jaws of a huge snake, its crown of feathers ruffled in the rising wind, its eyes the same bright red as Acamapichtli's blood, its fangs shining like pearls in the muck.

Acamapichtli was already headed towards the snake; I followed after taking the time to catch my breath – gods, how I hated that every step seemed to cost me, that even lifting the cane seemed to quench the breath in my lungs.

A familiar litany for the Dead was running in my mind – though my patron god Mictlantecuhtli wasn't there, couldn't ever be there.

"We live on Earth, in the Fifth World,
Not forever, but a little while,
As jade breaks, as gold is crushed,
We wither away, like jade we crumble,
Not forever on Earth, but a little while…"

The snake was half-sunk within the earth, its head facing the sky and the storm-clouds – so that its open jaws formed a cave. The higher ring of fangs looked as though they'd clamp shut any moment, and the lower ring was pierced through in the centre, leaving a space just large enough for a man to squeeze through, so that Acamapichtli and I had to enter single file, instinctively bowed, as if to protect ourselves against the fall of the huge teeth glinting above us.

Inside, it was dark and cool, smelling faintly of moist earth, with the pungent aftertaste of copal incense, a smell that clung to the inside of my mouth and throat as if I'd smelled nothing else for days and days – as I might have, for who knew what time the gods considered Their own?

"Ah, Acamapichtli," a voice said. I'd expected it to be sombre, vindictive – the way I still remembered it in my nightmares – yet while it was deep, reverberating in the darkness, there was nothing in it but mild interest, the same one a priest might have shown to an unexpected pilgrim. "What a pleasure to see you."

Acamapichtli had removed his sandals and set them aside; and he was crouching, his eyes on the ground – not grovelling, as he might have done before the Revered

Speaker, but still showing plenty of respect. I crouched next to him, setting my sandals aside.

"And you brought company, too," Tlaloc said. He spoke in accents similar to the Texcocan ones, reminding me incongruously of Nezahual-tzin – or perhaps my mind superimposed the accent afterwards, struggling for a human equivalent to the speech of the gods.

"My Lord." I looked down and did not move, not even when footsteps echoed under the ceiling of the cave, and a shadow fell over me.

Tlaloc laughed, and it was thunder over the lake. "Oh, do get up. I'm not Huitzilpochtli, and there is no need for ceremony, not for high priests."

Slowly, carefully, I pulled myself upwards with the help of my cane, and looked at Tlaloc.

He was tall, impossibly so, towering over us in the dim light – but then all gods were, especially in Their own lands. I caught only glimpses of His aspect: a quetzal-feather headdress streaming in the wind like unbound hair, fangs glistening in a huge mouth, a cloak that shifted and shone with the iridescence of a thousand raindrops, before I looked down. He was the rain and the thunder: savage, cruel and wild; one of the Old Ones who had been there since the First Age. Staring straight at Him would have been like looking at the face of the Fifth Sun.

"You know why we are here," Acamapichtli said.

"I know you are desperate," Tlaloc said. "Not many people come offering heart's blood." A touch of malice crept into His voice. "As your companion said, you are lucky not to have lost the hand, or worse."

"I live for Your favour."

Again, that terrible laughter – thunder and rain, and

the sounds of a storm heard from a boat adrift on the lake. "We both know you don't."

Acamapichtli didn't move. "I respect Your power, and Your will."

"Yes. That you do."

I hadn't spoken up – I had to steer this conversation back to its proper goal, or they would be talking to each other for hours to come. But the prospect of doing so, to have Tlaloc's undivided attention fixated on me, was enough to cause nausea in the pit of my stomach.

What in the Fifth World had possessed me to come here?

"My Lord," I said. My voice was shaking; I quelled it, as best as I could. "There is an epidemic in the city."

Even looking at the ground, I *felt* His attention shifting to me – the weight of His gaze, the air around me turning tight and warm, like the approach to a storm. "There is." His voice was mildly curious. "As, as High Priest of Lord Death, no doubt you feel it concerns you."

"It concerns us all," I said. The pressure around me was growing worse. Now I knew why Acamapichtli had gone so strangely inarticulate.

"Unless it is Your divine will," Acamapichtli said, from some faraway place.

This time, Tlaloc's laughter seemed to course through me – through my ears and into my ribcage, lifting my heart clear of the chest and squeezing it until it bled. The ground rose up to meet me, and I fell down – pain radiating from my left knee, echoing the frantic beat within my chest.

"My will? You know nothing about My will, save what you see in the Fifth World."

"I need to know…" Acamapichtli's voice drifted from very far away, but I was too weary to focus on anything but the grooves in the ground under my hands, and my cane – lying discarded some distance away.

"Know what?" Tlaloc's voice was mocking again.

"If we're setting ourselves against You." His words fell, one by one, into the open maws of silence.

"What a dutiful High Priest," Tlaloc said, at last. "Your companion, of course, isn't so enthusiastic." I'd expected malice, but it was a simple statement of fact.

"He's often a fool." Acamapichtli's voice came from somewhere above me. "But he means well."

I managed to move – pulling myself into a foetal position, and then raising my head up. Acamapichtli's bare feet seemed to be the only things within my field of vision. "Are we – setting – ourselves against – Your wife?" Each word, like raw chillies, seemed to leave a burning trail at the back of my throat.

There was a pause. "No," Tlaloc said. "You're not setting yourself against either Me or My wife."

"Someone – is using Her magic." I managed to extend my hands towards the cane, hooking the wood with trembling fingers – and haltingly started to bring it back towards me. If I could get up, if I–

"Yes." Tlaloc did not offer any more information – and Acamapichtli, the Duality curse him, didn't seem inclined to question this further.

"I don't understand."

The air tightened around me again. "There is nothing to understand."

And there was something – a familiar tone to the voice, even though it was deeper and stronger than any human voice: an emotion I'd heard all too many times.

"My Lord–"

"There is nothing to understand, priest. Now leave."

And there it was again: something I ought to have been able to put a name to, but with only the voice to go on, I might as well have been blind and deaf. Something was wrong. Something–

I needed to see – even if it burned my eyes, I needed to see His face.

The cane was almost within my reach… A last flick of my fingers brought it spinning towards me, raising a cloud of dust from the packed earth of the cave – and a sudden whiff of copal incense from the wood, a smell that didn't belong in Tlalocan, neither in the verdant marshes, nor in this dark and humid cave.

Slowly, carefully, I pulled myself up – my hands were shaking worse than ever, and I had to stop and start again more times than I could count. And of course, neither Tlaloc nor Acamapichtli offered any help. "If not Your wife," I said, slowly, "then who is it?"

And, shaking, I raised my eyes towards the hulking shape of the god, catching a glimpse of blue-streaked skin, pocked with dots, of a necklace of jade beads around His neck, each as big as a human skull, of two snakes on either side of the jaw, climbing upwards through the darkened cheeks, their tails wrapped around the eyes in perfect black circles – the eyes…

They were round, like sage seeds, like water drops, the blue of the sky, an instant before it darkened; the colour of lake waters, of turquoise stones, and at their hearts was a single dot of yellow – a kernel of ripe corn, moments before it was gathered up in the harvest, quivering in the warm breeze…

And I knew, in the instant before my vision was finally extinguished and darkness swept across the world in a great wave that swallowed everything up, that I'd been right – that I had read Him right, even though he was a god.

There had been fear in those eyes – not mild worry, nor annoyance at our trespassing, but a fear real enough to grip Tlaloc's whole being.

And, whatever was going on, if it was enough to scare a god, then it was more than enough to scare the wits out of me, too.

I regained consciousness in the Fifth World, my eyes itching as if someone had thrown chilli powder in them. I could see nothing of the world beyond pale shapes against the darkness. I fought the urge to bring my fingers to my eyes, knowing it would only make matters worse. It was my own fault for staring so long into the face of a god I didn't worship, and it would pass, in time.

At least, I hoped so.

Distant noises drifted: flutes and drums, and hymns to the Southern Hummingbird. It sounded as though we were back in the palace.

"Acamapichtli?"

I half-expected him to be gone, but finally he answered, his voice coming from somewhere to my left. "I am here."

"What... happened?"

"Nothing of interest." He sounded amused.

"You saw–"

"I didn't see anything."

He hadn't raised his gaze. He hadn't looked his god in the face – it was odd that he wouldn't, but then again, perhaps I was assuming too much from my own relationship to Mictlantecuhtli and His wife. I had never knelt to either Lord or Lady Death, and they would no doubt have laughed if I had removed my sandals and flattened myself on the ground. After all, what need was there for obeisance, when almost everything in the Fifth World descended into Mictlan at the very end?

"Well, what did you see?" Acamapichtli asked.

He hadn't moved to help me. His voice was relaxed, casual, as if I owed him everything – whereas I was the one who could barely see. But surely I didn't have to tell him? What could he do in his current state, hunted down by Tizoc-tzin's men?

But, if I did this – if I withheld information, playing games with the truth – then I was no better than he. "He's afraid," I said.

"Of us? That's ridiculous."

"Of what's going on," I said. "He knows something." Not that we were ever going to find out what: getting information from a god in Their own world was fraught with risk, as we'd amply demonstrated.

Acamapichtli sighed, rather more theatrically than was required. "I have to go. But I'll try to pass a message to my Consort to see if she can help you track down whoever is using Chalchiuhtlicue's magic."

"I thought they'd arrested her," I said.

"Not yet." He sounded smugly satisfied.

"Go… where?"

I imagined more than saw him make a stabbing gesture. "Back to my cell, before my clergy pays the price for my little… escapade."

He sounded almost sincere. "You don't care for your clergy. You never did."

"Don't I?" He laughed, curtly. "You're right. Perhaps I don't. Till we meet again, Acatl."

"Wait," I said. "I can't–" But his footsteps had already moved out of the room, and he wasn't answering me

241

anymore. Which left me alone – within a deserted section of the palace, cordoned off because of the plague.

Great. Now how was I going to get out and find Mihmatini?

I fumbled around, and finally found the cane – by touch more than by sight, since everything was still dim and blurred. Its touch was comforting, but I didn't use it to drag myself up just then – I suspected standing up was going to be near impossible without shaking.

From the lack of sounds nearby, it was the middle or the end of the night. The air was cold, without a trace of warmth, and what little I could see was unrelentingly dark: the middle of the night, then, and I was in no state to walk. And even if I had been, I was half-blind, weak and in no state to find my own way through a deserted section of the palace.

Trust Acamapichtli to abandon me in the middle of nowhere. Although to be fair, he hadn't known I was half-blind.

Fine. Much as I disliked the idea, it made more sense to sleep here. Now if only I could make my way to the wall in order to sleep against something hard...

Rising, under the circumstances, felt a little pointless. Using the cane as a prop, I half-walked, half-dragged myself across the room. At some point, I hit one of the mats, and felt the jewellery scatter with a crunching sound. But, after what felt like an eternity of shaking and dragging myself – to the point my legs barely obeyed me anymore, threatening to collapse altogether – my hands met the solid surface of the wall. I could have embraced it at that point.

Instead, I propped myself against it with the last of my strength, and settled down to sleep.

• • • •

I fell into darkness. In my dreams, the blurred shapes of the walls around me became the vast, watery shapes of Chalchiuhtlicue's Meadows: deserted Floating Gardens with maize growing in wide clumps, and canals over which hung mist and, in the distance, the silvery shape of a lake, where the *ahuizotls* – water-beasts – lay in wait, their yellow eyes barely visible below the surface.

There was someone pooling a raft in the canals, well ahead of me. I'd have recognised that haphazard way of rowing anywhere: Teomitl.

I wanted to call out to him, but darkness sucked me in again, and no matter how I called out I couldn't find him again.

Instead, I stood alone in the dark, and gradually became aware that I was not alone. As my eyes became accustomed to what little light there was, I caught a glimpse of polished bone – of a soft light, as yellow as newborn maize, glinting through hollow eye-sockets.

"Acatl," said a voice – one I knew as well as my own.

Mictlantecuhtli. Lord Death, ruler of the house of the fleshless, lord of mysteries and withered songs.

I did not bow, or make obeisance, for this He would not accept. "My Lord," I said. And, more slowly, more carefully, "This is a dream."

"Of course." Mictlantecuhtli said. He sounded amused – not maliciously, like Xochiquetzal or Tlaloc might have – merely like a man taking in a good joke. "We're not there yet."

Not there? "I don't understand," I said, slowly.

"The time of the jaguars, the time of the eagles – when gods will walk the Fifth World once more."

Its very end, and the birth of the Sixth Sun. "When is that?"

"Do you think I would tell you?" Amusement, again.

I knew He wouldn't. He did not gloat, or put Himself or His knowledge forward: what use, since everything came back to Him in the end? "I don't owe You any favours," I said, slowly.

"You never ask for any favours," Lord Death said, and He sounded almost sad. "I'll give you one never-theless." Before I could say anything, He'd reached out, with fingers of tapered bone, and touched me on the shoulder. Cold spread from the point of contact, not slowly, but in a swift wave of intense pain that seemed to seize every muscle at once, sending me writhing to the ground.

As I lay on the cold, packed earth, breathing dust with every spasmodic struggle to breathe, with darkness barely held at bay, I heard His footsteps: He was standing right by my side, watching. "A gift, keeper of the bound-aries," and His voice grew and grew until it became the whole world, and I knew nothing more.

I woke up gasping, in daylight, in a room which smelled of cold ashes and stale copal incense. My eyesight seemed to have returned, at least to some extent. I could see the adobe walls, and the frescoes, but everything was still slightly blurred. I couldn't remember if that had always been the case, or if some of the eye damage had persisted even beyond the events of the night.

My shoulder ached, and I felt... odd, stretched, as if the protection spell had returned, and I lay cocooned in Lord Death's magic. But no, it wasn't quite that.

Something was wrong. I reached out, wincing at the pain, willing all of it to Mictlantecuhtli Lord Death, an offering as suitable as blood, and rubbed the place where He had touched me in the dream.

There were three thin raised welts on my shoulder, almost like the marks of a whip – save that nothing had bled and they did not ache. They were cold to my touch, with the familiar feeling of underworld magic, and they did not seem to have had any effect on me.

Which was, to say the least, unlikely. If this hadn't been an ordinary dream – if Lord Death had been there with me, in this space out of the Fifth World – then He had given me something. A favour, a gift to His High Priest – dangerous, like all divine favours. It would be small, because things made in dreams couldn't endure for long in the Fifth World, but it wouldn't be innocuous.

I dragged myself up once again and went out in the courtyard.

Everything was deserted. The courtyard smelled of dried earth and packed ashes. Overhead, the Fifth Sun was descending towards the horizon, staining the sky with a deep scarlet colour like heart's blood. Using the cane, I made my slow way through the courtyard, and then through to another, and yet another, and they were all equally deserted – no, not quite, for there was the familiar, faint scent of death in the air; of corpses which had just started to cool. Through one entrance-curtain I caught sight of shapes stretched on a reed-mat, moaning and thrashing as if in the grip of a dream.

The sick. The dying. The dead. And I among them, all but blind. What a great combination.

Tlaloc had been afraid. Why – unless this was no ordinary sickness, but one that touched the very fabric of the Fifth World? I didn't like that. Gods were cruel and capricious, but not afraid. Never afraid – unless it was of something or someone more powerful than Them.

Something…

As I walked, fumbling my way through pillared porticoes, through empty courtyards – through the dry smell of dust and the moans of the sick – I slowly became aware that I was not alone. There were voices in my ears – faint at first, but growing in intensity until they seemed to fill the world. There was a smell like dry, stretched skin; and a wind that grew colder and colder; and ghostly shapes, walking by my side, as if exhaled by the underworld. They crowded around me, groping with cold hands, their faces obscured, their arms and legs translucent, like layers of water.

Was this Mictlantecuhtli's gift – to make me see the souls of the slain? But no, I had spells which could do that. Why waste His time giving me something I could attain for myself?

The ghosts didn't go away as I walked, but neither did they grow more solid. The voices wove in and out of my ears, and there was a hollow in my stomach, steadily growing and growing, even as the world wove in and out of focus – perhaps it was my eyes, but everything seemed to be spinning…

With some difficulty, I reached the next courtyard – the last one – crossing over a ghostly river, and found myself face to face with two of the She-Snake's guards, whose spears barred my way out of the wing.

"Look," I said, struggling, for behind the black-painted faces were ghosts, too – singing a wordless lament, whispering words of grief. "I need to get out. I am the High Priest for the Dead, keeper of the boundaries–"

The feeling in my stomach was worse; I wanted to curl up, to close my eyes until it was all over. I–

The boundaries.

I remembered lying on a cold stone floor, with everything spinning in and out of focus, feeling the hollow in my stomach grow and grow until it seemed to swallow me whole. It had been in the instants after the designated Revered Speaker Tizoc-tzin had died – when everything had hung in the balance, and the Fifth World itself had been close to tearing itself apart.

It had been worse, then. I had barely been able to stand up, and we had lain unprotected from the star-demons. Nothing like that here: the Fifth Sun was in the sky, and the star-demons' distant shadows cowering from His radiance.

But still… there were ghosts abroad, and the whispers of the dead, and – soon, perhaps – the panting breaths of beasts of shadow on the prowl.

Something was wrong with the boundaries.

"I need to get out," I said, again, to the guards.

They looked at me as if I were mad, with clearly no intention of letting me move more than a hand-span from them. "We have orders," they said.

"Then get me the person who gave you the orders."

They looked at each other, and then back at me. I saw ghosts drift between them, drawn like jaguars to a hearth-fire. My clothes were torn and slightly muddy from my visit into Tlalocan, but they were still the regalia of the High Priest for the Dead. "My Lord, we cannot…"

"Get me Quenami," I said, softly.

It might have been the tone, or the remnants of the regalia, but one of the guards left, looking distinctly worried.

In the meantime, I leant against one of the coloured pillars, desperately trying to look nonchalant, but the ghosts still hung in the courtyard like a veil of fog, and the slight nausea at the back of my throat wasn't getting better.

I'd expected Quenami to look smug or satisfied, but when he arrived, he merely looked harried. He wore his most ostentatious clothes – brightly-coloured feathers almost better suited for a Revered Speaker than for a High Priest – and his earlobes glistened with freshly offered blood. "Acatl. What a surprise to see you here." Even his sarcasm sounded muted.

I wasn't in the mood to play the dance of diplomacy. "Look, Quenami. There is an epidemic out here, and I don't need to be confined with the dying."

"Except that you might be sick yourself." His eyes were feverishly bright, his hands steady, but I could read the strain in his bearing.

"Do I look sick to you?"

"You never know. You might have it all the same."

He looked too worried – even for someone who had suffered the debacle in the courtyard. "It's worse, isn't it? It's spreading, and you have no idea how to stop it."

Quenami's head snapped towards me. "What do you know? You've been confined here since yesterday. I know you have. No one has seen you in that time; your own sister admits to knowing nothing of your whereabouts."

"I know enough," I said, softly. Gods, Mihmatini had been looking for me the whole time? She was going to flay my ears the next time we met. "Tell me it's better, that you have it all under control."

As Acamapichtli had; I hated that man's guts, but I had to admit he had a certain ruthless efficiency. Quenami was all bluster. "It's only a matter of time," Quenami said, haughtily. "The Empire is well protected, as you know."

It was – against star-demons and the celestial monsters

that would swallow us. But still... still, nothing prevented a resourceful sorcerer from sowing havoc. "You know the Southern Hummingbird won't protect us against a small thing like a plague." To a god, especially a war-god, hundreds of dead meant nothing. The great famine, the great floods, all had happened under the protection of a Revered Speaker. Huitzilpochtli the Southern Hummingbird only guarded from large-scale attacks which would annihilate the Fifth World or the Mexica Empire.

"What do you want, Acatl?"

"What I've told you. I want to get out, and I want to help. That's all. Is it really so hard to understand? I'm not working against the Fifth World."

Unlike you, I wanted to say, but I knew it wasn't the best time for airing this particular grudge.

Quenami looked at me, and back at the courtyard. "It's not safe..."

"No," I said, with a quick shake of my head – I'd never seen him so uncertain, and I wasn't sure what it presaged. "But for all you know, you might have it as well. Tizoc-tzin might have it as well."

"Very well," Quenami said at last. He made it sound like a special favour granted to me – as if he were Revered Speaker, and I a lowly peasant. "You may get out."

I didn't need to be told twice: I walked past the two guards, and came to stand firmly on the side of the healthy, the cane warm in my hands. Quenami made no comment, but let me follow him through a few courtyards – enough for me to realise the palace had grown uncannily silent, as if a cloth had been throw over everything. The servants wove their way among ghosts – not seeing them, but not saying anything in any case – and the few noblemen who were still out hurried past us, intent on not staying out any longer than they had to.

"How much worse is it?" I asked Quenami.

He shrugged – a contained movement, but I could still feel his anxiety. "The She-Snake says he has every thing under control."

Which wasn't the same thing as saying the problem was solved. "And what he has under control…"

Quenami shook his head – of course he wouldn't allow himself to look embarrassed. "About a fifth of the palace has been affected, and it sounds like it's spreading through the city."

"And you still think you can keep a handle on this?"

"Tizoc-tzin thinks so," Quenami said.

It was the closest he'd ever come, I guessed, to saying he didn't agree with his master. "And Tizoc-tzin still thinks it's a good idea to arrest the clergy of Tlaloc."

Quenami looked away, and didn't speak. At length he said, in a much quieter voice. "Your sister's priests are with us, to find rituals to slow this down. It will suffice. It has to."

But we both knew it wouldn't.

I detoured through the kitchens to find some food since, in addition to being weak and still wounded, I hadn't eaten anything since before leaving for Tlalocan. Then I made my halting way out of the palace, to check on Mih-matini and on my own priests.

The air was sweltering, wet and heavy, and the sky was an overbearing shade of blue, which promised no respite from the heat.

The ghosts didn't leave, though they did grow fainter, at the same time as the numbness in my shoulder faded. Mictlantecuhtli's gift, whatever it had been, was slowly returning to its maker. But it had accomplished its purpose.

A gift, keeper of the boundaries.

There was something wrong with the boundaries. Acamapichtli had said they were weaker; he had thought the plague had weakened them. I wasn't so sure. The hollow, nauseous feeling in my stomach – the one that was now slowly receding to bearable levels – was the same I'd had much earlier, when the army had returned, long before the plague was set loose.

There was something else, something we needed to work out with Ichtaca and the rest of the order.

I was munching on my tamales, enjoying the solidity of the maize sliding into my empty stomach – something firmly of the Fifth World, and not of Tlalocan or Mictlan – and slowly heading out of the palace, when someone grasped my shoulder. "Acatl."

If I hadn't been so bone-weary, I would have given a start. Nezahual-tzin moved within my field of vision. As usual, he was escorted by two Texcocan Knights, though he'd eschewed his regalia in favour of a more discreet cotton cloak and a simple headdress of mottled brown quail-feathers.

"Going round in disguise?" I asked.

His lips quirked up. "I could say the same thing about you."

I shrugged. If he wanted to make me angry, attacking my dress was hardly the best way.

"Your sister is waiting for you at the Duality House," Nezahual-tzin said.

And I could guess she wouldn't be particularly happy. But I didn't want to say this to Nezahual-tzin – who was

251

Revered Speaker of Texcoco, not my friend or equal. "Anything else I ought to know?"

Nezahual-tzin shrugged. We'd started walking towards the palace entrance, the two warriors following us. "I might have a lead on why Teomitl survived the sickness."

"A lead?" I said.

"I asked the stars," Nezahual-tzin said. It was probably literal, too – his patron god Quetzalcoatl was Lord of the Morning Star among His other aspects. "Magic flowed towards the Duality House that night."

"Hardly surprising," I said. With my healing, and our repeated attempts to heal Teomitl, the place must have been a riot of lights.

"Actually," Nezahual-tzin said, "it was Toci's magic."

That stopped me. "Grandmother Earth? Why would She–?" She was the Earth that fed the maize, that would take us back into Her bosom when the time came: an old, broken woman renewed with every offering of blood; a goddess born from the fragments of the Earth-Monster, eternally thirsting for human hearts and human sacrifices. And, in many ways, She was the opposite of the Southern Hummingbird, our protector deity: the incarnation of female fertility, the nurturing mother, whereas He was the virile, eternally young warrior. "Why would She want to heal Teomitl?" I asked.

"I don't know," Nezahual-tzin said. "But I intend to find out. It seemed to come from a house in the district of Zoquipan." His youthful face was that of an artisan, nibbling away at a massive block of limestone until the sculpture at its core was revealed. "Care to join me?"

I shook my head. "I have to get back to the Duality

House." That, or Mihmatini was finally going to lose patience with me.

Nezahual-tzin didn't look particularly disappointed. He did, though, walk with me up to the Duality House, claiming it was for my own safety. I wasn't sure of his motivations, but I welcomed the company, for I was none too steady on my feet.

We parted ways amidst a crowd of pilgrims carrying worship-thorns and balls of grass stained with blood – ranging from gangly adolescents barely old enough to have seen the battlefield to old men walking with canes, wearing long cloaks to hide the scars they'd received in the wars.

"Oh, one other thing," Nezahual-tzin said.

I stopped, and painstakingly turned around. "What?"

"You might be interested to know you're not the only one to have disappeared recently."

Acamapichtli? "I'm not sure–"

Nezahual-tzin's face was utterly impassive. "No one has seen your student since yesterday. Officially speaking, of course."

Of course.

"And you?"

Nezahual-tzin shrugged, casually. "I haven't seen him, either. But I have it on good authority some of the warriors under his command have gone missing."

He'd almost died. He'd said it to me, attempted to warn me: that he couldn't wait any longer for the things he thought were due to him. For the Mexica Empire to flourish under good leadership, and of course Tizoc-tzin's leadership was anything but brilliant. But surely he couldn't mean to… he couldn't want to sink us back into a civil and magical war…?

"I did warn you," Nezahual-tzin said.

And he had; I didn't want to hear it any more now than I'd wanted to hear it back then. "Yes," I said. "Thank you." And I pushed my way into the crowd of the Sacred Precinct without looking back.

FIFTEEN
Corpses and Curses

Contrary to what Nezahual-tzin had told me, Mihmatini wasn't waiting for me at the Duality House.

Instead, I found people grouped in the courtyard: mothers with children on their backs, entire families from the grandmother to the young toddlers, and quite a few warriors, who presented their emotions as an odd mixture of terror and annoyance – as if they were aware they should not have been so afraid of the supernatural. There appeared to be no sick people, but I strongly suspected those were being herded away by the priests of the Duality.

After many enquiries, I finally managed to get hold of Yaotl, my sister's personal slave, who looked at me with his customary sneer and informed me that she'd left for the city, in order to take a look at some of the sick.

"And Teomitl?" I asked

"He left yesterday," Yaotl said, curtly. "A couple of warriors came to pick him up."

Like the warriors who had removed their sandals? I didn't like this; I didn't like this at all.

I walked back to my temple in a thoughtful mood, but

found it flooded as well, my priests barely able to deal with the flow of supplicants, and Ichtaca himself having taken refuge in the shrine atop the pyramid, looking pale and harried.

"Acatl-tzin! We thought–"

I raised a hand. "It's quite all right," I said, thinking I was making a speciality of running out on them. "I ran into someone, rather unexpectedly, and spent the night stuck in the palace grounds."

Ichtaca looked bewildered. "We looked for you after the riot, but we couldn't find you."

"I was in Tlalocan," I said, briefly – ignoring the awe which spread across his face. "Not my idea. Acamapichtli's."

"But Acamapichtli-tzin–"

I mentally ran through the necessary explanations, and gave up. "Look," I said. "I promise I'll explain everything, but right now there is something slightly more urgent. I think there is a problem with the boundaries."

Ichtaca looked as if he might protest, and then he took a look down into the overcrowded courtyard. "It could be," he said, slowly. "It would explain why so many people have turned up here. They speak of ghosts, and of odd portents…"

"The boundaries are weakened," I said.

"But the Revered Speaker–"

The Revered Speaker should have been protecting us against that, yes. "I don't know," I said. "But it's the only explanation that fits." I thought of Tizoc-tzin; of the stretched bones beneath the sallow skin; of the shadowed eye-sockets that might as well have been empty. A dead man walking in the Fifth World.

"Oh, gods," I said, aloud. "We did it."

We'd brought him back, crossing the boundary between

life and death, and it had never closed properly. "It's something we did, with the spell to bring Tizoc-tzin back."

Ichtaca grimaced. He hadn't liked the story when I'd told it to him, but he'd had to bow down to my decision. To our decision. We had taken that as a group – as High Priests and equals, for once. "We don't have star-demons in the streets," he said.

"Because we have a Revered Speaker," I said. "The Fifth World is protected. But that doesn't mean things can't be wrong. Ghosts are hardly a menace."

I stopped, then – and thought of all the sorcerers we'd defeated – all the people who had died in our wars of the conquest, thirsting for revenge over the Mexica. I thought of how easy it was to call up a ghost and listen to their advice. No need to be a sorcerer frighteningly good at magic: our culprit merely needed to call on the right ghost.

Oh, gods. "I take it back. Ghosts *can* be a menace. A sorcerer advising someone…"

"Ghosts can't cast spells," Ichtaca pointed out.

"I know. But they can give the instructions, if you ask them the right questions." Oh gods. The living were quite enough to deal with; I didn't want to have to contend with the dead as well.

"Can you look into this?" I asked Ichtaca. "I need to know what exactly is wrong with the boundaries."

"You've stated it." He looked genuinely startled.

"I could be wrong." And I dared not, not on something this large. "I want to be sure."

He grimaced. "I know it's important, but–"

"There are other things, I know. You have to spread out the priests. I know you can do that."

"As you wish." He rose. "I was planning to direct the examinations of the bodies."

257

Ah, yes. The bodies. Finally, we had some time to examine them quietly, and to get a better idea of the nature of the sickness. "They're on an island in the Floating Gardens, if I remember correctly? I'll come with you," I said.

Ichtaca nodded, as if he hadn't expected anything less of me. It was a balm to my heart, in a time when my confidence was severely shaken.

Before we left, I took a moment to seek out the storehouse, and to help myself to a simple grey cloak, the one customarily worn by priests for the Dead as they walked through the streets of the city. I didn't look like a High Priest anymore, but at least I had lost the resemblance to a beggar mauled by a jaguar.

Ichtaca, of course, insisted I take the huge barge of the High Priest, with its highly-recognisable spider-and-owl design of Mitclantecuhtli, while he and the other priests sat in smaller reed crafts.

The priest with me was Ezamahual, the dour-faced peasants' son who always walked as if unbelievably blessed. He didn't speak as I carefully wedged myself into position within the barge – much harder than I'd thought possible, with my legs shaking.

He rowed in great, smooth gestures – a familiar rhythm for someone who had grown up at the river's edge – lulling me into a sleep that was almost restful… until I saw the first hints of ghosts trailing over the water.

The drowned, too, were rising up. This was more serious than a mere summoning from the underworld. Something was deeply wrong, and the gods knew it, from Mictlantecuhtli to Tlaloc.

And all, I suspected, because of us. It had to be – what else would cause such a massive disruption?

At the time, we'd thought it the lesser of two evils. The death of Tizoc-tzin, our newly designated Revered Speaker, had opened the gates wide to star-demons and their depredations. To name another Revered Speaker would have taken weeks – time we didn't have. Far better to seek the Southern Hummingbird's favour, and bring back Tizoc-tzin's body and soul from the heartland.

Except, it seemed, that it had solved nothing – merely sowed the seeds for further blood and fire in the Fifth World.

At this early hour, it made more sense to take one of the largest western canals, swinging under the Tlacopan causeway and continuing due south around Tenochtit-lan. The houses of adobe became mud and wattle – with coloured roofs at first. Then even those went away, and the crowds heading to the marketplace thinned out, until we reached the Floating Gardens: a network of ar-tificial islands used as fields for the planting of anything from maize to squashes. The farmers were up already, consolidating the ditches for irrigation and making sure the earth was well-watered in preparation for the plant-ing of maize.

The island that hosted the bodies was visible from afar, if only for the whiffs of Mictlan's magic emanating from it, as dry and as stretched as desiccated corpses.

The boat touched the ground between two willow trees: we all disembarked, and waited for Ichtaca to lead the way.

He looked at me enquiringly – unwilling to break the rules. I suppressed a sigh and went towards the centre of the island, towards the greater concentration of Mict-lan's magic. The bodies lay side by side in the hollow of a maize field, naked and bloated. The smell that wafted up to me nestled in the hollow of my stomach, strong enough to make me feel nauseous again. I might be used to handling corpses, but I'd never examined so many at the same time – and not in such a state. Thank the Duality it was the dry season now, and nowhere near as hot or as humid as it could get.

"If you'd do the honours…" Ichtaca said.

I didn't much feel like it, quite aside from my current weakness, but it would mean something to all of them, and especially to Ichtaca. With a sigh, I walked towards the bodies – cane in one hand, knife in the other.

The bodies lay on their backs in the mud of the Floating Garden, the willows at the edge of the island casting long, twisted shadows across their skins – and death, too, casting its own twisted shadows, in the form of blotches and bloated skins, all the signs of rot that we knew all too well.

Eptli's body was the worst: bloated and blue, barely recognisable as human. The others – the prisoner Zoquitl, Chipahua and his household – were not as bad. Chipahua and his companions in particular had the characteristic rigidity of the newly-dead, but their skins were dark rather than livid blue.

Before starting, I cast a quick spell of protection, calling on the power of the underworld to shield me. The noises of oars in the water receded, the peasants' tilling and digging became far away, and the sky itself became as grey as dust.

"Only here on earth, in the Fifth World,
Shall the flowers last, shall the songs be bliss,
Though it be feathers, though it be jade,
It too must go to the region of the fleshless."

I crouched by Eptli's body – the most important for us
– and considered. I had already examined it; I could cut
into the flesh, releasing the noxious air contained within,
but it was likely I wouldn't get anything more out of it,
not without magic. It had decayed too much.

So, instead, I moved to Chipahua's body – setting the
cane aside in the mud of the Floating Garden. He lay
against the radiant blue of the sky, his eyes wide open, seeing nothing of the Fifth World, his scar crowded by the
raised blisters on his entire face. They formed a faint pattern
that would have been vaguely reminiscent of a mosaic, save
that most of them had burst through the skin, bleeding into
the body. His entire skin had turned dark and the whites
of his eyes were now the red of blood. Blood had also
pooled below the other orifices – nose and mouth and ears,
eager to leave the body by whatever holes there might be.

The same pattern of burst blisters had also spread to
his limbs, though they were more dense on the hands
and feet than closer to the torso. Using the knife, I
slashed at his tunic to reveal the body underneath: more
burst blisters, and faint red spots covering the entire skin.
I moved to the groin area, lifting the penis to have a better look – and its skin came away in clumps, as neatly as
that of a flayed man, disintegrating like worn paper.

Breathe. He was dead; it wasn't as if anything worse
could happen to him.

Breathe. I needed to–

With some difficulty, I focused on the corpse again,
and looked at the penis and anus; both were flecked with
dried blood.

I fought a surge of fresh nausea. I had seen many
things, but not a corpse that looked as though every
blood vessel had burst or decayed.

"Ichtaca?"

"Acatl-tzin?" He'd been waiting on the edge of the Floating Garden for me to finish my examination.

"There are a dozen bodies here," I said. "If you and the other priests don't start examining them, we'll still be here tonight."

Ichtaca nodded, and started pointing to priests, assigning them bodies. He crouched by Eptli's body – trust him to take the hardest one – and drew his own blade, thoughtfully.

I didn't stare for longer – whatever mystery there was, he would solve it, and I needed to focus my energies on the body I was currently examining.

The mundane examination didn't seem overly conclusive; time for other methods.

I rubbed at my earlobes, dislodging the scabs from the previous offerings. With the blood, I drew glyphs on the backs of my hands – "one" and "knife", the week that was ruled by Lord Death. As the blood dripped down towards the hungry earth under my feet, I started chanting.

"In the land of the fleshless, in the region of mystery,
Where jade crumbles, where gold is crushed,
Where all our songs, all our flowers come to an end."

The glyphs on the back of my hand grew uncomfortably warm, until I could have traced them with my eyes closed. The rest of the world, though, seemed to cool – until the tips of my fingers felt burnt and pinched, and even the light of the Fifth Sun seemed dimmer.

"In the land of the fleshless, in the region of mystery,
In the house without windows, on the dais of bones,
The house of dust, the house of the fleshless..."

A green, mouldy light spread outwards from the glyphs, playing on my skin and on that of the body, until we both seemed equally leeched of life, and the smell in the air was dry and faint, like old codices buried in the desert.

Bracing myself against the pain that would come, I lowered my hands over the corpse and felt the jolt as the symptoms crossed into my own body – the salty taste of an unfamiliar magic, and the sense of vastness as the blood vessels enlarged and disintegrated – and then, as the shadows around me grew larger and larger, everything else caught on, the throat, the stomach, the entrails, every single membrane in the body...

I came to with a start, almost tempted to feel my torso to check that I still had my major organs – but that was foolish, since the spell only granted me an impression of what the death had felt like, and I had known in advance it would be unpleasant. So, I had a better idea of how Chipahua had died, but not of how he had caught the disease.

Still... something was staring me in the face, and I was far too weary to make it out.

I looked around: most priests seemed engrossed in the preliminary examination of the bodies, but a few – including Ichtaca – had moved to similar spells.

Ichtaca. I looked again at Eptli's corpse, which was bloated and blue, but the skin wasn't dark, and there was no blood on the face. And he had died almost instantly.

I dragged myself to the corpse, and put my hands over the face.

This time, the rush of magic was far stronger; it came from my outstretched hands, coursing through my entire body until my saliva tasted like brackish, muddy water, and my whole body started itching and burning up, and I felt the blisters on my mouth and tongue, and the rush of the shadows, the images of the flailing limbs, of the dying bodies – and everything was disintegrating again, but it was my heart that gave out first, collapsing on itself with the dissolution of the major arteries and veins...

Oh gods. There were two versions of the sickness.

I dragged myself to my cane, trembling with the memories of dying twice, in close succession, and limped to the other corpses, watching them.

The corpse of the prisoner Zoquitl was also devoid of bleeding and I got the same impression when I lowered my hands over it, the feeling of unfamiliar magic spreading from outstretched hands...

And the others... Chipahua's household, his companions, his wife, his slaves – I stood over them all, and over them all I felt the same thing, felt myself destroyed piece by piece, bleeding into my own body, exhaling nothing but my own debris and blood...

"Acatl-tzin!" Firm hands yanked me, jolting me out of the trance of the spell, and I lay gasping, the mud squelching against my skin, so cold as to make me shiver. The Fifth Sun overhead blurred, quivering, the willows spinning and bending as if in a great storm....

"Are you mad?" Ichtaca's voice asked – coming from very far away.

"Not... mad," I whispered, but he didn't seem to hear me.

"You were the one who said we'd examine them as a group, and then you go taking on their symptoms as if there were no tomorrow."

He sounded angry, but I couldn't bring myself to care anymore. I lay gasping and choking, trying to banish the memories of the shadows from my vision – feeling everything twisting and bursting within my body, as if I were the one on the edge of death.

That settled it: whoever had cast that kind of spell was thoroughly mad.

Some time later, Ezamahual helped me get up, wrapping my shaking hands around the cane and lending me his shoulder so that I stood more or less upright. The weakness was passing; the memories of so many deaths so close together were passing away, becoming a distant nightmare. Thank the gods for fallible memory – what would I have ever done, if I had remembered perfectly every single one of the examinations I'd practised?

"They're different," I said to Ichtaca.

He still looked angry, but he wasn't shouting at me anymore, which I guessed was an improvement. "Different how?"

"Eptli said he felt cold after touching something, and I think Zoquitl caught it the same way: from an object, not a person. Everyone else on this island caught it from someone already sick, just like Teomitl and I."

"So we're looking for an object impregnated with Chalchiuhtlicue's magic?" Ichtaca frowned. "That doesn't help much."

I shook my head. "Several objects. It's not something unique. And yet it was peculiar enough that Eptli remembered it, so most probably not an everyday object." And something else, too: this meant that Eptli and Chipahua had likely had direct contact with the sorcerer. "Did you learn anything else?" I refrained from adding "while I was unconscious", for both our sakes.

Ichtaca shrugged. "A better understanding of the disease, I guess. It's based on the liquids within the human body – spreading through the blood and coaxing everything into destroying itself in a rush." His round face was creased in distaste. "It's a horrible, useless way to die."

"But it brings power to Chalchiuhtlicue or to the sorcerer, if he knows how exploit it," I said, slowly. "Symbolically, they've all died of the water." I thought of whoever had attacked the Master of the House of Darkness, of the mask spreading across his face, blocking off his nostrils and mouth. A sacrifice to the goddess who ruled water; likewise, it would have brought power to Her – or to whoever stood between Her and the Fifth World.

Tlaloc had said the epidemic wasn't Chalchiuhtlicue's will, and in truth, I couldn't have seen why He'd have lied to us. So the most likely explanation was a sorcerer – one ruthless enough to steal from the goddess.

Which wasn't exactly heartening, as far as explanations went.

Ichtaca's grimace would have been comical in other circumstances. "Yes. How many victims have there been?"

"Too many," I said, thinking of the palace. "You know that as well as I do."

"It has to be contained." Ichtaca's face was set in a grimace. "Unless the Southern Hummingbird…"

I shook my head. "He won't intervene."

Ichtaca looked almost disappointed, but then, like Teomitl, he'd always been persuaded that our destiny was to conquer the Fifth World. I'd never been quite as enthusiastic. Like Coatl or Itamatl, I tended to think that wars were His province, and that He granted His favours as He saw fit.

Which didn't excuse murder, or the casting of dangerous spells.

Ichtaca, after the initial moment of uncertainty, appeared to have rallied. "Then it has to be contained."

"Easy to say. We're all working on it."

"I know," Ichtaca said. He flipped his knife upwards, staring at the blade. "You think it's Chalchiuhtlicue?"

"I don't think so." But still… one way or another, She was in the game, and Her magic was loose in the Fifth World, used against the Mexica Empire. And Her magic was tied to Teomitl, and She could drag him into Her little games – a train of thought I would gladly have done without.

"About healing the sickness…?" I asked.

"That's what your sister's priests are working on."

He'd always been much better at crafting new rituals than me. "I know. But Nezahual-tzin told me that there might be a way, with Toci's magic."

"Grandmother Earth?" Ichtaca shrugged. "Appealing to Her stability and solidity. Yes, it might work. At any rate, it can't make things worse."

"We need to try," I said. "There are two people in the palace–"

"I know. I'll see your sister's priests and see if we can work something together. What about you, Acatl-tzin?"

I looked at the bodies again, spread out pathetically in the sunlight, every one of them holding pain beyond my imagination, every one of them a sacrifice building power for someone who wished us no good. A few priests were still examining them – among them familiar faces, like Palli, a burly nobleman's son who had taken to the priesthood like an *ahuizotl* to water. His face was creased in a familiar frown, trying to work something out.

"I'm going to find some answers." I grasped the cane so hard my knuckles whitened.

Ichtaca frowned. "You should get a bit of rest. I'll call for a priest of Patecatl."

Why was everyone so suddenly concerned about my wellbeing? "There's more at stake than my health."

"Which doesn't mean it's unimportant." Ichtaca's face was disturbingly shrewd.

Ahead, Palli raised his head, and gestured towards us. "Acatl-tzin!"

"What is it?"

"You have to see this!"

"If it can be moved, bring it here," Ichtaca said, "Acatl-tzin is in no state to walk." He threw me a meaningful glance, almost a threat to get some rest.

Palli scrambled to his feet, and all but ran the distance that separated us, his sandals squelching in the mud. "Acatl-tzin." His hand was wrapped in cloth; and on the cloth was something – a small, shrivelled thing that stank of Chalchiuhtlicue's magic.

"I found it on Eptli," he said, almost apologetically. "Didn't dare touch it."

"What is it?" Ichtaca asked.

"The object," I said. "The vector of the sickness."

Palli angled it so that it caught the light: it was a small, translucent tube, with the remnants of a fine powder inside. And something else was carved on its flaring end – it looked like a hand, holding a stick?

No, not a stick. It was...

"This?" Ichtaca shook his head. "I can't possibly see–"

"I can," I said, darkly. "Before it was crunched up like this, it was a hollowed-out feather stem."

"Money?" Ichtaca asked. "But there is no gold inside."

No, and I couldn't identify the powder inside, which was an uncanny shade of yellow – a colour too light to be cacao, too dark to be maize flour. "It's symbolic money. The powder is probably the vector; the feather is the package. It gives it significance."

"You mean it represents money. I still don't see–"

"There is something carved on it," I said. "What do you think it is?"

Everyone squinted at it. At length, Palli said, doubtfully, "I think it's a hand holding a curved blade."

"I suppose so." Ichtaca didn't sound convinced. "Acatl-tzin, I don't understand…"

But I did. The hand holding a curved blade: the symbol of Itztlacoliuhqui, the Curved Point of Obsidian, god of frost and of justice – as cold and as unyielding as retribution. And the money: a single feather, an offering with the promise of more to come.

A bribe. Justice for a bribe.

Eptli had been greedy and arrogant, thinking money could buy anything and everything – even status. Even the war-council for his trial.

It looked like Xiloxoch's accusations of bribery hadn't been a lie meant to sow chaos amongst us, after all.

Ezamahual rowed me back to the Sacred Precinct in silence, but steadfastly refused to leave me alone after that. "You're in no state to walk, Acatl-tzin," he pointed out, his eyes averted from mine, but with an utterly stubborn expression on his face.

I gave in – we could have argued for hours, and I was feeling none too steady at the moment, as if I were still standing in the boat on the water. "Fine. Let's go to the Duality House."

I found the Duality House in an unusual state of feverish activity: in addition to the crowd of supplicants gathered at the gates, the clergy seemed to be busy. Sober-faced priests and priestesses carried armloads of fruit and flower garlands from the storehouse to the shrine in the centre, and every entrance-curtain seemed to be drawn open, revealing small but fervent gatherings – two or three priests crouching on the ground, listening to the orator in the centre with focused intensity. What sent my hackles up, though, weren't the priests, but the dozen Jaguar warriors among them – leaning against frescoes, casually hefting worship-thorns in callused, bloodied hands, and generally doing their best to appear innocuous, their visit merely a coincidence in the grand scheme of things.

I wasn't fooled, and I very much doubted Tizoc-tzin would be, either.

Mihmatini was in her rooms, and received me almost immediately. Under the feather headdress, her face was pale and drawn, the lines at the corners of her eyes making her seem much older than her twenty years.

"Acatl. Yaotl told me you were alive, thank the Duality." I'd expected a verbal flaying, but she merely sounded relieved.

"What's going on?" I asked.

"They're looking for Teomitl," Mihmatini said.

"Who isn't here." Yaotl had already told me he'd left.

"No," Mihmatini said. She exhaled, slowly and deliberately – an easy expression to read.

"I'm not the first one to ask."

Her gaze was bright, desperate. "No. The She-Snake was here."

Trust the She-Snake to always be near the heart of intrigues, but never quite embroiled in them. Careful and measured, like his father before him: the power in the shadows, never challenged or besmirched. "What else did he say?"

"You already know it."

"No," I said. "I'm not a calendar priest, and I've always been abysmal at divination. Tell me."

"He said… to be careful. That Teomitl was playing a dangerous game, and that we could lose everything." Her hand wandered to her cheek, scratched it. "And I said I didn't know what game, and he left." Her eyes wouldn't meet mine.

"But you know." And hadn't told me – I suspected perhaps not even admitted it to herself. Then again, had I been any better? I'd received enough warnings – both in signs and speeches – and hadn't heeded any of them.

"There have been…" Mihmatini shook her head, angrily. "The Duality curse me, I'm not about to behave like some gutless and bloodless fool. There have been signs, Acatl. Visitors at Neutemoc's house – Jaguar warriors and veterans, and too many noblemen to be relatives concerned with our old welfare. And an old woman, several times."

"An old woman?"

"Yes. Why are you interested in that? I would have thought the warriors were more significant."

"Significant, but not unexpected." My hands had clenched into fists; I forced them to open again – relaxed, carefree. "The old woman – you might know that when he almost died of the sickness, it was Toci's magic which saved his life."

Toci. Grandmother Earth. The aged, ageless woman; the bountiful and damaged earth that we broke anew with every stroke of our digging sticks. Most of Her devotees were women past their prime – the younger ones tended to call on the more youthful Xochiquetzal, like the courtesan Xiloxoch; the men chose other deities altogether.

"But I don't see what this has to do with anything," Mihmatini said, slowly and carefully, as if she stood on the edge of a great chasm, listening to the whistle of the wind in her ears.

"I don't know," I said. Gods help me, I didn't know. I just didn't like any of it. First, Jade Skirt's magic; now Teomitl's odd behaviour.

"Well, you might be content with that, but I intend to find out what's going on." Her hands shook, and for a moment there was a glimmer of tears in her eyes. "He always gets into scrapes bigger than he is. I… I need him back, Acatl."

"We'll find him," I said. "He's still my responsibility, remember?"

"You don't act like he is."

"He's my student, not my child," I said – and immediately regretted it: by becoming his wife and tying her garment to his, Mihmatini had taken on the responsibilities of both sexual partner and mother to him – nourishing him just as his mother had once done.

My sister grimaced, but said nothing, even though it cost her. I mentally vowed to have pointed words with Teomitl – plotting the gods knew what against his brother was one thing, but giving his wife sleepless nights quite another.

But I did need to check one thing, before it cost me my own night's sleep. "I need to ask," I said, spreading my hands in a gesture of apology. "Has he been talking about his brother to you – about our choice of Revered Speaker?"

"Not in complimentary terms, no…" Her voice trailed off, and she looked at me. "Acatl."

Much as I wished to, I couldn't lie to her. "You know what he wanted, more than anything else; you heard him as well as me. He wants things now, not five or ten years into the future."

"But…"

I couldn't think of any comforting lies. "We need to find him."

"Be my guest," Mihmatini said with a touch of anger. "He's hidden himself well."

Leaving all of us exposed – and the Duality House to become the rallying point for the discontent. Oh, gods – when I caught the fool I was going to pinch his ribs, hard. "I hadn't come here for Teomitl, originally."

"He does have a way of taking over conversations even when absent," Mihmatini said, her voice expressionless and flat – like glass, a moment before it shattered. "What did you want?"

"Two things. The plague–"

Mihmatini snorted. "Quenami is in charge, and making a mess out of it. Then again, he doesn't listen to half the things I'm saying."

So – panicked, but still not smart enough to see my sister as talented. "He's a fool."

"I don't care." Mihmatini's voice was grim. "Whatever he is, he's failed at containing this. That's his biggest fault to me."

"It's bad, isn't it?" I asked, cautiously – though I already knew the answer.

"As bad as it can get. Yaotl probably told you it's starting to spread within Tenochtitlan."

The last thing we needed. "Yes," I said, carefully, "Some of my priests might come by, later. We have an idea for a cure."

Mihmatini's gaze snapped up sharply.

"I don't want to give you false hope," I said. "It's quite possible it won't work at all."

"It's still going to be better than whatever Quenami's come up with," Mihmatini snorted. "And what was the second thing you came for?"

It took me a moment to remember what she was talking about. "Oh. Xiloxoch."

"The courtesan?" Mihmatini gave it some thought.

"Teomitl said he was going to arrest her, remember?"

"I do." Mihmatini puffed her cheeks, thinking. "I haven't heard any news – wait." She rose, and pulled the entrance-curtain to her chambers open. "Yaotl!"

"Mistress?" Yaotl came in wearing his palace vestment – an elegant, richly embroidered cloak – and streaks of blue and black across his cheeks.

"Acatl wants to know what we have on Xiloxoch."

Yaotl looked startled. "Nothing that I know of." He thought, for a while. "She did make an accusation against Eptli."

"When?" I asked. I hadn't thought she'd had time to see the judges before Tizoc-tzin worked himself into a rage over the clergy of Tlaloc.

"Before the clergy of Tlaloc was hauled in. For all the good it did her… It was dismissed summarily, like all the cases that didn't concern Acamapichtli's clergy."

Mihmatini shook her head. "She's a wily one. Neza-hual-tzin probably neglected to tell you she's been serving her goddess well."

Not surprising, though it was heartening to have a confirmation my suspicions were headed somewhere. "I presume she's been keeping an eye on the interests of Xochiquetzal while the Quetzal Flower is in exile from Tenochtitlan."

"That's what my priests have confirmed, yes," Mihmatini said. The Duality House was also the centre of a network of spies and magicians, whose only goal was to safeguard the balance. Her predecessor, Ceyaxochitl, had used this to terrific effect. Clearly, Mihmatini was learning fast.

"And this means?"

"Now? Nothing much," Mihmatini said. "It looks as though she's just watching and waiting."

"But you don't think she's involved in the plague."

"I haven't said that."

"I see." I thought of the snapped quill again. I couldn't see why Xochiquetzal would ally Herself with Chalchiutlicue, but the evidence spoke against Xiloxoch. "I need to find her."

Yaotl shrugged. "Try the palace. She'll be there – too canny not to be."

"Where is she?"

"I don't know. I'd try the palace, if I were you. If she wants to keep an eye on the Flower Quetzal's interests, she'll have to be at the heart of things."

Not the first place I wanted to come back to, especially with the plague raging within its walls. But still... I didn't have much choice.

Ezamahual didn't leave my side as we walked out of the Duality House. I leant on the cane, grateful for its support – but the Southern Hummingbird strike me if I was going to accept help from one of my priests.

"I'm going inside the palace," I said to Ezamahual. "You might want to leave."

He looked at me as if I were mad. "It's not a safe place," I explained, feeling increasingly flustered.

His look was the patient one of a mother towards a wayward child. "You're High Priest, Acatl-tzin. I wouldn't dream of leaving you alone."

Great, so much for that.

I half-expected the guards to challenge us as we climbed the stairs towards the entrance, but they seemed more bored than busy, leaning on their obsidian-tipped spears while gazing at the sky, looking through us, half-expecting us to provide some distraction. But we both looked like ordinary priests for the Dead, on errands that could only be menial – nothing worth salvaging from that, no fun or currency to be had.

Inside, the palace seemed empty and forlorn, the usual crowds subdued and silent, hurrying from courtyard to courtyard without looking up. A few artisans crept by looking as if they were trying to make themselves forgotten about altogether, and the judges and clerks walking with codices under their arms didn't look much more reassured, either.

I directed us towards the part of the palace where the young warriors usually congregated, thinking to catch if not Xiloxoch, someone who would tell me where she was – or perhaps our wayward Teomitl, who would laugh and toss his head back, and assure me that Mihmatini and I were being foolish with our suspicions. He would make it all go away, like an image in a darkened obsidian mirror…

We reached a smaller courtyard, which doubled as an aviary: wooden cages with quetzal birds surrounded a fountain. The gurgle of the water mingled with the harsh cries of the birds, the glimmer of sunlight playing off against the iridescent sheen on their emerald tail-feathers.

A warrior stood in front of the fountain, gazing into the water. He had his back to us, but even so, I would have recognised him anywhere: that arrogant, casual tilt of the head, that falsely contemplative pose... except that it was all subtly wrong, distorted as through layers of water.

"My Lord?" I asked.

Nezahual-tzin didn't move.

"My Lord?" A little higher-pitched – and a little more desperate. I could have dealt with his usual sarcastic, careless remarks, but at this moment I might as well have been talking to a stone effigy. I moved to the other side of the fountain and met his gaze, which was slightly vacant, as if he weren't quite *there*. I extended my priest-senses – wincing at the effort. There was a slight trace of magic; a touch of something. Not sickly and spread out like underworld magic, but instead firm and strong, as unmoving as a rock or as the Heavens above us.

"It's all in the water," Nezahual-tzin said. The vacuous smile on his face was so uncharacteristic I wanted to shake it out of him. "Can't you see?"

"No."

He smiled – dazzling, mindless. "He's coming, Acatl. He's coming. Neither walls nor lines on the ground – neither rivers nor marshes were enough to hold him – not even a fisherman's net."

I didn't waste time asking who "he" was. Instead, I rubbed at the scabs on my earlobes until they came loose, and said a short prayer to Lord Death, asking Him to grant me true sight.

As I'd thought, Nezahual-tzin was saturated with the dark brown of Toci's touch – a veil that hung around him like the vapour of the sweatbath, billowing in the warm breeze, lazily unfurling deeper hues of brown; the smell

277

of churned mud and dry, cracking earth, and in the distance, the faint cry of warriors fighting each other, for Grandmother Earth was also the Woman of Discord, She who brought on the wars we needed to survive.

What had happened to him?

He was still staring into the water, his grey eyes – a feature I'd always found uncanny – even more distant than usual, as if the fountain held the answers he'd always wanted. He was at rest, in a relaxed, non-threatening way that made my skin crawl. And where were his warriors – where was the escort, suitable for a Revered Speaker of the Triple Alliance…?

My gaze, roaming, found his hands – and the familiar, trembling haze of freshly-shed lifeblood. "They're dead," I said aloud. "Your warriors. Aren't they? Killed to cast the spell."

For a long, agonising moment, I thought he wasn't going to answer, but then, he looked up at me, his face cast into an expressionless mask once again – almost like the Nezahual-tzin of old. "Opened up like poinsettia flowers. Such speed and efficiency. One wouldn't think she'd be so fast…" His voice trailed off, and his gaze went down, towards the water.

She? Was it the same old woman who had visited Teomitl so often? What part did she play in this, other than seemingly ensorcelling two of the most important men in the Triple Alliance?

"Acatl-tzin," Ezamahual said. "What shall we do?"

I cast a glance around the courtyard. It was deserted, well away from the usual rush of people within the palace. But still…

His own people would probably know what to do with him, but they'd all be in the official residence of the

Revered Speaker of Texcoco – literally next door to our own Revered Speaker's apartments, high on the list of places to avoid in the palace. Still… He'd been helpful, if only in his usual, cryptic fashion, and my conscience balked at the idea of just leaving him here.

"Let's bring you home," I said to Nezahual-tzin. "Someone there will probably have a better idea of what to do."

We all but had to drag him away from the fountain, but once we were away from the water he relaxed in our grasp and seemed to follow us – more, I suspected, because he had nowhere else to go than out of any desire on his part.

"What's wrong with him?" Ezamahual asked.

"It's obviously a spell," I said, curtly. "But I have no idea how to dispel it." And, more importantly of where and how he had managed to get it cast on himself. What was its purpose? Simply to prevent Nezahual-tzin from tracking the mysterious summoner of Toci's magic? Did his pronouncements make sense, or were they just part of the delirium of the spell?

I didn't like any of this – then again, it wasn't as if the previous days had been particularly relaxing or likeable.

The Revered Speaker's chambers were in a large court-yard, on the first floor of a building which also hosted the war council, the council of officials that had elected him and that oversaw most of the daily life of Tenochtitlan, from religious worship to problems of architecture and city layout. On the first floor, three entrance-curtains marked the rooms of the Revered Speakers of Tlacopan, Texcoco and Tenochtitlan. The platform was overcrowded by warriors, and the general atmosphere was tense – none of the She-Snake's black-clad guards could be seen anywhere, and the warriors appeared to be arguing among themselves. In the courtyard, the crowd seemed to be dispatched in small groups, talking among themselves in hushed voices, throwing us harsh glances as we passed them by. The atmosphere was tense, as taut as a rope about to fray.

We made our way upstairs without being challenged. Nezahual-tzin drew a few passing glances, but no one seemed to know his face well enough, or at least they considered him not important enough. His gaze kept roaming – caught by the jade-coloured cloak of a veteran warrior, by the darkening blue of the sky above us, the smoke of copal incense hanging in the air, almost intense enough to be frightening.

There were two warriors on guard at the entrance-curtain of Nezahual-tzin's rooms; they only took a look at us and waved us through.

Inside, the chambers were as I remembered them: colourful frescoes of Quetzalcoatl the Feathered Serpent, depicting His descent into the underworld, the founding of His city of Tollan, and His departure onto the Eastern Sea on a raft of snakes – everything obscured by the potent haze of copal incense mixed with herbs and spices, a mixture that always made my head spin. I suspected Nezahual-tzin used it for entering divine trances, and wouldn't have been surprised to learn it had *teonanacatl* and *peyotl* mixed in – two hallucinogenic widely used by most priesthoods, but frowned upon by my own. One did not need trances or dreams to be reminded of the reality of death.

The low-backed chair – Nezahual-tzin's throne – was empty, the jaguar pelts on the dais meticulously cleaned by the slaves, who scattered away from us as we went deeper into the room.

Nezahual-tzin's breath had quickened; around him, something glimmered – the shadow of a great snake, slowly unfolding through my and Ezamahual's body, maw wide open, the feathers of its collar slowly gaining substance as we got nearer to the throne. The air was as thick as tar – tense, not with human intrigue, but with the growing presence of a god in the Fifth World.

Nezahual-tzin had gone completely limp, his eyes closed, lolling in our grip, much heavier than I'd thought possible. The snake came streaming out of his mouth, rearing its head through Nezahual-tzin's boyish face – the scales mingling with the skin, the feathers becoming the feather headdress at his nape, yet somehow larger and more defined. The only sound we could hear was Nezahual-tzin's quickening breath – far too fast for any-thing mortal.

The god Quetzalcoatl was trying to help his agent somehow; the one thing I did know was that we couldn't afford to be there when it happened. The Feathered Serpent might be the most compassionate of all the gods, but he was still a god – disinclined to take mortal frailty into account, especially when in a rush to dispel another god's interference.

I gestured for Ezamahual to hurry – we crossed the last few steps to the dais in what seemed an eternity, and dropped more than deposited Nezahual-tzin in his chair. Then we withdrew as fast as possible.

For a few moments, it seemed as though nothing would happen. The snake continued to solidify, some-what haphazardly – lidless eyes taking the place of Nezahual-tzin's grey ones; fangs appearing within the maw, as white as pearls fished from the depths. And then it reared up – not leaving the confines of Nezahual-tzin's body as I'd thought it would, but instead jerking the body upwards like a children's doll – there was a distinct crunch made by bones cracking, and Nezahual-tzin's head bent backwards at an angle that should have been impossible to maintain for a live human being. His eyes opened – and they were white, opalescent as a distant star, and his mouth was peppered with fangs, glistening with venom, the feathers of his headdress flaring outwards like a flower blossoming. He screamed, arms flailing and then falling down abruptly, released from the pressure that had held them – and then he crumpled like a rag on the dais, the snake fading away to nothingness.

I let out a breath I hadn't even been aware of holding. "My Lord?"

His breath again, loud, ragged. Gently, slowly, he pulled himself upright, his face paler than usual, but regaining colour with every passing moment until it was once more the dark of cacao beans. His eyes narrowed, the vulnerability gone in a moment, dispelled by a supreme effort of will. "Acatl. I see."

I didn't think he did. Ezamahual and I had both witnessed his weakness, and no amount of pretence would remove that fact. "Can you tell us what happened?"

Nezahual-tzin grimaced. "Not in so many words, no."

"You were in trance in front of a fountain," I pointed out. I glanced at Ezamahual; he had thrown himself facedown on the ground. Oh, gods, I should have remembered – Ezamahual was peasant through and through, and he'd walked with enough reticence through the palace. "Ezamahual, get up," I said.

"He's Revered Speaker…"

"And you're a priest of the Mexica. You don't answer to him."

"Not quite, but as a ruler of the Triple Alliance, I do appreciate the respect," Nezahual-tzin said. I threw him a warning glance strong enough to sear the feathers of his headdress, and he smiled back at me. "But Acatl is right. We can't possibly have any kind of conversation with you lying flat on the floor. Also, you did carry me from the fountain." He paused on "fountain", looking at me again, expecting further explanation.

I shrugged. "I don't have much to add. I met you earlier in the palace and you wanted to track down the user of Toci's magic."

"I remember that." Nezahual-tzin's voice was considered. "Not senile yet, you know. Quite the reverse, in fact."

As befitted a devotee of the Feathered Serpent, god of Wisdom and Knowledge. I doubted he'd ever have many memory problems. But, if another goddess had interfered...

"You lost two warriors," I said. "I suspect they were sacrificed to put the spell on you."

"I see." He raised his hands, looked at them in the light. His face had gone hard. "And what are you doing in the palace?"

"Looking for Xiloxoch," I said, as bluntly as he'd asked. "And for Teomitl."

"You'll have gathered there are better places to be, in the current context."

I would have pointed out that he'd stayed within – but of course he was Quetzalcoatl's agent, and probably immune to the plague altogether. "My sister told me Xiloxoch would be in the palace, but I couldn't find her."

"I'm not surprised." Nezahual-tzin's voice was curt. "I can enquire after her."

I shook my head. I'd already stumbled up the stairs of

283

Tizoc-tzin's private chambers with the Revered Speaker of Texcoco – a man I'd been accused of collusion with a few months before. The last thing I needed in this time of paranoia was more fuel for that particular accusation to surface again.

Though it might be too late for that. "Don't bother," I said. "We'll find her ourselves, if she's in the palace."

Nezahual-tzin frowned. "I dislike unpaid debts."

Which might or might not be true; I didn't know him well enough to say. He probably had an interest in investigating all of this, though I couldn't think why – and we wouldn't find out until it suited him to reveal his intentions. "Well," I said – half-suspecting I would end up regretting this, "you can look for Teomitl."

Nezahual-tzin's grimace was almost comical – but then what he was saying sank in. "I can't involve myself with this."

"Why not?"

His gaze was level. "You know why, Acatl. I gave fair hints, but I can't do more. Tizoc-tzin is Revered Speaker of the Mexica, my peer in the Triple Alliance. What I think of him – doesn't play a part."

"You're not saying–"

"I'm saying what we all know. Teomitl has always been frustrated by his brother's behaviour. I wouldn't blame him for attempting to displace him, but I can't condone the attempt."

"I can't either," I said. "I want him stopped before this foolishness takes its course." I wasn't even sure if that was the reason he had disappeared; if my worst fears were true and he had finally set himself irrevocably on this – at odds with the safety of the Fifth World – and with me. I–

"As I said–" Nezahual-tzin shook his head. "I can't take part in this."

Because – because, when and if the dust settled, and we had a new Revered Speaker, he needed to have remained neutral in order to ingratiate himself to whoever it turned out to be. "You have neither face nor heart." The words – the insult – were out of my mouth before I could think.

Nezahual-tzin watched me, and said nothing. "Will that be all?"

Why had I ever thought he could help in anything? I bowed, sarcastically, before my temper could fray any further. "That will be all, my Lord."

I was so annoyed by the conversation with Nezahual-tzin that we went through several courtyards before I became aware the world was swimming again around me.

Oh no, not again. What was wrong with me? This time, Lord Death hadn't touched me, and there were no shadows nearby.

And yet… I had the same hollow in my stomach, the same slight sense of nausea, as if the Fifth World would tear itself apart at any moment – as if we danced on the brink of the abyss, unaware that the slightest step out of place would send us all tumbling down into darkness.

Ezamahual seemed unconcerned – in all likelihood, he wasn't sensitive enough; he hadn't been there last year atop the Great Temple, when the hole in the Fifth World had gaped open, and I'd almost collapsed.

But why here, of all places?

Xiloxoch was not among the young warriors laughing and lounging near the steambaths. For that matter, neither was Teomitl, though the startled looks I got when asking about them looked slightly too guilty for my own peace of mind.

One warrior, though, remembered Xiloxoch had come by, and had walked off in the direction of the prisoners' quarters – which was a better lead than no lead at all.

As we walked back to the prisoners' quarters, leaving behind the bustle of the various courts, the sense of oppression didn't diminish. If anything, it became worse, pressing against my chest, making the air in my lungs sear. I felt as if my skin were sloughing off, coming away in flakes and whole pieces, and there was a vague sense of something, just beyond the borders of my perception – something huge and unspeakable that would swoop in at any moment, taking me with it.

"Ezamahual?" I asked through gritted teeth.

His face swam out of the darkness, eyes wide open in concern. "Is something wrong, Acatl-tzin?"

Yes. No. Why was I the only one to feel this? "Yes. I need – to – stop for a while."

I staggered into the nearest courtyard – which was next to the book-house and, at this late hour of the day, filled only with a few astronomers, staring thoughtfully at papers laid on the ground.

"Forgive my imprudence," I said to the one who seemed the eldest – a wizened old man who was tracing glyphs within the grid of a calendar. "I need to cast a spell." Even the cane felt heavy in my hand. "It's – somewhat pressing."

He looked up at me. "To Lord Death?" I nodded. "Just do it away from the book-house, will you?"

We walked away from the book-house, to a relatively quiet part of the courtyard. One of the astronomers got up, throwing me a sympathetic glance, and went to sit closer to his companion.

I laid the cane aside for the spell; to my surprise, I could stand well enough without it, with barely a tremor in my legs. Then I slashed my earlobes with my obsidian knife, and carefully drew a circle on the ground in my own blood, calling on Lord Death to bless this place – where my blood met the ground, the stone hissed like a scalded jaguar – the magic of Mictlantecuhtli Lord Death meeting that of the Southern Hummingbird.

> *"Only here on earth, in the Fifth World,*
> *Shall the flowers last, shall the songs be bliss,*
> *Though it be feathers, though it be jade,*
> *It too must go to the region of the fleshless…"*

Silence seemed to spread from within the circle, along with a green, sickly light which oozed from beneath the ground, like sulphur from the cracks of a volcano. And when it touched me – when it wrapped itself around me, cocooning me in a magic as familiar as my own blood, my own skin – I breathed in a sigh of relief.

We set out from the courtyard. I was still leaning on the cane for support, but I found it much easier to breathe. The familiar magic of the underworld wrapped around me, as intoxicating as *peyotl* or *teonanacatl* – stretched, dry emptiness I'd known all my life, the hollow taste of grief, the sharp tang of our own mortality, a gulf in my stomach.

Even so, the pressure remained: a thickening of the air, a slight buzzing in my ears that got worse as we approached the prisoners' quarters.

Within, the atmosphere – reverent, distant – remained the same; the prisoners watched us warily, as if our mere presence was enough to shatter the peace. One of them was playing the flute, a simple, haunting sound which climbed higher and higher like a cry of devotion.

All of this lasted for no more than a handful of breaths – and then the peace was shattered by loud voices. A man and a woman – the woman was Xiloxoch, but I couldn't place the second voice, though I knew I'd heard it before. They both came from within a building – in fact, the very building that had hosted the unfortunate Zoquitl; the conversation sounded… animated, to say the least.

"I know my rights." Xiloxoch's voice was low and almost toneless. "You should go away."

"And why would I do that?" The man's voice whipped through the air like a sword's blade.

If there was an answer, I didn't wait to hear it. I flung open the entrance-curtain with as much force as I could muster – gods, I hated melodramatic entrances, but I had to concede they weren't without effect.

They both turned, then, to look at me. One, as I had known, was Xiloxoch, wearing a drab tunic and skirt like a demure housewife; the other was Pochtic – Master of the House of Darkness, his face still swathed in bandages, his skin sallow against the vibrant colours of his feather headdress.

"Well, well." His voice was deeply mocking. "Our High Priest for the Dead. You're too late; they've taken the corpse away."

"I was aware of that," I said, but didn't elaborate. "What are you doing here?"

Xiloxoch shook her head. "I know my rights," she said, again. In her hands was a golden trinket, shaped in the likeness of the Fifth Sun.

The things of the dead man: taken by the courtesan who had ministered to him and thus customary for sacrifices. "Only if you slept with him," I said. "Did you?"

"I brought him comfort," Xiloxoch said. Her hands tightened around the trinket. What was so important about it?

And, more pressingly, what was Pochtic doing here? "The work of the Master of the House of Darkness," I said, very slowly, "doesn't include the care of prisoners."

Pochtic threw me a pitying glance. "A prisoner died, and both I and Coatl were attacked."

"Coatl is ill," I said, slowly. "It's not quite the same."

"He's right." Xiloxoch's voice was malicious – the trickster, closing people's eyes with burning coals, stirring up filth and ashes. "You shouldn't be here. Neither you nor Coatl." She spat the word. "Not after what you did."

"I can't speak for Coatl, but you're mistaken–"

"Am I?" Xiloxoch opened her hands, angling them so that the light coming in through the entrance curtain glimmered on the gold, so that, for a moment, everything shone as yellow as the Fifth Sun. "Gold and jade; precious stones, precious stones. Was that all it took, my Lord?"

Pochtic's bandages shifted; his lips tightened in pain. "You will not speak to me like this."

"Why not?" Her voice was mocking. "Will you call me a whore and despise me, like they all do? I am a priestess, too." She threw her head back, her long hair shifting like a cascade of crows' feathers; for a moment, she was bathed in a warm, pulsing radiance that wasn't hers – something that smelled of the jungle, humid and primal, the odour of churned earth, of rutting beasts, and of jaguars slithering in the shadows, just out of sight.

Even through the bandages, I saw Pochtic's eyes narrow. "Your… goddess…" he spoke the term as if it were an insult, "doesn't frighten me."

Xiloxoch smiled, licking her lips, her teeth wide, and as black as obsidian. "Pity. Try another god, then. Itztlacoliuhqui."

The Curved Point of Obsidian, god of frost and ice, and of blind justice – of victims lashing out in pain, back at their tormentors. "You have nothing," Pochtic said. He brushed off some invisible dust from his clothes, and walked out without a word for either of us.

Xiloxoch spat on the ground. "As wily as a beast."

I watched Pochtic's back – remembered the tense set of his hands, the false assurance in his voice. He might have been no better than an animal, as uncultivated as fallow fields, following the roads of the deer and the rabbit, but he was something else, too: scared.

Because of the plague? But he had not been among its victims. And why come here, to see the prisoners? Was he hoping to find an explanation into deaths that shouldn't have been concerning him?

Huitzilpochtli strike me down, why was everyone running scared?

"I need to talk to you," I said to Xiloxoch.

She sighed, raising her eyebrows as if it were a performance within her temple. "If you must."

I opened my hand – the one that wasn't clenched around the cane – to reveal the twisted feather stem, still wrapped in a cotton cloth.

Xiloxoch looked at the feather for a while. Her face was expressionless – remote, as distant as if she were the goddess herself. "What of it?"

"You know what this is."

She shrugged. "Not in so many words."

"Then you're a liar," I said. "Because I knew what this was as soon as I saw it, and I'm not that knowledgeable."

Xiloxoch's lips turned downwards, a small, dainty grimace. "Fine. It's a broken feather stem, like the ones that hold gold dust. It was used as the vector for a spell."

"And you had nothing to do with this?" I asked.

"Why should I have anything to do with it?"

"Money. Bribes. What Eptli gave to the judges. It would have been poetic, wouldn't it, if he had died by touching tainted money? Worthy of flowers and songs, all the way to the underworld."

Xiloxoch's face shifted – reducing itself to a single, powerful emotion that was gone in an instant. Anger, or fear? "I can tell you what I see, not how to interpret it."

Still evading me? "I need interpretations," I said, dryly. "That's what we thrive on. For instance, tell me what kind of illness would kill Eptli and Zoquitl – and then spread to all our warriors?"

"You're mistaken."

"I see," I said. "You protect your goddess's interests, but I don't know what She wants."

Xiloxoch's lips were curled in anger. "I can swear this to you: I have nothing to do with this."

"As Pochtic had nothing to do with the bribe."

That, if nothing else did, went straight to her guts. "Pochtic is an arrogant fool, and one day he'll get what he deserves."

Not while Tizoc-tzin was Revered Speaker. Something of what I thought must have shown on my face, for Xiloxoch said, "Tizoc-tzin isn't eternal."

I surely hoped so – no one was, even those returned from the world of the gods – but... I watched her face, the carefully blank expression. Something wasn't quite right. "Are you saying he's vulnerable to the plague, like everyone else?"

Her eyes narrowed – a fraction too long – before she shook her head. "Just that he's mortal, like the rest of us. You, of all people, should know."

I did know – all too well. But that wasn't the point. She'd said that he wasn't eternal with a definite tone – as if Tizoc-tzin's death were weeks or days away, not years ahead of us.

As if… "Where is Teomitl?" I asked. The words were out of my mouth before I could stop them.

Xiloxoch shook her head. "Teomitl? I don't know, Acatl-tzin. I haven't seen him since the tribunal." And her voice sounded utterly sincere – curious, even, I could see her mind working, wondering how she could take the best advantage of this.

"You haven't," I said, flatly. Then who had Teomitl teamed up with? What in the gods' name did he think he was doing?

Xiloxoch smiled. "No. Did you have any other questions, Acatl-tzin?"

I didn't. I toyed with seizing her, there and then, but whatever was going on was obviously bigger than a single courtesan; if I'd started to arrest everyone who seemed to have a connection with the plague, I'd never have stopped.

"Till we meet again." Her voice was low, mocking, as she walked away.

I stood for a while, breathing in the atmosphere of the courtyard, which was as thick as tar, and filled my lungs with hot, dusty wind. The feeling of being observed and weighed had diminished, but only because I was protected. Something – something was wrong here. And either Xiloxoch or Pochtic – or both – had known it.

I walked among the prisoners until I found Cuixtli, the Mextitlan man who had given us Xiloxoch's name. He was sitting cross-legged on the ground, in an attitude of meditation, hands outstretched, eyes open but looking at nothing in the Fifth World.

Cuixtli didn't look up as I approached, but when my skin brushed a little too close to him, the magic of my protections hissed like a snake about to strike, and Cuixtli shook his head, annoyed. His eyes slowly focused on me. "Priest."

"I have this privilege, yes."

"Why are you here?" Cuixtli unfolded his lanky body, and stood, looking up at the sky. The Fifth Sun had set, and only a glimmer of His light remained in the world; in the courtyard, servants moved to light up the braziers, filling the air with the scent of smoke. "Why are any of you here?"

I shrugged. "We're trying to help you. Find out what's going on."

His smile was pitying. "You help yourself, priest. I – or the others for that matter – have no interest in solving mysteries."

Of course not – to one who would be with the Fifth Sun soon, honoured as a god, why should any of the Fifth World matter? "I'm not sure," I said, slowly. "Something is wrong in this courtyard. You might not be safe here."

"Do Mexica not respect those who offer their lives?"

"I don't know." As Teomitl had said, they were the worthiest men – the ones selfless and brave enough to give their lives for the continuation of the Fifth World. And yet – yet they were captured foreigners, not from

Tenochtitlan, not even from Tlatelolco. Many would see them as nothing more than tools, faceless sacrifices, living witnesses to the greatness and glory of the Mexica Empire. "The Duality curse me, I don't know. Why were they here, Cuixtli?"

His face was contemplative. "The official and the courtesan?" He pursed his lips. "Much for the same reason, I should imagine."

"What, to gather Zoquitl's things?"

"The official obsessively searched every corner of this courtyard for something he wouldn't name. But I think he was checking spells."

Spells. Spells to do what? "What do you mean?" I asked, as a fist of ice tightened around my heart.

"You are High Priest, are you not? One of the three who determine the destiny of your Empire, of your Alliance."

If only. "Perhaps."

"Then you should see it." He rose, fluid and silent, almost inhuman, like a bird gliding through the air – and before I could stop him he had laid his hand on mine, at the level of the scars from my blood offerings. When he touched me, they pulsed, and my skin crinkled and reddened like copper in the fire. But there was no pain. Only a distant hiss in my ears, and then the sense of the world falling away from me, as I stood high above the earth, held by some impossibly distant star, except I hadn't moved, I was still standing in the courtyard, still looking at the adobe walls with their rich frescoes, the gods shifting and turning until even I could no longer recognise them – their coloured faces merging with one another's, the rich backgrounds running like raindrops until the walls were once more blank, leaving nothing but a couple of glyphs, stark red against the paleness of the adobe.

A pyramid temple, with flames coming out of its shrine; a slave's wooden collar and paper clothes; a heart struck in four bleeding pieces...

May your reign not last: may the cities you hold fall one after the other. May everything you start turn against you, wither into dust, into filth. May you be left without faces or hearts, thrown in the mud with the god's shackles weighing you down...

And it all shone green, the green of algae, of jade – the same light that filled Teomitl's eyes from corner to corner when he got angry.

Jade Skirt's magic.

My hand hadn't left the cane; but I held it so tight my fingers hurt. "How long has that been in the courtyard?"

Cuixtli shrugged. "I don't know."

"But you could see it."

"No." He smiled. "I can see *you*, priest. I can see the way the magic pushes against you, looking for another way in. It's touched you before, hasn't it?"

The plague. The night of fever, the squirming bodies pressed against mine – the pain like nails scraping corn from my belly. "I'm not entirely sure I see what you mean." What was I doing, taking advice from a foreign warrior – one of our sworn enemies?

No. I was being ridiculous. That he was a warrior or a foreigner had ceased to matter: days before his sacrifice, he stood above us, below us – closer to the world of the gods than any priest or sorcerer.

I walked, slowly, painfully to the walls, ran my hands on them – felt the magic deep within, quivering with anger and rage, like waves in a stormy lake – felt it shiver at my touch as though it recognised me – like a jaguar scenting a wounded prey. "And you think they were here for the spells."

Cuixtli didn't answer for a while. "The official was clearly looking for them, though they didn't affect him as badly as they did you."

Spells of rage and anger, to unseat the Mexica Empire – to unseat Tizoc-tzin. Who hated us enough for this?

Xiloxoch, or Yayauhqui. I didn't think Itamatl had had enough rage in him for this.

"And the courtesan?" Cuixtli had disapproved of Xiloxoch.

"I don't know. She might just be what she seems, picking up Zoquitl's things."

"But–?" I asked, hearing the scepticism in his voice.

Cuixtli shrugged. "She brims with magic, too – and she's far too curious."

I nodded. "Do you think she has something to do with the spell?"

Cuixtli's hands pointed, briefly, towards the wall. "I don't know. Whoever drew this is angry. They want justice."

Justice for what? For the Empire? For Eptli's transgression? The Duality take me, I had even fewer answers than before.

SIXTEEN
The Gates of the Fifth World

On the way out of the palace, I met Yayauhqui, the Tlatelolca merchant. He was at the head of a group of similarly-clad men, carrying heavy baskets bulging with clothes.

"Acatl-tzin, what a surprise."

I wasn't altogether sure it was a coincidence; I was uncomfortably reminded of Nezahual-tzin's warnings about the Tlatelolca. "What are you doing here?"

Yayauhqui shrugged. "Paying tribute."

"I didn't know you did that."

"Ordinarily, no. But our governor has had... an accident."

"What kind of accident?"

Yayauhqui gestured at the palace. "The same kind of incident you have within, I'd guess. He's very ill."

That didn't seem to fit in with the Tlatelolca plot – unless they were punishing the governor for collaborating with the Mexica? "You know more about this than you're telling us."

Yayauhqui looked surprised. "No. Why would I?"

"I'm told you were far more than an ordinary warrior of Tlatelolco."

Yayauhqui's face didn't move, save for a slight tightening around the eyes – it was uncanny to see the amount of control he could exert on his own emotions; or, rather, the effort it took him to display any strong feeling. "What if I was?"

"You were of imperial blood," I said, slowly. "And your own family was cast down."

His lips quirked up in a smile. "My family had given up on me long before that, Acatl-tzin. Any branch that bore no flower was pruned at the roots."

"And you'll still pretend to me Tlatelolco's defeat meant nothing to you?"

Yayauhqui's face did not move. "Of course not. I've already told you what I think about that. But, really, what does it change whether I was of imperial blood or not? Do you think it's no less the city of merchants and peasants than it was that of the Imperial Family?"

My own parents had been the first to praise the wars we waged – and to feel proud of what our warriors achieved. "You're right," I said, slowly. "But still – you had more of a stake in the existence of Tlatelolco as an independent city-state."

Yayauhqui shrugged. "We can argue politics for a while, but we'd both be bored."

As usual, his perception of his opponent bordered on the uncanny. "Humour me," I said.

"What do you want to know? Personally, I think Moquihuix-tzin was a fool." He must have seen the shock on my face, for he laughed. "He wasn't my brother or my uncle; just a distant cousin. And yes, most of us knew, or suspected what he was up to."

"Which was? "

"The plot." He snorted. "Moquihuix truly loved his

city, and I can't blame him for that. But he always had delusions of grandeur – wanting to make us bigger than we could bear. In many ways, he was thinking too much like a Tenochca."

I didn't react to the jab against us. Not that I approved of delusions of grandeur, in any case. "And he failed."

"As I said." Yayauhqui shrugged. "He wanted us to take our place in the Triple Alliance, rather than remain subservient to you."

"And you didn't approve?"

"No, it was a great idea," Yayauhqui said. "But, as I said, it required planning, and strategy, and careful political manoeuvring. Moquihuix planned well, but he counted too much on people's loyalty – thinking everyone loved his city as he did. And he never really stopped to consider that the smallest thing could trip him up."

"His wife?" I said.

He shrugged. "It's old history, but she was no fool. Any man could have seen that, but Moquihuix was too wrapped up in his plans for the future. He had... a presence, something that made people agree with him regardless of what he said; he relied too much on that. You cannot influence people all the time. He saw us at the head of the Triple Alliance, raking in the tribute that went to Tenochtitlan. And of course, he never did listen to anyone who dared to tell him otherwise." His lips quirked up. "I'm afraid I made a poor warrior, Acatl-tzin. I fought for my city, but not for my ruler."

Other people had done the same – were doing the same. But I didn't say so – didn't dare to acknowledge this. "It doesn't change–"

"No, we're agreed." His gaze was almost mocking. "It doesn't change anything. You should recognise that."

But I still couldn't quite resign myself to the idea.

"I'll have payment for Tlatelolco, Acatl-tzin. But not upon mortals: upon the god who betrayed me."

"That's–"

"Blasphemy? Do you truly think I care?" He grimaced. "What can They do to me, that hasn't already been done?" His companions were carrying the baskets into the palace, under the wary eyes of guards.

He looked intense and driven, but not, it seemed, by what preoccupied us all. Still... still, I didn't like the thought of him loose. "Can you stay around the palace for a bit?"

His gaze was withering. "Until you've found out who causes the plague?"

"I can ask more forcefully."

"I have no doubt you can." He sounded almost placid. "Fine, for a bit. I'll be in the merchants' quarters."

And he walked away, humming a song under his breath. I wasn't sure whether I'd successfully confined him, or merely given him a pretext to install himself in the palace.

Ezamahual – who had been silent during the entire conversation – insisted on accompanying me all the way to my house, uncomfortably reminding me of the way Teomitl had nagged at me to get some rest.

In truth, the last thing I wanted to do was rest. Thoughts chased one another in the confines of my mind, each one more panicked and incoherent than the rest. And when sleep finally came, I saw again Teomitl pooling his craft through the canals of Chalchiuhtlicue's country, and heard the hymn of the Blessed Drowned.

"In Tlalocan, the verdant house,
The dead men play at balls, they cast the reeds,
Go forth, go forth to the place of many clouds,
To where the thick mists mark the Blessed Land…"

I woke up. The sky was still dark, but I couldn't sleep anymore. My back ached like that of an old woman, and I fought a twinge of pain when I hauled myself to my feet. The Fifth Sun wasn't yet up, but I nevertheless offered Him my blood, to sustain Him in His fight against the darkness, singing a low hymn under my breath.

I got up, and dressed, finding by touch my wicker chest of clothes, and the spare grey cloak with owls that would mark me as High Priest for the Dead – and the mask lying on the ground after I'd discarded on the previous night. I left the mask hanging on my waist – tying it with a piece of rope – and set out into the Sacred Precinct.

At this hour of the night, all but the most dedicated of pilgrims had left – though torches and braziers still lit up the night, showing the way for the novice priests running around the Serpent Wall. Ahead, on the shadowy mass of the Great Temple, sacrifices were still tumbling down, with the familiar thud of dead bodies coming to rest on the stone at the bottom of the steps. The smell of copal incense hung heavy in the air – and it seemed that everything was right with the world.

If only.

I made my way to my temple, which – of course – wasn't deserted, even this early: further supplicants had come, and offering priests stood in the courtyard, coaxing them into entering one of the examination rooms so they could have a quieter conversation. The pilgrims' faces were taut with fear, their bearing subdued, deliberately muted in order not to draw attention to themselves. I had never been so glad of my grey cloak, which disguised my identity as High Priest: a few of the more adventurous tried to seize me as I moved towards the centre of the courtyard, but I managed to gently direct them towards more available priests.

I repaired to one of the smaller examination rooms, which was currently unused – no bringing the sickness into our own temple. Powdered dust lay thick on the altar, and the image of Mictlantecuhtli looked at me – hollow-eyed, and yet somehow drawing all the light to Himself. My shoulder itched, where He had touched me.

A gift, keeper of the boundaries.

He didn't grant favours, or magic; didn't choose an agent in the Fifth World, or play the power games of the other gods.

And yet... and yet, knowing I was under His gaze was comforting – He was there, waiting for us to come down to Him in the end. He would always be there, and He would never judge, or strike at the unworthy.

"My Lord," I said, aloud. "Thank You."

There was no answer, but I felt a little better after that.

I climbed to the shrine atop the pyramid temple – where, to my surprise, I found Ichtaca still there, sitting behind one of the pillars with the registers of the temple on his knees, staring at the coloured glyphs on the maguey paper as if he could coax them into speaking. He rose, hastily, when my cane scraped on the floor. "Acatl-tzin."

"Did you stay up all night?" I asked.

He shook his head. "I couldn't sleep."

"You and me both," I said, sombrely. "Something is going on in the palace, on top of everything else." I explained, briefly, what I'd felt in the courtyard of the prisoners' quarters.

When I was done, Ichtaca's face was grave. "Those are serious matters."

"I know," I said. The Duality curse me, I knew all too well. "I guess you must have news."

Ichtaca grimaced. "In many areas, yes. If we start by the smallest – I sent a couple of offering priests to the Duality House, to see if we could heal the sick."

"And?"

"I don't know. They haven't come back. I suppose it's a good thing."

"I suppose so."

"And the rest?"

He wouldn't look at me. "I haven't gone very far, but I think you're right about the boundaries. They're weakened."

"And am I right about the causes?" I asked, even though I already suspected the answer.

Ichtaca didn't answer for a while.

"Ichtaca, it's past time for respect. If it's my fault, I'd rather hear it now, than have you not say anything out of respect. That helps no one."

He sighed. "It is as you said. There is a dead man among the living. This creates a hole."

"But not what we had last year."

"There is a Revered Speaker," Ichtaca said. "He keeps us safe from star-demons. But his very existence…"

It reminded me of an old story Mother had used to tell me, about a man clinging to a branch above an abyss – save that the branch was a tree-snake. He could haul himself up, but the moment he released the snake, the creature would wrap itself around him and choke him to death. Or he could, of course, let go, and fall into the chasm; in the end, he had to take the risk to be choked by the snake, for he wouldn't survive the fall. "By his very existence, he's weakening the boundaries," I said.

"Yes." Ichtaca would not look at me, or at my sandals. "There is a door open, and ghosts are coming through, and the plague."

I shook my head. "The plague is a spell, not a summoning. It's not coming from the weakened boundaries." But it might be spreading faster because of them: none of the usual barriers against spells were in place anymore. And the ghosts... the ghosts were an additional confusion we didn't need. "Doors can be closed," I said.

"It would kill him."

And, once more, leave us defenceless against star-demons, until weeks of bickering had passed and the council finally designated a new Revered Speaker. "Then left ajar," I said. "With a smaller opening. It's wide open right now, isn't it?"

Ichtaca sighed.

"It could be done," I said. If the plague didn't kill us first. "There are spells, in the codices..."

"There might be. But they're going to require time."

"Then let's take it. I don't much like the alternatives," I said.

Ichtaca was silent, for a while. "I'll set the offering priests to researching the matter. Those who are not busy elsewhere."

There was no sarcasm in his voice, though from where we sat, we could see the crowd in the courtyard, and hear the faint voices raised in argument.

Ichtaca looked up at the night sky – at the stars, which were the eyes of monsters. "Something is going to happen, Acatl-tzin. I can feel it in my bones. Something in the palace."

His tone was earnest, and I felt some of his unease. "We can't actually move on premonitions." If they'd been genuine visions, which were rare enough, it would have been another matter...

My eye was caught by some movement near the entrance: it looked like priests from our order, struggling to go through the crowd. "Ichtaca?"

He stared down. "Those are the priests I sent to the palace," he said. "Something is wrong."

SEVENTEEN
The Coward's Way Out

When we arrived at the palace, I immediately felt the sense of wrongness. It wasn't the hushed quiet – which by now had become the norm – or the atmosphere of reverent fear, which suggested the sickness had propagated yet further. Rather, it was the sense of purpose: people were still hurrying through the courtyards and the corridors, but they were mostly going in one direction, and their faces were grim.

"Acatl-tzin," Ichtaca started, but I shook my head. Whatever was going on, we'd find out soon enough.

The flow of people was going towards the quarters of the Revered Speaker, though that particular courtyard appeared much the same as ever. We followed a stream of minor noblemen in cotton clothes to a smaller courtyard decorated with rich frescoes and elaborate carvings. The smell of pine needles hung in the air, but even from where we stood – pressed in a crowd of noblemen, warriors and officials – Ichtaca and I felt it. The passage of Xolotl, Taker of the Dead, always left a particular trace in the air.

The crowd was thickest on the pyramid shrine at the centre of the courtyard. Without needing to glance at each other, Ichtaca and I sliced at our earlobes, and whispered an invocation to Lord Death, feeling the keening cold of the underworld spread over us like a mantle: the sharp touch of the Wind of Knives as He flayed the soul, the fear that seized the heart on hearing the howl of the beast of shadows; the dry, cold touch of Lord Death's skeletal hands.

The crowd parted before us like a flock of quails, and we climbed the staircase easily, stopping, for a brief moment, at the entrance to the inner chambers before the black-clad guards of the She-Snake decided we were entitled to be there, and waved us in with a wave of their hands.

Inside, the atmosphere was stifling, both because of the sheer number of people packed into such a small space, and because I could feel the death – taste it on my tongue like some rotten fruit, like something stuck across my windpipe, all but choking the life out of me.

I'd never seen that – not at any death scene I'd attended, no matter how protracted or painful the agony had been. Beside me, I felt Ichtaca pause, his gaze roaming left and right, trying to understand what had happened. If I joined him and we pooled our forces, it would be child's play to work it out – to see what was fundamentally wrong, grating at me like a missing limb…

No. I was High Priest, and my place wasn't at the back, but further ahead in the press, where the most important men would be in attendance.

The people gathered around the reed mat were familiar: Tizoc-tzin and his sycophant, Quenami; the She-Snake, and the familiar, coolly relaxed countenance of Nezahual-tzin – in addition to several warriors who served as escorts, and two frightened slaves who were doing their best to look innocuous.

In fact, it almost looked like the last time, save that the man in the centre – Pochtic – looked quite past any kind of help. Death had relaxed the muscles, so that the small obsidian dagger in his hand now lay half-across the stones of the floor. Like Acamapichtli, he'd used it to brutal efficiency – not slashing across his wrists, but digging deep inside to reach the arteries. The blood had spurted in great gouts, staining the floor underneath, but I could feel no magic, no latent power within. Either he'd offered it to a god as he died – which would have been odd, as he'd stated quite clearly the god he worshipped was Tezcatlipoca, the Smoking Mirror, a god of war who preferred human hearts as sacrificial offerings, and not something as cowardly as the slitting of wrists. Or…

Or something else had been wrong with him. He could already have pledged himself as a sacrifice, been a dead man walking, like the council two months ago – a sacrifice in abeyance, payment for a task already performed.

One thing was sure: his death wasn't making our Revered Speaker any happier. "I want to know who did this." Tizoc-tzin's face was livid. "I want them arrested, and punished – wood or stone, it wouldn't matter. I want them gone."

The wood of executioners' maces, the stones cast at adulterers and murderers.

The She-Snake was kneeling on the ground, his gaze fixed on the body. I'd expected to see Teomitl, but he still wasn't there. What in the Fifth World was he up to? Too much, I guessed. "By the looks of it, my Lord, I would say there aren't many people to punish," the She-Snake said.

"What do you mean?"

The She-Snake saw me approaching, and threw me a glance that was almost apologetic. "It was by his own hand."

There was silence. "Coward," Tizoc-tzin said, voicing what everyone thought.

I knelt by Pochtic's side, looking at the body. Neat cuts, without any flinching. I hadn't thought anyone could do that, but it certainly couldn't have happened in a fight. Nevertheless… there were ways and means to force compliance. But no, I couldn't feel any magic in the room.

No… not quite. There was something: a thin thread of brown and a reddish-yellow colour, a twin invocation to Grandmother Earth and Tonatiuh the Fifth Sun. Odd. Joint magics were so rare as to be…

Wait a moment. I stared at the face for a while, but saw nothing but the slackness of death. His earlobes, like mine, were covered in scar tissue from his many blood offerings, and there were more scars under the lip, but nothing…

Gently, I tipped the head towards me – the rigidity of Xolotl's passage hadn't yet settled in, and I managed to open the mouth. The light of braziers glimmered on the congealed saliva within the palate, but the bulk of the cavity was occupied by the tongue, which had swollen to more than twice its normal size. My fingers caught on the raised trace of a wound: it had been a single hole at one point, but repeated passages of some foreign object had enlarged the wound to a gaping hole–

Penance. And a rather extreme form. If he had been a priest, it would have been normal, but he had been a warrior and an official. Which left the other explanation.

I got up, brushing dust from my cloak, and turned around, taking in the scene. The brazier was piled with resinous wood, and the air still smelled faintly – not only of the acridity of copal incense, but also of a more unfamiliar mixture.

"He saw a calendar priest, to speak to Tlazolteotl," I said, aloud.

"To confess his cowardice." Tizoc-tzin's voice was scornful.

Nezahual-tzin – who hadn't said anything so far – looked sceptical. I felt much the same. Confession to Tlazolteotl, the Eater of Filth, served but one purpose: to void the justice of the Fifth World, by cleansing away the impurities of sin.

"There are more pressing matters. Such as conspiracies within the palace."

And the plague within the palace didn't matter, perhaps?

"My Lord…" The She-Snake said cautiously, like a man crossing a bridge of frayed ropes. "Nothing so far has suggested that there is a conspiracy."

"I can feel it," Tizoc-tzin hissed. "And so can he." He stabbed a finger in my direction.

Every single pair of eyes – from the She-Snake to the councilmen – turned in my direction, making me wish I could open a portal and disappear into Mictlan. "I'm not sure what you mean," I said, cautiously.

"You've been investigating. Tracking down the enemies of the Mexica Empire."

Well, lost for lost… I found my voice from the faraway place where it had fled. "Pochtic took a bribe, my Lord. So did Coatl."

There was a pause. "Ridiculous. You're mistaken, priest."

"Those are serious accusations," the She-Snake said, gravely. "But it's not the first time they have been made, which I suppose lends them some credence. Nevertheless – I fail to see what this has got to do with anything."

I had to admit he had a point – the Duality curse me if I could see what the bribe had to do with anything, either.

A tinkle of bells: the entrance-curtain was lifted by a pale hand, and, to my utter surprise, Coatl entered, leaning on a cane and looking none too steady. He was followed by two of my priests, Palli, and a younger offering priest, Matlaelel.

Ichtaca, who had been looking at the frescoes and muttering to himself – a sure sign that he had found something wrong – nodded to me when Coatl entered.

"My Lord," Coatl said, bowing to Tizoc-tzin – and then to everyone else in turn. "I was informed of what happened."

"You were sick," the She-Snake said.

Coatl nodded. "Until I was cured." He was thinner than I remembered, his rich cotton cloak hanging loose on his shoulders, his hands shaking on the cane, showing the translucent shape of bones. In fact...

I looked from Tizoc-tzin to him – pale faces, with the cast of the skull barely hidden under the stretched skin; the eyes shadowed, almost subsumed; the fingers almost too thin and sharp to be normal; leeched of colour like bleached bones.

In fact...

He looked as though he'd risen from the dead – which ought to be impossible. "What do you remember?" I asked.

"Nothing."

I continued to stare at him, until he finally gave in. "There was a dog, howling in the wilderness – if he caught me, I would be gone forever..." Every word seemed to come with difficulty, dragged from weak lungs, or a crushed throat. "And canals in sunlight, but I couldn't reach them, there was no time..." He stopped, then. "Why are you asking me this?"

I shook my head. "I need to know–"

"What we need to know is the truth." The She-Snake's voice was as cutting as broken obsidian. "Did you take a bribe, Coatl?"

"A bribe?" he sounded sincerely surprised. Either he was a better actor than I suspected, or he was telling the truth. "No. I've never taken a bribe in my life." Again, the ring of truth – an answer coming neither too quickly nor too slowly, without perceptible hesitation, or the lifeless tone of things learned by rote.

His gaze was on Pochtic – not on Tizoc-tzin or any of the other officials. "He's dead." He sounded utterly surprised. Had the healing – whatever it was – affected his memory?

"It might have something to do with Eptli's death."

"Eptli." His face darkened – in anger, in hatred? Whatever it was, it seemed to be directed at something beyond the dead warrior. "I remember Eptli. What a waste. And Pochtic–" His eyes narrowed and glimmered – one shaking hand went up to his face, wiped them clean. "This shouldn't have happened."

"We're wasting our time," the She-Snake said. He looked from Pochtic to Coatl, and then back to Tizoc-tzin. "My Lord… if there is a conspiracy against you, I very much doubt it's here."

For a moment, I thought Tizoc-tzin was going to argue, but then he shook his head. "You're right. Whatever he did, it wasn't against me. Let us go. We need to focus on more pressing matters."

He swept out of the room, followed by Quenami and the other officials.

I caught the She-Snake before he left. "Acatl," he said, His voice was courteous, suggesting, nevertheless, that I'd better have a good reason for disturbing him.

"You'll want to keep a watch on the prisoners' quarters."

"Will I?"

For a moment, I thought of warning him about Teomitl – about what might be brewing in the palace at this very moment. But my stomach heaved at the thought of betraying my student on so little evidence. There had to be a reasonable explanation for his disappearance and odd behaviour. "There is a spell in the courtyard," I said. "Written in blood over the adobe – by someone with no love for the current Mexica Empire."

"I see." He didn't argue with me, thank the Duality. "Who is casting the spell?"

"I don't know. I'm working on it."

The She-Snake grimaced. "I have far too few men as it is, with this whole business. But I'll put those I can spare on this."

I bowed. "Thank you."

He shrugged. "We both serve the same cause, Acatl. Now, was there anything else?"

I hesitated, but still the words were out of my mouth before I could call them back. "What about – Acamapichtli and the clergy of Tlaloc?"

This time, he wouldn't meet my gaze. "I don't know. Tizoc still thinks they might be guilty of something."

Of many things, probably, knowing Acamapichtli, but that was missing the point. "We need them here – serving the same cause. You know that – a priest for the war-god, a priest for the weather and the peasants..."

"And one for those who have moved on. Yes," the She-Snake said. "*I* know that."

The implications of the sentence were clear. "Do what you can."

"I will." He left with a nod of his head, not looking back.

The room felt much less crowded once they'd gone, leaving me free to talk to Palli. "I'm impressed you managed to heal him," I said, with a jerk of my chin towards Coatl, who still stood, looking at Pochtic's body as if he couldn't quite believe what was happening. "But what did you do, exactly?"

Palli looked nervous. "Is anything wrong?"

I was about to say he hadn't taken a good look at Coatl – until I realised that only the higher orders of the clergy knew that Tizoc-tzin wasn't quite a man anymore, but something else, a soul held in the body only through the favour of the gods. "Never mind," I said. "I need to know what you did."

Palli shifted uncomfortably. "Nothing wild, Acatl-tzin. Just calling on Toci's favour."

"How?"

He grimaced again. "Human sacrifice. We tried animals, but it was obvious there wasn't enough power."

"You sacrificed a life to save a life?"

"An important life." I hadn't seen Ichtaca creep up behind me – but suddenly he loomed behind me, as forbidding as a god. "I needn't remind you of who Coatl is."

Deputy for the Master of Raining Blood, member of the war-council – moving among the turquoise and jade, the brightest lights and most shining mirrors of the Mexica Empire. "I know. I don't care. A life for a life is wrong."

"Then what? Do you want us to kill him again? It won't regain the sacrifice's life. Besides," Ichtaca said, "he knew what he was doing."

How could he be so high in the hierarchy of Lord Death, and fail to see the problem? "That's not the point. All lives are equal and weighed the same – separated

314

only by the manner of their deaths." I felt like a teacher in the calmecac, repeating obvious truths to boys not old enough to have lost their childhood locks. To give one's life to the gods was the greatest sacrifice, but to do so in favour of another human being, to rank human lives by importance, like *things*...

Ichtaca's lips pursed. His rigid sense of hierarchy – what had caused him to put Coatl ahead in the first place – wouldn't let him contradict me, his superior. "As you wish," he said.

The Duality curse me if I let him have the last word. "It was good work," I said to Palli. "But I don't think it would make a viable cure."

He looked disconsolate, and I couldn't think of anything that would change matters. "Look into it again," I suggested. "There might be a way around the human sacrifice."

"I suppose."

I wished I could offer more – but black was black and red was red, and he shouldn't have done that. I guessed my point had come across clearly enough. "Ichtaca?"

"Yes, Acatl-tzin?" His face was smooth, expressionless.

"There is a man you need to track down – someone who came here earlier. A calendar priest."

"He will be under the seal of secrecy." He didn't say "you should know that", but it was abundantly clear.

I shook my head. Yes, the priest wouldn't be inclined to reveal the contents of the interview. But still... a drowning man couldn't afford to be choosy about which bit of driftwood to cling to. "He might still give us something to understand Pochtic. It looks as though Pochtic did the prescribed penance, and then still committed suicide." Which, to be honest, made me wonder if the offence hadn't been too grave to be forgiven – which suggested either something large, or something that went against the will of a powerful god.

"Hmm," Ichtaca was still looking at the walls – which reminded me that he'd been muttering earlier.

"Something the matter? Here, I mean."

His gaze suggested he thought more was the matter than a deserted room containing the body. "I don't think – something is odd in this room, Acatl-tzin. I can't quite pinpoint what, but…"

I sighed – assessing my meagre resources. "Palli, can you see about tracking down the calendar priest?"

Palli pulled himself straight, almost to attention. "Yes, Acatl-tzin!"

I could feel Ichtaca's discontent as I moved into the room, leaning on my cane – Storm Lord's lightning strike me, I was looking the same as Coatl, though perhaps not quite so battered.

Coatl still stood where we'd left him, looking down at Pochtic's body. His eyes, dark and shadowed, were all but unmoving, his gaze expressionless. But tears had run down his cheeks, staining the black face-paint. "That's not how it happens." His voice, too, was expressionless – too carefully controlled.

"How it happens?" I asked.

"We die in wars," he snapped. "Caught by spears and cut by obsidian, our souls taking wing on the courage of eagles, the ferocity of jaguars. We don't–" His hand rose towards Pochtic, faltered. "We don't just end it like this."

"No," I said, at last. "I know it's not much, but I'm sorry you had to see this."

He shrugged. "Doesn't matter now. You can't erase the memory of it, anyway. Was there anything else, Acatl-tzin?"

I bowed my head, as gravely as I could. "Yes. I apologise for bringing this up," we both knew I wasn't sorry, not by a large margin, "but I need to know what you can remember about the sickness."

The tremor in his hands was barely visible. "Not much. I... I couldn't breathe – as if I were in water or mud. And there were... bodies." He inhaled, sharply. "Dozens and dozens of bodies, all burning with fever. I've walked battlefields, but this was–"

"Different."

"Yes." Gently, he knelt by Pochtic's body, his fingers probing the wound that had slashed the arteries. "That's all there is."

"I see." It was consistent with my own symptoms – with Teomitl's. And all consistent with Jade Skirt's involvement – water or mud, and the sensation of choking. But it was nothing *new*, though.

"And Pochtic?" I asked.

"I thought I knew Pochtic." His gaze was distant. "Obviously, I didn't."

"So you don't know why he might have committed suicide." I was only stating the obvious there, in the hopes that it might help.

"No," Coatl said. He rose, picked up his cane again – his breath fast, laboured. "He was a man who enjoyed life. Too much, perhaps. I don't think he understood what lay beneath as well as some."

"You mean?"

"He knew it was for the glory of the gods, for the Fifth Sun and Grandmother Earth. But I think, all too often, he saw his own glory first." He sighed, again, as if he were a calendar priest, closing the divination books on Pochtic's life. "Ah well. It doesn't matter, now. Never will again."

Suicides, like the rest of the unglorious dead, went to Mictlan. Given enough time, we could summon the dead man's soul, find out what he had known.

I suspected we didn't have that kind of time.

"If you didn't take a bribe…" I said, slowly.

He looked up, with a brief spark of anger in his eyes – nothing unnatural or false there. He may have been acting, but I'd interviewed him earlier and had seen that, while he might have many talents, subtle acting wasn't among them. "How many times will I need to tell you I didn't?"

"It's not that," I said, throwing up both hands like a shield. "My point is that someone still accused you of taking it."

"Who?"

Judging by the gleam in his eyes, I wasn't sure I ought to tell him. But still, he'd find it easily enough. "A sacred courtesan, Xiloxoch. And it looks like several of you were approached with this. By Eptli."

"Eptli." Coatl's voice was bitter. "He's been a worse companion dead than alive, I have to say."

I had to agree there. "And you don't remember this, either?"

Coatl shrugged. "I know what you want." For the first time, there was anger in his gaze. "Eptli was one of my men, and whether he's dead or not, I won't see his name being soiled by chaff and straw. If I have nothing to say against him, I won't invent calumnies."

"Look," I said. He'd just been healed from the sickness, and he couldn't possibly have understood how everything had gone wrong. "Chipahua and his household are dead. The Master of the House of Darts has vanished. We have further warriors with the illness, and someone has been writing threats against the Mexica Empire in the prisoners' quarters." Gods, put like that, it became rather overwhelming.

"And you see me sorry for it," Coatl said, "but there is nothing much I can do to help you."

I could recognise obstruction when I saw it. "Fine," I said, stifling a sigh. "If you can think of anything that would shed light on those matters, keep me in mind."

"Of course," he said, but we both knew he was lying.

EIGHTEEN
The Dead Man's Confession

Palli caught up with me as I was walking out of the palace – we'd left Ichtaca with Pochtic's body, still mumbling to himself. I wasn't sure how much of it was sheer annoyance at my position on the healing ritual, and how much was his detecting a genuine problem.

Never mind. We could both argue until we ran out of breath, but I wouldn't change my position. I had the uncomfortable feeling Ichtaca wouldn't, either.

"Acatl-tzin," Palli said. "I know you asked me to track down the calendar priest, but it's likely he'll be at his temple. We can go together, if you want."

I glanced at the sky: the hour of Xochipilli the Flower Prince, with the Fifth Sun at His zenith. Palli was right: most of them would be having lunch. "Let's have a look."

We stopped for a quick lunch, buying spiced tamales from a vendor and eating the warm food with relief.

The calendar priests had their own temple, a low complex with a small pyramid shrine. As Palli and I walked in, a priest was busy directing a painter to add day-signs to a fresco; others were carrying copies of the sacred calendars back to storage rooms, while novice priests ground pigments in the huge stone mortars. A few more sat cross-legged, annotating horoscopes and pondering favourable dates for their supplicants' endeavours. The air smelled of fried maize more than copal smoke, an odd change after the atmosphere of the Sacred Precinct.

The first calendar priest we found directed us to his superior – who directed us to his superior in turn, until we found ourselves facing the head of the order, a portly man with a stern face, who looked as displeased by our request as by the prospect of being disturbed at his lunch.

"Acatl-tzin." He managed to radiate disapproval even over his utterance of my name. "I'm told you're looking for a calendar priest."

I nodded, and wasn't surprised when he launched into a speech on confession. "As you're well aware, the priest is but the vessel through which confessions are made to the Eater of Filth. He may not repeat the words, for they haven't been spoken in the Fifth World…"

I used the pause in the discourse to insert a few words of my own. "I know that, and I don't want to know the contents of the confession. I just want to speak to the priest who received it."

That stopped him. "Why?"

"The words are out of the Fifth World; the offence, too. But there are other things I might learn."

His eyes narrowed. "Thus going around the interdict. I thought you a more devout man, Acatl-tzin."

One could say I had elevated our survival to a devotion. I bit back a sharp retort, and said only, "Most men who call on the Eater of Filth don't commit suicide afterwards."

He clicked his tongue in a falsely compassionate way. "I see your problem. However, I don't think I can be of help."

The calendar priest who had referred us to him – their equivalent of a fire priest – hadn't left; he was standing by the entrance-curtain, his face set in the peculiar expression of people working hard at concealing their thoughts. "I see," I said, rising from the mat. "My apologies for taking up your time."

I let the other calendar priest escort us out – sounds of mastication behind us, coupled with the strong smell of spices and grilled maize, made it clear the head of the order had gone back to his delayed lunch.

"It sounds like serious business," the calendar priest said. He sounded wistful. "Most of us just get called for adultery, or some other petty offence. You'd think a once-in-a-lifetime confession would be more exciting."

"But it's not," Palli said. "Like most dead bodies turn out to have died from natural causes." He sighed. "And sometimes, of course, it all goes wrong like a dash of cold water, and you wish it could all be normal again."

"I guess." The priest sounded sceptical. "Still... as you say, not every day you have a suicide."

"The Master of the House of Darkness, no less," I said, sombrely. "In the wake of threats against the Mexica Empire."

His face lit up. "Really. And you need to speak to a calendar priest for that?"

I felt dishonest. Likely, it would come to nothing, and we'd have stoked his wrong ideas about the priesthood. But still... given the stakes...

I was going to regret this. "The calendar priest who saw Pochtic-tzin would be useful, yes. He'd probably have a good idea of what's going on." Better than mine, possibly.

"Look..." The calendar priest wavered. I gave him an

encouraging smile that felt false from beginning to end. "I didn't tell you this, all right?"

Palli shook his head. "Nothing gets out. Our word on it."

"Quauhtli was called for a reading at the house of some nobleman." The calendar priest frowned.

"That's odd, isn't it? A reading at noon?" Not everyone had lunch, but most people preferred to wait until the heat of the day had dissipated before getting on with serious business like divination.

"Happens," the priest said. He sounded less and less certain. "I think. Most people don't ask for a particular calendar priest, though – and they don't send warriors to escort him to the house."

Warriors. Why? "Where did he go?"

Something of the worry in my voice must have reached him; he was wavering, wondering if he hadn't made a mistake in talking to us. "He might be in more danger than you think," I said. I kept my voice slow and quiet, despite what it cost me. "But if we act now, we might be able to get him out."

"Er... south edge of the Sacred Precinct, I think." He gave us a quick description of canals, which I did my best to commit to memory – as well as a brief description of Quauhtli, though it was generic enough to be pretty much useless. "Thank you," I said.

We walked through the crowds to the southern edge of the Sacred Precinct, passing by the bone-rack, on which priests were adding a fresh row of bleached skulls from human sacrifices – someone had obviously failed to clean the skulls properly, judging by the rank smell of rotting flesh which rose from between the wooden posts. Palli grimaced; I looked on, preoccupied by other things.

The calendar priest had spoken of a house on the south-eastern edge of the Sacred Precinct – in the district of Zoquipan, the same location Nezahual-tzin had been investigating before someone had cast a spell on him.

It could have been coincidence, but there had been precious few of those lately.

Outside the Serpent Wall, the rows of noblemen's houses started up again, each encased within high, stuccoed walls – with steambaths, from which wafted the white vapour, and the smell of spices. Everything seemed silent. We trod our way past deserted canals, where boats bobbed at their anchors under the withering gaze of the Fifth Sun, following the priest's instructions until we stood in a street that seemed much the same as the others. The walls were blank, or decorated with frescoes, and nothing called to mind our missing calendar priest.

Palli looked at me questioningly. He was about to be disappointed – what good could a crippled High Priest do? Unless…

I put the cane on the ground, hand-spans away from the canal, and withdrew a knife from my belt. Then, quickly, I spoke a hymn to Lord Death.

"We all must die,
We all must go down into darkness…"

The familiar veil descended over the world, throwing everything into insignificance – the adobe becoming the colour of yellowed bone, the water in the canal darkening to the colour of a corpse's blotched skin, the smells of maize and steam receding to become the familiar ones of rotting meat and flesh.

This deep within the streets inhabited by noblemen, magic was everywhere, the various trails crisscrossing in the air, shimmering in the water like spilled cooking oil. Huitzilpochtli the Southern Hummingbird, Tezcatlipoca the Smoking Mirror, Xochiquetzal the Quetzal Flower, Tlaloc the Storm Lord, everything merging like a hundred drumbeats on the night of a festival. I stood still, and didn't move – waiting for the discordant beat, the colour slightly out of place.

There was a faint trail alongside the canal – a smell of algae, of churned mud; a sensation of quiet, muffled sound in a universe where everything was at peace forever. I teased it out, followed it. It wove between houses, in and out of the steambaths, dipping into canals like a girl testing the waters, twisting in the mud at our feet like a snake.

The scent died at the gates of a mansion much like any other – blank-faced, drawn back on itself with no hint of what lay inside. But the smell in the air was familiar, quivering on the edge of recognition.

"Acatl-tzin…" Palli said, behind me.

I realised that I stood defenceless – a cane and a bloodied obsidian knife my only weapons.

Never mind.

The warrior by the gate was a veteran with the whitish scars of sword-strikes on his legs: he displayed them proudly, not bothering to hide them beneath a cloak. "Yes?" he asked, making it clear we were wasting his time.

I smiled as brightly as I could. "We're looking for a calendar priest."

That, if nothing else, threw him. He hadn't expected brutal honesty. "Not here. Now go away."

"That's hardly polite," I said. Behind him, from within the house, another three warriors were emerging – not the friendly-looking kind either, but beefy thugs that wouldn't have been out of place at a pillaging.

"What's all the fuss?" the leader of the warriors asked.

"They say they're looking for a priest."

"Are they." His gaze narrowed, focused on me – appraising my worth. "The High Priest for the Dead." He jerked a thumb in the general direction of the inner courtyard. "What a happy coincidence. As it turns out, you're expected in here."

In here? Three of the burly warriors had deployed in the courtyard, looming over us, and their leader was grinning like someone who held all the weapons, and knew it. "Fine," I said. "I might as well not keep your master waiting."

They laughed at that, as if I'd said something witty – which I'd clearly not done.

I felt as if something had changed when we entered the house – something indefinable, which tightened the air and made it harder to breathe. The courtyard was sunny, and as we passed through two more it seemed like a nobleman's house – with slaves grinding maize into flour, women weaving maguey fibres with the familiar clack of their looms. Except... except that there were warriors everywhere, casually leaning against pillars – hefting their *macuahitl* swords with wistful smiles, and watching us like turkeys among jaguars and eagles.

Palli had gone rigid – I focused on my breath, coming in and out of my lungs; on the faint touch of Lord Death on my skin, a wind that raised goosebumps on my arms. I was High Priest for the Dead, and they couldn't touch me – they wouldn't dare.

At last, we reached the centre of the house. A small flight of steps led to a grander room, wide and airy with rich frescoes. At the back of the room, seated on a low-backed chair, was the owner of the house.

She was a woman – and old enough to be my own grandmother, with bent limbs and hundreds of wrinkles on her round face. But the gaze she directed towards us was sharp, and, when she moved, she exuded enough magic to choke the life out of us.

I knelt on the mat before her – couldn't help noticing the stains of blood, scrubbed but never removed. Was this where Nezahual-tzin's missing warriors had died? The air seemed to shimmer with the heaviness of the grave – the magic of Grandmother Earth, who had birthed us and would receive us all.

"So you're the priest." Her voice was mildly curious – kind, almost, save that her tone was firm, and obsidian lay beneath every word, sharp and cutting.

"We're looking for a priest," I said, slowly.

"And with no more idea of the stakes than a child breaking maize stalks before the harvest."

That stung. "You're the one who sent Nezahual-tzin back, weren't you? 'He's coming.' He said what you told him to say."

"A warning you'd do well enough to heed." She rose – I could feel her more than see her, but she moved with a grace and fluidity uncanny for her age. Her shadow fell over me, and she seemed so much larger than she ought to have been – the room smelled of dry earth, of rotten leaves, and the hand she laid on my shoulder was curved claws, pricking my skin to the blood. "You have little idea of what you're playing with, priest." I heard a sound, a breath coming in rapid gasps – and it was mine, it had always been mine...

Far, far away, someone pulled an entrance-curtain, the tinkle of bells a muffled sound that could not impinge on her presence, on the five fingers laid on my shoulder, each a sharp, painful touch on my exposed skin.

"He's mine."

"Yours?" The hand withdrew; the presence, too. My heart thudded against my chest, begging to be let out of its cage of ribs.

"Of course. Aren't you, Acatl-tzin?"

Slowly, carefully, I rose – for I knew the voice, as well as my own, all too well...

Teomitl stood framed in the doorway, his feather headdress of quetzal plumes, his cloak a deep, almost turquoise blue, and with jewellery shining at his throat and wrists. Clothes fit for a Revered Speaker; the old, thoughtless arrogance transfigured, too, into deliberate authority.

"You–"

He waved a dismissive hand, and the air seemed to tighten with each sweep of his fingers. "Not here, Acatl-tzin. Come. We need to talk."

Did we indeed. I brushed dirt and dried blood from my cloak, stood as straight as I could – not shaking, not shouting, standing with a calmness I didn't feel, not one bit...

"Teomitl-tzin..." There was someone else behind him – a calendar priest, judging by his garb. Our missing priest, Quauhtli. And something about him...

Teomitl shook his head. "I've got all I need. Thank you."

Quauhtli's face lit up, far too fast and too strongly to be a natural feeling. "It was my duty, Teomitl-tzin." His eyes were open slightly too wide; his gestures, as he moved into the room, were those of a drunken man, and

I didn't need true sight to see Jade Skirt's magic etched in every limb and every muscle.

"You–" I started, but Teomitl shook his head.

"I told you. Not here. Let's go out."

I thought we'd be alone, but two warriors followed us at some distance – close enough to hear everything. Teomitl made no remark, merely accepted their presence with the same ease Nezahual-tzin accepted his own bodyguards. He looked – leaner, somehow, more dangerous than he had, as if something had broken irremediably within him.

"We've been looking for you," I said. It seemed like such an inadequate way to express the turmoil within me.

He shrugged. "I had things to do. To safeguard the Empire."

"Such as suborning calendar priests?" I shouldn't have antagonised him this early in the discussion, but I couldn't help it.

Teomitl's face set in a grimace. "We've already had this talk, Acatl-tzin. I'll do whatever is necessary to protect the Mexica."

Go on, I thought. Say it. Teomitl was, if nothing else, scrupulously honest; these… evasions ill-suited him. "And you think you know better than your brother?"

He grimaced again. "Tizoc? We can dance around like warriors at the gladiator-stone, and it won't change the truth. My brother is a sick man."

"Unfit to rule," I said, slowly, softly. "Is that what you think, Teomitl?" I knew it was; I just hadn't thought he would voice it, much less act on it.

"Isn't that what you think?" His voice was fierce, as cutting as obsidian shards. "Don't look so surprised. I've seen you, Acatl-tzin. You brood like a jaguar mother over a lame cub. You wonder if you were right to bring him back."

"No," I said. "I brought him back with the Southern Hummingbird's sanction, with the blessing of Izpapalotl, the Obsidian Butterfly. You can't change the truth, Teomitl. I'm a priest, and when the gods speak, I obey."

"They're not your gods."

"They're the gods of the Mexica Empire." Didn't he understand anything? "The ones who protect us, who bring us victory after victory, who gather in all the tributes from the hot lands and the deserts. What I think of them doesn't intrude. It shouldn't intrude."

"Then you're a fool."

Was I? "If I am, it's no place of yours to tell me."

"Because I'm your student? No longer."

I thought of the calendar priest's vacant gaze; of Teomitl's voice, a lifetime ago. *Do you think me wise, Acatl-tzin? Wise enough to handle Chalchiuhtlicue's magic?*

"No," I said. "I should think you've made it abundantly clear." I raised a hand to forestall his objection, and miraculously, he stopped. "Listen to me – as a parting gift, if nothing else. The Empire dances on a knife's edge, with a Revered Speaker half-back from the land of the dead. And you – you'd think to replace him, as easily as you spend breath. Except you can't. You just can't. We've barely recovered from one disaster already, and to depose the Revered Speaker will cause an upheaval we're not equipped to deal with."

"Still the same." Teomitl's lips were two narrow lines, as pale as those of a drowned man. "You're too cautious, Acatl-tzin. Moments should be seized; opportunities should be wrestled into fruition. I'll not wait in my brother's shadow for years on end, wondering when he'll have the decency to complete his journey into the world beyond. I will act now."

One Revered Speaker deposing another was bad enough – "And what – kill him?"

His gaze didn't waver. "As you said: he's already halfway there."

To kill his own brother... But then I remembered that they'd never been close; that Tizoc-tzin's persistent mocking of Mihmatini had driven the final wedge between those two.

"You're mad."

"Desperate," Teomitl said. "It's not the same."

"Fine." I said it more acidly than I meant it. "But you can't count on me."

His gesture was dismissive – as if he'd never counted on me at all. How dare he?

"I have all I need here."

"You have a wife." Again, more acidly than I meant to. "Do you think she would approve?"

For the first time, I saw doubt in his face – swiftly quashed. "She's Guardian. She knows that I only act in the best interests of the balance."

"If you say so. Do tell her that – because I most certainly won't." And I could guess how Mihmatini would react – enough to make sure I was some distance away when she got the news.

Again, that small, dismissive gesture – a curt brush off, a judgment that I could offer nothing of value. "You've made your position clear. Will that be all, Acatl-tzin?"

He stood, just a few paces from me, decked with finery fit for a Revered Speaker; escorted by warriors in his own house, doing the Duality knew what with his magical practitioners. I wanted to scream at him not to do anything foolish – not to break us more than we already were, to pay attention to the magical currents he so casually ripped through – but, as he had said, I had already made my position clear.

I could have asked him what the priest had said, but then I would have been party to his violation of the divine secrets.

"No," I said. "You're right. There is nothing more I can do here."

I did go to see Mihmatini – after dropping off Palli at my temple. I had no idea what he'd seen or heard while I was away, but he wouldn't stop shivering, and every time his eyes strayed to the ground he would give a little start, as if waking from a nightmare.

I found the Duality House much like the air before a storm: very little activity, but every gesture charged with a meaning and import I couldn't decipher – and, throughout, a leaden weight, a sense of something large and unpleasant about to happen, lodged in my throat and chest. Mihmatini was in her rooms with Yaotl. She was staring at a divination book, impatiently turning pages as if each of the hollow-eyed deities had offended her.

"Acatl." She looked up, a smile starting to tease the corners of her eyes, and then her face fell. "You haven't found him."

I took the coward's way out, and said nothing; it must have been answer enough for her. "You look tired," I said, sitting by her side.

She waved a hand – in a gesture eerily reminiscent of Teomitl. "I've been busy." She stabbed the paper. "I have to do something, or I'll burst. So I've been looking into matters. It's not good, Acatl."

"Not good?" I hadn't thought my stomach could be colder. "Chalchiuhtlicue's power has been increasing these past weeks," Mihmatini said. "It is the Ceasing of the Waters: a time for propitious sacrifices."

"You think—"

"Something is going to happen. Something bad."

"The prisoners," I said.

"The She-Snake moved them to different quarters; we've warded them pretty tightly." Mihmatini puffed her cheeks, thoughtfully. "I don't think they'll go that way. It's like water – they'll find the path of least resistance."

Which, by definition, we wouldn't have considered. Great.

Mihmatini tapped the book again. "I just wish – there's something about this that should be obvious."

"The date?" I asked, a tad too sceptically.

"Most priests consider dates important. And I'm pretty sure most High Priests, too."

"What can I say; I've never been a good candidate for the position."

"We'd got that," Yaotl said – mocking and sarcastic, as always.

Mihmatini looked up again, frowned. "You're the one who looks tired. Don't get me started again on the skeletal look."

It was a running joke between us – usually when I hadn't got enough sleep or food: I was High Priest of Mictlantecuhtli, not Lord Death himself.

I could just shake my head, pretext fatigue after the illness – and take the coward's way out. It would be so easy – just a few words, a nod in the right place…

And I'd never dare to look her in the face again, if I did that.

"I found Teomitl."

In the silence that followed, you could have heard maize bloom.

Mihmatini's face had gone as flat as polished obsidian. "And it didn't occur to you to tell me before?"

"I'm telling you now." If you'd told me, a year ago, that Yaotl, always so ready with a jest, would be coming to my rescue...

"Where is he?"

I picked my words carefully. "There are some things you need to hear first."

"No. I need to see him first," Mihmatini said.

"Look," I said, slowly, aware that every new word was another weapon I handed her. "You know he's never liked Tizoc-tzin – and with the failure of the coronation war..."

Mihmatini's face had gone as brittle as obsidian. "He wouldn't. Teomitl wouldn't..."

I spread my hands, wishing I could make another answer – heard her breathe, slow and even, her face growing more still and unmoving each time, as if someone were leeching all humanity from her. "Where is he?" she said at length.

"A house in Zoquipan," I said. Mihmatini was still watching me, with an odd expression in her eyes – anger, tenderness? Something halfway between the two. "Look." I took a deep breath. "Promise me something?"

She cocked her head, like a bird about to fly – an eagle, not a timid sparrow or a harmless turkey. "It depends."

"Take Yaotl," I said. "And two priests."

"Why?" And then she worked it out. "Acatl, you're a fool. He wouldn't harm me."

"He wouldn't, no," I said, finally – though he had changed much. "But he's not alone in this." The old woman, whoever she was, the warriors of his entourage, and whoever else in court might be supporting this little power-grab, or whatever else he might have planned.

The Duality curse me, I should have asked him for more information – no, I couldn't have done that, not manipulating my own student into admitting the truth.

Mihmatini folded the calendar, carefully. "Right. I'll see him," she said. She took a deep breath and for a moment, an achingly familiar moment, she seemed to loom larger, her arms spread wide enough to hold the Fifth World – no longer my younger sister, but a reflection of the gods she served – a living reminder of her predecessor Ceyaxochitl, who had been small and frail, except in moments such as these.

It wasn't until Mihmatini took a step forward that I became aware of the burning sensation in my throat. Ceyaxochitl had been dead a few months, and grief still caught me at odd times, hooking me like a barbed spear. "Be careful," I said.

"Thank you for the advice, but I don't think I need it," Mihmatini said. She cast a glance around the room and picked up a vivid blue shawl, which she held against her chest, thoughtfully, then folded it back again on top of the reed chest. "Let's go."

Yaotl followed his mistress out of the room without demur – which left me alone in my sister's deserted apartments, with a folded calendar and nothing useful to do.

I took a look at the calendar out of sheer conscientiousness. I was no calendar priest, but I could see the same things as Mihmatini. Jade Skirt's influence was rising throughout the month, and it was culminating today, on the Feast of the Sun.

Something bad was going to happen, but I couldn't see what. Something to do with the prisoners – neither the She-Snake nor I were infallible, and there had to be something we hadn't thought of. Another outbreak of the epidemic? We couldn't afford to sacrifice a life for a life. If more people fell ill in the palace, what would we do?

No, I knew what they would do. Both Tizoc-tzin and Quenami, who thought themselves so much above the common folks – they would order us to heal the sick noblemen, not the peasants or the merchants. That wasn't the question. The real question was, what would I do?

And I didn't have any answer. The death of officials would send the Empire into chaos, but to buy our salvation by trading one death for another...

At length, I rose and went back to my temple. I barely had time to check the shrine and our registers before a commotion in the courtyard brought me out. From above, I could see the grey cloaks of my priests, arguing with what looked like a nobleman – quail-feathers' headdress, richly embroidered cloak – and another man in grey clothes.

As I descended, though, they swam into focus – Quenami, looking harried and wan, and Ichtaca, whose round face was grim. By their frantic breaths, they had run all the way there.

My heart tightened in a clench of ice.

Quenami all but grabbed me as I came down the final stairs, his hands scrabbling at my cloak with the coordination of a drunken man. "Acatl." He drew a shuddering breath, but for once he seemed at a loss for words.

"What happened? The prisoners..."

It was Ichtaca who answered, his eyes as hard as cut stones. "No, not the prisoners, Acatl-tzin. The priests."

The priests? The clergy within the Sacred Precinct? But surely that was impossible? "I don't understand."

Quenami took a step backward – and, with an effort akin to wrenching a sacrifice's heart from his chest, pulled himself together to look once more stern and arrogant. "Of course you wouldn't. We mean the clergy of Tlaloc."

Acamapichtli. Tapalcayotl. All of them, cooped up in their cages, stripped of their finery and of their powers. Perfect targets. "How many?" I asked, but Ichtaca shook his head. "You have to come, Acatl-tzin."

How many priests had been in that courtyard? A hundred, perhaps more? I'd talked to Tapalcayotl, and had barely paid enough attention to the others caught in this sordid power-play. But surely there had been dozens of cages: the clergy of Tlaloc was the second most numerous, after that of Huitzilpochtli the Southern Hummingbird.

Say two dozen. That was already too much. Every death would have increased the powers of our sorcerer, and brought their plans this much closer to fruition.

I thought of Mihmatini's calendar, and of the sense in the air of the calm before the storm. Well, lightning had struck, and we were, if not lost, dancing on the edge of the chasm already.

NINETEEN
The Water's Influence

It was carnage. Granted, I wasn't a warrior and hadn't walked the battlefields, but I imagined it couldn't get much worse than this. It wasn't the blood scattered on the ground: I had seen enough of it in devotions or large spells. It wasn't the body parts, either: again, I was no stranger to violence.

What made my stomach heave was the sheer scale. The courtyard had been lined with cages, and all of them had been hit at the same time, by what seemed to be a much faster variant of the plague. The bodies lay contorted on the ground, blackened with internal bleeding – and I remembered from the autopsy how much it had hurt, every organ breaking down and leaking into the body. The faces were turned upwards, the nostrils and mouths ringed with blood; the eyes, wiped clean by the blankness of death, had red corneas, and scarlet tears ran down the cheeks.

Near the back, under the pillars, I found the cage where Tapalcayotl had been. He lay still, almost unrecognisable with the flow of blood that had puffed up his cheeks, all his haughtiness and aggressiveness gone forever – one arm still extended outwards, with a carved amulet that had rolled away on the stone floor.

So much blood; so much magic, shimmering in the air, so much raw power devoted to Chalchiuhtlicue. The sorcerer would be gorged with it, ready to move against the Empire if necessary.

I knelt, and said the words, the ones I always said – the litany for the Dead – even though they'd died for Jade Skirt, and would be in Her land now, rowing boats among the eternal canals, harvesting always-ripe maize. But I couldn't leave them without a guide, and there were no priests of Tlaloc left, not in the whole of Tenochtitlan.

> "We leave this earth, we leave this world,
> Into the darkness we must descend,
> Leaving behind the precious jade, the precious feathers,
> The marigolds and the cedar trees…"

Footsteps echoed behind me. I'd expected Tizoc-tzin, but it was the She-Snake, his face grave. "I trust you've seen enough."

No, I hadn't. "How did this happen?"

"I don't know," the She-Snake said. "But I'm not surprised. They were jailed pending trial, not kept under a magical watch." His gaze was dryly amused. "No one is going to care if malfeasants fail to survive until they appear before the judges, after all."

Of course he was lying, and of course he knew what I'd think of this. I bit back on an angry remark – he hadn't been the one to arrest the clergy, after all – and said, instead, "I trust that's made Tizoc-tzin realise that the clergy wasn't involved with any of this."

The She-Snake raised a mocking eyebrow. "It might

have. I wouldn't know. We've all advised him to remain in his quarters for the moment. If whoever has done this is moving against the Mexica Empire, then they'll target its head, sooner or later."

"That's not enough," I said. I tasted bile on my tongue. "You've seen what they can do. Tizoc-tzin has to leave Tenochtitlan." I didn't like this; among other things, it would leave Teomitl a freer rein than I liked, but it had to be done. We couldn't afford to lose the Revered Speaker – never mind that most of this was his fault, that Tapalcayotl and Acamapichtli were dead, the clergy of Tlaloc all but reduced to small, unimportant priests in far-flung cities, and that it would take years for it to rebuild itself, if it was rebuilt at all...

No. I was High Priest. I'd let my feelings and my urge for justice distract me once, and the results had been disastrous. The truth was, there was as much justice as we could make, but preserving the balance of the Fifth World was more important than even that.

It was a thought that hurt like a knife between my ribs, but I had to hold it. I had to believe it.

"He can't–" The She-Snake considered for a while. "I can't be the one to suggest this. In his absence, I would represent him in the city, and he knows it. He'll see this as an attempt to seize power." His face was unreadable; I'd never really understood what motivated him; if he didn't, deep down, yearn to be more than viceroy, more than a substitute for the Revered Speaker.

"Then ask Quenami." Given his state, I didn't think he would protest, for once.

I didn't look to see if he was following. He could deal with the politics, as if he had been born to. I, in turn, would deal with the magic.

I stood in the centre of the courtyard, breathing in the rank smell of blood – it had started to change already in the sunlight, like butchered meat going bad. So much of it, such a sickening waste...

Cuixtli wasn't here: there was no other power to show me the way. But I knew what to look for, now. I slashed the back of my hand, letting the blood drip onto the ground, and said a hymn to Lord Death, feeling the cold of the underworld rise up, the keening lament of the Dead become the only sound in the courtyard. Everything seemed to recede into insignificance, save the corpses in the cages, limned with green light, the eyes bleeding and weeping, as if they could still see anything in the Fifth World. Faint traces of light hovered over the bodies: the remnants of the *teyolia* and *tonalli* souls, gathering their scattered pieces before entering the world of the gods – close enough to touch, if I were so minded. But their words would be garbled and confused – their selves incomplete – and I would learn nothing.

Instead, I focused my attention on the pillars. Magic pulsed from them, an angry, steady beat – as I walked closer, the frescoes mingled and merged with each other, receding away until all that remained were the red glyphs, their contours bent like maize stalks in strong sunlight: a pyramid surrounded by smoke, a temple pierced by arrows, a body lying on the ground, torn into four hundred pieces...

May everything you start turn against you, wither into dust, into filth. May your priests lose the black and red of the ancients – their codices, their memories of knowledge and ritual. May you be left without faces or hearts, thrown in the mud with the god's shackles weighing you down...

Jade Skirt's magic, washing over me like waves in a stormy lake – flashes of writhing bodies, contorting in the agony of drowning, of *ahuizotls* feasting on the eyes and fingernails of bloated corpses...

Enough.

I drew a shuddering breath and stepped away from the wall.

Ichtaca was waiting for me at the courtyard's entrance. "I need to know who came here."

He raised an eyebrow. "Half the palace. They were on trial, and I'm sure neither Tizoc-tzin nor the court would have deprived themselves of the opportunity to mock them."

"You don't understand. Someone engraved a spell within this courtyard, and they had to have done it after the cages were set up."

His face set in a grimace. "Acatl-tzin–"

"I'm sure of it."

Xiloxoch. Yayauhqui. Which of them had it been? I had been weak, and ineffective. For once, Teomitl had the right of it: we had to act. "You need to arrest people," I said to the She-Snake.

"You know who is responsible for this?"

"No," I said. "But it's too late for those considerations."

The She-Snake grimaced; I could tell he didn't entirely agree. But, like me, he had to bow to necessity. "Who?"

"A courtesan named Xiloxoch, and a Tlatelolca merchant. Yayauhqui."

Which, of course, might stop nothing, even if it was one of them. If they had accomplices, the plague would go on.

No, not only the plague. They'd made a deliberate sacrifice to Jade Skirt, gathering up power with those deaths packed so close by. The plague wasn't the finality: our sorcerer was preparing for something much, much worse.

"I'll try to locate them. But you must know–"

That the palace was large, and in utter chaos; that they might not want to be found. "I know." But it had to be tried, all the same.

"I'll inquire," Ichtaca said. He looked at the She-Snake, who still stood near the empty cages, looking at the corpses as if it could all make sense. But of course it would all make sense, once we caught the culprit. Once the Mexica Empire was safe. "One more thing, Acatl-tzin. About the Master of the House of Darkness."

"Pochtic?" Our mysterious suicide, who was probably mixed up with all of this.

"Yes," Ichtaca said. "I examined the room in which he died, as you requested me to."

I hadn't – not exactly – but the gods knew I wasn't about to begrudge him for taking initiatives. "And?"

"There is something I have to show you."

"Ichtaca, there is no time – " I started, but his face was set.

"I could tell you, but I need your opinion."

I sighed. "Fine," I said. "Let's go." At least it would get me away from that courtyard and that pervasive smell of meat and blood – else I was going to retch up the little I had in my stomach.

Pochtic's rooms were deserted, the focus of attention having moved elsewhere. We climbed the stairs of the pyramid, passing by a couple of bored-looking guards – and found ourselves in the room again.

The body had been removed to our temple, and everything smelled – stale, neglected, as if reflecting the misery and despair that had led Pochtic to commit the sin of suicide. The braziers had been extinguished, and the smell of copal incense had turned into the unpleasant one of cold ashes. The frescoes, though, were as vibrant as ever – the painted faces of the gods such as Tezcatlipoca the Smoking Mirror looking back at us, at the stains of blood that had changed the colour of the floor – mocking and empty-eyed, as if They knew secrets we weren't worthy of.

Tlaloc the Storm Lord had known something – something that had scared him. And if a god, one of the Old Ones, could be scared of something...

The Duality curse me, I didn't want to think about that, not now.

Ichtaca stopped at the back of the room, near one of the windows, looking down at the blood-stained sleeping mat. "Here," he said. "Can you look at this?"

I still had Lord Death's true sight upon me, and for a moment, all I could see was death – the memory of blood spurting out from cut arteries, of a soul sleeping away into the underworld. "Not the blood," I said.

"No," Ichtaca said. "Beneath."

Beneath... There was something – not an image, but the faint memory of a smell, something I'd seen before, sweet and sickening...

Jimsonweed. Peyotl. Teonanacatl, the gods' food, the sacred mushrooms – a compound of powerful hallucinogens that pierced the veil between the Fifth World and the world beyond. So close to a sleeping mat. "Dreams," I said. "Portents. He was in contact with the spirit world."

Ichtaca grimaced. "Yes."

He had been seeking it, deliberately. "Taking advice from someone dead?" I shuddered to think of all the

344

sorcerers whom he could have contacted, with the boundaries weakened. At least the dead who descended into Mictlan didn't survive for more than four years – after their journey through the underworld, they dissolved at the foot of Lord Death's throne. But the other dead – the ones who went to the Fifth Sun's Heaven, or into Tlalocan – they were still there, waiting to be summoned, or freed.

"There's something else, too."

Something else… I extended my senses, probing at the edge of the cloud. Something sharper, like pieces of a broken knife – corrupted almost beyond recovery. "Wards?" I asked. "Some kind of spell…"

"Yes," Ichtaca said. "I was hoping it would remind you of something."

Not that I could think of. "Wards aren't my specialty," I said, almost sheepishly. "Have you asked a priest of the Duality?"

"I tried, but they're too busy warding off the epidemic from the rest of the population."

"I've seen them somewhere, that's the trouble. Something much like it, but I can't pinpoint…"

"It'll come back to you," I said, finally. I looked at the pieces again, but they had faded too much, and unlike Ichtaca, they didn't remind me of anything at all.

What could Pochtic have done, which would require guidance from the dead? I thought back to when I'd seen him in the courtyard of the prisoners' quarters. Cuixtli, the Mextitlan prisoner, had said Pochtic had been looking for a spell.

Looking for a spell, or… or making sure everything was as it should have been?

"He cast the spell," I said, slowly. It made sense – an altogether chilling kind of sense.

But why? Why would the Master of the House of Darkness, one of the four on the war-council, seek to act against the clergy of Tlaloc? Some old rivalry I hadn't known of? Some grievance? It all sounded too extreme.

"What spell?" Ichtaca asked.

"The one in the prisoners' quarters. The one that took the lives of Tlaloc's priests."

There was silence. "He did what?"

The voice wasn't Ichtaca's; it came from behind us, from the entrance to the room. And I knew it.

I turned around, slowly, and watched Acamapichtli limp into the room. Like his priests, he was all but un-recognisable – his face scarred, his movements slow and stiff – and the eyes...

The corneas had burst, drowning the irises. "You–"

He fumbled his way into the room, tapping the floor with a wooden cane – his other hand wrapped into something I couldn't see. Behind him was a black-clad guard, not his jailer, but his only help to move, to climb stairs – to see anything at all. The steady tap of the cane against the stone floor was all I could hear as he made his way towards us. "I caught the sickness, yes. But, as you can see, it passed me by. Almost."

Almost – and it had left its mark everywhere. And it had damaged his eyes, too. I had been blind for a while, after entering Tlaloc's world – but I had recovered. For Acamapichtli, there would be no such grace.

"You–" He was alive – alive, ready to help us, to rebuild his own clergy. But the cost, oh gods – the cost...

"Always be prepared," Acamapichtli said. His voice was raw, as if he hadn't spoken for a long time – I thought of blood, dripping down his throat, of vocal chords distended as those few blood vessels within burst, and bled, and left whitish scars everywhere within. "I–" He stopped in the middle of the room, the cane finally falling still – blessed silence flowing all around us. He un-clenched his hand, revealing the bone-white shape of an amulet. "Always be prepared." There was a shadow of the old, mordant sneer on his face, if not in his voice. "It's served me well, as you can see."

"You're alive," I said – stupidly, because it seemed to be the only fact filling my head. "I thought–"

"That I was dead?" He grinned, a truly frightening ex-pression – his thin lips parting to reveal teeth, covered in the blood that had leaked from his gums. "Not such luck, I'm afraid. I'm a hard man to kill." He tapped his cane against the ground, once, twice. "Now, what were you saying about the–" he paused there, his hands shak-ing "the deaths of the clergy?"

"I think," I said, slowly, "that the Master of the House of Darkness was involved. I don't know if he cast the spells or made sure they were in place – but he certainly played his part in them." And *that* – not the deaths, those were part of the ritual – but the betrayal of the Empire and the Fifth World – that would be a sin the gods might forgive, but that Tizoc-tzin wouldn't, and he had already seen how much score Tizoc-tzin set by priests and by the gods' rules. He had to have known, even after his penance, that it wouldn't keep him safe, that nothing would ever keep him safe from Tizoc-tzin.

But why had he thought…?

Oh, of course. I had come into the prisoners' quarters and challenged him, and he had assumed I knew some-thing. He had been wrong, of course. I ought to have felt sorry, but the memory of the priests in the courtyard made it all but impossible.

"I see," Acamapichtli said. "Can you summon his soul?"

"I don't know–" I glanced at Ichtaca, who still hadn't moved. We'd already summoned the soul of one victim, and it hadn't been of great help. "I need preparations for that; it certainly won't be until tomorrow."

"I don't care. This – rabbit-faced coward has just played his part in all but exterminating my clergy." Acamapichtli gripped his cane – he was still a blind, scarred man with a limp, but power shimmered in the air around him, a reminder the enemy underestimated him at his peril. "Anything we can do to avenge this…"

I could understand – I'd had some of the same burning hunger within me, and knew how much worse it would all be for him – but we couldn't afford anger; we couldn't afford revenge. "It's not over yet, that's the problem. The deaths were just the beginning. They're the fuel for another spell."

Acamapichtli said nothing for a while – his ruined eyes staring straight ahead. "I want revenge."

"I know. But the Fifth World–"

"–can take are of itself?" He laughed, sharp and bitter. "Probably. But they were my priests, Acatl. They will *not* be used for some ritual against us. Tell me how I can help."

I shook my head. "You need to find your Consort," I said. "If she's still alive. We need to understand what kind of ritual we're dealing with. Ichtaca, can you set up the summoning?" I asked.

He grimaced. It was far from a straightforward thing – the body was unwashed and unadorned, and the vigils hadn't even started. And we both knew how important procedures were, at a time like this. "I'll see what I can do," Ichtaca said. "In the meantime–"

I glanced at the darkening sky – the air as heavy as before a storm. "I have an errand to do. I'll see you afterwards."

TWENTY
The Jaguar Knight's Brother

It was late by the time I arrived at Neutemoc's house; and in the darkness, the leaping jaguars painted on the gates seemed as luminous and as threatening as haunting mothers hovering on the edges of the Fifth World. Faint voices wafted out from the courtyard, and the laughter of children – for a moment, it seemed as though I had gone back to a few years before, when there had still been a mistress of the house, and my brother had epitomised the success I'd never know as a priest without possessions.

In the reception room, Neutemoc was sitting, nibbling on a fried newt; the laughter came from Necalli and Mazatl, who sat listening to Mihmatini telling a story – though my sister herself wasn't laughing. Her eyes were red, and it was obvious her mind lay elsewhere.

"Brother." Neutemoc lifted his bowl towards me – a salute, almost. "Be welcome."

I sat next to him, helping myself to a handful of maize flatbreads. For a while, neither of us spoke; the children squealed and laughed as Mihmatini mimicked a bumbling warrior seeking to eat dried-out corn, and a merchant obsessed with counting his feathers and gold quills. It was all… so hauntingly familiar, a reminder that outside the tensions of the Imperial Court and the threat of our extinction, there were still flowers and songs, still quetzal feathers and precious jade. And yes, they wouldn't last, they would be soiled and marred – but did that make them less valuable, while they still shone brighter than the Fifth Sun?

"How is she?" I asked.

Neutemoc made a stabbing gesture with one hand. "Brittle. Be careful what you say."

I grimaced. "I'm always careful."

"You know what I mean." Neutemoc turned, to look at me for a while. "You look melancholy as well. Still that warrior's death?"

"I don't know," I said. I'd walked back there, rather than my temple, and to be honest, I still didn't know why. I could have made four hundred excuses about needing to talk to Mihmatini, or to keep contact with my family, but there had been no such rationality in my choice. Like a hunted beast, I'd gone to ground in familiar surroundings, and those had turned out to be my brother's house. "There is too much going on."

Neutemoc was silent for a while. "There is always is, isn't there? The gods move and plot, and we are the pawns on the patolli board." He raised his bowl again, as if addressing an invisible assembly.

"You know–"

"–that you don't think that." The ghost of a smile quirked up his lips. "But still… they talk, in the Jaguar House."

"Of the deaths?"

"That, yes." Neutemoc laid his bowl on the mat, between the jug and a plate of tamales. Then he looked at me sideways, from the corner of his eyes. "There are a

351

lot of Knights missing, too. Officially, they've gone back to their families for the Feast of the Sun."

"I can't–" I started. I wasn't supposed to be telling anyone about Teomitl; the gods knew we had too many people, from Nezahual-tzin to the She-Snake, who already suspected. But if I didn't speak out, the weight on my heart would blacken and tear it. "They went to join Teomitl."

Neutemoc's face went deathly still. "He has desires beyond the House of Darts, then?"

"I don't know," I said, a little more annoyed this time. "He's not involved in this." It might have been his goddess' magic, but he'd almost died. No, he had nothing to do with the sorcerer. But he was making use of the chaos for all it was worth. "But the situation suits him, and he is taking advantage of it."

"And you never foresaw any of this," Neutemoc said – displaying a disquieting shrewdness for a man who had once been oblivious to the goings-on in his own household.

"No," I said, at last. "I don't understand–" I didn't understand how both Mihmatini and I could have failed to see anything – to interpret the signs, the portents; to peer into the shape of the future and see how it inevitably led to this, brother against brother.

"He was your student," Neutemoc said. "Your beloved son, if you want to go that far – and knowing you, I suspect you would. But even beloved sons go astray, Acatl. It's the nature of raising children." His lips quirked up again, in what might have been a smile if it wasn't so weak and devoid of emotion. "Our parents might have had a few things to say about that, had they lived."

But it wasn't that – what Teomitl was doing went against everything I'd been trying to teach him. I poured myself cactus juice into another bowl, letting the sharp, pungent aroma waft up to me, washing away all other smells. "Yes," I said, sarcastically, raising the bowl towards him. "They might." Look at us now, the priest they'd always disapproved of, and the bright warrior all but disowned by his own order.

Mihmatini rose, leaving Ollin and Mazatl on the mat – both curled up and sleeping. Like Quenami, she quelled the shaking of her hands well, but she couldn't quite disguise it.

"You saw him," I said.

"Of all the stubborn-headed–" she stopped herself, and sat by our side. "I can't… I just can't make him listen."

"You're his wife," Neutemoc said, finally. "He'll heed your opinion, but not on this."

She took a deep breath. "I thought–" She blinked, furiously, her eyes wet – and for a moment I wished Teomitl were there, so I could shake some sense into him.

"He loves you," Neutemoc said, gently. "But he wasn't always smart, that one."

Mihmatini said nothing – her hands clenched, briefly.

"Did he…?" I hesitated. "I'm sorry, but I have to ask. Did he tell you anything?"

I had to repeat the question twice before Mihmatini could bring herself to answer it. "Say anything? No, nothing useful," Mihmatini said. "But the chaperone is the driving force behind this."

"The old woman?" I asked. She had been the one to see him; the one that had set him on his bid for the Turquoise and Gold Crown. "Who is she?" She'd exuded Toci's magic, as naturally as we breathed – as if nothing stood between her and the goddess. Another agent we knew nothing of? Unlikely: few gods ceded Their powers to mortals, and Toci – the hungry earth, the broken furrows – tended to keep Herself to Herself.

Mihmatini grimaced. "His sister. Always had a bit of a weakness for her brother – though really, he's almost young enough to be her nephew, or worse. And she doesn't look like she likes Tizoc-tzin – or Axayacatl-tzin – very much, for that matter."

More palace politics? I hid a grimace. The last woman who had interfered in imperial succession had been by far the more successful and canny claimant – even though she had failed, in the end. An old imperial princess would be as sharp as broken obsidian – and as dangerous as a jaguar mother deprived of her children. "Between both of them, they might just get what they want." That was, in the case of the princess , the support of the palace; for Teomitl, that of the army. And Tizoc-tzin out of the city... Had I done the right thing?

But no, I had to. We couldn't afford to have our Revered Speaker fall to Chalchiuhtlicue's magic, not so soon after the last one's death – and with him unconfirmed, too, devoid of anything but the simplest magics of the Southern Hummingbird.

Mihmatini shook her head. "There has to be something I can do, Acatl."

Was there? I couldn't be sure. "You know him better than anyone else," I said, slowly. "You'll think of something."

She took in a deep breath. "I guess." But she didn't sound convinced.

"I need your help," I said to Neutemoc.

Neutemoc raised an eyebrow. "That's... unexpected."

"I'm not finding this funny."

"Me neither." There was a flash of something in his eyes, as if he remembered for a moment that I was part of the reason his wife was dead, and his house deserted. "What do you want?"

"Nothing much," I said. "I need you to look into Eptli."

"Why? The man has been dead long enough, surely?"

"I don't know," I said. "I've got a gut feeling he wasn't picked at random." The first victim of the disease would have had a high symbolic weight, if nothing else – but something in the way he had been set up suggested personal rancour, and if it wasn't Chipahua, or the merchant Yayauhqui, or Xiloxoch, then I couldn't understand why anyone would hate him.

"I can ask," Neutemoc said. "But unless you can think of something more specific…"

"Anything that would have made him an enemy."

"Still rather broad." Neutemoc grinned with far too much amusement.

"Look, if I knew, I wouldn't be here. I don't think it's anything obvious, like people who couldn't stand him as a warrior. If it were, we'd have found out by now. It has to be something more insidious; some secret of his past we haven't found."

Neutemoc sighed. "I'll see what I can do."

Afterwards, I walked with Mihmatini in the courtyard, under the gaze of the white moon – Coyaulxauhqui, She of the Silver Bells, who was the Southern Hummingbird's sister and His bitterest enemy.

"He loves you," I said in the silence. "But–"

"But not enough to listen to me? I don't know if that's love." She sounded miserable. "He's doing a foolish thing."

"The gods come first." They always did – except my own god, who always came last. "The Mexica Empire comes first."

Mihmatini shivered. "He belongs to the Southern Hummingbird after all, doesn't he?"

I was silent, for a while. "You have to realise it's not only the Southern Hummingbird who drives the Mexica forward. The other gods feast on our offerings as well, and would crush anyone foolish enough to try and get in their way."

"But other people would make them just as well, wouldn't they? We're not the only ones worshipping Tlaloc the Storm Lord, or Xochiquetzal."

"No," I said. I stopped by the pine tree, ran a hand on its rough bark, breathing in the smell of crushed needles and dry wood.

"It's not fair."

"It's not about fairness. It's about balance first."

"And you believe that?"

"Yes." I had to – or what else could I cling to? "What are you going to do?"

"I don't know. That's the problem, Acatl – I just don't know." Her face in the moonlight was gentle, and she seemed not so much the Guardian or a priestess, but just my sister, as bewildered as the day the dog had bitten her. "There has to be something..."

I didn't know what to say. I could have lied, and told her it would get better, but that would have been wrong.

She sighed, at length. "Never mind. Let's see what to-morrow will bring. Good night, brother."

"Good night."

I emerged from dark, deep dreams of the plague sweeping through Tenochtitlan – among which swum Acamapichtli's blind face, his hands questing for my own, never quite meeting them – and found myself in a sunlit room, with one of Neutemoc's slaves waiting by my sleeping mat. "Acatl-tzin, there is someone to see you."

"Someone?" I rolled over painfully – I no longer needed the cane to stand up, but I did still feel as though I'd been pummelled repeatedly. "I'll be outside in a moment."

Alone, I pulled myself upwards – reached out for my obsidian knife and offered up my blood to the Fifth Sun and Lord Death.

I didn't know who I had expected – Ichtaca with further news, perhaps, or the She-Snake, come to apprise me of yet another disaster. But the person waiting for me in the courtyard was Xiloxoch – her face painted the yellow of corn, her hair unbound like that of a young courtesan about to dance with warriors. "Acatl-tzin." She smiled, uncovering rows of black-stained teeth – unfortunately for her, so much seduction was wasted on me. I had once faced the goddess she worshipped, and compared to Her raw power, artifices were rather paltry.

"I hadn't expected to see you again."

She raised a thin, artful eyebrow. "Why not?"

"The She-Snake's guards are looking for you."

She had the grace to look amused. "Let them look. It's you I've come to see."

"To mock me? I'd have thought you'd played your part," I said.

"My part." She tossed her head back, in the familiar fashion of courtesans trying to appear coy. "And what do you think my part is exactly, Acatl-tzin?"

"False accusations. Sowing discord." When she said nothing, I added, "And attempting to steal sacrifices."

That got a smile, if nothing else. "Please. I wouldn't attempt to scrape corn from the belly of another god. The sacrifices were merely… irresistible."

Irresistible. The proximity of death; of godhood – and

something else, something in the way she said it... What hadn't I seen? "Sex," I said, flatly.

"I prefer the term 'lust'," Xiloxoch said. She smiled again, stroking the pine tree as she'd hold a lover's arm. "My mistress takes power where She can."

Small, paltry offerings of semen and vaginal secretions – nowhere near full blood sacrifices, but perhaps enough to keep an exiled goddess satiated.

"I could call the guards," I said.

"Ah, but will you do such a thing, without even listening to me?"

"Perhaps I don't want to listen to you," I said. But my curiosity was too strong – even though I suspected she was going to feed me more lies. "Fine. What do you want?"

Xiloxoch tossed her head back. "Oh, Acatl-tzin. This isn't about what *I* want. This is about you."

"You have nothing I want."

"Do I not?" Her eyes were mocking – and for a moment, they reminded me of Xochiquetzal's burning gaze, of Her face in the moment She'd risen from her low-backed chair to confront me, the embodiment of a force beyond human imagination or control. "Or perhaps I do. Perhaps it's time to make alliances, Acatl-tzin."

"Alliances." I dragged my voice back from where it seemed to have fled. "Alliances. I don't need help."

"You don't? I'm glad to know you have a good understanding of what's going on, then." Her lips quirked up. "Tell me you do, and I'll leave you alone."

And she knew very well that I wouldn't, the Duality curse her. "What are you offering?" And at what price?

"A little help," Xiloxoch said. "A little... destabilisation for certain parties."

"You speak in riddles."

"Of course." She smiled again. "Why should I make life easier for you?"

"Then why are you helping me at all?"

She smiled again; her blackened teeth seemed to have turned into the maw of a jaguar. "Because I don't particularly appreciate any of the sides taking part in this. Because as long as you're all weak, Xochiquetzal is strong."

And as long as she could lead us astray, she would. "You'll forgive me for not feeling particularly trusting."

"No matter." She leaned against the pine tree, looking at the sky. From the slaves' quarters came the rhythmic sound of maize being pounded into flour. "I'll give it to you regardless."

"At what price?"

"I told you. As long as everyone is busy…" She opened out her hand, revealing a bundle of cotton clothes. "I thought you might want to see this."

When I took it from her, I felt the weight of Chalchiuhtlicue's magic, a smell like brackish swamp water, or the bloated flesh of drowned men. Carefully, I unwrapped it, and found a torn feather quill, filled with powder, which looked for all the world like the one Palli had found on Eptli's body. Except that the powder was a different, richer colour, more dark orange than yellow: I'd have said cacao, except that it was not dark enough for that.

I wasn't crazy enough to rub it between my fingers. "Where did you get this?"

Xiloxoch pursed her lips, which were as red as chafed skin. "You'll remember I collected Zoquitl's possessions. This was among them."

"And we didn't see it."

She smiled, as if my scepticism was of little matter. "It was well hidden, and you didn't search the room that well."

I wasn't altogether sure I believed her, but then I couldn't see why she'd want to give this, and how she'd have filled it with Chalchiuhtlicue's magic. "You have the bravery of warriors about to die, then. The sickness–"

"Please. I have my own protections. In any case," she smiled again, an expression that was no doubt meant as seductive, but was starting to be decidedly unpleasant, "it's all yours. You'll know what to make of it."

Other than the fact that it had been the vector for the sickness, and slightly different from the one that had killed Eptli... no, I didn't. "Well, that was helpful. I certainly feel more knowledgeable."

"Make of it what you wish. I could tell you you're looking in the wrong place, but you already know that."

"Yes," I said. "Was that all you had to say? You're wasting my time, once again."

"Once again? Whenever did I waste your time, Acatl-tzin?"

"The bribe," I said. "It was all a fiction you devised to keep us running in the dark."

She smiled again, as radiant as the rising sun. "I sow chaos, Acatl-tzin. I do my goddess' will. You know all this. Does it matter if I lied to you?"

"It might make me slightly distrustful," I said, darkly.

"You're a disappointment. Too frank, that's your problem. I lie when it suits me, and tell the truth when it doesn't. And, right now, the truth is more convenient."

I'd had enough. "If you're just here to mock me, you might as well be gone."

She shrugged. "Fine. But remember what I've given you."

She was gone in a heartbeat, but, just as she'd intended, she'd sown the seeds of doubt.

TWENTY-ONE
Merchants and Warriors

After Xiloxoch was gone, I stared at the powder for a while, but try as I might I couldn't make anything of it.

"Up already?" Mihmatini's voice asked.

I sighed. "And already swamped with problems."

"As usual." Mihmatini settled on the rim of the well, watching me with bright eyes – her hair neatly brought up in two horn-shaped buns, the traditional style for married women. "The problems don't go away, you know. You might as well enjoy the quiet bits in the middle."

"You're one to talk," I said, sharply, looking at her.

Her face was dark – as taut as a rope about to snap. "Perhaps I'd like to be able to take my own advice." She stopped, her gaze dragged to the thing in my lap. "What in the Fifth World is that?"

"A parting gift," I said. "One of the vectors for the sickness." It might have been an elaborate lie from Xiloxoch, but then why give us two, one on Eptli's body, and one directly? The most likely explanation was that it really was the vector of the sickness.

"This?"

"Yes," I said, gloomily. "It's meant to be money from a symbolic standpoint, but what's inside is not gold. I can't figure out–"

My sister made a sound – I thought she was going to cry, but after a while I realised she was laughing. "Oh, Acatl. Sometimes, you're such an idiot."

"What?" I asked, looking at the cloth again – what had I missed.

"Men," Mihmatini snorted. "You're all the same. What was the last time you actually entered the slaves' quarters?"

"Fairly recently."

"For an investigation, right?" She wiped tears from her eyes. "Sometimes, I swear, you're useless."

"If you're finished with the mocking," I said, strongly suspecting I was going to end up looking like a fool again, no matter what I did – why could I never win anything against her? "What is so funny?"

"If you cooked at all, or dealt with food at all, you'd know what the powder is."

"I cook," I said, stiffly.

"Only when you can't find food at your temple or at the palace kitchen." Mihmatini shook her head, amused. "The powder is cacao pinolli – cacao powder mixed with maize flour."

"It's a drink."

"And a base for flatbreads, yes," Mihmatini said.

"Someone is killing people through food?" It made no sense. "Try this one," I said. I gave her a brief description of the other powder, the one Palli had found.

"A deeper yellow than maize flour?" Mihmatini asked. She puffed her cheeks. "It could be many, many things, and I can't be sure without having a look at it. But I think it's chia pinolli – chia seeds and maize flour."

"I detect a pattern," I said. Unfortunately, it was the kind that stubbornly refused to coalesce into anything coherent.

"Yes, me too, but why would anyone want to use those for propagating a sickness?"

"I don't know," I said. I rose, wrapping the broken quill into a piece of cloth, and tucking it into my belt. "If anything occurs, do tell me. I'll be at the palace." I needed to speak to Coatl again – and to see what I could get from either of them about the bribe.

In the corridors and courtyards, the bustle was worse than ever, and the crowd abuzz with the rumours of Tizoc-tzin's departure. Apparently, he'd left at dawn with a close circle of his faithful, leaving Quenami and the She-Snake in charge – a radical departure from tradition, and one that had tongues wagging from the military courts to the treasure halls.

When I reached Coatl's quarters, though, he wasn't there. According to the slaves, he'd left in the night and hadn't come back. "He's going with Tizoc-tzin?" I asked.

The slave shook his head. "Not that we know of. We have received no orders for the removal of his household."

Not knowing what else to do, I went to see the She-Snake, but he was busy with Quenami, and the line of supplicants and noblemen was already overflowing the courtyard of his quarters. I chatted, briefly, with one of his slaves, but it didn't look as though his guards had even started looking for Xiloxoch or Yayauhqui.

Coatl had left. No matter how I turned this around, I didn't like it. He'd said he hadn't taken the bribe, and he was honest, I was sure of that. But why leave at all, in such circumstances? He might have been frightened of the plague, but in this case he would have removed his whole household, not disappeared himself.

Why?

I walked out of the palace, preoccupied, back to my temple, where – to my surprise – I found Neutemoc and Mihmatini in discussion with Palli.

"What are you doing here?"

Neutemoc was dressed for war in the fur-suit of Jaguar Knights, with his helmet tucked under his arm and his *macuahitl* sword in his right hand. And Mihmatini wore her Guardian clothes; her slave Yaotl trailing behind her, holding a basket of fruit and flowers – offerings for calling on the power of the Duality.

"Mihmatini told me about the powders," Neutemoc said. "Why didn't you ask me?"

"You know about cooking?" I couldn't hide my surprise.

His lips quirked up, in that smile that wasn't a smile. "It's not about cooking." His voice took on the singsong cadences of sacred texts. "Forty baskets of cacao pinolli, and forty baskets of chia pinolly every eighty days, eight hundred mantles of cotton every eighty days, and eighty white and yellow cuextecatl costumes every year."

"It's a tribute list," Mihmatini said. "For Tlatelolco. For the last eight years they've been paying this every year."

"Tlatelolco?" The merchant, Yayauhqui.

"Yes. I asked about Eptli," Neutemoc said. "Other than what you told me, nothing much that was new. Except this: his father was a messenger, originally. He was the one who carried back the news that Moquihuix-tzin, the Revered Speaker of Tlatelolco, was plotting against the Mexica Empire. That's how he became a nobleman."

"Tlatelolco." I took in a deep breath. No wonder they'd wanted our fall, our failure in everything. "Let's go."

"Where?"

"To find and arrest someone, before it's too late."

Yayauhqui was not at his stall, and when we inquired at his household, we found him absent there too. The slaves showed us into the courtyard and served us bowls of chilli-flavoured cacao. After a while, a middle-aged woman by the name of Teyecapan came to see us, looking distraught. "They've told me you're looking for my husband. I can assure you, he's done nothing wrong."

"Then let us see him," I said gently. "He can tell us himself."

"He's not here," she said. She looked at us as if we were addled. "It's the Feast of the Sun. He'll be in the slave market, buying a sacrifice victim for the merchants."

Neutemoc threw me an exasperated glance as we walked out. "I'm getting tired of walking back and forth between the houses and the marketplace."

"Not to mention hot," Mihmatini said, hiding a smile. And, indeed, the Jaguar Knight's costume might have looked grandiose, but it was no more comfortable than my High Priest regalia: we were both sweating quite profusely under the withering glare of the Fifth Sun.

Tlatelolco was nowhere as deserted as Tenochtitlan. But for the sick governor, the plague appeared to have touched it little – which made sense if Yayauhqui was behind it all. There were fewer people in the marketplace, but I suspected the missing were mainly Tenochcas.

In the marketplace, the slave section was filled with merchants, discussing in small groups, looking at the slaves for sale – nearly all burly, unblemished men kneeling on the reed mats with the distant gazes of people who expected to be kneeling all day.

Yayauhqui was easy to find: he towered over the other merchants by a head, and, with the true sight on, there was an empty hole where his souls ought to have been.

"Acatl-tzin?" His gaze moved from Neutemoc to Mihmatini, and then back to me. "I did wait for you in the palace, but it was a while and you didn't come back..."

The other merchants were frowning at us – their gazes were sharp and inquisitive, if not yet hostile. "Can we move away a little?" I asked.

Yayauhqui smiled. "It all depends. What do you want?"

"You're under arrest," Neutemoc said, curtly and harshly.

"I don't understand." He sounded genuinely puzzled.

"The plague is linked to Tlatelolco."

"And you come to me? Do you have any idea how many people of Tlatelolca blood are around here?"

"Few who knew Eptli, I'd wager," Mihmatini said.

Yayauhqui considered her, thoughtfully. At length, he bowed. "I'll grant you this, my Lady, but I had little to do with Eptli, and certainly nothing to do with his death."

And he sounded sincere. I knew he was a great liar, but surely, if he'd that much hatred of Mexica – if he was that much closer to his goal of unseating us – surely he would have shown some glee, some excitement? "Come with us," I said.

He shrugged. "It's a nuisance, and I assure you I'm innocent."

"Then you won't mind coming with us until it's all over." A matter of days, or perhaps of hours.

His face darkened, slightly. "I do mind. I have business, and other things to attend to. But if that's what it takes to convince you..."

He walked ahead of us on the way to the palace, his head thrown back, as casually arrogant as any warrior.

"Are you sure it's him?" Neutemoc said.

"He might want to be coming back to the palace," Mihmatini said, slowly, but she didn't sound convinced.

I wasn't, either. If all he'd wanted was to get back into the palace, he could have walked. And someone who could paint spells into the remotest courtyards didn't need a pitiful excuse like an arrest to be at work within the palace complex. "Something is wrong."

"We have the wrong person," Neutemoc said. He shrugged.

"No offence to him, but Yayauhqui is a merchant. Your plague sounds like it's been orchestrated by a warrior with a good grasp of strategy."

"He used to be a warrior," I reminded Neutemoc. "All Tlatelolca were both – merchants and warriors."

"Don't lecture me." Neutemoc looked amused. "I know what you mean, but I still don't think it's him. Call it a gut feeling. He just doesn't seem to have the right mindset."

I wasn't sure how much my brother's gut feelings were worth – but when it came to warriors, they had to be better than mine.

Which left us, it seemed, with not much more to go on.

TWENTY-TWO
Beyond Death

At the palace, we dropped Yayauhqui off into a room for "guests", and I managed to find one black-clad guard willing to keep an eye on him. Though Yayauhqui himself didn't look as though he had any intention of moving: he'd picked up ledgers from his merchant peers before leaving, and he was now sitting cross-legged with the papers spread in his lap, thoughtfully annotating them with a writing reed.

It could have been an elaborate deception, but the most likely explanation was that it was all the truth, and that we'd been mistaken by picking him as the instigator of the plague.

But, if not him, who else? As he had said, we did not lack Tlatelolca. Another of the former imperial family, with more military training, and a stronger will for revenge?

Pochtic would know.

We walked back to Pochtic's rooms, where Ichtaca had readied everything for the spell: my priests had brought back Pochtic's body from the temple, and laid it again in the position in which he had died: readying the *teyolia* – the spirit that travelled the world beyond – for being

369

summoned. Around him they had traced the glyph for *ollin* – movement, the symbol of this Fifth Age – and around the glyph a circle which encompassed the whole room, a symbol for the rules and rituals which bound us all. Now nine of them – one for each level of the underworld – were chanting hymns to Lord Death, beseeching Him to help us summon the dead man's soul.

> *"In the region of the fleshless, in the region of mystery,*
> *The place where jade crumbles, where gold is crushed,*
> *The place where we go down into darkness..."*

"I think we'll wait for you outside," Neutemoc said. He shifted uncomfortably – unused, I guessed, to the matter-of-fact way with which we treated death.

Mihmatini shook her head. "You wait outside. I want to see this." Her gaze was hungry, feverish, and I thought I could name the reason for her impatience – she'd leap on anything we could use to make Teomitl see reason.

"Don't overdo it," I said.

Her gaze was hard. "I know what I'm doing."

I sighed, but said nothing. I couldn't push her any further. We walked into the room together – to find Ichtaca on the edge of the circle, watching the ceremony. He bowed to Mihmatini, with the look of uneasy reverence he always had for his magical and political superiors – excepting me, of course.

"You don't look convinced by the ritual," I said.

Ichtaca shrugged. "You know why."

After death, the souls that went into Mictlan lay in scattered shards – not like the sacrifices or the dead in battle, who opened up wings of light to ascend into the Fifth Sun's Heaven, nor the drowned men, who entered

Tlalocan whole. Rather, those souls destined for Mictlan needed to strip themselves of every remnant of the Fifth World, pulling their essence from the corpse that had hosted them. It took a few days for that transformation to be complete, but this assumed proper rituals – the washing and laying-out of the body, and the vigil: all the small things that kept reminding the soul of the next step in its journey. Here, there had been time for nothing of this; the body had been moved, cutting its link to the place of death.

"Two days," I said, aloud.

"It will have to suffice," Ichtaca said.

We waited side by side, until the chanting subsided; it was time for me to take my place at the centre of the quincunx.

Pochtic's body lay on the ground – not the pale, contorted thing I remembered, but something else. Palli and the others had dressed him in a semblance of a funeral bundle – given the little time they'd had, I suspected there were rather fewer layers of cotton than Pochtic's status warranted; fewer amulets and pieces of jewellery as well.

I inhaled – feeling the cold of the underworld gather itself from the circle under my feet. Green light had seeped from the dried blood on the ground, until it seemed as though I stood in mist. Everything smelled faintly humid – like leaves on the edge of rotting. Then, with one of my obsidian knives, I drew a line across the scarred back of my hand, letting the blood fall onto the floor, drop after drop. There was a small jolt every time a drop connected, and the mist opened itself up to welcome it, with a hunger that was almost palpable.

"From beyond the river,
From beyond the plains of shards,
I call you, I guide you out…"

The light flared up, coming to my waist; I could see faint smudges within, and hear the distant lament of the dead; shapes moved within the mist – there were hints of yellow eyes and claws and fangs, and the distant glimmer of a lost soul, like dewdrops on flower leaves.

"Past the mountains that bind and crush,
Past the wind who cuts and wounds,
Past the river that drowns,
I call you, I guide you out…"

Nothing happened.

Or rather: the mist remained, and the feeling of emptiness arcing through me, telling me passage into the underworld was open. But no soul came; no vaguely human shape drew itself out of the murky darkness.

The Storm Lord strike me, Ichtaca was right: we were too early, and the soul was still in four hundred scattered pieces.

But no; there was something… some resistance, as if I'd hooked a fish at the end of a line, or rather, more than one fish: I could feel the pulling, the scrabbling of several smaller things trying to get out of the way, with the same intelligence as a shoal of fish or a flock of sparrows.

I grasped my obsidian knife, letting the blade draw a bloody line within my palm – waiting until the obsidian was tinged with my blood. Then I wove the knife up, heedless of the small pinprick of pain that spread from my open wounds – up, and around, as if cutting into a veil.

The air parted with a palpable resistance, and the pull I felt grew stronger – and then, in a moment like a heart-beat, *something* coalesced in the midst of the circle.

The souls I had seen had been human, but this clearly wasn't. It moved and shimmered, barely within the Fifth World – I caught glimpses of wings and feathers within its ever-changing shape, as if the soul wasn't yet sure how it had died.

"Priest?" It whispered. The voice was to Pochtic as a codex picture was to a god – small and diminished, its timbre extinguished. "Where–?"

"The Fifth World – but only for a little while," I said. "Everything must tarnish and fade into dust, and you are no exception." My voice took on the cadences of the rit-ual – for this had to be done properly, lest Pochtic never achieve oblivion in Mictlan. "The blood has fled your body; the voice of your heart is silent. The underworld awaits you."

The soul shifted and twisted. If he had been a man, he would have hugged himself. "I'm dead?"

Quite unmistakably so. "Yes," I said.

It moved again, extending tendrils of light to wrap around the funeral bundle – and withdrawing as soon as it touched it, as if it had been burned. "Dead…" it whispered.

What a contrast to the vibrant, arrogant man Pochtic had been, but then, few spirits maintained their cohesion into death. I had only met one, and he had been Revered Speaker of Tenochtitlan, schooled in propriety and ritual since his birth.

"Dead," I said. And, because strong emotions could survive even into Mictlan, "You committed suicide."

A brief flare from the soul; a shifting of lights to become darker. "I did." There was a pause. "I… I was afraid."

I said nothing, not wanting to break the fragile process of gathering its memories.

"He was going to find me – arrest me, kill me. The Revered Speaker..." It paused, shifted again. "I... did something. I–"

It was silent, then – hovering over its own corpse, not daring to touch it. At length, it whispered, and it was the voice of a broken man, "It can't be forgiven. It can't ever be forgiven."

If it still had eyes, it would have wept.

And, if I didn't vividly remember the carnage in the courtyard, perhaps I would have bent or relented – but Tapalcayotl's face was in my mind, black and twisted out of shape by sores, and the memories of a dozen bodies scattered like a grisly harvest, and the vulnerability in Acamapichtli's eyes. "What did you do?"

"I– I– " Its voice was low, halting – ashamed? "He was talking in my sleep, always – whispering, suggesting, threatening – always talking, until I couldn't take any more of it. I just couldn't! He – he wanted me to help him, to get revenge, and I couldn't say no."

Talking. Dreams. "You had herbs, in your room," I said. "Jimsonweed, and *teonanacatl*. You were speaking with the spirits." But even as I said that, I thought of the decayed wards – they *had* been familiar, but they weren't for better communication with the departed. They were the reverse: walls to keep the spirits out, attacked until they'd ruptured. We'd had backwards: it wasn't the living seeking to spread the plague with the help of the dead. It was the dead seeking revenge, and influencing the living to get it.

"He found you," I said, slowly. "A tool for his plans. And you helped him," I said. From the start – giving the feather quills to Eptli, to Zoqutil, engraving the spells within the palace – corruption in our midst, like the rotten core of a cactus.

"I–"

"Tizoc-tzin won't forgive; the Southern Hummingbird doesn't forgive." It was a lie, for his soul would go down into Mictlan, where there was no judging, no weighing of deeds – where everyone, prince or nobleman or peasant, was equal. "Who was he, Pochtic? What did he want?"

"I–" Something rippled across the soul, as if it were caught in some inner struggle. Vaguely, I heard Ichtaca cry out from beyond the circle. "Revenge, but I can't say anything – I can't, he would kill me…"

"You are already dead," I said. "Wrapped in the bundle of your funeral pyre, awaiting entry into the land of the dead, the land of the fleshless, the land where jade crumbles and feathers become dust." Every word fell into place with the inevitability of a heartbeat – further ritual, hemming the soul in, reminding it that there was no escape. "And he can't harm you anymore, whoever he is."

"You're wrong – wrong, wrong," the soul whispered. Around it, the circle was crinkling inwards – the green mist receding into the stone floor, to reveal once more the frescoes of the gods on the walls. "Wrong…"

"No," I said. "You're dead – you belong to Lord Death now, and to Mictlan. No one can take away from you, and no one can reach down into the underworld. What does he want? Tell me."

The soul shifted, twisted – writhed, trying to escape – the wings were falling away, and the outline of arms and legs were forming, flailing wildly as if in great pain. "He – revenge," he whispered again. "On all of Tenochtitlan, if need be. May the cities you hold fall one after the other; let the temples be awash in fire and blood…"

I was losing him. The time for the ritual was past, and he was going away from me, gathering himself for the plunge into Mictlan. I needed to get something, and fast. "What does he want, Pochtic?"

The soul was unravelling like a skein of maguey fibre, faster and faster – drawing away from the corpse, coalescing into the shape of a man, but growing fainter and fainter the whole while. "Pochtic!"

But he was gone, and I remained alone with his corpse, within a circle that was stone again. The room was cold; and the wind on my exposed arms chilled me to the bone.

Something was left behind, a mere whisper on the wind: a name, quivering out of existence with each spoken syllable. "Moquihuix-tzin."

"Moquihuix-tzin?" Mihmatini asked. She sat on the terraced edge of Pochtic's quarters, looking down into the courtyard. Neutemoc was by her side – as if standing guard. "That's the last Revered Speaker of Tlatelolco. He's–" she stopped. "It doesn't matter whether he's dead, does it?"

I grimaced. "Partly. The dead can't cast spells, or summon creatures. But they can influence." And Moquihuix-tzin had been a strong character – both Nezahual-tzin and Yayauhqui had described him as a man used to getting his way. No wonder Pochtic had been such a pliant tool.

"Which isn't helping us, is it?" Mihmatini said. "With Pochtic gone, he could be influencing pretty much anyone."

Below, a few noblemen were crossing the courtyard, and a couple was coming towards us, the woman ahead of the man – her face utterly unfamiliar, as sharp and rough as broken obsidian, her clothes slightly askew, as if she'd dressed in a panic.

They were almost upon us when I realised that the man behind her – tall and unbending, with a headdress of heron feathers – was Acamapichtli. He stood once more with his old arrogance, as if his scarred face and sightless eyes meant nothing. He wore a carved fang around his neck, a beacon of power I could feel even without my true sight, and he moved confidently, as if being blind were no trouble at all.

"Further evidence of your charms?" I asked.

He shook his head, impatiently. "Behave, Acatl. This isn't a time for levity. I've brought my Consort, as you asked."

The woman bowed to me. Up close, the lines on her face were clearly visible – she would never be called beautiful, but she was striking as only priestesses could be, secure in her identity and power, which gave her a place in society above the common folk. Two black lines ran on her cheeks, calling to mind the face of the goddess Herself – whom I had seen once, more than a year before, when Teomitl had been granted his powers. "Greetings, Acatl-tzin. I am Cozolli, priestess of Chalciuhtlicue, and Consort of Tlaloc."

"No need to be formal," I said. Acamapichtli shot me a quick look; I didn't know what he thought of the position of women in the clergy – who, save for the Guardian, could only ever be the inferior of their male homologues.

"Fine, fine," Acamapichtli said. "We can dispense with the idle chit-chat, Acatl. We've come here because we have news."

"And from the look on your face, not good," Mihmatini interjected.

Acamapichtli turned in the direction of her voice. He was silent for a moment. "Oh, I see. The Guardian. What a pleasure." I expected him to be mocking, but Mihmatini's strength must now be evident, and he had always been a man to respect that.

Mihmatini looked less happy – much as if she'd swallowed live eels. "Acamapichtli." She made no pretence of respect to him, though, and to my surprise he nodded, as one equal to another. "What do you want?"

"The boundaries are breached, Acatl. That's why the gods are so scared."

Even blind, he must have felt by our silence he wasn't achieving quite the effect he'd intended. "We know this," I said, wearily. "We're working on how to fix this. If you're here, you can confirm something for me."

Acamapichtli turned his face towards his consort; who said nothing. "Go ahead."

The entrance-curtain tinkled, letting Ichtaca through. He had changed out of the formal regalia, and his hands were now clean of the sacrifice's blood. He nodded, curtly, towards Acamapichtli and Cozolli, and sat cross-legged, patiently waiting for us to finish.

"I need to know if your god had Moquihuix-tzin's soul in His keeping."

"The Revered Speaker of Tlatelolco?" Acamapichtli looked surprised. He shrugged. "How would I know this?" But his consort nodded.

"He died by the noose," she said, curtly. "Every priest knows that."

The jab completely bypassed Acamapichtli. "And how does this help us, exactly?"

"It doesn't, per se," I said, slowly. Why was I bothering with this? There was only one thing which should have mattered to me. "We need to close the boundary." I turned to Ichtaca, who had remained silent until then. "You had started working on that."

Ichtaca grimaced. "Yes. It's far from being a simple problem. The gates need to be drawn close without being shut – leaving just enough magic for Tizoc-tzin to exist, but not enough for widespread ghosts."

And even that would still leave a risk – summoners would find it slightly easier to work, and there would be more creatures slipping through the cracks. But it was still better than star-demons.

Pretty much anything was.

"And?" Mihmatini asked.

"I think–" Ichtaca said, slowly, "that it would take the three High Priests, again – as it took them to open it in the first place."

Three High Priests. I had a mental vision of trying to convince Quenami he needed to work with us. "It won't work," I said. "Even if Quenami is still here. We need mastery, and subtlety." And, while he might be a fine diplomat, the events of the previous days had proved, quite unequivocally, that he didn't have much magical expertise.

But Ichtaca was right – what had taken three to do couldn't be undone by two. We needed... someone to stand in for Quenami. Someone linked to life, virility and good fortune.

"If you want to keep it open, you can't close it from the Fifth World," Acamapichtli said, acidly. "You have to be on both sides, to keep control over what you're doing."

"On three sides," I corrected, distractedly. "To rebuild the tumbled one, you do need three people. One in the Fifth World, one in the underworld. And one astride the wall."

Mihmatini's gaze was harsh. "Why do I get the feeling you're going to be the one astride the wall?"

"Look, that's not what matters."

"What about the Heavens?" the Consort Cozolli asked. "They're also open."

"Symbolically, it's a single boundary," I said gently. "Between the Fifth World and the world above, the world below. All you need is one person outside that boundary."

"Hmm." She didn't appear wholly convinced, but I was.

"We need a third person. Mihmatini–"

She shook her head. "I stand for all gods, and none. I can't complete your triad."

Then – I looked at Cozolli – she was only a Consort, and was symbolically tied to Tlaloc through her worship of Chalchiutlicue. No, she wouldn't do either. "Then it'll have to be Quenami. " I stopped, then, thinking of someone else who stood for a god – who might as well be High Priest, given his close relation to his patron. "The breath of sickness in the Fifth World," I said. "Death astride the wall. And the breath of life in the underworld."

The breath of life. The wind, Ehecatl-Quetzalcoatl, the Feathered Serpent. "Nezahual-tzin." Mihmatini's voice was grim. "Fine – if he hasn't run away as well. And what about our troublesome ghost?"

"If we find him, we'll work out how to deal with him," I said. The truth was, I had no idea how you killed a ghost. I could banish them – but that just sent them back into the Heavens, ready to come back again.

Unless…

Every ghost disappeared before the throne of Lord Death – if it came to that, we might be able to do something.

Save that it was a favour, and I had no wish to incur more debts with my god.

"It might not work, Acatl-tzin."

"I–" Ichtaca looked at me, halfway between admiration and horror – not an expression I felt altogether comfortable with.

As usual, he'd managed to make his doubt evident while outwardly agreeing with me. I shrugged, and spread out my hands. "The boundaries have to be closed. That's our role. Do you have a better idea?"

Ichtaca looked dubious. "No," he said at last. "You're going to require the help of the order."

I smiled. "I wouldn't have had it any other way."

Mihmatini looked wistfully at her feet – where the pale trace of the thread tying her to Teomitl coiled on the ground. Then she sighed. "I have to come with you. I can help to make the spell stronger."

"Are you sure?"

"No," she said, curtly. "Don't ask, or I might just change my mind. I hope it's going to work, but it's really uncertain." Mihmatini pursed her lips. Clearly, she didn't much care for asking Nezahual-tzin's help once again. She looked back and forth, from Acamapichtli and Cozolli to me. "How come your order doesn't have a Consort anyway?" Mihmatini asked. "You seem to be the only exclusively male priesthood in the Empire."

Ichtaca jerked as if stung; I merely nodded, looking slightly away from her. Acamapichtli just looked smug. It was public knowledge, but still, never brought out in such an open fashion – like pointing out to an aged relative that they were senile. "There was… a problem with the Consort, a dozen years ago. She did – let's just say she got involved in activities she shouldn't have."

Meaning that she'd dabbled in the wrong kind of magics, made the wrong kind of alliances, and set herself to fold the entire Fifth World into Mictlan.

Mihmatini grimaced. "And she was killed? And the female priests?"

Ichtaca spoke, slowly, measuredly. "Not killed – exiled. And the corruption went deep into the clergy. It was, ah, cleaner to remove the branch than try to prune sprig by sprig."

Mihmatini grimaced. "I've heard it said you're sick people, but this is the first proof I had." She shook her head, as if removing water from her hair. "Never mind, that's all pretty unimportant right now. Acatl?"

I shrugged. "I don't have a better idea."

"If you need someone in the underworld and someone on the boundary, you'll need a gate into Mictlan. Opening one isn't cheap or easy," Ichtaca said.

"No, but we can manage." Provided nothing went wrong.

Ha ha. I knew the answer to that one, too.

Finding Nezahual-tzin turned out to be more difficult than we'd foreseen. He wasn't in his quarters, which lay empty and deserted, like those of the Revered Speaker. He wasn't in the steambath, or in the various Houses of Joy, and neither was he in the tribunal, listening to the various magistrates argue in search of truth.

I could tell Neutemoc was starting to get frustrated – no wonder, he was a warrior, and such footwork was merely the prelude to the fight – and even Mihmatini's temper was close to fraying. Acamapichtli, to my surprise, was more equable, in fact, he and his Consort were worryingly silent, following us with alert faces, their gazes moving, as if they could track dead spirits.

And perhaps they could, too. Knowing Acamapichtli, he wouldn't have chosen a weak or ineffective Consort.

The priests behind me, Palli and Matlaelel – who carried the supplies we'd need for the spell – didn't look enthusiastic, either.

"He didn't exit the palace," I said at last, as we looped through the same deserted courtyard for the fifth time. "The guards didn't see him."

Neutemoc grimaced. "I'm not convinced they'd have seen him."

"The Revered Speaker of Texcoco?" Mihmatini shook her head. "No, they'd have seen him. If only to warn Tizoc-tzin." She grimaced. "And with the number of people left…"

I said nothing. The atmosphere in the palace was somehow different – there were still people wandering the corridors, from magistrates to noblemen, from feather-workers to officials. But still…

Still, it was like a man with a removed heart – he might flop and writhe for a bare moment on the sacrificial altar, but there was no doubt that he was already dead.

Had Nezahual-tzin left the palace? He'd proved before that he came and went as he chose – sometimes in disguise, if there was need. He might have gone past the guards…

Something stopped me – a thought that slipped into the tangle of my mind like a sharpened knife. We were all acting as if the palace was impervious, and the guarded entrance was the only one – but the truth was, it wasn't anymore. Not if you could brave the power of Chalchiuhtlicue and enter the tunnel Teomitl had created – in the women's quarters.

And the gods knew Nezahual-tzin liked his women.

I bit back a curse. "Let's go."

"Where?"

"Women's quarters. I'll explain later."

The women's quarters did not give off the same atmosphere as the rest of the palace: in the courtyards, life seemed to go on as it had always done, with the regular clacking of weaving looms as the girls learned to spin cotton and maguey fibre, and the subdued laughter of conversations drifting to us, about servants and men, and impending births. A woman I'd already seen, her belly heavy with child, was coming out of the steambath – walking slowly with her attendants, glaring at us for daring to impugn on her dominion.

As we entered one of the more secluded courtyards, Mihmatini's head came up, as if scenting the air. "You're right. He's here."

"You can feel his powers?" Neutemoc asked.

Mihmatini laughed, briefly. "No. I know what the place looks like when there is a man around. I always thought he had guts, but to use Tizoc-tzin's absence…"

"He's probably visiting relatives," I said, though I didn't really believe any of it.

Mihmatini walked to one of the closed entrance-curtains, and wrenched it open without ceremony. A jarring, discordant sound of bells accompanied her inwards – we could hear a woman's voice, arguing but growing fainter, and then another sound of bells, followed by Mihmatini's voice again.

Then silence.

Neutemoc and I looked at each other uncomfortably. "Maybe we shouldn't be here," Neutemoc said.

"I don't have a better plan," I said with a sigh. "But you can go home, you know."

He grinned – his face transfigured into that of a boy. "It's more interesting here."

The entrance-curtain tinkled again, letting through Mihmatini and Nezahual-tzin – who looked as though a jaguar cub had just pounced on him and settled down to maul him. "What is the meaning of this?"

"The meaning of this is that we get you out," Mihmatini said, with an expansive gesture of her hands. "And then, once you're safely out of here, we can worry about explaining to Tizoc-tzin what you were doing in the women's quarters."

"Nothing reprehensible," Nezahual-tzin protested – as smooth and arrogant as always.

"You can be sure Tizoc-tzin isn't going to swallow this," Mihmatini said, grimly amused. "Now–"

Something crossed the air, like the shimmering of a veil – everything seemed to ripple around us, as if we were underwater – and then it was gone, but the air was wrong.

Mihmatini stopped; Nezahual-tzin's eyes rolled up, showing the uncanny white of pearls. "Acatl…"

They came into the courtyard three at a time, fluid and inhuman – their bodies the black of a starless night, their faces both ageless and wrinkled, like those of drowned children; the hand at the end of their upraised tail twitching, moving and opening as if eager to rip out eyes – moving like lizards or salamanders. They fanned out, blocking both exits to the courtyard – I could see Neutemoc's lips moving, keeping track of them all, but there must have been more than a dozen of them already, watching us with white, filmy eyes – hunger and hatred in their gazes.

Ahuizotls.

Teomitl…

But the one who strode into the courtyard after them wasn't my student. Rather, it was Coatl, but he moved with a grace I'd never seen from the warrior.

"Coatl?"

His gaze moved from one end of the courtyard to another, watching us. "A warrior. A Guardian. And priests. Is that all the Mexica will field, to defend the Triple Alliance? Where are your She-Snake, your Revered Speaker – your Master of the House of Darts?"

Mihmatini's hand tightened around my wrist. "Acatl–"

He had died, and been brought back to life. That was what Palli had thought; what we had all thought. But what had come back – what had walked and talked, and smiled and wept – it hadn't been Coatl at all. It had been another soul. A dead soul trapped within Tlalocan.

"I know," I said. "Moquihuix-tzin!" I called.

He jerked, slightly, but his attention was still fixed on Nezahual-tzin.

Nezahual-tzin's opal-white eyes moved towards Coatl, steadily held his gaze. "I don't believe we've been introduced."

Coatl's broad, open face turned to look at him – the eyes were more deep-set than I remembered, and dark, as if he stood within a great shadow. "You wouldn't know me, pup."

Teomitl would have lashed out; Nezahual-tzin merely raised an eyebrow. "Pup? That's not setting up a felicitous acquaintance." His hand moved, to encompass the *ahuizotls* gathered in the courtyard. "Though those are hardly friendly."

"He's here to kill us, you fool," Mihmatini said. Power was flowing to her – ward upon ward to defend herself, an impregnable force against the *ahuizotls*.

"Me as well?" Nezahual-tzin looked shocked – his eyes reverting, briefly, to their clear green-grey shades. "I haven't done anything to you that I would know of."

While they were arguing, I gestured to Palli and Mat-laelel. We spread out in the courtyard, drawing obsidian knives from our belts, cutting deep into the palm of our hands – where the veins flowed all the way to the heart – and let the blood drip onto the ground, forming the first hints of a circle. I eyed the *ahuizotls*, which still hadn't moved. I didn't think it was going to last long.

"Whoever gets to Nezahual-tzin first–"

Mihmatini shook her head. "Drags him into Mictlan, yes. For that, we need your gate, Acatl."

"And you need to stay here," I said to Acamapichtli.

He snorted, like a Revered Speaker amused by a peasant's joke. "I had the general idea, don't worry. Now concentrate on your work, High Priest for the Dead."

"You know what they say about the taint of your ancestors," Coatl hissed. "It was your father who undid us – who sided with the Tenochcas instead of following the path of justice."

Nezahual-tzin laid a hand on his *macuahitl* sword – slowly, casually. Beside him, Neutemoc did the same. Acamapichtli and his Consort nodded at each other, and both simultaneously drew obsidian daggers.

"I believe," Nezahual-tzin said, slowly, carefully, "that this taint is washed away at birth. I certainly would hope the midwife acted suitably when I was born."

Coatl's face distorted in anger. "You – you mince words as if they meant anything. Will words bring back my people, pup? Will they invoke the dead back from the Fifth Sun's heaven; heal the raped women and all those taken slaves?"

"Your people? You're not Coatl, are you?" Nezahual-tzin's eyes narrowed; the sword's wooden blade came up, its obsidian shards glinting in the sunlight; and he took a step in Coatl's direction.

"You waste my time." Coatl brought his hands together, and before we knew it the *ahuizotls* were flowing towards us, the hands on their tails going for our faces.

TWENTY-THREE
Blessings of Mictlan

I took a swipe at the first *ahuizotl*, sending it leaping back
a few paces – but not slowing it down, as its legs bunched
up for another assault.

I'd never liked the things – they might have been
Teomitl's, but they were creepy, and that was saying a
lot, since I knew most of the beasts that haunted each
level of the underworld. But never mind that, my goal
wasn't to kill them – with the power that coursed
through Coatl, he could surely summon more with a
mere snap of his fingers – but to complete the circle, and
open the gate into Mictlan.

The *ahuizotl* leapt again – I ducked, feeling clumsy next
to its fluid grace. Power shimmered in the air around me
– and over me reared a huge shadow. I guessed that
Nezahual-tzin was calling on his patron god, the Feathered Serpent Quetzalcoatl; I could also guess that
Neutemoc, Mihmatini, Acamapichtli and Cozolli would
be fighting the rush of *ahuizotls*. What I needed was…

I evaded another leap of the *ahuizotl* – the Duality
curse me, the thing was fast – and glanced around the
courtyard. The blood we'd already spread shone in the

sunlight, bunched up in three bundles, nowhere near the circle we needed.

What we needed was…

A distraction.

I waved my knife at the *ahuizotl* – catching its attention, as well as that of two of its neighbours. As my gaze roved, I caught bits and pieces of the scene, what looked like Palli's flailing arms as he waved an obsidian dagger, and Matlaelel's face, as pale as muddy milk. Then I was diving for the entrance of the courtyard, but more of the beasts were flowing up, barring my passage, and at the last moment I altered my trajectory, crashing into the entrance-curtain. The bells danced above me, their voices shrill and unpleasant; a prelude to the rough, jarring sound the three *ahuizotls* made as they tore through the cotton.

Having little choice, I retreated deeper into the shadows, holding my knife like a shield.

The room smelled of copal incense and food gone stale – hints of cold maize porridge, of amaranth seeds and the faint memory of spices. And I knew there had been someone – two women. "I apologise, but–"

A hiss came from the darkened centre. I steadied myself, preparing for the onslaught of the water-beasts – and met the glowing eyes of Chantico, She Who Dwelled in the House. Her hands wrapped around live coals, daring me to steal Her things.

A fresco. It was only a fresco. The goddess couldn't be here. "Get out!"

Too late. The *ahuizotls* were coming – one headed straight for me, and two others for the women. I couldn't spread myself so thin – it was all I could do to fend off one, struggling to stab the hand which terminated its tail – it

390

leapt, bearing me down, and I was on the floor, squirming, while the hand swept down, aiming straight for my eyes – I raised the knife, whispering a prayer to Lord Death, and sank it to the hilt into the palm of the hand.

I'd expected blood, but of course nothing like this flowed – only weak ichor, as thin and as brackish as marsh water. The *ahuizotl* cried out like a hurt child – the Storm Lord strike me if I was going to fall for that. I raised my knife again, and while it was still wailing, transfixed it between the eyes.

It dropped like a log, trapping me underneath its corpse. The magic ebbed out of it in a painful tingling rush – the power of Chalchiuhtlicue was as much anathema to me as that of the Storm Lord Her husband, or of the Southern Hummingbird. I lay breathing heavily, struggling to collect myself.

The women.

I rolled the corpses of the *ahuizotl* off me, ignoring the ache in my arms, and stood up, fully expecting to see a pair of water-beasts feeding on corpse.

Instead, I met the irate eyes of a woman who looked formidable enough to take down the gods. "And the meaning of this is?"

I pointed to the dead *ahuizotl* – behind her, her attendant was kneeling in a quincunx glowing with the familiar heat of living blood, and the other two beasts lying dead at its centre. "Sorry. It was the nearest refuge. I thought…"

I paused then, wrenching my mind into another alignment. My sister was a powerful priestess in her own right, and Xiloxoch had brimmed with the power of her goddess. Why had I thought of those women as defenceless? "I apologise for disturbing you – you'd best stay there. There are people trying to kill each other outside."

The woman rolled her eyes, in a way that suggested this happened all the time. "Men. We're sealing this place, so I won't say it twice. You'll want to head out."

I certainly wasn't about to argue. Gingerly, I bowed to her, and walked out of the room – back into sunlight through the torn entrance curtain. I felt a breath at my back, and a hint of something large and angry beneath my feet – before the entrance-curtain fell again.

The courtyard was a mess: the fountain had been blown to pieces, and the wind was lifting up a cloud of dust that prevented me from seeing much. But magic still glowed within, and I could follow the progress of the circle: it was three quarters complete, its largest missing chunk right behind Coatl's greenish radiance. Not surprising.

I hefted my knife closer to me – feeling the stretched emptiness of Mictlan gather in my chest, the familiar sense that I'd never breathe again in the Fifth World – and went straight into the dust.

Shapes moved: moaning faces, flailing limbs, as if I were back within the fever-dream, weighed down by four hundred thousand bodies. I felt the sickness, curled at the edge of my thoughts, questing for a way in. I'd had it once and survived, which gave me an edge, but I couldn't count on this.

Also, the *ahuizotls* had to be somewhere, and I certainly didn't have an edge against them.

I had gone perhaps three paces when I found the first body – blackened by the plague, blood streaming out of its orifices. It was the young offering priest, Matlaelel, the whites of his eyes completely red, blood welling up from under his nails and nipples. His mouth opened – blood had run down from his gums, staining his teeth – and his lips shaped a word I couldn't understand – my name, perhaps? I fought the urge to lay my hands on him, to whisper the litany for the Dead and grant him safe passage into the World Beyond.

I said the words, regardless – because I was High Priest for the Dead, and it was my province, and because I had dragged him into this, and I owed him at least this.

"We live on Earth, in the Fifth World,
Not forever, but a little while…"

Shadows moved within the murky gloom. I made for the only thing I could see, which was the gaping emptiness within the circle.

"Acatl-tzin!" Palli's hand on my arm almost made me jerk in surprise.

He was pale and wan, but more from loss of blood than anything else – and covered in the brackish ichor of wounded *ahuizotls*. Blood covered his hands, welling up from a dozen cuts.

"We need to finish the circle," I said. "Coatl–"

"Nezahual-tzin and your sister are keeping him busy," Palli said grimly.

Mihmatini? I ought to have known.

"Fine. Then we're headed for the other side of the courtyard. Can you see it?" I assumed Acamapichtli would be able to take care of his own problems; perhaps a mistake, but he certainly wasn't incapable.

"Yes, but–" Palli's face was pinched with fear.

I could have lied, made promises about how the plague couldn't touch him, but I had never had the ruthlessness for that. "We need to close that circle," I said. "Or more people will die. Not only us, but everyone here."

Palli grimaced, but he nodded. "Let's go."

As courtyards went, it wasn't a large one – at least, I was sure it hadn't been. As we fumbled around in the dust cloud, it didn't appear so small anymore. The shadows twisted and shifted, and even Palli seemed impossibly far away – I soon lost him, as veil after veil of reddish dust rose to cover everything. A dark silhouette loomed through the fog: a huge snake which had to mark Neza-hual-tzin's location. My gaze swept left and right – where were the *ahuizotls* – surely they hadn't disappeared? But all I saw were the faces, slowly coalescing into focus, distorted with pain, their mouths open in soundless screams – men, women and children, with the shadows of rich headdresses and jewellery.

I couldn't tell at which point the nagging suspicion at the back of my mind coalesced into certainty as heavy as a stone in my belly – perhaps it was the woman, with the fine line of cuts across her face, or perhaps the child with sticky blood clogging his hair, gathered all in the place of the single wound that had dashed his brains out, or perhaps the dour warrior who looked hauntingly familiar, until I realised he could have been Yayauhqui's father.

Tlatelolco. The dead of Tlatelolco, weighing us down like stocks on a guilty man's neck. But there hadn't been so many of them – and they were dead, they had been dead for years and years, enough time for their souls to have moved on, found their true rest…

I'd been wrong, then. This was a plague passed on by the dead, by all the ghosts flittering through the diminished boundaries. It couldn't have existed without what we had done, Quenami, Acamapichtli and I.

Focus. Focus. Breathe, slowly, calmly – every step I took seemed to be through mud or tar; the faces swam in and out of focus, all crying out for revenge.

I wasn't a warrior, or a devotee of Huitzilpochtli the Southern Hummingbird. But, in the end, it didn't matter. The god had chosen us, and favoured us, and we had grown and grown, taking over our neighbours. It was sheer survival: everything that lived had to grow, or ossify and die. Nevertheless... I could understand their anger at what had been done to them.

I could have told them this, but they wouldn't have listened, or understood.

I walked on. The dust thickened, and every step seemed to cost me. The dead wailed and screamed and pleaded, demanding to be acknowledged – but I closed my ears to their pleas, and went on.

Ahead, the circle shimmered – broken still. I couldn't see Palli, but the three darker silhouettes shimmering with magic were presumably Mihmatini, Moquihuix-tzin and Nezahual-tzin. I passed them by – a hair's breadth away, and I thought they would turn, or feel me, but they were too engrossed in flinging magic at each other.

I trudged on – only walking mattered, step after tottering step, ignoring the dead and their twisted faces, ignoring the memory of Matlaelel's blood-filled eyes. When my feet finally met the edge of the circle, it felt like a miracle, like a god's blessing descended to me, who had least deserved it.

I knelt in the dirt, and rubbed open the previous slash across my palm – there was a slight stinging pain, such as when I made an offering to the gods, and then blood flowed again.

The faces in the dust hovered closer – it shouldn't have been possible, but they were pressing against me, their mouths opening as if to taste my blood. If they did so – I didn't even want to think about it. Blood was many

395

things, among which an entry point into the body – and the illness, carried through my veins, would surely kill me as it had killed Matlaelel.

There was no time for finesse – I rubbed at the wound again, feeling it open further, the blood greedily pouring out – and tottered across the circle, trying to seal it shut before the plague faces could touch me – I could feel their foul breath on my skin, smell the dry, musty smell of their approach, like fire-crinkled mummies suddenly springing to life…

Step after step after step – the circle grew wider and wider, and it was almost complete…

The woman with the cut-up face was a finger's width away from my bleeding hand. I could see her body now, pulling itself out of the morass of faces, her arms and legs covered in similar wounds, her breasts hacked away and a pulsing mass of blood between her legs….

Almost there… The words of the hymn welled up as irrepressibly as the blood, spilling out into the Fifth World as the woman's teeth brushed my skin.

"Above us, below us,
The heavens, the place of heat,
Above us, below us,
The region of the fleshless, the land of mystery…"

I felt the plague, coursing within my body – the pressure in my veins and arteries, travelling to my heart and liver – my vision blurred and became red, and my body shook, and I was on my knees, struggling to remain standing…

"The path out of the Fifth World, into the city of the Dead
The city where the streets are on the left, where the houses have no windows…"

Dark green light washed across the pattern – starting at the circle and rising like an unstoppable tide as the sounds of battle receded and became a lament for the Dead, and the stretched emptiness of Mictlan expanded, shrivelling my heart a fraction of a moment before the rising tide of blood caused it to burst.

And then everything went blessedly dark.

There was dust in my eyes and a gritty taste in my mouth, but the air smelled wrong – too wet and scorching to be that of the underworld. I lay on something hard and un-yielding, feeling the Dead passing through me – hearing, like a distant mumble, their endless prayer to Lord Death:

> *"Not forever on Earth, but for a little while,*
> *Even jade crumbles, even gold is crushed,*
> *Not forever on Earth, but for a little while…"*

Hands held me down – stroking me like a mother stroked her child – there was something wrong with them, but I couldn't remember what…

Everywhere they touched, fire blazed – not the confla-gration of war, but rather that of a funeral pyre, tightening and drying flesh, shrivelling bones. Something impossibly heavy was tightening around my chest, squeezing my lungs until it hurt to breathe – and before the flames, the last touch of the fever on my mind receded, crushed into utter insignificance; there was nothing left but a familiar, stretched emptiness in my bones and sinews.

I opened eyes gummed with secretions, struggling to form anything from the blurred darkness around me. But I knew, or suspected, what I would be seeing.

"My Lady. My Lord."

The hand on my arm had the sharpness of finger bones, and a skeletal face swam in and out of focus – Mictecacihuatl, Lady Death, Her grin the wide one of skulls – and behind Her, looming out of the darkness, Her husband Mictlantecuhtli, fingering the bloody eyes of his necklace.

"Acatl. What a surprise."

My vision was returning, little by little – I stood on the dais of bones that marked Their seat of power; below me was a sea of pallid souls, ghostly hands lifting up the offerings that had been buried with them, from sewing tools to toys, from *macuahitl* swords to fragments of weaving looms. A cold wind blew through them all and lifted up the faint, translucent shapes of bodies to face the gaze of the gods, under which they seemed to shrivel and vanish.

Mictlan. The deepest level of the underworld – no, wait. If I focused enough, I could hear the sounds of battle, the cries of *ahuizotls*, and Acamapichtli's sarcastic laughter. "I stand on the boundaries," I whispered.

The underworld wavered, in and out of focus; the bare outline of the courtyard began to appear again, with the shadowy shapes of *ahuizotls* leaping onto the beaten earth. I banished it with an effort, to focus on the scene before me – my gods required no less than my full attention.

"Of course you stand on the boundaries. You always have," Mictecacihuatl said, shaking Her head.

"I – " Everywhere I turned, I saw only the Dead – an innumerable crowd flowing from the shadows of ruined buildings – the furthest ones mingling together like the waters of some great rivers, their faces receding into featurelessness – they whispered and sang, and prayed to Lord and Lady Death to grant them oblivion, at the very last. "I came with some people–"

Mihmatini. Nezahual-tzin. Where were they?

A sound, from Lord Death's throne, echoing amongst the skulls and femurs that made up His chair: laughter, coming from His vestigial lungs, lifting up his prominent rib-cage. "You come here for Our favour?"

Amongst the massed dead, a space was clearing up – silhouettes flickering in and out of focus, moving like shadows in the background of a fresco. Coatl – no, not Coatl anymore, but a tall, stately man with a feather headdress, and a cloak of turquoise, who wielded not only a sword, but a flint cutting axe, its blade shimmering with all the colours of oil on water.

Moquihuix-tzin.

The scene was, for a single moment, mercilessly clear – it wasn't Nezahual-tzin that Moquihuix-tzin was facing, for the Revered Speaker of Texcoco lay unconscious at the feet of the combatants.

It was my sister.

She moved slowly and a touch awkwardly, but somehow she always managed to be there when he struck. She didn't have a sword, but both her hands held daggers – mismatched ones, the one in her left hand small and mundane, looking more like an everyday knife for cutting maize and tomatoes than a real weapon; the other was a longer knife, and a translucent snake curled up from the hilt to the point of the blade, shimmering with the radiance of the Feathered Serpent's magic – she must have picked it up from Nezahual-tzin's body.

She fought better than I'd expected, but it was clear that they were mismatched. Her opponent was a warchief and a sorcerer; Mihmatini's only experience with weapons must have been in the Duality House. Her stance was purely defensive – it *was* a dance to her, I re-alised, and she sidestepped the blades, but couldn't bring herself to break the pattern by stabbing her partner – surely she had to realise she couldn't hold – surely she had to shift her stance?

Neither of them looked up to the dais – they flickered in and out of existence, and I was beginning to suspect that they couldn't see us at all. Within a god's world, the gods made the rules – and Lord Death could alter reality as it suited His whim.

The Storm Lord's Lightning strike me, where was Neutemoc when you needed him?

"Guests," Mictlantecuhtli said, behind me. "What an odd thing to bring here." He sounded genuinely puzzled.

I needed – I needed Nezahual-tzin awake, to complete his part of the ritual – if Mihmatini had managed to speak with him at all, before they tumbled into Mictlan. I needed Acamapichtli – as I thought this, the scene in front of me wavered, and I stood once more in a dusty courtyard, watching an *ahuizotl* leap straight for me. With an effort, I shifted – making the beast vanish as if into smoke – and shifted again.

The courtyard was shrouded in greenish mist, but as I stood within the gate, I saw Acamapichtli standing within the circle, hefting his blade thoughtfully. Besides him, Neutemoc and the Consort Cozolli were fighting two *ahuizotls*, albeit with difficulty. "Acatl!" Acamapichtli said.

I made a gesture with my left hand. "I'm working on it."

"You'd better work fast."

I didn't brother to protest. Instead, I banished the scene again, and turned back to Mictlantecuhtli – who stood watching me as if nothing had happened.

"You warned me the boundary was broken," I said, slowly.

"A favour." He smiled – revealing teeth as yellow as corn, and stars caught within his throat. "For you, who never asked for any."

"I don't understand."

"You're our High Priest," Mictecacihuatl said. She stretched out a bony hand, to point at the dead. "Most people in your place would scheme and intrigue."

Why was She telling me this? "But that's not what you need," I said, slowly.

"That's not what you can give us, either." Mictlantecuhtli waved a dismissive hand. "We don't ask worship. We ask for you, as our High Priest, to keep the boundaries. Do you know why?"

Was this really the time for childish questions? "Because the Fifth Word will end if they're not maintained."

I heard a sound, then, a clicking like bones rubbing together, and it was a while before I realised He was laughing. "Oh, Acatl. Have you learned nothing? We ask you to keep the boundaries because there is no life without death, and no death, either, without life. What is Our dominion, if the dead can come back into the Fifth World when they will it?"

"Then…" I said, slowly, "then… you don't approve of this, either."

The combatants flickered into existence again – Mihmatini had lost the shorter blade; she clung to the other one in bleeding hands, holding it in front of her like a shield.

"Of the plague?" Mictecacihuatl asked.

Of what I had done, bringing Tizoc-tzin back, I thought, but could not voice the sentence aloud. Mictlantecuhtli's face was turned towards me, but I wouldn't look at the shadowed eye-sockets.

"Acatl," He said gently. "Do not torment yourself. We do not stand against the will of the Southern Hummingbird."

"But–" But that wasn't what I wanted to know. I realised I'd meant to ask Him if we'd made the right decision, but stopped myself in time. He would have had words, and they would have been wise and detached. But the truth was, it was past time to be selfish and worry about my conscience, or dwell on things I could not take back. A course had been set, and we would not turn back.

Mihmatini blocked a strike that would have decapitated her; her eyes were wild, looking right and left, as if she expected to see me.

Time to end this. I took a deep breath. Even if Nezahualtzin woke up, he wouldn't be able to do his part in the ritual, not while Mihmatini was still pressed by the fight.

The fight needed to end, first. Moquihuix-tzin needed to die. And for that…

"My Lord," I said, slowly. "I ask for no favours; merely for things to take their course. I want what should happen here, on the ninth level of the underworld, to happen." For the dead – the defeated – to find oblivion at Mictlantecuhtli's feet.

"Why?" Again, genuine puzzlement. "Would you put your sister in danger?"

He was a god – had been mortal, once, in the beginning of the Fifth Age, before He gave his blood to move the Fifth Sun across the Heavens. He couldn't understand us, not any more – couldn't understand fear and hope and despair, and the knowledge that I needed to bargain for this now before knowing who would win the fight – that I needed to put my own sister's soul in the balance, agree to consign her to Mictlantecuhtli's oblivion if she lost the battle – so that the Mexica Empire could be great, could follow the destiny set by the Southern Hummingbird – guzzling human hearts and captives like a glutton, taking in riches from the northern deserts and the southern jungles until it choked on them.

I–

"Acatl?"

They were shadows again – the fight a hint, like a painting hidden underneath a layer of maguey paper – and all I could do was guess, and hope against all hope – and do what was needed.

"My Lord." I kept my voice steady, focusing on the polished bones of the dais, on the musty smell of earth and dry corpses. "A soul that comes before Your throne finds oblivion."

"That is truth." I felt Him shift, high above me – waiting as He always waited, for everything to come to an end.

"I–" The words caught in my throat – I kept my thoughts away from the fight, focusing them on the memory of the dead and the wounded – of Tapalcayotl, of Chipahua, of Acamapichtli. "What of a soul who dies before Your throne?"

There was silence – flowing like the calm after a successful birth. At length, Mictlantecuhtli made a sound I couldn't interpret – a bark of laughter, of anger? "Look at Me, Acatl."

"I–"

"You're asking for no favours. You never do. You merely want Me to take my due as I have always done. You know as well as I do that there is no ceremony in Mictlan."

Slowly, carefully, I pulled myself up – how was Mih-matini doing? Could she hold out for that long? – and looked him in the eye.

His face was smooth, polished bone, His cheekbones spattered with drops of blood; His headdress was of owl feathers and paper offerings; His teeth were white, and as sharp as those of a jaguar. His eye-sockets weren't empty like those of a skull, but rather filled with a soft, yellow light, like the Fifth Sun at the end of the afternoon.

"Few have asked this. Your need must be pressing." Between His teeth glittered light, too – a hundred stars, caught in His throat, in His empty rib-cage, imprisoned there to keep the Fifth Sun safe.

"I do what I must." The words were ashes in my mouth.

"For the Fifth World?"

I could have said the Empire, but it would have been a lie – I wasn't sure I could believe in that anymore, not with our current Revered Speaker. Or perhaps I needed to believe in it – in the idea rather than the man, to make it all somehow palatable. "For balance, and our survival. And justice." For the warriors and the crippled clergy of Tlaloc, and all those dead before their time.

"I see." His eyes were – no, not warm, for He was death, and would ever be cold – but there was sadness in them, and sympathy, and for a bare moment, as we looked at each other I had the feeling that He encom-passed me, and weighed me, and understood me better than anyone ever would, and it was a thought as bitter as raw cacao. "I said it before, Acatl, it is not a favour – mainly an extension of rules."

"Then You agree?"

He was silent, for a while. "It sets an uncomfortable precedent. But you are My high priest, and I know your need. So go, with My blessing." He smiled – a bare uncovering of the stars that whirled within Him. "For what it's worth, Acatl."

Something shimmered and tightened in the air. When I turned around, the fight had stopped shivering in and out of reality, and had become entirely real.

"We shall meet again, Acatl." They were fading away, leaving me on an empty dais – with a sense of odd warmth running through me.

Not a promise; a mere statement of fact. Almost all the Dead were His.

I didn't move. I couldn't, for I stood on the threshold of the gateway, and I couldn't enter one world or another, lest the ritual fail. I kept my eyes on the fight ahead – Mihmatini was moving yet more awkwardly, stumbling every other step. On Coatl – Moquihuix-tzin's – face was nothing but sheer determination. He had lost his sword, but wielded the axe with the ease of one of Chalchiuhcutlicue's devotees – thank the gods he couldn't use his magic, not here in the underworld where Lord Death's wards were at their strongest.

I called up the courtyard, briefly, and met Acamapichtli's exasperated eyes. The *ahuizotls* seemed to be all dead, though Neutemoc was limping, and Cozolli held her arm awkwardly. "Any time you feel like starting the ritual…"

"We still have – a problem," I said. "Hold on, will you?"

In the underworld, Nezahual-tzin was stirring, dazedly pulling himself up – and they were all so far away, stuck as if behind a pane of glass, neither of them seeing me – I would have screamed, but even as I shifted, Moquihuix-tzin sent Mihmatini's dagger flying – and closed in for the kill.

"Mihmatini!" The scream was torn out of me before I could think, fear and rage mingling in one primal, unstoppable force that seemed to take its substance from my wrung lungs. "Mihmatini!"

At the last moment she sidestepped and, for a moment, her eyes met mine, and saw me. She smiled, shaking her head – that same expression she had whenever I tried to mother her.

Oh, Acatl. You're such a fool sometimes.

It happened in an eye-blink – she rolled to the ground, avoiding the axe stroke which would have split her skull; her outstretched hand met Nezahual-tzin's, and she rose, holding something sharp and white – the aura of Duality magic around her flaring like the hood of a snake, an expenditure of power that must have utterly drained her – and, grasping the axe in one hand, used the other to drive her weapon into Coatl's chest.

He gasped, and collapsed like a felled tree, while Mihmatini stood over him, her face expressionless, her hand dripping blood from the deep wound she'd taken from seizing the axe.

She smiled up at me, then turned to Nezahual-tzin and pulled him towards the dais. I couldn't hear them at first – my sister seemed to be whispering furiously, and Nezahual-tzin, still dazed, mostly nodded – a fact which must have pleased her no end.

At last, they stood below me. Nezahual-tzin smiled up at me. "As timely as ever, I see."

I shook my head – now wasn't a time for jibes. "Are you–?" I asked Mihmatini. "I thought he was going to kill you." I thought I was going to lose her forever, that I'd bargained for nothing but one more death. "I–" It hurt, to breathe.

"Oh, Acatl." Her voice was pitying. "Have more faith."

I said nothing – I couldn't think of any smart answer to this. Instead, I turned to Nezahual-tzin. "Have you–?"

He nodded, brusquely. "Let's get to it, shall we? I don't know how long I can stay upright."

The courtyard shimmered into existence again – except that I stopped it halfway through, before it became fully material. I could see Nezahual-tzin, slowly breathing – calling down the Feathered Serpent's power until his skin glowed with pulsing magic – and Acamapichtli, his blind eyes thrown back, looking up at the sky, which slowly filled up with storm clouds. There was a noise like wings unfurling, and the distant rumble of thunder.

And I – I, who belonged in neither of those worlds – felt the touch of Mictlantecuhtli spread from the marks on my shoulder, a cold that seized my bones and muscles, and then my heart until I could no longer feel it beat. My hands curled up into claws, my skin reddening against the cold.

"I stand on the boundaries,
  On the edge of the region of mystery, on the edge of the house of the fleshless,
  I stand on the boundaries,
  On the edge of the gardens of flowers, of the expanses of grass..."

And, as I spoke the words of the hymn – as Acamapichtli and Nezahual-tzin joined me – light slowly appeared, washing us all in a radiance that was neither the harsh one of the Fifth Sun, nor the green mouldy one of Mictlan, but something that had been there for the birth of the Fifth World, something that would always be there, underpinning the order we kept.

"We stand for sickness, in the house of the living,
For the breath of the wind, in the region of the fleshless,
For life and death, caught on the threshold…"

And there was… something, like a tightening, as if a loose garment had just readjusted itself: the world knitting itself back together. My gate wavered and shrank, and the nausea that I'd carried with me all this time finally sank down to almost nothing.

"With this we will stand straight,
With this we will live,
Oh, for a while, for a little while…"

And then the feeling was gone, and I sagged to my knees like a wounded man whose feverish rush of energy had just worn off. "Acatl!"

"I'm fine, I'm fine," I said, but I could barely pull myself to my feet. I shouldn't have left the cane behind us. I turned back, to stare at Moquihuix's body – and, to my surprise he stared back at me, his face clouded with the approach of death. The weapon Mihmatini had used to stab him – a sharp reed which shone as if it had been dipped in gold – was still embedded in his chest.

He didn't look like Coatl at all, but like his true self, a Revered Speaker lying in the dust of Mictlan. "Priest." His voice still carried far, as if he were addressing the crowd from atop his pyramid temple. His lips curled up, in a smile that was painful. "It is Tenochtitlan's destiny, indeed, to rule over the valley of Anahuac, to expand into the Fifth World and make everything theirs. I wish you joy."

"Wait!" I said, but his eyes had closed, and his body was already shimmering out of existence, his limbs growing fainter and fainter, followed by his torso, and, last of all, the turquoise cloak which had marked him as a Revered Speaker and his quetzal feather headdress, crumbling into a fine powder which mingled with the dust.

A wind rose, carrying a faint, familiar smell – rotting maize, or leaves – and his soul rose upon it; not the faint memory of a human, but a bright radiance made of hundreds of people: the people of the plague, the dead that he carried with him. He rose towards the dais, and was lost to sight.

When I turned around, Nezahual-tzin and Mihmatini had both joined me on the dais. Nezahual-tzin was binding Mihmatini's wound, with a mocking smile. She was glaring at him, daring him to make a comment.

"You'll be fine?" I asked.

She shook her head. "Of course I'll be fine, Acatl. Don't fuss like an old woman. It doesn't become you."

"Sorry," I said. "It's just that–" I saw, then, that her free hand was shaking, her back slightly arched, and I could only guess at the effort she used to hold herself upright. "Never mind. Let's go back."

We came back to the Fifth World in the same courtyard we'd left from. It was bathed in sunlight, the corpse of Matlaelel and the bloody remnants of a few *ahuizotls* the only signs of the battle. And another corpse, too, shrivelled like a dried fruit, who might have been Coatl, who might have been Moquihuix-tzin: it was hard to tell anymore, with the decay.

I'd expected a crowd of noblewomen, irate at our intrusion upon their lives – who were, I was beginning to understand, neither as weak nor as defenceless as I'd allowed myself to think.

I hadn't expected the warriors: an army large enough to fill the place, their *macuahitl* swords glinting in the sunlight – and, at their head, the old woman and Teomitl – and my brother Neutemoc and my offering priest Palli, standing in their path with the desperate assurance of doomed men.

TWENTY-FOUR
The Revered Speaker

We'd appeared behind Neutemoc and Palli – which meant that the warriors saw us first, and, as their faces widened in incredulity, Neutemoc turned round to face me. "Acatl!"

He looked exhausted – his jaguar's furs bloodied, his helmet split with a blow that must have narrowly avoided cleaving his skull. Palli himself was holding himself with easy, casual aloofness, as befitted both his position and the situation, but beneath it all, he had to be no less tired than my brother. "What in the Fifth World...?"

I looked for Acamapichtli – who had withdrawn between the pillars, and was on his knees, helping his Consort bandage her wound. His gaze was mild, sardonic: it said, quite clearly, that he would take no part in this, that, Master of the House of Darts or Revered Speaker, it made no difference to him at all, and that the Fifth World would endure as it always had.

Not unexpected, sadly.

Teomitl moved, as fluid as a knife through human flesh – kneeling by the charred body of Coatl-Moqui-huix, which lay between the warriors and us. "He's dead," he said. He wore rich garb – not quite that of the Master of the House of Darts, not quite that of a Revered Speaker, as if he were still uneasily caught between both functions. But his attitude was regal.

The old woman inclined her head. "Good. That leaves only one thing."

Teomitl pulled himself up. His gaze was unreadable; his face turned away from me or Mihmatini. "I know."

I heard Mihmatini's breath quicken. She looked from Neutemoc to Teomitl. For a moment, anguish was written on her face, but then her hands clenched, and she wrenched herself from her immobility. She bypassed Neutemoc before he could stop her, and came to a stop in the centre of the courtyard – standing under the warm gaze of the Fifth Sun, which shimmered on the hundreds of wards she was weaving around her. "We won't let you pass." Her voice shook, but her hands were utterly steady.

"We?" the old woman's voice was sarcastic. "I can't see anyone with you, girl."

Mihmatini flinched – I couldn't see Teomitl's face, but never mind, it was too late for that; far too late. Slowly, with as much dignity as I could master, I walked in my sister's wake, ignoring the sharp glance Neutemoc threw at me – and came to stand by her side – blood to blood, brother to sister.

The old woman cocked her head. "Two doesn't make an army."

"Listen to me," I said. "This is foolishness, Teomitl. You can't possibly–"

"We've already had this conversation." He still wouldn't look at me; his voice was low, emotionless, instead of the anger I'd expected. "This is what the Empire needs."

"You know it's not."

The old woman smiled. "You know he has a destiny, priest. You can feel it, hanging over him."

Right now, all I could see was the jade cast to his features, the living remnants of Jade Skirt's magic, which had given us so much pain. "Yes, he would rule the Mexica, and rule them well. But not now. Destiny is for fools to manipulate."

"He'll never be this ready."

"What do you gain?" I asked.

She laughed – low and without joy. "Tizoc is no better than his brother. They both used me and discarded me without a second thought. Now I grow old in the shadow of Mictlan, and I would see the better brother made Revered Speaker."

As I had thought – an imperial princess playing at politics – and she was saturated with the magic of Grandmother Earth, probably what had aged her until she seemed old enough to be a generation above Teomitl.

"As Guardian of the Sacred Precinct, I won't let you pass," Mihmatini said. She masked her hesitation well, but I wasn't sure whether it would be enough – the old woman was a canny practitioner.

"Mihmatini…" Teomitl looked straight up, but his eyes were as shadowed as Coatl's had been, and I could read nothing from him. The Duality curse me, when had I ceased to understand him? "You have to understand."

"I… I understand, but I don't approve. You'll break the Fifth World, Teomitl, worse than anything he's ever done." Her hands swung, pointed to the charred body on the ground. "And he hated us – hated us so much…" She couldn't quite repress the shiver that ran through her. "All

413

that for what? To grasp a toy you can't have now, like a spoiled child?"

"You know Tizoc," Teomitl said. "You know his mere presence opens up the breach, that there will be more demons in the streets, more beasts of shadows taking people." He swung to look at me, and the light of the Fifth Sun dispersed the shadows over his eyes, letting me see the anguish in them. "You know this, Acatl-tzin. You know he'll kill us slowly, take us apart piece by piece. You know there's no other choice."

"This will break us," I said, finally. What did he want from me? My approval? I was no longer his teacher; that much had been made abundantly clear. "You know it will."

"I know." His voice was an anguished cry. "But there is no other way!"

The old woman said nothing; she merely stood, looking smug.

"I have to do this," Teomitl said, slowly, carefully. His voice gained strength as he spoke – becoming once again the confident one of a man who moved in the highest circles of power. "This is right." He hefted his *macuahitl* sword, holding it as if he could draw power from within the obsidian. His skin had the greenish cast of jade, of underwater algae, and his aura of magic had grown stronger.

But I knew he had doubts, that there was a crack. I could – no, I might find it, but I needed to find it fast.

"You have to step aside."

"I can't."

"You–" His face twisted. "Why do you keep involving yourself in this, Acatl-tzin?"

Because… because it was the Fifth World, because I knew it would collapse if Teomitl did this. And something else – as usual, in the end, it is the smallest and pettiest things that define us. "You're my student. Whatever you do is what I taught you."

"Do you truly believe that?"

"I–" He was my beloved son, as akin to me as the blood of my blood; he made my face widen with pride, gave me the satisfaction I would never have as a childless priest. Neutemoc had said children went astray, but most children didn't end up endangering the safety of the Fifth World. It was his pride, his accursed pride, and his desire to do what he believed was for the good of the Mexica – regardless of whether it actually was good for them.

But...

He did have doubts. I had seen them. There was a crack.

Tizoc-tzin. He did all this because of Tizoc-tzin – because the man he had admired, the man who had taught him politics and tactics, had turned out to be such a disappointment. He did it because he didn't want Tizoc-tzin to rule us.

"There was someone else who reached for the Turquoise and Gold Crown in a time of turmoil," I said, slowly. "Someone who thought it had been denied to him for too long, and grasped it before he was ready."

Teomitl paused – his hand frozen in the act of lifting up his blade.

"If you do this, if you seize power now, when we're most vulnerable, then you'll be just like him. Just like Tizoc-tzin – throwing the Mexica Empire in disarray just for the sake of something you think should be yours."

"Don't listen to him." The old woman's voice was low and fierce. "He doesn't know what he's talking about. He's a priest who won't join the heights of the powerful; a poor, sad little dove who keeps looking down at the

ground whenever an official passes him, doomed to always be carried in someone's arms, like a child wrapped
in a mother's mantle."

Teomitl turned, halfway, to look at both of us. In the
warm light of the afternoon, his haughty profile had
never looked more like Tizoc-tzin's. "You're wrong," he
said – not slow or stately, he'd never been much for either. "Both of you. I… I do it because there is no other
choice. Because Tizoc will lead us into ruin." He turned,
to look at me – his eyes wide, his face ordinary again,
with no trace of Jade Skirt's magic, but his gaze as piercing as a spear. "Don't you believe this, Acatl-tzin?"

"You know what I think."

"No," Teomitl said. "I know you think the Fifth World
can't take another change of Revered Speaker, not so
soon. But what do you think of Tizoc?"

"I–" I was taken aback at the question – and the only
thing that occurred to me was the truth. "He killed the
clergy of Tlaloc, as surely as if he'd cast the spell himself."
Over and over, we had seen evidence of his growing
paranoia, of his instability.

"And you believe he should rule, until such time as
he dies?"

"No." The truth, out of my mouth before I could call
it back. "But I can't condone this, Teomitl. I can't – one
doesn't become Revered Speaker or receive the blessing
of the Southern Hummingbird by feats of arms."

"Ask the coyote's son," Teomitl said, with a small curl
of his lips. I could feel Nezahual-tzin's presence behind
me, but he was silent – as if this were merely between
Teomitl and I. He had said, many times, that he wouldn't
interfere. "He who came to his mat borne on the shoulders of Tenochtitlan's warriors."

"That's—" I took in a deep breath. He — I thought of Tizoc-tzin again, of the paltry forty prisoners, who hadn't even been sacrificed; of the confirmation that wouldn't even have the semblance of a real war, coming on the heels of a failed coronation war and a failed investiture ceremony. But I was High Priest; I served the Mexica and the Revered Speaker — it had been one thing to oppose Tizoc-tzin when he had been Master of the House of Darts, but now that he was Revered Speaker my loyalty was to him, and, like the She-Snake, I might disagree with his actions, and try to steer him back to the right path, but to conspire in order to depose him? It would have been against any order, any balance that I served. Teomitl was wrong: this was no way to solve the problem.

"I—"

I thought of the star-demons; of the plague; of Moqui-huix-Coatl and the chaos in the city. Did I really want this — more souls creeping back through the cracks in the world, creatures of the underworld amongst us? I kept the balance — which was my duty, my destiny.

Just as ruling the Mexica Empire was Teomitl's destiny.

As he had said, there was no solution — no clean, clear-cut way out of this tangle we'd worked ourselves into. Seeking to preserve the balance had led us to opening the rift, and this in turn had led to the plague.

We did it, Acamapichtli had said. I'd said we'd done the right thing, and not believed a word of it. Teomitl wasn't blameless, but it was also our insistence on pre-serving the balance at all costs, our fear of breaking the Fifth World's equilibrium, which had led us to this.

And, really, how long could we continue like this?

"You'll rule," I said, to Teomitl. "She's right, it's your destiny."

417

He grimaced. "If it's to tell me to wait, I've heard it all."

"I'm not asking you to wait for Tizoc-tzin's death." The words were lead on my tongue. "Let it pass, Teomitl. Wait until Tizoc-tzin is confirmed as the Revered Speaker – until he has a stable reign." And pray, all the while, that there would be no other major disaster. The breach was diminished, and the likelihood of this ever happening again was low – but low didn't mean non-existent.

"You're asking this as my teacher?"

I could have said yes, and we both would have known it for the lie it was. "No. You haven't been my student for a while." All children grew, and went astray – unable to fulfil their parents' dearest dreams. All students became men, and young girls grew and changed, too.

You're such a fool, Acatl, my sister's voice said in my mind. Always blind to change.

"I'm asking this as one man to another," I said.

Teomitl looked from me to the warriors – and then to Mihmatini, who still stood rigid, with her hands clenched into fists. "You're my wife. You wouldn't–" he said, and then shook his head again, recognising that she would. "Everything came together so beautifully."

"No. You only thought it was coming together. We saw everything coming apart." Mihmatini's voice was low and intense. "If you take one more step, I'll fight you, I'll swear."

I said nothing. My own position was already abundantly clear.

Teomitl looked from us to the old woman, who stood defiantly, her wrinkled face alight with a fierce passion. "You have to seize the moment, or you'll never amount to anything. You know it." Her voice rose, dark with hatred and spite. "He asks you to wait, but will you ever have such a great opportunity again? Tizoc has fled the city with the priests of Huitzilpochtli, the clergy of Tlaloc and of Mictlantecuhtli are busy with the breach, and you have warriors behind you. Such a situation will not occur again, you know it. They never do."

Teomitl was silent, for a while. At length, he looked up – at the Fifth Sun resplendent in the sky. "No," he said. "You're right. It won't happen again."

Her face split, in a wide, unpleasant grin of triumph, but Teomitl went on, "But I'll make it happen. Someday."

"You can't–"

He raised a hand, and even from where I stood I felt the pressure of Chalchiuhtlicue's magic – a shockwave that all but sent her sprawling against the pillars of the patio. "Don't think of telling me what I can and can't do."

The old woman sprang up, the magic of Toci rising around her in a tide. The shadows that rippled around her were the colour of earth, as brown as cacao beans or pinolli. "You–"

Teomitl's lips quirked up. "You wield the magic of Grandmother Earth, but I have other ones. And do you truly think the army would follow you, Chalchi-unenetl?"

For a moment, they stared at each other, and then the old woman looked down with a grimace. "You win this. For now. Don't mock Grandmother Earth, boy. She'll come for you, too."

"In the end, we all come to Her embrace," Teomitl said. He appeared unperturbed.

"My Lord? " the leader of the warriors said.

"You heard," Teomitl said. "Go back. Tizoc-tzin is the rightful Revered Speaker. I'll take no action against that – for now." His eyes drifted, for a moment, in my direction:

they were jade from end to end, the cornea drowned in murky reflections.

"You mean we came here for nothing?" The other warriors nodded, staring at each other with a definitely hostile mood.

Teomitl drew himself up, the jade-coloured light spreading from his eyes onto his face until he seemed a statue – and further, the whole courtyard dancing on the rhythm of underwater waves, everything smelling of brackish water and churned mud. "There will be no battle today," he said, and his voice, ageless, malicious, was no longer wholly his. "Leave this place."

The warriors looked from him to the old woman – whom they clearly didn't appreciate. Their faces were drained of colour in the light of Jade Skirt's magic, like those of drowned men, and they breathed heavily, as if something were constricting their lungs.

Faster than I'd thought possible, the courtyard emptied, until we were the only ones remaining – and Teomitl, still in the thrall of the goddess.

"Well, well," Nezahual-tzin said, speaking up. "Allow me to congratulate you on a wise decision."

Teomitl looked at him, as if unsure whether to strike him down.

"Teomitl!" Mihmatini said, sharply. "Let go."

He shivered, and sank to one knee, the divinity draining out of him like blood from a torn vein. His eyes rolled up, became brown once more. "Don't toy with me," he said to Nezahual-tzin, rising up in a fluid movement.

"Of course I wouldn't dream of it."

"Acatl-tzin. Nezahual. Acamapichtli." He bowed to us, and then, very stiffly, to Mihmatini. "If you'll excuse us."

She nodded. I watched them both walk away, into another courtyard. They were not holding hands. I wondered what they'd say to each other; wondered if, as with Tizoc-tzin, Teomitl's rash actions had created a chasm that would never heal.

Acamapichtli was speaking with his Consort in a low, urgent voice, with no eyes to spare for us. The old woman – Chalchiunenetl – had stayed. She was standing, looking at the charred corpse of Coatl-Moquihuix-tzin, the expression on her face indescribable.

"He was her husband, you know," Nezahual-tzin said, conversationally.

I hadn't even heard him come up to my side, but suddenly, he was there. "Her husband," I said, flatly. It couldn't be – she looked far too old for this – and then I remembered that served Grandmother Earth, and that her magic had probably aged and twisted her. "Does it matter?"

"Not anymore, no." Nezahual-tzin smiled, as dazzling as usual. "Well, I'll leave you to clean this up. The next few years should be… interesting."

There were explanations, and consequences, and, as Nezahual-tzin had foreseen, a substantial amount of formalities.

The plague didn't vanish altogether, but it became less virulent, less contagious. Of those not already dead, many would recover. But still – many would not, and many more would not rise at all from their sickbeds. The toll had been heavy.

Tizoc-tzin was coming back, and the She-Snake was making sure everything was ready for the confirmation ceremony. They'd bought slaves from the Tlatelolco marketplace, to replace the warriors who had died – ironic, in so many ways, but the priesthood seemed to be the only ones aware of this. Otherwise, things seemed to go on as they should.

Mihmatini had gone home, after a very lengthy conversation with Teomitl – and a glance cast in my direction which expressed more than words. Whatever rift Teomitl had opened in their marriage was going to need more than a few hours' talk to solve.

Neutemoc, surprisingly, had barely said anything: he'd helped me argue with Quenami, shaking his head at some of the latter's more arrogant pronouncements, and remained behind in the palace, talking to his fellow warriors, and generally making sure that Tizoc-tzin, outwardly, would find the support he craved – an illusion that wouldn't hold for long, as we now all knew.

I, as usual, retreated with my priests in my temple, to begin the vigil for Matlaelel, and tidy things up in my own domain.

I was settling down with the temple accounts when I heard footsteps outside, and a hand drew aside the entrance curtain. "Acatl." The tinkle of bells didn't mask Acamapichtli's voice.

I bowed my head, not knowing if he'd see it or not. He was still wrapped in layers of Tlaloc's magic, but I couldn't be sure what he was saying.

"I thought I'd find you here. Ever the busy clerk." His voice had the old, mordant sarcasm.

"Ever the same," I said, but it wasn't quite true.

He'd brought chocolate, and maize cakes; we sat together atop the platform of the pyramid shrine, looking down on the temple complex and the shadows of my priests below as they went for their funeral vigils, and the haunting sounds of the bone whistles started to echo around the courtyard.

422

"So we closed it."

Acamapichtli grimaced. "We did. Well, not quite. You know we couldn't. But it was good that you killed Coatl."

"Thank my sister," I said, gloomily.

"I already did." He shrugged. "Don't look so sad. I can recognise power when I see it. She might be young, she might be a married woman, but it changes nothing. She's for great things, you know. Perhaps even greater than her predecessor."

"I don't know," I said. It made me feel uncomfortable to dwell overmuch on Mihmatini right now – because of Teomitl, because there was nothing I could do about their marriage. Whatever they did, they'd have to work it out by themselves. "So we're safe," I said, to change the subject.

"I guess. But not as safe as we once were."

"Do you…? " I stopped, unsure of what to say. "Did you ever stop to think what we'd done? That we'd–" That we'd break things worse than ever, cause our own doom just as Tenochtitlan's invasion of Tlatelolco had paved the way for Moquihuix-tzin's revenge?

Acamapichtli sighed. "A word of advice, Acatl: don't dwell on what is past." His sightless eyes looked west, towards the setting sun, and his scars seemed to shine in the dim light. "You'll only hurt yourself."

"But…" But I had to know; had to see whether I was right, whether my decision would heal us in a few years' time, or throw us into worse chaos. But Acamapichtli didn't know any of this, nor could he understand it.

Acamapichtli's smile was wide and sarcastic. "We all blunder through life, Acatl, making the best we can with what we have. That's all the truth there is." He rose, wiping his hands clean of cake crumbs.

"Where are you going?"

He smiled again, like a jaguar showing his fangs. "You'll want to be alone."

"Acamapichtli!"

There were footsteps again, on the pyramid stairs; brash and impatient, and I would have known them anywhere. I heard the entrance-curtain to the shrine tinkle as Acamapichtli withdrew for good, leaving me alone, staring at Teomitl.

He wore the garb of the Master of the House of Darts: the Frightful Spectre costume, his face emerging from the jaws of the skull-helmet, the quetzal feathers of his headdress fanning down like unkempt hair; the slit over his liver, symbolising the sacrifices he was making for the Mexica, seemed to glow in the dark. "Acatl-tzin."

I sighed. "Come on. There are some maize cakes."

"I've come to apologise–"

I shook my head. "No need for that. I think we've both made mistakes that we shouldn't have. The important thing is that we're safe." Safe, but not as before; safe, but trembling on the edge of extinction.

Teomitl sat down, looking at the maize cakes with studied intensity. "I'll give it a few years," he said. "If we hold that long."

"I know."

"You disapprove."

"I don't know." Not anymore; I was the one adrift without anything to cling to, the future only a terrifying blank. "The Duality curse me, I don't know."

Teomitl broke the maize cake in two, watching it. "I don't think Mihmatini will ever forgive me."

"Give it time," I said. I didn't know. Out of all of us, she'd probably been treated the most shabbily, and I didn't know how far her love extended. "I can't help you there. I don't think, in fact, that I can help you much at all. You were right in one thing: you're far too adult to have a teacher."

He smiled – with a shadow of the old carelessness. "You said things as one man to another. That won't change, Acatl."

"No," I said. "I guess not."

Teomitl was silent for a while. He poured chocolate into a bowl, and breathed in the bitter, spicy smell, but didn't drink. "When Tizoc comes back…"

"Yes?" I'd expected something about apologies, but he didn't even broach the subject.

"I'll ask him about Tlatelolco. It's high time that wound was healed. We can't keep making them pay for something that happened thirteen years ago."

"What did you have in mind?"

"I don't know," Teomitl said. He smiled again, and I couldn't help smiling in return. "I'll think of something."

He rose with the bowl in hand, and came to stand near the edge of the platform. Below, the city of Tenochtitlan was bathed in the last light of the setting sun, and the familiar sounds wafted up to us: the splashes of the boats being polled home; the murmur of the crowd offering its last sacrifices in the Sacred Precinct; the harsh cry of the conches and the melancholy roll of the drums that marked the end of the day, and the setting of a sun that would rise, again and again. "It hasn't changed," he said, almost in wonder.

The last light of the Fifth Sun bathed him, surrounding him in a glow like molten gold, and all of a sudden I saw the ruler he'd become, the one his sister had believed in so desperately – not who he was now, but who he would be, in a few years' time: a man brimming with the power of the gods, smart enough to forge his own alliances and make his own opinions, respected and feared by the army, quick to love and quick to hate – a man who would lead us all to the Southern Hummingbird's promised glory, whose name would spread far and wide, like smoke, like mist – who would make the Empire great and wealthy, and eclipse the name of Tizoc-tzin as if it had never been.

"No," I said, "it hasn't changed." But he had; oh, he had, and the world seemed to blur and bend a little as I looked upon him.

Neutemoc had said that even beloved sons and beloved students went astray – that, like I and my brother, they ended up a bitter disappointment to their parents or teachers.

And sometimes, they outgrew us, and some of their light shone back upon us, making our faces widen with pride – far more than anything we could have done on our own.

About the Author

French by birth, Aliette de Bodard chose to write in English – her second language – after a two-year stint in London. Though she has trained as an engineer (graduating from Ecole Polytechnique, one of France's most prestigious colleges), she has always been fascinated by history and mythology, especially those of non-Western cultures. Her love of mysteries gave her the idea to write a series of cross-genre novels which would feature Aztecs, blood magic and fiendish murders.

She is a Campbell Award finalist and a Writers of the Future winner. Her short fiction has appeared or is forthcoming in venues such as *Interzone, Realms of Fantasy*, and *Fantasy* magazine, and has been reprinted in *The Year's Best Science Fiction*. She lives in Paris, where she has a job as a computer engineer.

aliettedebodard.com

AUTHOR'S NOTES
The Historical Setting

As in previous volumes, I took some liberties with naming conventions: the Revered Speaker of Texcoco is Nezahualpilli-tzin, but I shortened the name to Nezahual-tzin. I also kept the convention of referring to the inhabitants of Texcoco as "Texcocans" rather than the more proper "Acolhuas", and once again used the "tzin" like Japanese honorifics , to mark respect, rather than as permanent titles. My main concern, again, was to keep the text readable and understandable, in order not to add confusion to an already complicated universe.

This volume is most concerned with war, a central concept in Aztec society: more specifically, Tizoc-tzin's coronation war, which is recorded in the annals as a disaster. The coronation war was more properly a confirmation war: once the new Revered Speaker was invested, he had to lead his men into battle: this served the double purpose of confirming him as a leader of warriors, and of securing enough prisoners for the public celebration of his accession to power.

Again, what we know of the organisation of the

Aztec army is fragmentary: I mostly used Ross Hassig's *Aztec Warfare* as a source for practical details of campaigns, chain of command, and matters of discipline, such as deciding to whom a prisoner belonged.

The war council was essential in Tenochtitlan: it consisted of four members – their names and functions have been reported in differing fashions, depending on the source. Given that titles such as Master of the House of Darkness seemed to have been attributed much like titles in Ancient China – ie, names chosen for specific acts of valour rather than functions which had to be always filled – I chose to pick among the recorded members of the war council those names which seemed most attractive to me.

Together with the war council, the Revered Speaker and the She-Snake made up most of the high ranks of Tenochtitlan: therefore, they could not all be absent at the same time. While the Revered Speaker was on campaign, the war council split in half: two of its members remained behind in Tenochtitlan – they were replaced by two deputies within the army. The other two would march along with the soldiers. This ensured that, not only did the city keep functioning smoothly in the absence of the Revered Speaker; but also that in case of attack, there were strategists and veterans ready to organise the defence of the city.

War, of course, permeated every layer of Aztec society: the merchants I mention also doubled as spies and as advance units, and they sometimes had to disguise themselves while on missions in foreign cities, in order not to be summarily executed. The tension between them and the warriors is well-documented, and I had

Eptli voice a lot of the clichéd insults traded between both groups.

Tlaltelolco, which turns out to be crucial to the plot, was Tenochtitlan's sister city: it was founded by a splinter group some kilometres away from the Mexica capital; and, as time passed, both cities grew to abut each other. Where Tenochtitlan was a city of warriors, Tlatelolco was known for its merchants, and its marketplace had the dimensions of a small city. The war between Tenochtitlan and Tlatelolco is also reasonably documented: it went on pretty much as I described it, though it is likely that Tenochtitlan's growing role in the Triple Alliance and the management of the Mexica Empire drove a lot of Moquihuix's plotting (and it's still not really clear how much of the so-called plot was Moquihuix seeking to strike before he was struck).

As mentioned in the novel, Texcoco's role was crucial: had Nezahualpilli's father not chosen to honour his old alliances ands side with the Mexica, it's likely the war (and victory) would have gone the other way. I did tweak history slightly by having Moquihuix die strangled – the record of his death is confusing, with no less than three different accounts, but in none of them does he die of strangulation.

It is worth noting that Teomitl/Ahuizotl did indeed make a headstart in healing the breach between both cities, by marrying a Tlatelolca princess. Their son, Cuauhtemoc, would become joint Revered Speaker of Tlatelolco and Tenochtitlan – though, sadly, this was at the time of the conquest, and he is more known for being the last Mexica Revered Speaker.

The epidemic Acatl, Mihmatini and Teomitl have to

face is also, unfortunately, quite real: I derived its symptoms from smallpox, a sickness which was brought over by the Spanish and devastated the Aztecs – who, having no livestock, had never had to face the disease. It turns out that there are quite a few different varieties of smallpox, and – sadly – I did not have to exaggerate in order to make the epidemic deeply horrific (the hallucinations of diseased corpses, though, are my own invention in order to give the illness supernatural weight).

On the role of women in Aztec society, I once again cheated: though there were priestesses, none of them had even a fraction of the liberty and power enjoyed by Mihmatini and Acamapichtli's consort. The female priesthood was very much inferior to the male clergy – its members shared in the deprivation, but were far less visible in ceremonies, and wielded very little power. It is, though, a recorded fact that High Priests were the only members of the clergy allowed to have a spouse: this is most probably for the reason I advance here, to have representatives of both the male and female sides of the deities at the highest levels (much like the Revered Speaker and the She-Snake functioned as two halves of a male/female duality).

I have had questions about the hymns: they are not real – as in, they were never spoken by bona fide Nahuatl speakers. I write them myself, using a reference the very real hymns contained in books such as *The Flayed God*, or *Aztec Thought and Culture*. The main reason I do this is because, like most religious hymns, Aztec hymns are highly language-specific, and translate very badly to English (most literal translations come with reams of translator's notes), all the more so when one does not have the cultural references necessary to understand things.

It is, for instance, highly counter intuitive that the Nahuatl expression "to bear fruit" actually has a negative connotation: the verb in this expression carries the entire meaning of flowering, ripening, bearing fruit and then falling to the ground and rotting away; it was mainly used about high officials that were dismissed because of their reprehensible actions. Likewise, many Nahuatl expressions either do not have an English equivalent, or would require paragraphs of explanations to make sense. I sometimes can manage to put in entire Nahuatl phrases, and I try to do this whenever it is possible; but it is far from being always the case.

Further Reading

Paper Sources
Manuel Aguilar-Moreno, *Handbook to Life in the Aztec World*, Oxford University Press, 2006

Elizabeth Baquedano, *Eyewitness: Aztec*, DK, 1993

Frances F Berdan, Patricia Rieff Anawalt, *The Essential Codex Mendoza*, University of California Press, 1997

David Carrasco, *Religions of Mesoamerica: Cosmovision and Ceremonial Centers*, Waveland Pr Inc, 1998

Inga Clendinnen, *Aztecs: an Interpretation (Canto)*, Cambridge University Press, 1991

Laurie Coulter, *Ballplayers and Bonesetters*, Annick Press, 2008

Nigel Davies, *The Aztecs: a History*, University of Oklahoma Press, 1973

William Gates, *An Aztec Herbal: the Classic Codex of 1552*, Dover, 2000

Ross Hassig, *Aztec Warfare: Imperial Expansion and Political Control*, University of Oklahoma Press, 1988

David M Jones & Brian L Molyneaux, *Mythologies des Amériques*, EDDL, 2002

Miguel Leon Portilla, *Aztec Thought and Culture*, University of Oklahoma Press, 1990

Miguel Leon Portilla, *The Broken Spears: the Aztec Account of the Conquest of Mexico*, Beacon Press, 2006

Roberta E Markman & Peter T Markman, *The Flayed God: the Mythology of Mesoamerica*, HarperSanFrancisco, 1992

Jacques Martin & Jean Torton, *Les Voyages d'Alix: Les Aztèques*, Casterman, 2005

Colin McEwan & Leonardo López Luján, *Moctezuma Aztec Ruler*, The British Museum Press, 2009

Mary Miller & Karl Taube, *The Gods and Symbols of Ancient Mexico and of the Maya*, Thames & Hudson, 1997

Jacques Soustelle, *Daily Life of the Aztecs*, Phoenix Press, 2002

Michael Ernest Smith, *The Aztecs (People of America)*, , Wiley-Blackwell, 2002

Thelma D Sullivan & Timothy J Knab, *A Scattering of Jades: Stories, Poems and Prayers of the Aztecs*, University of Arizona Press, 2003

Online Sources
Aztec Calendar – *http://www.azteccalendar.com*

Sacred Texts – *http://www.sacred-texts.com* (most particularly the "Rig Veda Americanus" by Daniel G Brinton)

Mexicolore - *http://www.mexicolore.co.uk* (in particular the article on Tlaloc)

Acknowledgments

As always, I remain deeply indebted to the people who helped me with this book, either during the pre-writing brainstorming, the actual writing, and the post-writing process, aka the painful dissection of the bits that weren't working. The sixth Villa Diodati workshop helped me brainstorm my ending: Stephen Gaskell, Ralan Conley, Ruth Nestvold, Nancy Fulda and Sara Genge dissuaded me from having yet another epic battle between various private armies (though, sadly, the stakes in this prevented me from having the quiet, intimate ending I'd first envisioned; next time, I swear...).

Various people kept me going while I was writing: Stephanie Burgis, Patrick Samphire, Neil Williamson, the late Colin Harvey, Gareth L Powell, and the entire gang at Codex, who listened to me vent my frustrations online.

My most excellent crit group helped me salvage the disaster of the first draft: Dario Ciriello, Juliette Wade, Keyan Bowes, Doug Sharp, Genevieve Williams, Janice Hardy, and TL Morganfield. As always, Traci Morganfield was a treasure trove of information, a great help for brainstorming, and a wonderful friend whose enthusiasm helped me navigate the troubled waters of writing this book.

The response to the books has been wonderful so far, and many people have publicised *Obsidian and Blood* online. I don't have space here for everyone, but here a few people I'm deeply indebted to: Charles Tan and Lavie Tidhar at the World SF blog, Josh Vogt of *examiner.com*, Ove Jansson at *cybermage.se*, Duncan Lawie of Strange Horizons, Lauren from Violin in a Void, Ros Jackson of Warpcore SF, Brad P Beaulieu and Gregory A Wilson from Speculate! for a truly epic set of podcasts, Cheryl Morgan (and co-conspirators Mike Carey, and Jon Courtenay Grimwood), Jenny Barber from the British Fantasy Society, Seb Cevey and his co-conspirators at Angle Mort, Rob at Val's Random Comments, Emmanuel Chastellière of Elbakin, Brenda Cooper, Jonathan Crowe, Gemma Files, Rose Fox, Russ Gray, Alethea Kontis, Jason Loch, Henry Lopez, Anne Lyle, Gillian Pollack, Jason Sanford, John Scalzi, Angela Slatter, Fred Warren and the rest of the gang at Liberty Hall...

Special mentions to everyone who took part in the Great Honeymoon Giveaway competition on my blog; to the numerous people who entered my goodreads giveaway for Harbinger of the Storm; to the people involved in the Codex Blog Tour (Colin Harvey, Lawrence M Schoen, Nancy Fulda, and Doctor Grasshopper) and to everyone who attended Eastercon, the SFWA Nebula Awards Weekend, and Imaginales – and actually managed to make me feel like a rock star.

And since space is limited, and I don't have enough of it to mention you all, a big blanket thanks to everyone who read the books, blogged about them, lent me some space on the web for guest posts, or boosted the signal in some other way. You all rock, and I definitely wouldn't be here without you.

Special thanks to Rochita Loenen-Ruiz, Chris Kastensmidt, Floris Kleijne, JK Cheney, and Justin Pilon for being around and providing much needed friendship and support when I needed it; and to friends closer to home (Charles-Eric Drevet, Clémence Lê, Alexandre Mège, Fabien Terraillot, Mathieu Leocmach, the ex-police interns/Binet Robot team, and the various members of our Nephilim roleplaying group) for reading and promoting the books.

As always, I owe a lot to the Angry Robot team – Overlord Marc Gascoigne, Lee Harris, Mike Ramalho, and John Tintera – and to my wonderful agents at Zeno, John Berlyne and John Parker, for the dedicated work and the awesome advice.

And, last but not least, to my family – to my grandparents and my parents and my sister – for always nurturing me, and for propagating my reputation as a writer all over France, Europe and Vietnam. And to my husband, Matthieu, for the brainstorming, the crits – and the general awesomeness.